THE
WILD
COURT

THE WILD COURT

BOOK THREE OF *THE COMING OF ÁED* TRILOGY

E.G. RADCLIFF

FIRST EDITION

MYTHIC PRAIRIE BOOKS

BISAC: YOUNG ADULT FICTION / Fantasy / General |
YOUNG ADULT FICTION / Fantasy / Dark Fantasy |
YOUNG ADULT FICTION / Legends, Myths, Fables / General

Mythic Prairie Books
154 W Park Avenue #141
Elmhurst, IL 60126

info@egradcliff.com
www.egradcliff.com

First edition

Library of Congress Control Number 2021905178
ISBN: 978-1-7336733-7-2 (pbk)
ISBN: 978-1-7336733-8-9 (ebook)

Edited by Kelsy Thompson & Margaret Diehl
Cover design by Micaela Alcaino
Illustrated by E.G. Radcliff

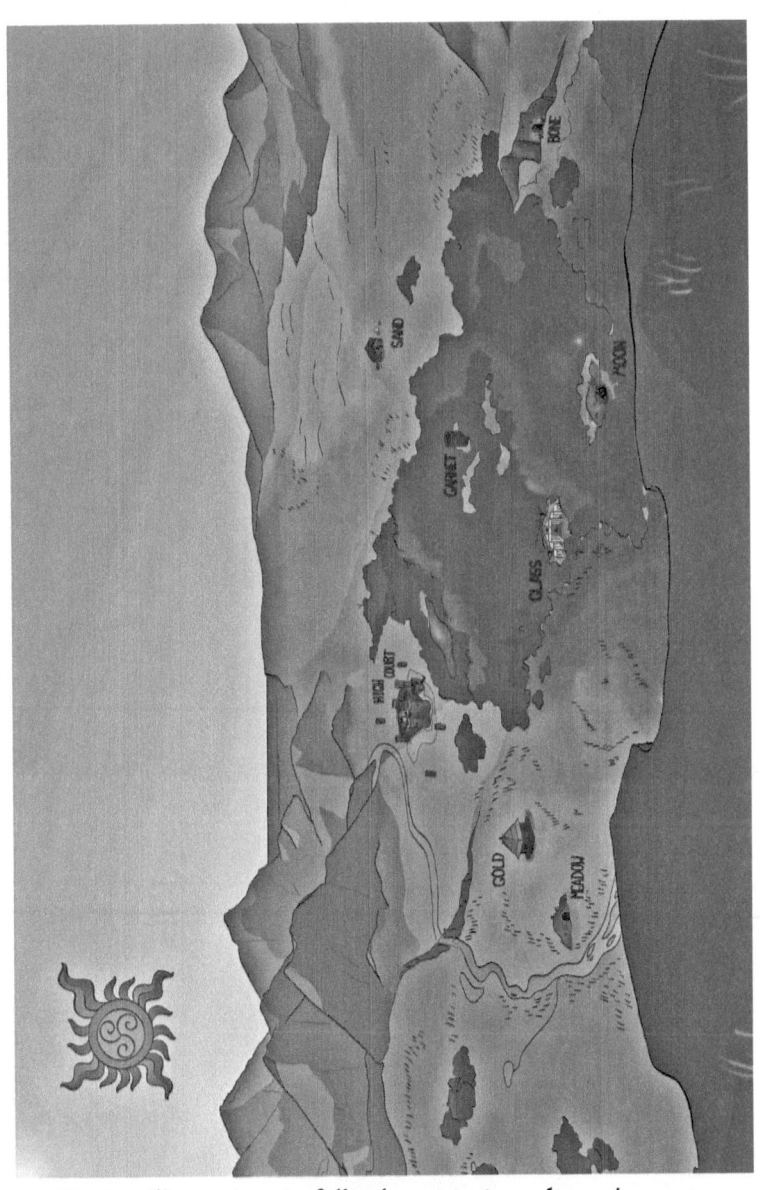

To view illustrations in full color, visit **tinyurl.com/twcart.**

GLOSSARY

Amadán:	Fool
Ceann beag:	Little one

PRONUNCIATION GUIDE

Áed	Aid
Eamon	Ay-mon
Lachtna	Lahkt-na
Neasa	Nya-sa
Fionnuala	Fin-noola
Fionnlagh	Finn-lee
Iarlaith	Eer-lah
Echdían	Ekh-dee-un
Róise	Ro-ish-a
Niamh	Neev
Rian	Ree-in
Síofra	Shee-fra
Líadan	Lee-din

CHAPTER ONE
ÁED

Áed started the day with a headache.

He'd woken too early in the morning, sheets tangled enough that he nearly dumped himself onto the floor when he tried to sit up. His first thought was that something was nagging at him; there was uneasiness seated deep in his chest, as if something was about to happen.

Perhaps that made sense. He'd been anticipating this day for months.

The sun hadn't risen yet, but when Áed disentangled himself from his bedding and stumbled blearily to draw the curtains, the autumn sky was a paling, rosy indigo and still sparkling with a few early-morning stars. The air in his room was crisp and chilly.

Shivering, he dragged a blanket off the bed to drape over his bare shoulders and crouched before the hearth. Years ago, he'd instructed his servants to let him take care of this chore himself. It took both hands to move a log from the woodpile to the fire grate, but it took only a thought to send fire rolling over the kindling. It popped and crackled, and the bricks of the fireplace heated up quickly. The fire

1

danced; Áed let it flicker over his crumpled hands, in the ever-stiff muscles of his forearms and wrists, warming him from inside and out. When the flame shimmered too close to his blanket, Áed drew the heat back, watching it twine over his fingers and flutter until all he saw were his bones glowing through his skin.

He closed his eyes and let out a slow sigh, pressing his still-smoldering palms to the tops of his bare feet and wondering if he should just get up and put on socks instead. At the very least, he would need to get dressed at some point. It was a festival day—the Festival of Souls. This was the festival for the coming of winter, for the memory of the dead and the wait for rebirth. It came with its own set of expectations. Even beyond that, though, this one was uncommon in its own right. The past summer, Ronan had come of age at fifteen—or at least he had approximately done so. Nobody knew his real birthday. All the same, at this festival, Áed would be officially declaring him Crown Prince of the Gut. He wasn't sure how Ronan actually felt about this since as long as Áed was King, Ronan's life wouldn't change much, but for Áed, it felt like an important milestone. Sometimes, he still marveled that seven years ago, the two of them had been little more than street rats.

A knock sounded on the door of the suite, echoing through the downstairs rooms and rolling around the high ceiling.

With a sigh, Áed pulled back the heat from his hands entirely and, standing, dropped the blanket back onto the bed in favor of a proper robe. He slipped out of his room and padded down the curving staircase to the door. The royal chambers were quiet. Sometime earlier that morning, the servants had clearly been in; the curtains had been drawn open to welcome the morning sun, and a bowl of apples, just harvested, sat on the table. "Who's there?" Áed called. He kept his voice soft since Ronan would still be asleep at this hour, piled under an unmade mess of blankets in his own bedroom.

"Page, Your Majesty," the voice came beyond the door. "Message for you from one of your advisors. The, uh… the Master of the Northeastern Quarter."

Éamon. Áed smiled to himself as he cracked open the door and accepted the note from the nervous-looking page. Of course, Éamon would be up this early, probably working on something. Áed wasn't even surprised. "Thank you."

Áed unfolded the paper easily—once, several years prior, Éamon had noticed Áed struggling to turn pages in a book he'd been reading and since then had folded his correspondence loosely. He even used a smaller seal so that Áed could more easily break the wax without uncooperative hands tearing the paper.

Áed—

I was wondering if perhaps you would like to meet for the festival tonight. I overheard a few of the other councilors talking about their plans, and they promise to be a bore—I'm sure they mean to corner you after Ronan's ceremony this evening. If you'd prefer not to spend your festival discussing their proposal (which is about the sewer system under the coppersmiths' guild, and they have stronger feelings about it than they should), it would be my pleasure to assist.

Yours,

Éamon

Áed smiled to himself, refolding the note and setting it to the side. The page was still waiting, fidgeting with his sleeves. "Would you get a message back to Lord Éamon, please?" Áed said, and the page nodded. "Tell Éamon that we're friends," Áed said, "so he doesn't need to keep making excuses to see me. I'd love to meet for the festival, boring councilors or otherwise."

The page nodded again, already moving back down the hall. "Of course, Your Majesty. Thank you, Your Majesty."

Áed had stopped trying to convince the palace staff to call him by his given name a long time ago. It seemed to make them uncomfortable, which was worse than the weight of a title.

When the door swung closed again, Áed stretched, trying to decide if it was worth it to go back to bed. Today was one of the few days on which he could let himself relax; ordinarily, he'd have meetings to attend with his Council of the King, audiences to hear, judgments to pass. That wasn't to say he *minded* those things, of course. Seven years hadn't dulled his desire for progress, and as long as there was work to be done, he would do it. The Maze was more prosperous now since Áed had provided incentives to trade salt and fish with the White City. Travel between the two settlements was now more accessible, as Áed had directed royal funds toward opening routes that were physically easier to traverse. It wasn't easy to govern the Maze as a King. Áed had taken to addressing the gangs; they were the closest thing to a government that the city had had in centuries, and thanks to Ninian, Áed knew a thing or two about how they operated. The going was slow. But it was going.

All of that just meant that Áed wouldn't mind a day of rest. The only thing that he needed to do today was name Ronan Crown Prince, but that on-edge feeling hadn't diminished. It was making him antsy.

Vague sunlight was beginning to float in through the lead-paned windows, illuminating motes of dust hanging in the air. Áed scratched absently at his forearm, feeling the scarred ridges of tattoos beneath the sleeve of his robe. Antsy feeling or no antsy feeling, he supposed there was nothing for it but to start the day. Ronan would be awake soon anyway, and Áed could at least get some festival preparations out of the way.

He took a deep breath and squared his shoulders.

It was going to be a good day.

CHAPTER TWO
ÁED

Áed was staring at Ronan. Ronan stared back at Áed, so innocently that it felt like a challenge, but Áed wasn't about to back down. "I know you're going to be late."

Ronan was sitting on the edge of his bed, pulling on a pair of tall boots. As usual, he was early to be dressed for the festival, wearing a berry-red cloak and a mask looped, for the moment, around his neck. And, also at that moment, he was using the whole power of his earnest, innocent face to blink at Áed. He even managed to look affronted at Áed's accusation.

Áed scoffed. "Don't give me that look. You've run off at every festival for the past three years."

"Well." Ronan frowned, green eyes wide. Áed wasn't falling for it. "I'm still all right, aren't I?"

"I want to keep it that way." Áed crossed his arms. Once Ronan had turned twelve, three years past, Áed allowed him to take part in the White City's common festivities instead of the more-reserved palatial ones on the condition that he had at least two guards with him at all times. It hadn't seemed fair to deprive Ronan of real celebration. The veil would be opening, and worlds would collide. It was a liminal night. An important night. "Be *safe* and come back to the palace in time for the ceremony. That's not just me telling you. That's a whole royal order."

"That doesn't work on me."

"Does, too. I outrank you." Áed set his jaw. "I mean it. Do you understand?"

Ronan nodded.

"So, are you going to try and run off?"

Ronan hesitated. "No."

Áed pressed a knuckle to his forehead with an exasperated sigh. "See, what you just said was *fully* not true."

Dropping the innocence, Ronan slouched, glowering a little. "I go off on my own all the time. And I'm fine. I mean, I even did it in the *Maze*. When I was a *kid*."

"Well, you were raised by starving teenagers." He and Ninian had taken care of Ronan as well as they could, but now that Áed had the means to do better, he was not about to pass up the opportunity. He had been trying to impress this upon Ronan for seven years now. "You are a *prince*, Ronan. People have more reason to come after you than they did when you were just another street orphan."

"We've had this conversation," Ronan mumbled.

"I keep hoping that this'll be the time you *finally* listen." Áed raised an eyebrow. "I could make you stay with me at the palace celebration."

"Oh, Gods, no."

"Then don't run off. And get back on time."

Ronan finished lacing his boots and sighed. His hair, ever the color of crow's wings, was plaited back into a long braid, which he flicked back when it slipped over his shoulder. "Fine."

"Liar." Áed rubbed his temples; his headache had only gotten worse as evening approached, and this conversation wasn't helping. The antsy feeling hadn't left, either. If anything, they were building in conjunction. "Gods. At least bring something to defend yourself with."

Ronan pulled a short knife out from under his pillow. "I always do."

"You sleep with that in your *bed*?" Áed shook his head. "You know what, don't answer that. Just come back safe before the ceremony starts. Promise me."

"I promise."

Áed made a mental note to tell Ronan's guards to be extra vigilant. "Good. I'm holding you to that." He moved to the doorway.

"Wait, where are you going?" Ronan sprang to his feet. "Are you meeting Éamon for the palace festival?" At Áed's nod, Ronan gave him an exasperated look. "And you're wearing *that*?"

Áed looked down at his clothes. He had prepared for the festival in the ways that had become habit for him, which meant letting Ronan hang up a carved turnip and hammer a rowan branch over the lintel of the royal apartment. Áed wasn't overly partial to either since the rowan made him dizzy every time he went through the doorway, and in secret, he thought the turnip was marvelously ugly. Most importantly, however, he set an empty third place at the table when he and Ronan ate. It was always something of a somber dinner.

The point was, other than donning the crown he'd wear for the festival, he hadn't given much thought to his clothing.

"What's wrong with this?"

Ronan looked at Áed like he'd turned into the turnip. "What's wrong with it? The fact that you wear that every day?" Ronan grabbed Áed's sleeve as he marched out of the room, dragging Áed with him. "It's a festival, and you're meeting Éamon. Don't be boring."

"Boudicca's been rubbing off on you, I see," Áed complained as Ronan led him into Áed's room. "And what exactly does this have to do with Éamon?"

"You're very dense."

"Excuse me?"

Ronan ignored him in favor of crossing to Áed's closet and frowning at the contents. "Why is all of this black? Or... what is this? Earth-toned?" He rifled through a few shirts. "This one isn't horrible."

"None of them are horrible."

Ronan didn't acknowledge that he'd spoken, tossing the shirt over his shoulder. "Here, put this on."

Áed looked at the garment that landed in his hands. It was a thin, fitted black turtleneck. "Okay, I was wrong. This one's horrible." He held it up. "Ronan, this is sleeveless. Why do I own this?"

"Because it'll look good. Put it on." He dug around in the closet a little more. "And here. This, too." He lobbed another bundle of fabric at Áed, who barely caught it. It was a sweater, soft and moss-green.

"I've changed my mind. You're *worse* than Boudicca."

Ronan didn't answer, merely watched critically as Áed, glowering, put on the clothes he'd picked. It was easier than arguing. Ronan had always been willful, but as he'd grown, he'd gotten *stubborn*.

The turtleneck fit snugly, and the sweater slipped off Áed's shoulders, revealing bare upper arm on at least one side no matter how he tugged it. The sharp, black lines of his tattoos cut across his uncovered skin.

"Hm." Ronan looked pleased, and then once again, Áed was being dragged down the hall. Ronan positioned him in front of his wide mirror, which was larger than Áed's own. "There. See?"

The sweater hung comfortably around him, loose and not

too formal, and the turtleneck beneath hugged his chest enough to catch the shape of his collarbones. It wasn't flashy or particularly eye-catching, but... "Ronan, I can't go out like this."

"What? Why not?" Ronan put his hands on his hips, still clearly proud of himself.

"I—"

Ronan perked up as the sound of knocking came from downstairs. "Don't have time to change!" He grinned. "It sounds like Éamon's here. Don't worry!" Ronan started shoving Áed out of his room, toward the stairs. "He'll like it!"

It was kind of ridiculous, Áed thought, that he was letting himself be pushed around by a fifteen-year-old. But his head really did hurt, and if Éamon was already there, Áed couldn't keep him waiting—would Éamon mind waiting? At the very least, Áed didn't *want* to keep him waiting.

Ronan opened the door, still grinning, to reveal a startled-looking Éamon. "Here you go!" Ronan chirped innocently, thrusting Áed through the door with two hands on his back. "He's ready for you! Have fun!"

The door slammed closed, leaving Áed and Éamon in the hallway.

For a long second, Áed didn't think either of them blinked.

A faint smile was playing on Éamon's face. His ivory hair fell over his right eye, as usual, obscuring the scar that split his eyebrow and cheek. He was dressed in a tunic of pinkish linen, tied with the belt and embroidered with gold, and the shade made the periwinkle of his visible eye stand out. "What was that about?" Éamon blinked, seeming to take in all of Áed. "You look nice, by the way."

Áed chuckled uncomfortably. "Ronan got to me."

When Áed was with Éamon, he could feel himself relax. He didn't necessarily want to think about it too much, but he couldn't deny that Éamon's presence combated a loneliness that seemed to come from living in the White City. Áed supposed it made sense; he was friends with a few of his council members, but not particularly close. When all was said and done, the responsibility of ruling fell to him alone. Not to mention that raising Ronan on his own was difficult—Ronan had some friends among the pages, and the domestic staff was very fond of him, but he still came to Áed for everything important. People turned to Áed when they needed things. It made Áed all too aware that he had no family to turn to for himself. So he turned to Éamon.

The two of them made their way down the stairs and across the open, columned walkway that crossed the palace courtyards. The wind blew cold, smelling of the coming winter, but the sweater Ronan had chosen was thick and warm. Except, of course, for Áed's shoulders, which quickly grew icy.

Éamon seemed to notice. In the next moment, he had swept his own cloak off his back and draped it over Áed's shoulders. As much as Áed felt he should argue for the sake of politeness, the comfort of having his blackened scars hidden was undeniable. Besides, he was quickly distracted as his eyes caught on something that had been hidden beneath Éamon's cloak. "What's that?"

Éamon followed Áed's gaze, and his face slid into a lopsided smile. "Oh, that?" He patted the leather bag hanging over his back, which was clearly weighted with something. "I may have brought a bottle of wine."

Áed felt himself grin. It was easy enough to notice the ways he himself was different from the person he'd been seven years earlier, but Éamon... well, the Éamon of seven years ago, struggling under the thumb of his father Elisedd, most certainly would not have been comfortable doing half of the things Áed loved him for. Flouting decorum. Dropping by past midnight so that he and Áed could wander the gardens and chat about nothing important. Arguing in the council chamber. Áed had to admit that while he'd been fond of Éamon back when they first met, his friend had positively blossomed since Elisedd's banishment. "Share?"

Éamon swung the bag around to his front to tug loose the drawstring and free the honeyed alcohol. Textured glass glimmered in the dim light. With a smile and unnecessary little bow, he uncorked the bottle and handed it to Áed, who accepted it with both hands. It was spiced and sweet, like autumn sun.

Áed passed it back to Éamon, who took a drink of his own. "I don't suppose we should finish it before we get to the festival."

"Best not," Éamon agreed. "I think we'll want it."

The sound of voices and music began to reach them as they arrived at the ground floor of the palace and made for the entrance to the gardens.

The palace gardens were large and edged with trees, an earthy oasis amongst white-brick buildings. The surrounding walls were high and covered with ivy that whispered in the wind, and within those walls, people moved against the light of the central bonfire, constructed where there was ordinarily a fountain. Water had given way to flames that bathed the entire garden in warmth and unearthly, flickering shadows. The people were dressed in fur capes, masks, and cloaks of heavy fabric. The odors of smoke and wine curled through the air.

Guards posted at the entrance to the garden fell into step beside Áed as soon as he and Éamon passed the threshold, and Áed looped his arm through Éamon's to prevent the pale-haired councilor from being lost to the crowd outside of the guards' protection.

As King, Áed needed to make an official appearance at the celebration. Hopefully he could get it over in a few minutes, but he didn't expect that would be the case. He turned to Éamon. "I have to go talk to people. Do you want to come with me or make your escape while you still can?"

"I'm staying with you, of course. Why do you think I came?"

Áed felt a smile steal over his face even as, with every passing minute, the tension in the back of his head grew more powerful. He was grateful for Éamon's arm still looped through his own, steadying.

It took almost an hour for Áed to make his rounds through the courtyard, but it wasn't nearly as strenuous as it could have been. The air of the festival was cheerful and darkly intoxicated, and musicians played on harp, pipes, and drums. By the time Áed finished greeting everyone and accepted another drink of Éamon's wine, the sun was well below the horizon. "Ronan should be here soon," he said. "I told him the ceremony would be at sundown."

"He doesn't seem excited to be Crown Prince," Éamon observed.

Áed sighed. If he were honest with himself, he knew Éamon was right. He leaned against the trunk of one of the garden's great trees, looking out over the celebration. Unlike the festival that would be taking place in the city streets at that moment, nobody was dancing. "I remember when he was younger, and he found out he was going to be a prince. He was thrilled."

"That was then." Éamon took the bottle back and swallowed a mouthful of wine. "I don't know what child *wouldn't* want to find out they're royalty. Especially when they're used to living the way you lived. You know."

Áed sighed heavily. "Do you think he's even going to come tonight?"

Éamon shrugged. "Give him another hour, maybe."

"I'm not putting too much pressure on him, am I?"

It was Éamon's turn to sigh, and the councilor leaned up against the tree next to Áed. "I don't know what else you're supposed to do. He's your heir. He just came of age. And if something were to happen to you…" He shook his head as if banishing that thought. "Well, you remember what happened after Seisyll died, before you took the throne. The city was a disaster."

"It isn't like it changes anything, right?" Áed held out his hands for the bottle, and Éamon obliged. "So long as I'm still here, Ronan doesn't even have to do anything differently. It's just a title."

"He only has fifteen years," Éamon said. "Titles can be heavy."

Áed groaned. That was something he knew well. "I have to do this. If something happens, and he takes the throne, his first act can be to name his own heir and abdicate. I don't care. But I can't leave the kingdom in uncertainty, Éamon. I've worked too hard for it."

Éamon patted his shoulder comfortingly. "I know."

"He's not coming."

"I know," Éamon said again.

Áed tipped his head back against the tree's rough bark. The crown he wore wasn't the same as the one used at his coronation—it was simpler, intended for less formal use. He could feel the simple gold band press against his forehead and temples as he rested his head against the tree. "He doesn't have to be present for the ceremony to be binding," he said quietly. "I'm the King. When I announce it, it's law." He looked up into the branches above, watching black leaves flutter against the starry sky. "But I'd wanted him to be here."

"Tomorrow, you should talk to him." Éamon gave his shoulder a supportive squeeze. "Do what you have to do tonight, but tomorrow, sit down with him. I think it's a good idea."

Accompanied by Áed's guards, he and Éamon made their way toward the center of the gardens, where the fountain-turned-bonfire radiated brilliance and blessed heat. Before the fire, close enough to make Éamon cast a worried look at the leaping flames, a short dais had been constructed. Áed stepped onto it, and Éamon took up a spot beside it, as far from the flames as he could get. Áed took just a moment to savor being taller than his friend before he turned to address the gathered crowd. The wave of attentiveness began at the foot of the dais and spread outward; within three breaths, the entire garden had fallen silent.

"Welcome, all," Áed announced, fixing a smile on his face. Gods, but he was grateful for Éamon's cloak. The moon was high in the sky, cold and waning, but it didn't feel peaceful. Even aside from his headache, Áed was still jittery. He couldn't stop his eyes darting over the crowd. "Tonight was intended to be both a festival and a ceremony." He drew the cloak a little closer. "Unfortunately, His Highness Prince Ronan is unable to attend. The ceremony will continue in his absence."

He scanned the crowd one more time, searching for a familiar red cloak, but finally let out a breath. Ronan wasn't there. He must have given his guards the slip again.

"My time as your King has been immensely fulfilling. I see my position as a privilege, and I hope that I will not need to relinquish it anytime soon." He crossed his arms behind his back. "However, hope amounts to nothing when no preparations are made. Now that your prince is of age, it is the time to make those preparations." He took a deep breath. "From this moment on, I declare Prince Ronan heir to the throne of the Gut." His head was beginning to feel staticky; the fire behind him cracked and popped, and the wind blew. "The Crown Prince will rule in the event of my absence, or my removal from the throne due to inability or... death..." He blinked, giving himself a little shake. "I expect you to treat him with the same respect..."

He broke off, feeling his eyes unfocus without his permission. A jolt of pain, like a spike driven behind his eye, speared his head, and he sucked in a little gasp.

Suddenly, the night felt very alive. He looked around, struggling to bring the world into clarity.

"Áed?" Éamon's voice came to him, sounding concerned. "Are you all right?"

There was something in the air, all around. Something familiar and unfamiliar, and something that was *pressing*.

Áed felt himself stagger.

"Áed!" Someone caught him—Éamon caught him, that was Éamon's hair falling away from ultraviolet eyes and one deep, jagged scar.

"Éamon," Áed managed. The night itself looked like it was shimmering, warping and dancing like the air over a fire. "Something's coming—"

"What's wrong?" Éamon sounded terrified as he guided Áed off the dais, and Áed's guards were hovering close. "What's happening?"

It was all Áed could do to clasp his ruined hands to his temples and squeeze his eyes shut.

And then the world exploded.

CHAPTER THREE
ÁED

Scenes came to Áed in fragments.

A billowing plume of fire rolling across the garden, leaving a blackened wake of grass smoldering behind it.

Arrows flying indiscriminately, crackling with blinding sparks of flame.

Shadowed forms writhing with fire—or perhaps they were haloed with it, ringed in flaming coronae that lashed out in the forms of whips, or swords, or nets.

And in the chaos and the darkness, between the panicking nobles and bursts of wild firelight, there flashed pair after pair of ember-red eyes.

Éamon was standing over Áed protectively, but he looked transfixed, his eyes wide and glassy. He wasn't moving, only staring unblinkingly at the flame-gilded chaos that had overtaken the night. "Éamon!" Áed could feel magic hanging heavy in the air, fire and desperate emotion cascading from the open veil and the fae who came through it. Too powerful for any human to bear. Protectiveness poured through Áed, acutely enough to make him gasp, and he grabbed Éamon's hand with both of his own. As Áed dragged Éamon to a crouch, the sheer quantity of magic around them made his head spin. He wanted Éamon to be safe from this. He wanted him *protected*.

As the intention hammered through his mind, Áed felt his hand grow warm. It didn't feel warm in the way his fire did—instead, it felt like his own emotion was spilling through the connection between his hand and Éamon's.

He had never felt anything so strange.

At Áed's touch, the councilor seemed to come back to himself. "Áed?" Wildly, he looked around. Screams were splitting the air; the garden was full of smoke, and the sounds of coughing and crying came from every direction. As Áed watched, a woman's figure, red eyes alight with internal luminance, tripped over the edge of the dais. Áed shoved Éamon back into the shadow of the nearest tree, praying that the faerie wouldn't look two feet to her left. The woman instead scrambled to find her feet, her face a mask of terror, and, gathering her skirts frantically, sprinted away across the darkness.

Áed stared after her.

"Áed," Éamon managed. "What's going on?"

Áed spotted his guards standing by the dais, mere silhouettes against the raging bonfire—was it his imagination, or was that fire dancing higher than it had before? As Áed watched, one of the guards clutched desperately at another before their hands moved to grasp at their head. A moment later, their knees seemed to buckle, and they sank slowly to the ground. From his vantage point in the shadow, Áed could see the glassiness in their eyes. Across the field, nobles were scrambling to evade bursts of flame in gold and white, but before his eyes, he watched them stagger, one by one. Éamon squeezed his hand, bringing him back to the moment. "Áed?"

"Don't let go of my hand," Áed gasped. He gripped Éamon's fingers as tightly as he could.

"Why?" Éamon looked panicked, his back pressed to the tree. Firelight and shadow made his face look unearthly and sharp. "What is *happening*?"

Fire.

Illusions.

Madness.

The weight of fae magic was hanging heavy over the night, thick as the smoke from a burning house. Áed had never felt anything this potent, and Gods, his head wasn't done spinning. The only magic he'd ever experienced was Boudicca's healing spells and whatever power lived in his own diluted blood, but this... *this* was the tension that had been splitting his head since that morning. He didn't usually sense any difference when the veil thinned, but with this much magic actively in use just on the other side, he could understand why it would be different. No *wonder* he'd had a headache. It was gone now, as if pressure had been relieved—the way a great river might be released when a dam gives way.

What was going *on*?

"I—I'm shielding you," Áed managed. "I think."

"You're *what*?"

A blast of fire, so dense it looked like flickering red water, engulfed the dais. Behind Áed, Éamon cried out and covered his face from the heat.

Áed pushed Éamon deeper into the shadows. "Are you okay?"

"I'm—Gods, define 'okay!'"

"Do you think it's like this over the whole city?"

"I don't know! Áed, what—" Éamon froze as a burning arrow whizzed over Áed's shoulder and embedded itself in the oak tree not two inches from his face. Áed caught a whiff of burning hair.

"Fae," Áed said. He couldn't tell if Éamon heard him over

the roar of fire and the shrieks of people all around them. "We can't stay here. Don't let go of me!"

Áed wrenched Éamon to his feet, and then they were sprinting across the garden toward the palace.

"They're—they're *fae?*"

Áed only nodded, gripping Éamon's hand so hard that his bones protested.

They were fifty feet from the door.

Twenty.

Ten.

Without warning, Áed found himself thrown to the ground. His side skidded over the cold, hard earth, and his breath left him in a choking wheeze. Éamon crashed down beside him, still holding Áed's hand in a death grip. Gasping, Áed scrambled to his elbows. He tasted blood, and through the high of terror singing in his veins, he could tell his shoulder and hip were bleeding too, skinned from the impact with the half-frozen ground. He looked up frantically, trying to find what had hit him.

All he could see was white fire.

The blinding light resolved around a figure, wreathed with flames so stunningly bright that Áed winced at the pain of his pupils contracting. The faerie's face was hidden by a featureless black mask, and as he stood above Áed, the night sky was blotted out by the brilliance of his ice-white flame.

He raised a hand, and the flame flowed along the course of his outstretched arm.

Where it became a blade of fire.

Áed's eyes widened. He rolled to the side just as a burning blade sunk deep in the earth where he'd lain a fraction of a breath before.

The faerie was unreadable behind his mask. Éamon hauled Áed up as he clambered to his feet, but the faerie only slid his sword out of the ground and raised it again.

And then he froze.

Áed and Éamon watched, motionless, as the white fire haltingly stuttered out. The faerie collapsed to his knees.

He slumped face-first onto the ground, a knife embedded firmly between his shoulder blades. Behind him, a faerie whose hand shone with red fire stood wide-eyed, still frozen in the position of throwing a knife. For just a moment, his eyes met Áed's. "Thanks," Áed managed. He was dazed. The word made no sound, and then the faerie was looking over his shoulder fearfully and taking off into the night.

In the next heartbeat, Áed and Éamon were once again dashing for the palace door.

Inside, the hallways were chaos. Áed saw more white fire punctuating the bursts of gold and red, and screams echoed through the corridors. A pair of fae, one of them clutching a sobbing child protectively to his breast, bolted for the door to the garden, but they skidded to a stop in front of Áed and Éamon.

The one with the child addressed Áed, sounding desperate. "Did you just come from the outside? Can we make it?" His voice was accented in a way that sounded lilted and musical, but that did nothing to mask the fear in his tone.

"Make it where?"

The child let out a terrified wail, and the faerie shushed her frantically. "Anywhere safe. Is there anywhere safe?"

"Not outside," Áed answered automatically. "I don't know what the rest of the city is like—*fuck!*" His mouth fell open. "Ronan! Where's Ronan?"

The faerie without the child winced. "Did you lose someone?"

"We're missing a member of our party, too," said the one carrying the little girl. He'd started making a low purring sound deep in his chest, clearly meant to comfort his child, but it was choppy with his own fear and uneven breathing. "She was supposed to cross with us, but I don't know where she came through."

"Or if she even did," said the other. "They were ready for us."

A shout came from the end of the hallway. The fae family startled, fear etched into their faces. "Is there *anywhere* safe?"

Áed had no idea what was happening, but his head was buzzing with magic and adrenaline, and he heard himself reply. "Left here, down the stairs. There are lots of empty rooms. Maybe you can hide."

The childless one looked near tears. "Goddess bless you. Good luck!"

Éamon stared at Áed incredulously as the trio ran off in the direction Áed had indicated. "You just gave a faerie directions!"

"No time!" Áed yanked Éamon down a side hall, and then they were running again. This passage had windows that looked out over the garden, at the fiery carnage raging there. The sound of screams penetrated the glass, and the air hung heavy with the smell of smoke. Some of that smoke was clearly from *things* burning—wood, fabric, grass. Some of it, however... Áed's stomach turned. He caught more of those blinding white flames, saw more figures running for cover. Half of the trees were on fire. "I need to find Ronan!"

"Do you think he ran off?"

"Yes! Probably! Definitely!" Áed couldn't keep the panic out of his voice, and he didn't try. "The whole city could be like this! Éamon, I don't know where he is!"

"Where was he *supposed* to be?"

A blast of fire collided with the windows immediately behind them, shattering glass inward over the floor in a deafening explosion and a spray of shards. Áed tripped, and Éamon jerked him upright. "Anywhere!" Áed shouted, feet crunching over the broken glass. He could feel a bleeding laceration on his shoulder blade, but his frenzied mind blocked the pain. "So long as he keeps with his guards, he can go anywhere! But he never keeps with his guards, so now he's anywhere and *alone*!"

"In here!" Éamon said urgently. He shouldered open a door along the hall, and they both tumbled in. Still holding Áed's hand, Éamon slammed the door shut and fumbled the knob until it locked. "Help me move this bookshelf!"

"We can't barricade ourselves in! I have to find Ronan!"

"Áed." Suddenly, Éamon's face was inches from Áed's. "You cannot go out there."

Áed snarled. His eyes were hot, but with tears or magic, he couldn't tell. "I can, and I will!"

"No!" With the hand that wasn't holding Áed's, Éamon gripped Áed's shoulder. "Áed, did you see what they were doing?" He gave Áed a little shake. "Did you?"

"I—"

"Most of them were *running away*. The white-flame ones with the masks were attacking the other ones, did you see it? The fae were going after each other. Each other!"

Áed stared at him as the pieces began falling together. They didn't make a shape he recognized.

"They aren't targeting humans. For all we know, you and I are the only humans in the whole Gut that aren't just *asleep*. At first glance, they'll assume we're fae since we're awake, but they aren't actively attacking anyone who's passed out!"

Áed's brain wouldn't slow down. "I can't leave him out there." Even if Éamon was right, and fae were fighting fae, there would still be collateral damage. If this had extended to the city, then it was safe to assume there were fires breaking out all over the White City and probably the Maze.

"Are you listening to me?" Éamon looked desperate, too. "You! Will! Die!" Éamon's eyes were wide; his hair, damp with sweat, was pushed off to the side to reveal both eyes at once, and both were frantic. "He's probably passed out on the ground with everyone else, but if you go out there, you're going to wind up on the end of a *sword made of fire!*"

Both of them jumped at the sound of another explosion outside the door, followed by screams. The screams fell silent within a heartbeat, and then the crunch of a heavy tread on broken glass sounded from down the hallway.

"Help me move the bookshelf," Éamon whispered sharply. "*Please.*"

Haltingly, Áed lent his weight to the side of the heavy furniture. Éamon was stronger than him, but it still took both of them to slide it in front of the door.

Áed's breath was shaky as he and Éamon stood motionlessly in front of the barricaded door. Outside, regimented footsteps continued down the hall until they turned and faded out of earshot.

Éamon sank to the floor. Still holding his hand, Áed bent over before giving up and collapsing.

He had never felt so helpless. Ronan could be *anywhere*; he could be injured, he could be dead. He could be frozen on the floor of a burning building, fire creeping closer and closer until it caught the end of his braid and began licking toward his body.

Áed shuddered violently, clasping his free hand over his mouth and squeezing his eyes shut with a violent gasp.

He couldn't do this.

"Áed?" Éamon said concernedly.

"Let go of my hand."

"What?"

Éamon would be safe in this room. Without Áed dispelling the magic—however he was doing that—his mind would slip away like everyone else's, overwhelmed by the power of the magic pouring from the fae battle. Áed could... could what? Comb the entire city district by district, street by street, building by building? He had no idea where Ronan was. But he had to find him.

Éamon only redoubled his grip. "Áed, I don't know what the hell is going on, but I am *not* letting you go out there."

"Éamon—"

"Morning is only a few hours away. The veil won't stay open much longer." Éamon's eyes were wide and haggard. "I have family out there too." His voice was unyielding. "We'll look in the morning."

Áed's stomach curdled. "I had Cynwrig supervising the guards at the palace gate. Where was Boudicca going to be tonight?"

"I don't know."

The silence that followed hung heavy.

The only source of light was a vent that connected the room to the windowed hallway; in moon and firelight, it was just enough to see by. Smoke wafted in under the door that was mostly blocked by the bookshelf, and periodically, more screams echoed from farther away. After a while, Áed found that Éamon's head was on his shoulder, his bone-white hair streaked with soot and his eyes half-mast. Áed focused on combing the flecks of ash from his friend's tangled curls, concentrating on the repetitive motion and trying to force himself not to imagine Ronan dead in a thousand increasingly more horrible ways.

⸹⸹

Hours later found them sitting against the bookshelf.

The world was finally silent.

"Do you think it's safe?" Áed asked. The words came out flat, but he could feel the tension behind them. Éamon startled, jerking his head off Áed's shoulder with a gasp, and Áed regarded him with some surprise. "You managed to sleep?"

Éamon blinked. "I guess I did." He paused. "It's quiet."

"I think we can leave." He glanced to their hands, still clasped. Áed's bones were aching. "I want to see if it's safe for you to drop my hand."

Slowly, Éamon loosened his grip until Áed's hand slid free. He blinked a few times, as if his eyes were re-focusing. "Whoa."

"Are you all right?"

"I—I'm fine." He shook his head. "Dizzy. You don't feel this?"

Áed shook his head. "The magic must be lightening. You can function?"

Éamon clapped his palms to his face a couple of times. "I can function." He shot Áed a glance. "You will explain this to me later, won't you?"

"Later." Áed walked around to the side of the bookshelf and put his back to it to push. "Help me?"

The bookshelf screeched against the floor as they pressed it away from the door, a few tomes tumbling from the shelves and landing, undignified and flapping open, on the ground.

Morning light spilled through the doorway as Éamon turned the knob, and they squinted as the scene came into focus.

Éamon swore quietly.

Most of the windows along the hallway were shattered, glass blown both inside and out in long, deadly shards. Scorch marks scored the floor and walls, deep enough that the burnt stone crumbled under Áed's touch, and in the garden, Áed could see at least three trees felled, their trunks burned through. The marble floor of the hallway was cracked and stamped with streaky footprints, cast in blood and ash.

"Everyone's still in the garden."

Áed blinked, looking past the destruction. Sure enough, the slumped figures of humans were sprawled here and there across the grounds. They were concentrated where the crowd had gathered the night before, around the bonfire long since reduced to a pile of embers. For a moment, Áed thought they were still unconscious. Then, he saw that the person nearest them was entirely carbonized. White teeth grinned at him from a charcoal face. Another had been crushed under the burnt shell of a great oak tree.

Áed had to look away, bile rising in his throat.

Éamon took a deep breath and stepped carefully through one of the broken windows. He stepped carefully through the broken window and walked to one of the nobles on the grass who looked mostly intact. "So this is fae magic," he said grimly. He found her pulse with deft fingers. "She's alive. Is she... asleep?"

"In a sense, I think." Áed made his way out of the window as well, looking around through the fine morning mist and ignoring the pointed, inquisitive glance Éamon sent his way. There wasn't a single faerie to be seen, and he could feel the enchantment wearing out of the air. People would be coming around. "Come on. We have people to find."

Éamon looked a little guilty about leaving everyone lying helplessly, but he stood without complaint. "Let's find Cynwrig first. He should be closest. He can help us look."

Áed nodded, gritting his teeth. This was overwhelming on a level he'd never faced before, and anxiety was tightening his breath. He forced himself to move with purpose, concentrating on the next step. "Right. Follow me."

CHAPTER FOUR
ÁED

They found Cynwrig slumped against the palace's main gates. A fine trickle of blood had dried along his hairline from a cut on his brow, but otherwise, he looked uninjured. Breathing a sigh of relief, Éamon dropped to his knees next to his stepbrother, and Áed followed.

"Cynwrig," Áed said, pushing up the general's sleeve instead of trying to remove his gloves. He pressed his crooked palm to Cynwrig's forearm. "Hey. Wake up."

For a moment, nothing happened. Then Áed remembered the feeling of extending a shield over Éamon through their linked hands, the powerful oddness of projecting a feeling beyond his own body. He closed his eyes for a moment, trying to reclaim the way it felt to extend an emotion of *protection*. After a moment or two, Cynwrig's eyelids fluttered. His ice-blue eyes opened slowly, a look of confusion stealing over his face.

"Welcome back," Éamon said. His voice sounded strained.

The general sat up slowly, looking around, and his expression grew steadily more shocked. "What *happened*?"

"Fae," Éamon said, looking to Áed as if for affirmation.

Áed nodded. "Ronan's missing. We don't know where Boudicca is, either."

Groaning, Cynwrig got to his feet. He blinked a few times like Éamon had when he broke contact with Áed's hand, shaking his head as if to clear it. He still looked like he was processing the chaos of the palace grounds, but... well, if Cynwrig was anything, he was a professional. Áed could detect the moment the general pushed aside his confusion, squaring his shoulders and taking a short, sharp breath. "If we rouse some of my men, we can cut the search time."

As Áed went around hurriedly waking unconscious members of the August Guard—they weren't hard to find, given how much security the palace celebration demanded—Éamon filled in Cynwrig on the events of the previous night. Once Áed had gathered some two dozen guards, they reconvened at the gate.

"Right," Áed said, turning to the guards. He could feel the sleepless night making the edges of his mind frizz, catching on every reason to panic, but he schooled it with the thought of Ronan. "Your priority is finding the prince. And Lord Éamon's stepsister, the healer Boudicca." He made himself stand straight, trying to imitate Cynwrig's posture. He was a King. He was supposed to be calm in crisis. Pretending to be confident helped him gather his thoughts. "If you find anyone in immediate danger, do your best to ensure their safety before continuing with the search." He turned to Éamon. "Can you wake people?"

Frowning, Éamon knelt next to a fallen guard whom Áed had not yet roused. He gave them a shake, patting their face. The guard didn't stir, and Éamon looked up. "I don't think so."

Áed took a deep breath. "All right. We'll just have to wait for the magic to keep fading. It seems like once people are awake, they can stay awake, but waking them isn't easy. Don't try. Don't waste time." He swept his gaze over the assembled guards. "Understand?"

He was answered with a chorus of "Yes, Your Majesty."

"Good. Go."

The guards, Cynwrig in the lead, filed through the palace gates and into the city.

"Are we following them?" Éamon asked uncertainly.

"I'm not. You can go where you like," Áed said, suppressing a pang of nervousness at the thought of Éamon leaving his side. "If we cover ground that they aren't searching, we'll have more luck."

"Twenty-odd guards can't sweep the whole city."

"And once people start waking up, there'll be a panic. I know." Áed knelt next to another guard, brushing his hand over her forehead until she woke, blinking. "I'm going to get more people," he said, helping the guard to her feet and moving to another. "Then I'm going to start looking anywhere Cynwrig's party hasn't reached."

"I'll come with you," Éamon said, and Áed couldn't deny the wave of relief that rolled down his spine. Éamon crouched next to an unconscious noblewoman, her dark curls ornately braided and sprawled over the ground. Áed watched out of the corner of his eye as Éamon gave her a shake with no response, and then hesitantly raised a hand. He brought it down across her face in a sharp slap.

She didn't budge.

Éamon looked up to where Áed was still moving between dark-suited guards, leaving blinking, confused figures in his wake. "Why can't I do anything?" he asked, sitting back on his heels. He glanced back down to the noblewoman he'd failed to rouse. "Are you the only one who can?"

Áed looked away, concentrating on the next guard. The

truth was, he wasn't entirely sure what he was doing. Fae magic wasn't something that he'd ever had the opportunity to study; there just weren't any materials to learn from. But just because he didn't know the mechanics didn't mean he couldn't guess why his touch would be different. And that wasn't something he could just *say*. "I… later." He stood, looking around for any more guards. "I'll explain later."

Éamon, to Áed's gratitude, clearly had too much on his mind to press.

Áed repeated his instructions to the blinking, disoriented guards, and then they too were off, hurrying through the gates. Áed turned to Éamon. "Ready?"

"Let's go."

And together, they set off into the city streets.

〉〈〉

Áed had been right about the rest of the city being the same as the palace.

Blackened starbursts decorated the walls of the buildings, and the remains of festival decorations—tables of food, garlands, food vendors' stalls—were upset across the streets. Rowan boughs hung at uneven angles from doorways, and people lay everywhere, surrounded by dropped cups of ale, broken plates, fallen hats. It was difficult to tell who was unconscious and who was dead, except in the situations where it was so obvious that Áed had to look away. They passed a tailor shop that Áed knew was run by an immigrant from the Maze, and Áed grimaced to find that flames had hollowed it out from the inside. Fires danced through piles of rubble on the side of the road, and over the buildings, Áed could see columns of smoke rising into the sky.

For the first hour, Áed and Éamon combed every street that Ronan and Boudicca were known to frequent. They ran into a few guards, also searching, and relayed their routes, sharing which places had turned up fruitless. Two hours later, a guard approached them to breathlessly report that they had found Boudicca and were transporting her to the palace. She couldn't be woken, but she appeared only mildly injured. Éamon had looked to Áed helplessly, and Áed had nodded. Éamon had turned back to the palace at a run. The guard had stayed with Áed to continue the search for Ronan.

Three hours after that, there was still no sign.

The longer they looked, the harder it was for Áed to maintain hope. He could feel himself fraying a little more at every body-scattered street that remained empty of his ward.

Two more hours, and the sun was getting low in the sky. Áed was struggling to hold a thought, his mind doing a poor job of fighting off vivid scenarios of Ronan's burned, broken form trapped somewhere Áed would never find him. He squeezed his eyes shut, gritting his teeth against the roll of nausea that rose in his throat.

There was a moan from behind them.

Áed and the guard jumped in tandem, and Áed whirled toward the source of the sound, heart pounding.

A woman was moving. Her eyelids fluttered as she pressed a palm to her forehead with a little groan, and she lifted her head weakly.

Down the street, another person began to stir. Then another, and another. "Your Majesty," Áed's guard gasped. "They're waking up."

"Noted." Áed took a step back, strangely unnerved by motion breaking what had been eerie stillness moments before.

"I must advise we return to the palace, Your Majesty," the guard said nervously. "I'm not equipped to protect you."

Part of Áed knew the guard was right. With this level of destruction all around, the confusion that would ensue could quickly lead to panic. The King was easily recognizable, and he was meant to protect the city from disasters like this, or at least know how to fix them afterward. When they found out he didn't have any answers, desperation and terror could easily curdle into something more violent. It wouldn't be safe for him. But... "Ronan's still out here."

The guard bit her lip. "Your Majesty, with all due respect... once His Highness comes around, don't you think the palace is the first place he'll go?"

Áed pressed his lips together. That was probably true. "What if he's injured?"

"The August Guard will keep searching, Your Majesty." She cast a concerned glance around them. "Please, Your Majesty, let me keep you safe." She looked nervous. "Besides, um. You... you look like you're about to drop."

In all honesty, Áed felt like it, too. The terror of the sleepless night and the miles of walking that day, combined with staving off the magic from Éamon's mind and waking the guards, had left him exhausted. "I've felt worse."

"I know, Your Majesty." The guard looked down. Well, of *course*, she knew. Stories of Áed's time in the dungeons, as well as tales of his life before—often making up with inventiveness what they lacked in detail—were common in pubs, around bonfires, among the kitchen staff at the palace. "Please. If you return to the palace, you can send out more search parties, now that people are coming around. That will do more than the two of us can."

Áed pressed his palms into his eyes. The guard's logic made sense, even if dropping his own search made it feel like his chest was constricting with every beat.

But he had to be pragmatic. For Ronan.

"Right. Okay." He dropped his hands and blinked spots out of his vision. "Take me back."

}}}

Áed had scarcely made it through the palace gates with his guard before he was accosted by a small division of men. "Your Majesty!" cried the one in front, jogging up with four more guards behind him. "Your Majesty, you're back!"

The palace grounds were swarming with guards and healers. Most people seemed to have *some* idea of what to do, but nobody looked like they knew what was going on. The city had been even less organized, from what Áed had seen on the two-mile walk back. Pockets of panic had been bubbling; a few brave civilians were trying to keep order, and kindhearted souls were doing their best to administer aid to any wounded and cover the dead. A few had spotted Áed and hurried over desperately. It hurt to see in their eyes the hope that Áed, their King, could make everything better with a metaphorical snap of his fingers. He *wished* that was how royal power worked. Instead, he'd had to tell them that he was doing his best, and to please stay calm, that he'd be sending relief as soon as he could. Fortunately or unfortunately, they hadn't turned on him. Instead, he had to watch their faces fall. They'd lost homes. They'd lost loved ones. Their festival night, a celebration of the beloved dead, had turned into a harvest of new spirits.

Áed tried his best to turn his attention to the guards. "Yes. What is it?"

"It's the Crown Prince, Your Majesty!" the guard said urgently. "He's here, at the palace."

"What?" Áed demanded. He broke into a run toward the main door, making the guards follow him. "Where? Is he hurt?"

"He returned only a few minutes before you did, Your Majesty," the guard managed. "He's in the throne room, which is being kept empty. And he's being attended by a healer as we speak."

"Attended—*hell*!" Áed fumbled the elaborate doorknob with both hands. It made sense that there wouldn't be doormen stationed at their posts just then, but the extra obstacle was about to push him over the edge. "What's happened?"

"Nothing serious," the guard hastened to assure him. "He may have sprained a wrist, that's all."

Áed swore again, finally managing to wrestle the doorknob into submission and plow his way inside. His voice echoed in the marble halls. "And you didn't *lead* with that?"

"Well, Your Majesty, that's, um—" The guards were keeping pace as Áed hurried for the throne room. "The other thing is that he's brought someone back with him."

Áed frowned, trying to figure out why that would be significant enough to mention with such a tone of trepidation. "Who?"

The guard glanced to his comrades. "Well, um…"

"It's a faerie," one of the others blurted. "He brought back a faerie."

That nearly brought Áed to a dead stop in the hallway. "What?"

The first guard nodded. "Don't worry, Your Majesty, she's in custody—we have her in a holding cell. Away from anything flammable, of course, and one of my men, brave soul, has bound her hands—"

From down the hall, the tall throne room door burst open with an indecorous *crash*, and a slight, dark-haired figure tripped out. "Áed!" Ronan's hair had come loose from its braid, hanging long and wild down to his ribs, and he shook off an irritated-looking healer as he sprinted down the hall. "I knew I heard you!"

"Ronan!" Áed gasped. He ran to meet him, wrapping his arms around Ronan as the boy collided with him, and squeezing him so tightly his arms shook. "You're safe! You're all right? You're not hurt?"

Ronan returned the hug, trembling slightly, before he squirmed out and faced Áed with green eyes blazing. "Áed, you've got to order them to let Erin out!"

"Erin?"

"The faerie," one of the guards confirmed.

Ronan nodded frantically. "She's hurt, and she didn't do anything wrong, please—"

Áed turned to the guards. "Where is this faerie?"

"Dungeon, Your Majesty," the guard answered. "First level."

Áed took a deep, steadying breath. "The *Crown Prince* brought her back, and you locked her in the dungeon?" He narrowed his eyes. "And then ignored *His Highness's* orders to the contrary?"

The guard looked confused and a touch guilty. "Her lot is responsible for the... for everything. I thought..."

Áed waved a hand. "I understand. I'm sorry; I'm on edge." He shook his head. "I need to talk with her." If he spoke with someone who could answer a few questions, maybe this wouldn't be such a mind-bending mess. From what he'd experienced the previous night, most of the fae involved hadn't seemed like they wanted to be, but come daylight, he hadn't found *any*. They had either crossed back over the veil or vanished deep into the recesses of the city. "Bring her somewhere comfortable and be gentle with any injuries. Have a healer waiting for her." He had no idea if human healing magic would even work on someone who was full fae, but a decent healer would at least know how to set a bone or bandage a wound.

Ronan slumped with relief. "Thank you. Gods."

The guards tramped off to follow Áed's orders, and for a moment, Áed just let himself breathe in the stillness of the hallway. Then he glanced sideways at Ronan. "For the record," he said sharply, "this is why I tell you to stay with your guards."

"Er…" Ronan rubbed awkwardly at the back of his neck. "Sorry."

"And you didn't show up last night."

Ronan looked even more abashed. "Did you still announce me Crown Prince?"

Áed nodded. "I wish you'd been there." He took another deep breath and let it out slowly. "But it's nothing to worry about now."

Ronan perked up slightly. "You know, if I hadn't run off, then I wouldn't have met Erin." He looked at Áed seriously. "You'll want to talk to her. I mean it."

"Will she be able to tell us what happened? And maybe why?"

Ronan swept his hair over one shoulder to fidget with the ends. "I think so." He sighed. "She didn't talk to me much. I think she has a fractured rib or something, and she's really scared."

"You helped her back here?"

Ronan nodded, face growing agitated. "I told her she was going to be safe, and then they threw her in the dungeon."

Áed sighed heavily. "Gods. Nobody knows what to do."

"You do, though, right?"

Áed ruffled Ronan's hair, making a few long locks fall directly into his eyes. "Unfortunately, mate," he said wearily, "I'm still 'nobody' in this situation." He sighed again. "Come with me. I have to send out healers and give some direction to the guards."

"Why do I have to come?"

"Because I'm not letting you out of my sight." Áed dropped an arm over Ronan's shoulders to punctuate his point while Ronan grumbled. "Come on."

CHAPTER FIVE
ÁED

"Let me talk to her first."

Ronan stood next to Áed outside one of the palace's many rooms—a room that ordinarily housed nothing but an empty bed and some shelves gathering dust, but which at that moment was home to one faerie. And two healers. And three guards. And so much human-cast protective magic that Áed thought it was a wonder anyone inside could breathe. "Do you think she'll want to talk?" Áed asked. Ronan was fidgeting nervously with his hair, now pulled back into a hasty ponytail.

"I hope so," he said. "Gods, I hope she's okay."

Áed glanced at Ronan sideways. Ronan had always been empathetic, so the fact that he cared so much wasn't a surprise, but something was different. Ronan himself was confused enough that Áed couldn't get a good read on what, but he had a hunch based solely on the flush in Ronan's cheeks. For the moment, he put it aside. "How did you meet her?"

"After I woke up," Ronan said, "all I knew was that I had to get back to the palace. I was real foggy, at first." He bit his lip. "Everyone was nervous, you know? But then I saw her in an alley—the one between the bookshop and that tea place with the hanging plants—and she looked *terrified*." He frowned faintly. "She was hurt. So I went to help."

"I don't know whether to praise you for that or tell you it was dangerous."

"Oh, come on," Ronan complained. "It's what you'd have done."

Áed couldn't combat that. He shook his head. "You can talk to her first."

Ronan's face lit up. He didn't need any further prompting to dart through the door.

Áed slumped against the wall with a heavy sigh. His injuries were minor, but he hadn't had a chance to get them looked at, and they were smarting. The cut on his back from the blown-in window was the worst, but his sweater, torn from the impact with the ground when the white-fire faerie had attacked, revealed raw skin on his shoulder. He was sure his hip was the same. Now that Ronan was back at the palace safe and sound, all Áed wanted to do was sleep.

Doubtful he'd be able to, though. He'd already started a list in his head of everything he needed to do, and that list was long. His people were suffering. He needed to start with relief.

Inside the room, he could hear muted voices. It sounded like Ronan was doing most of the talking, occasionally interrupted by a female voice. Áed closed his eyes instinctively, trying to figure out what they were saying, but as soon as he did, he felt his mind wandering. Gods, he was tired.

His eyes flew open at a sharp yelp from within the room. Even through the wall, he could feel the wave of fae magic that caused it. The feeling of human fear hit him shortly afterward, sharp and almost tangy. He whirled to the door, scrambling to open it.

Every human in the room was frozen. Their faces were masks of abject terror, and as Áed watched, Ronan sank to his knees, clutching his head. He was shaking.

On the bed, the fae girl was sitting up, one hand fisted on the blankets and the other held out in front of her, trembling. Her teeth were gritted, and her crimson eyes were wild. She looked like she was in pain, but her strong magic poured over the room. Áed could feel it himself, pulses of unnatural fear encroaching on the edges of his awareness as the girl's power twisted his undefended, human emotions.

"Stop!" he cried.

The girl's focus snapped to him.

Her mouth fell open, and the magic fell away. "Thank Goddess," she gasped. She spoke in the same musical accent as the fae Áed had met as they fled during the festival. Her hair, in long dreadlocks down her back, had fallen out of the twine that held it away from her face—a fine, pretty face, beaded with sweat and full of relief. She sat up further and winced. "Do you know what's going on? I got hurt, and—oh, no, they're coming around already." She raised her hand again.

"Erin, wait!" Ronan managed from his knees. "Please—"

Another wave of fae magic, laced with Erin's own fear, buffeted the room. Ronan let out a terrified cry, and one of the guards bolted for the door. The healers weren't far behind, stumbling out into the hallway. Two guards remained, trembling but stalwart, and after another heartbeat, Erin collapsed over her knees, and the magic lifted again.

Áed crossed to the bed in two strides, and the faerie made a faint, animal whine at his presence. Áed knew, some deep instinct rising from dormancy, that the sound meant she was glad of his presence. That she was afraid. That he was somehow a comfort. "You need to stop that," he said. He put a hand on her shoulder, firm but gentle. "You're just exhausting yourself."

"But—"

Áed turned to the guards. "Leave us."

The guard nearest the door furrowed his brow, looking worried. "But Your Majesty—"

Áed shot him a hard look. "Thank you for your concern. Leave."

Obediently, the guards trooped out, casting confused glances over their shoulders. Unsteadily, Ronan used the edge of the bed to push himself to his feet.

Erin was looking at Áed with an expression of bafflement. "They... take orders from you?" She looked lost. "They called you 'Your Majesty?'"

"Erin, this is Áed," Ronan supplied shakily. A faint sheen of sweat had broken out on his brow, and he wiped it away with his sleeve. "My guardian and the King of the Gut."

"He's—you're—" Erin looked entirely lost. Another whine sounded from somewhere in her chest, and this time, Áed knew that she was distressed. It was intuitive in a way language simply wasn't, more instinct than intention. She spoke over the noise, and it continued quietly behind her words. "*What?*"

Áed took a deep breath, trying to ignore how strange it was that he could so naturally comprehend her nonverbal vocalizations. He had never *met* a full faerie, and the way Erin had looked at him—like he was kin—had made his heart twist in a way he hadn't felt before. "Like Ronan said. My name is Áed, and yes, I'm the King." He sank to a weary seat on the edge of the bed. "I'd really like it if you could help me answer a few questions about what happened last night."

"About—" Erin seemed to be struggling to assemble a

sentence. "But—don't you already know? Aren't you—you're—"

Áed's head was starting to hurt again, but this time, he was pretty sure it was just lack of sleep. And maybe a bit of dehydration. "Ronan, would you check the door, please?"

Ronan turned the bolt in the lock.

"Right." Áed turned his attention back to Erin, who was staring at him with an incomprehensible array of emotions. He kept his voice low to avoid the ears of anyone lurking at the door. "I'm half-fae, to answer the question I think you were trying to ask. In the palace, only Ronan knows. I was born on this side of the veil, and no, I don't know what happened last night." He pushed his hair back from his face, noting with absent familiarity how Erin's eyes immediately locked on his hand's crumpled form. "I've never met a full faerie before tonight, and I can't say it was a great experience. But if you don't plan on trying to hurt us, then I promise you that you're safe here."

For several long moments, Erin just stared.

"I think that might have been a lot," Ronan ventured.

Erin whispered under her breath, entirely to herself: *"The human King is half-fae..."* She blinked, looking between Áed and Ronan. "Someone must have known this."

"I've tried very hard to avoid that," Áed said, but Erin shook her head.

"No, I mean one of us. One of us must have known. They should have told someone." A look of frustration was growing on her face. *"Someone* must have known. Who's your fae parent?"

"I never knew her. Hey—" Áed leaned forward as Erin looked more agitated. A strange chuffing sound came from deep in his chest without any permission from his brain, and he knew right away it meant *soothing*. He nearly clapped his hand over his mouth in surprise.

Erin only replied with a faint, distressed whimper.

"H-hey," Áed said, trying to focus over the internal noise of his rational mind panicking. "Calm down. It's all right."

"It's not!" Erin's hands moved to her neck to fidget unhappily with her necklace. It was pretty, crafted of what looked like sea glass charms. "If we'd have known, someone might have sent an envoy, and—and maybe—" There were tears beading in her eyes.

"Erin," Ronan said concernedly, but Erin was still talking.

"We just wanted to be safe." She wiped away tears with the backs of her gloves. "We didn't mean to hurt any humans. We're not trying to take over, we're just trying to *hide*, and maybe if we'd have known the King was *fae*, we could have… I don't know, planned something differently!"

"Please slow down," Áed said, trying to keep his voice calm. He hadn't known if he'd be able to sense the emotions of a faerie, but he could certainly feel Erin's distress rolling off her. "Could you start from the beginning, please?"

The faerie took a deep breath. Her hands had moved from fidgeting with her necklace to fidgeting with her turquoise sweater. "You're low-court, right?"

Áed blinked. "I'm what now?"

Erin shook her head. "Just show me your fire."

Ronan glanced over as Áed held out his palm and let a few flames gather over it. He snuffed it just as quickly.

Erin nodded, her shoulders sagging with what Áed identified as relief. "You're low-court, all right."

The temptation to simply sit down and spill every question he'd accumulated over the years was nearly overwhelming. He'd never had the opportunity to speak with one of his own like this. Instead, Áed tucked his hands into his pockets. "How do you know?"

Erin held up her own thin hand, and a few tongues of

red and gold fire danced over her fingertips. "Your fire's not white. Easiest way to tell." She sighed and slumped back into the pillows, propped against the headboard. "There are other ways, too. Like, you'll never see a high-court faerie with a physical flaw." She narrowed her eyes. "Hm. I should have known from your freckles, I guess. Though those could be from your human side." She shook her head. "Beyond that, high-court fae have white fire. Horrible white fire that burns faeries like me. Like you." A shudder ran through her shoulders, and she growled softly. "You've seen it, haven't you?"

Áed realized he must have made a face, or perhaps Erin had sensed his immediate reaction. "Yeah," he said. "Yeah, one of them came at me last night. With a… a flaming sword."

Erin's lips pressed together. "Be glad they didn't hit you." Her eyes, as red as Áed's, were shadowed. "You'd be dead."

"Wait," Ronan interrupted, sounding alarmed. "*Dead?*"

Erin ignored him. Ronan blushed, embarrassed. "High-courters don't usually cross the veil at festivals," she went on. "They have their own celebration in the Queen's court. Some low-courters go to that too, I guess, but we're never very welcome. So we cross."

"Hold on," Áed said. "Queen?"

"You really don't know anything."

"I wish I did." He leaned against the edge of the headboard. "Never mind. Tell me what made last night different."

The faerie sighed. She closed her eyes. "There's been fighting." Her head tipped back onto the pillows. "War, really. If you want to call it what it is. Between the high and low courts."

"Why?"

Erin ran the tip of her tongue over her lips. "The Queen

had this… this consort." She looked to the ceiling. "Real powerful." Her lip twitched into the hint of a sneer. "We called him the Cur. The Queen's dog, did anything she wanted. He's evil."

Ronan frowned from the end of the bed. "Did he do something to the low courts?"

Erin huffed a short, humorless laugh. "Yeah," she said. She lifted her head. "He left."

Áed's confusion was mirrored on Ronan's face.

"Yep." Erin laced her hands over her chest. "Just took off. Abandoned post and position. Nobody knows why."

"Then what's wrong?"

"What's *wrong*," Erin said, sitting up again, "is that the Queen thinks one of the low courts kidnapped him or something." She threw up her hands. "As if we even could!"

"So she's attacking you because she thinks you have him?"

"Hard to say," Erin said. "We've told her we don't have him, and we couldn't be lying. But she hasn't stopped accusing us." Once again, she dropped back against the pillows. "A lot of us couldn't take it. We're not all fighters, you know?" A hint of a smile flickered over her face. "Could still kill most of your lot without much trouble."

"Please don't."

The faerie exhaled shakily, perhaps with the barest hint of a laugh. "Anyway. We planned to take refuge in this realm. Cross the veil and just… lay low. Until we could go home again." Her expression had begun darkening again, growing sadder. "But it was the Queen's perfect opportunity." She rubbed at her mouth, eyes welling with tears again. Áed could tell she was exhausted. "There were a lot of us in one place."

Áed thought back to the fae woman tripping over the dais and stumbling up frantically to sprint away, the panicked fae couple with the child, the terror in their eyes. "I'm so sorry."

Erin sniffed. "If we'd have known this place had a fae King, maybe you could have helped. We could have asked, at least." Her damp eyes were bright. "Wouldn't you help your own?"

Áed took a long breath. He wanted to. He did. But... "Ronan," he said slowly, "stay with Erin. There'll be a guard outside if you need anything." He stood from the edge of the bed. "Erin, I'm going to send the healers back in to look at your injuries."

Erin looked confused, and also like she was trying to suppress the soft, unhappy keening sound that trembled from her throat when Áed made to leave. "Where are you going?"

Áed ran a hand down his face. "The city—*my* kingdom—is terrified. And still on fire." He turned for the door. "I'll come back, I promise. I want to talk about this more. But I have to take care of what I can right now."

"He gets like this," Áed heard Ronan murmur. "He's stressed."

"Will he help?" Erin whispered back. Her voice shook a little.

When Ronan spoke again, his tone was hard. "Don't worry," he said. "He will."

CHAPTER SIX
RONAN

Ronan found Áed in one of the stairwells later that evening, dead asleep.

He was still wearing the turtleneck and sweater Ronan had picked for him the night before, and where the sweater had torn, Ronan could see that Áed still hadn't gotten his own injuries treated. His hair was uncombed, and Ronan could see the dark circles under his eyes.

Ronan let out a short breath. He himself hadn't even been *conscious* for the exciting part of the past night; one moment, he'd been hurrying through the festival, enjoying being overwhelmed by lanterns and masks, music and dancing, and the next, he was coming around on a soot-blackened street. Everything had smelled like smoke, his wrist hurt from where he'd apparently tried to break his fall—and yeah, it had been pretty terrifying—but he'd been *fine*.

If he had to bet, he'd put very good money on Áed having been up all night. And Ronan knew he'd searched frantically all day.

So… yes. Áed had definitely sat down for a moment's rest on the stairs and simply fallen asleep.

The right thing to do might be to let him sleep. Ronan

had a pretty good idea of the state Áed must have been in for the past day and night, and it almost made him feel guilty for sneaking away from his guards. He had just wanted a bit of freedom, that was all. All he'd intended was a hint of rebellion, the sort he *knew* was pathetic, but that he couldn't seem to help. He'd just wanted one night where he could be Ronan, the stranger-boy who'd accept a dare and dance with a couple of pretty girls, who'd be an adventurer someday, and who *definitely* wasn't His Highness the Crown Prince, stuck between marble walls. He hadn't imagined the night would turn out the way it had.

He pressed his lips together. Áed would want to be woken up, whether he needed sleep or not.

Gently, he shook Áed's shoulder, the one that didn't look like it had been skinned on the ground. "Áed. Wake up."

Áed stirred with a groan. Slowly, his eyes blinked open. "Ronan?" he mumbled. A hand went to his back, which had been resting on the stairs. "Ugh. Ouch." He reached out a hand, and Ronan took him by the wrist and helped him to his feet. "What time is it?"

"Probably about midnight."

Áed swore. "I was going to check back in with Erin."

"Don't worry about that now," Ronan said. "She's asleep."

"How is she?"

Ronan thought for a moment. When Áed had left, Erin's features had been nearly unreadable. Fear, confusion, exhaustion… Ronan couldn't tell what people were feeling the way Áed could, but he didn't need that uncanny ability to know that she was a mess. She'd fallen asleep an hour after the healers finished up. Ronan had left her alone to rest. "Her ribs are better," he said finally. "The healers' magic works on her."

"Good," Áed said. He still looked a bit disoriented from

having been asleep. "That's good."

"We have to help her, you know." Ronan plucked at the hems of his sleeve. There was something to that idea, he thought, of diving into a quest for the sake of somebody else. It sounded courageous. It also sounded like the right thing to do. "We can't just leave all those people to get attacked like this." He pointed at Áed. "And didn't you say one of the high-courters tried to kill you last night?" He crossed his arms. "That makes it personal."

Áed sighed heavily, rubbing at his eyes with crooked thumbs. "It was personal the moment they came into my cities." He leaned a hip onto the banister. "We can handle refugees. At least…" Apparently giving up, he sank back to a seat on the stairs. "At least, we *could* have handled refugees. Now half the city is burning, and nobody even knows yet how many are dead."

Ronan winced. All he could think of was Erin's terrified face. She wouldn't have tried to hurt anyone; he was sure of it. "That wasn't the low-court fae's fault."

"I didn't say it was." Áed rubbed at his eyes again. He did look positively haggard. "Right now, my responsibility isn't to take sides. It's to make sure that something like this never happens again." He gritted his teeth. "I've worked so hard, Ronan. This is devastating for the White City—can you imagine what it's done to the Maze? It's going to be hard enough to put everything back together again this time. This can't *happen* again."

"It's not going to stop, though," Ronan said helplessly. "As long as their war is going on, it's going to spill over on the festivals." He slid to a seat a few steps below Áed. "We could order a lockdown four times a year for the festival nights, but there's still going to be damage. There's nothing you can just *do*." He felt his eyebrows come together. "Besides, don't you feel *anything* for them? For Erin?"

"Of *course,* I do," Áed snapped, and Ronan realized that he'd probably sounded more accusing than he'd meant to. "I was there, you know. I was awake. There were faeries fleeing for their *lives.* Parents with children. Families broken up. I'm—I'm not *heartless*, Ronan." He took a deep, steadying breath. His eyes' ordinary luminosity was dulled with weariness. "But I don't know what to do right now."

Ronan played with the ends of his hair, twisting the strands into little braids and then brushing them through with his fingers. His lips pursed thoughtfully. "Let's talk to Erin again. She probably has more to say, once she's feeling better."

Áed nodded. "That's all we can do right now."

⇟

Ronan was fairly certain that if Éamon hadn't come by a few hours after sunrise to see how Áed was doing, Áed would have slept until the stars came out that night. Ronan had been busy running back and forth between the royal chambers and Erin's, each time hoping that *one* of the people he was thinking about would have come around. Each time he checked on Erin, the healers shooed him away and told him the faerie needed rest. And Áed was snoring softly behind the door to his private room. Given that Ronan maybe did feel just a little bit bad about giving his guards the slip, he didn't want to disturb the King.

Fortunately, real cause presented itself in the form of Éamon. The white-haired councilor knocked on the door to the royal chambers shortly after Ronan, having sprinted up the tower stairs for the fourth time that morning, had decided to take a quick break. Áed hadn't even needed to be woken; a few moments after Ronan invited Éamon inside, a sleepy and disheveled King emerged from his room.

"How is Boudicca?" Ronan asked as Éamon bowed unnecessarily to Áed, who was coming down the stairs.

"She's all right. Mostly worried about everyone else." Éamon sighed. "You know how she is."

"She's like Áed, then." Ronan tucked his loose hair behind his ear. "I only got him to rest last night when I found him asleep on the stairs."

"I had things to do," Áed grumbled, slouching in and reaching past Ronan for one of the green apples in the bowl on the table. "I *have* things to do. Good morning, Éamon."

"I don't get a good morning?" Ronan protested.

Áed took a bite of the apple and spoke around it. "I'm still upset with you, remember?"

Ronan sulked. "I said I was sorry."

"I'd say that I'll believe you when you prove it, but you won't have a chance. You're not leaving my sight for the foreseeable future."

It didn't seem important for Ronan to mention that he'd been running around the palace all morning without Áed knowing, so he didn't say anything. Instead, he turned to Éamon. "What brings you by, my lord?"

Éamon rolled his eyes at the title. He'd clipped his curls back to his left temple, leaving hair to hang only over the scarred side of his face. Ronan had never fully understood why both Éamon and Áed were so adamant about hiding their scars, but then again, he didn't have any of his own. Maybe it was just one of those things that didn't make sense until it happened to him. "I just came from an emergency council meeting. The August Guard is distributing supplies as Áed ordered, but we don't have enough for everyone who needs it. People are getting frustrated." He let out a heavy breath. "Things are getting more intense. I wanted to check in on both of you."

"Well, *I'm* fine." Ronan grabbed an apple himself and leaned on the table. "But Áed needs a hug."

"I'm fine," Áed said quickly. "What I need is to get to work." He set aside the core of his apple. "I can start by talking to Erin again. I'm going to go get dressed. Excuse me." He fixed Ronan with a swift glare before Ronan could even open his mouth. "And *no,* I do not need your help. I had to wear Éamon's cloak for the whole festival, thanks very much." He glanced to Éamon, his gaze losing its ire. "It's ripped, by the way. I'll buy you a new one. I'm sorry."

"Áed, wait." Éamon seemed to catch himself reaching out and drew back his hand. "I also wanted to know if maybe you had any answers for me. About… the festival. What you could do."

Ronan frowned, looking to Áed. "What did you do?"

"He protected me from the fae magic," Éamon said. "And he was the only one who could wake the unconscious ones."

Ah. Well, that certainly wasn't something Ronan was going to touch.

For his part, Áed only looked away. "I haven't quite figured it out yet." Ronan knew him well enough to notice him trying not to fidget. "I'm sorry. I'm not… completely sure."

Éamon looked faintly disappointed. "Well. I'm sure there are more important things anyway."

Áed hastily retreated upstairs to dress, leaving Éamon and Ronan at the table.

Éamon took the opportunity to look after Áed, a faint crease between his eyebrows. "Who's Erin?"

"Oh, you didn't hear?" Ronan munched his apple, unable to keep the shine out of his eyes. "She's a faerie."

Éamon's visible eye widened in a way that Ronan found rather gratifying. "A *faerie*?"

Ronan nodded. "I found her when I woke up after the festival."

Éamon looked a bit stunned. "And she's *here*? In the palace?"

"Sure is." Ronan pulled out a chair and flopped into it. "Áed's talking to her about what happened when the veil opened."

"Is that *safe*?"

Ronan crossed his arms. "She's just scared. More than we are, probably."

"Scared and fae." Éamon looked a bit disbelieving. "That's a dangerous combination, I think."

"Erin wouldn't do anything." Ronan looked at Éamon stubbornly. "She's a good person."

Éamon's eyes narrowed a degree. "Good person or not, be careful. And by the Gods, keep her a secret. The last thing the people are going to want to hear is that the palace is working with one of the creatures who just torched half the city."

"Erin didn't do that," Ronan protested. "She said she didn't, and faeries can't lie. She's nice."

Éamon pursed his lips for a moment, wary, and then closed his eyes and let out a short sigh. The corner of his lip twitched up. "And what does she look like, this Erin?"

Ronan sat back, toying with his unfinished apple. "Well. She's got long hair—not as long as mine, but it's really curly, so actually, maybe it's longer—and she's a little taller than me, and her fingernails are painted black—or maybe they just *are* black, who knows? Do full fae have black nails? And her eyes are awfully big… and…" He trailed off, realizing that he'd started rambling.

Éamon looked faintly amused. "She's pretty, huh?"

Ronan blinked, feeling his cheeks warm up. "I never said that." He took a defensive bite of his apple. "And anyway," he said, casting around for something to say, "she's my age." He pointed at Éamon, wagging his finger. "That's creepy."

The councilor held up his hands in surrender, chuckling. "So you're sweet on a faerie."

"I am not."

"Sure."

Ronan crossed his arms again, fuming a little. "Why is this fun for you?"

"You're sweet on a faerie."

"So are you," Ronan grumbled under his breath, too low for Éamon to hear. Then, louder, "I only met her at the festival, anyway. I just want to help."

"Of course," Éamon ceded magnanimously. "Your motives are pure."

"Of course, they are." He raised an eyebrow. "Are yours?"

Éamon cocked his head. "Beg pardon?"

Ronan leaned back casually. "You're here to visit Áed, aren't you?"

A faint pink rose in Éamon's cheeks. "You're implying something, aren't you?"

"Am I?"

"You're a brat, you know that?"

Ronan grinned. "I'm on your side, *my lord*. How'd you like Áed's festival outfit?"

The blush deepened, just a little. "Áed hated it."

"Irrelevant." Ronan waved a hand, inadvertently sending an apple seed across the room.

Éamon *hmph*ed, looking away. "I remember when you were quiet and adorable. What changed?"

"I'm still adorable. Now, do you have a plan?"

"I do not need a fifteen-year-old to help me with my love life."

Ronan snorted. "Apparently, you do. You've been pining over Áed since I was quiet and adorable."

Just then, the door to Áed's room opened, and Éamon quickly stood, face flushed. "Áed!"

Áed stopped in the middle of looping a scarf around his neck and glanced between Éamon and Ronan. "What did I miss?"

"Nothing!" Ronan chirped. "Áed, are you ready to talk to Erin?"

Áed cast one more suspicious glance between Ronan and Éamon, and then he nodded and finished tucking in the end of his scarf. He slid down the banister instead of taking the stairs, which Ronan only ever saw him do when he was in a hurry or a very good mood. Ronan suspected that any good mood likely came from Éamon's presence, and haste was probably the more important factor. "Ronan, you're coming."

Ronan hopped to attention while Áed turned to Éamon.

"I don't want to overwhelm her," Áed said thoughtfully, "but if you wanted to meet her, maybe you could. I should talk with her first, but—"

"Oh, no," Éamon said with a nervous laugh. "I'm all right. Thanks." He plucked at his sleeve. "Not sure I'm really up for—" He swallowed. "That is, I think I saw plenty of fae at the festival. Don't need to see any more."

Áed's face fell faintly. "Right. Of course."

"I'll still walk down with you, though," Éamon said quickly. "I came over to see you, after all."

"Great!" Ronan interrupted before Áed could respond. "We'll be off then? Yes?" He hurried to the door and opened it. "After you? Your Majesty? My lord?"

Áed muttered something with a roll of his eyes before he and Éamon started down the tower stairs.

Ronan bounced on his toes as he followed them down the stone spiral staircase. Light slanted in through the occasional narrow window—as well as cold air because those windows were drafty—and made the stairwell glow in the marble sun.

It took far too long, in Ronan's opinion, to reach Erin's room, but he supposed that Áed and Éamon weren't as partial to running everywhere. When they arrived, the healer stationed at the entrance stood from where he'd been sitting against the wall, obviously dozing. "Good morning, Your Majesty," he said, blinking sleep out of his eyes and doing his best to stand at attention. "Your Highness. My lord." He bowed. "The faerie girl is awake. I've checked her injury. It's healing well." He rubbed at an eye. "Please forgive me for drifting; I'm afraid I was up all night."

"Thank you," Áed said with a warm smile. "We'll see her now, if you think that might be acceptable."

The healer looked askance. "Your Majesty, if I may ask..." He tucked his hands into his loose sleeves. "Why are we treating her?" Immediately, he shook his head. "I'm not disloyal. Your Majesty knows best. I only wonder because—" He swallowed. "If I may share, Your Majesty, my cousin died last night. I only wonder why we're treating one of the people that did it before we're treating our own citizens. Your Majesty."

Áed closed his eyes, and Ronan saw his head bow a degree. "I'm so sorry for your loss," he said quietly. "I promise, I'm doing everything that I can. I think this faerie girl has answers for us, which is why I need her in health." He opened his eyes. "I appreciate you speaking so plainly."

The healer nodded, looking at the ground. "Of course, Your Majesty. And I... I do trust you." He looked up. His eyes were enormous through the thick glass of his spectacles. "I warn you, though, Your Majesty, that many besides me are suffering."

Áed looked physically pained. "I know."

At that, the healer stepped aside with a short bow. "It should be all right to see the faerie, then, Your Majesty. Only try not to agitate her. For both her sake and yours."

Outside the door, Éamon stopped. "Is it all right if I wait here?"

Áed nodded, though Ronan saw the tautness of his mouth. "Of course. Wouldn't want to make you talk to a faerie."

Ronan thought Éamon noticed the hint of tension behind Áed's words, but he only stepped aside so that the stationed guard could open the door for them.

Inside, the room was dim. The window faced westward, away from the rising sun, so the morning light was diffuse and peaceful. The air smelled like herbs and candle smoke.

Erin was sitting up in bed, and she opened her eyes at Ronan and Áed's entrance. They flashed red, brighter than the pale light should have allowed. It sent shivers down Ronan's spine. Erin came from across the *veil*. It had taken all of Ronan's self-control not to bombard her with questions about the marvels she must have seen. She was injured, and she was surrounded by soft palace bedding, but she still had an air of wilderness about her. "You're back."

Ronan hovered by the door while Áed pulled over a seat left by one of the healers. *So she's pretty.* Éamon's words ghosted through his head, and he felt his cheeks warm slightly. It wasn't *wrong*. Objectively.

Áed crossed his legs, propping his elbows on his knee. "Let's talk."

Erin's delicate fingers, seemingly without any conscious thought, moved to worry at her sea-green necklace. "Really?"

Her eyes narrowed, clearly distrustful, and she hummed. It was a low, peculiar sound. "Because yesterday, you didn't seem terribly keen.'"

"I'm sorry." Áed's eyes were earnest. "Yesterday was... a lot."

"You're telling me."

"Right. Of course. My apologies." Áed sighed. "I want to make a plan. Something that will hopefully benefit both sides of the veil. But I can't make any decisions without knowing what you have to say, so..." He nodded to Erin. "I'm here to listen."

For a moment, Erin just scrutinized his face. "What do you want to hear?"

"Anything you can tell me." Áed gestured to Ronan. "Ronan tells me that you're trustworthy, so I'm trusting you."

Erin frowned thoughtfully. "Well, for starters, you ought to know that I'm sort of nobody." She glanced between Ronan and Áed. "If I knew how to end the war, I'd have said something. I'm not a court leader or anything."

"That's fine." Áed beckoned Ronan over, and Ronan realized he'd still been standing awkwardly by the entrance. He folded himself into a cross-legged seat at the end of the bed. "Maybe you can start by telling us about the courts."

Erin seemed to catch herself before commenting on how little they knew. "So, uh. You already know about the high and low courts." She held one hand below the other. "Most of the low courts are literally underground, and the rest don't have a permanent mound. Like I said earlier, low-courters have red fire and usually physical imperfections." She tapped one of her ears, and for the first time, Ronan noticed that its tip folded over itself. His first impression was that she'd slept on it wrong.

Cute, his brain supplied, and then he promptly pretended he hadn't thought that at all.

"There are seven low courts," Erin went on. "Each one has a chief; the more powerful chiefs have their own families, too. That metric doesn't apply to the high court, of course—the Queen just goes through consorts. No children, no real family, and she's still more powerful than any of us."

"Tell me more about her?" Áed asked.

Erin shushed him. "You wanted me to tell you what I know. I'm doing that. I'll get there."

Áed held up his hands in surrender, and Erin went on. "Anyway. Seven courts. I'm from the Sand court." She traced a symbol in the air, fiery lines hovering behind her fingertip and revealing a sigil of shifting dunes. "Then there's Gold. Glass. Meadow, Moon, Garnet. And… Bone." The last word left her lips accompanied by a smoldering outline of an animal skull—a dog, perhaps, or a fox. "Áed, do you know which your mother was from?"

Áed shook his head, and Erin frowned.

"By your freckles, I'd guess Meadow. But with that hair, maybe Gold?" She looked him over thoughtfully. "It's not quite the right shade. And you're taller than most of the Gold fae I've met. But most of the Meadow folk have darker skin." She shrugged, clearly moving on. "Who knows. Anyway, the low courts have all allied. Most of them stand behind either Moon or Bone—Moon because it's powerful, Bone because it's vicious. Any questions so far?"

Ronan thought he had several thousand, but before he could isolate just one, Erin had moved on.

"All right. Now, the *high* court is a different story. There's only one, and the Queen leads. The Queen—the Queen of the past thousand years—subjugated the lower courts a few centuries ago." She rolled her eyes. "We're supposed to tithe to her at festivals, present our children to her for blessing, follow her laws."

Áed looked like he wanted to be taking notes. "You said

the war started because the Queen's consort went missing?"

"Yes." Erin's expression turned stormy, and a low rumble started in her chest. Ronan was getting used to her strange noises—when he'd found her, she'd been crying keening wails of pain that had sounded *distinctly* inhuman—but some were easier to interpret than others. He supposed it was a *fae thing*. "She's accused every low court of treason, ordering him found on pain of destruction."

"Sounds rational," Ronan muttered, and Erin rolled her eyes.

"Yeah, well. None of us have that bastard, or we'd have given him back. And wherever he is, he *definitely* knows about the war. He hasn't returned to stop us from getting massacred, so. Shows what kind of person he is."

Ronan raised his hand but didn't wait for acknowledgment before he interjected. "It seems like maybe you need help."

Erin glanced at him suspiciously as if she was trying to discern whether he was making fun. Apparently satisfied, she slumped against the pillows. "We need a lot of things," she mumbled. "Troops. Weapons. Bone and Moon are trying to supply the courts behind them, but... well, we're already at a power disadvantage. High magic is devastating, and even a military like Bone's can only do so much." She huffed, clearly frustrated. "A lot of us just want to be *safe*, but that isn't an option anymore. As things are, the Queen's forces will destroy us before long. For each victory we take, she takes three."

Ronan looked pointedly to Áed.

Áed sighed, avoiding Ronan's eye. "I just have a few more questions."

"Go ahead," Erin mumbled.

"The fae who crossed at the festival," Áed said. "Do you know where they are?"

"If talking to them is what you want, good luck," Erin

replied. "They'll have gone into hiding by now. Could be anywhere." She scowled. "Unless they got caught by the high court, in which case… who knows?"

"I'm sorry," Ronan said. He meant it, but Erin just looked away.

"Anyway," she said shortly. "Is that all?"

It wasn't, of course. Ronan was sure of that. But it felt like he had to absorb what he'd heard before he could think of asking anything else. He shook his head.

But Áed didn't. "Erin," he said slowly. His emotions were obscured behind unfocused eyes, but it was clear that he was thinking. "I know it isn't a festival. But…" He scratched at the back of his head, frowning with contemplation. "Is there a way for us to cross the veil?"

CHAPTER SEVEN
ÁED

Áed had really expected Erin to shake her head. Or maybe shake her head after giving him a look as if he were a moron, something she'd already done a few times.

He'd been properly surprised when instead of doing either of those things, she pinched her lower lip thoughtfully. "It was something I know people were talking about," she said after a moment, "when we were planning our escape."

Áed glanced to Ronan. Ronan had been staring at Erin like she was either the most fascinating or the most beautiful person he'd ever seen, and that expression had yet to leave his face. For her part, Erin seemed to be actively avoiding Ronan's eyes, stealing glances only when she didn't think he'd be looking.

Funny.

"We stopped discussing it after a while," Erin continued, interrupting Áed's observations. "It goes the wrong way—into the fae realm, instead of the human one. Wouldn't work."

Áed blinked. "But there *is* a way?"

"Well… yes." Erin tugged absently at one of her dreadlocks. Her carnelian eyes met Áed's and held them. "It just isn't easy." She frowned at him. "Why? Will you send us troops? Because I don't know how well a human army will stand up to *high-court faeries*." Her eyes narrowed. "But weapons would help. Do you have weapons?"

Áed shook his head. "We do. But that wasn't the idea."

Erin deflated, but Áed was still thinking. "I can't contribute to your military." The kingdom simply couldn't afford to spare the resources. Beyond that, he couldn't *imagine* trying to bring that up to the council, much less the general public. A King whose people hated him was not the kind of leader he wanted to be. "But it sounds like that isn't the only way."

Ronan, still sitting at the end of the bed, looked at Áed curiously.

Áed took a moment, trying to gather his thoughts. The first priority had to be diplomacy: crossing the veil with the intention of speaking to *someone* about making sure no more damage spilled into the human realm. That was the bare minimum. But if more could be done—if the war could be *ended*—well, that would be even better. Áed rubbed the back of his thumb pensively against his lips. "You're focused on the military," he said. "Which makes sense. You're being attacked." He hesitated. "But has anyone tried to find the consort?"

For a moment, Erin blinked at him. "I mean, the Queen sure has."

Áed shook his head. "No, no. I mean, has anyone from the low court tried to find him. To return him to the Queen."

"And give the Queen what she wants?"

Áed shrugged. "Maybe, but wouldn't it end the fighting?"

Erin twisted one of her dreadlocks between her fingers. "Suppose we did try that. How would it work?" She shook her head. "If the *Queen* hasn't found him, how would we?"

At that, Ronan's eyes widened. He leaned forward, his

mind clearly whirring. "Wait a minute," he said. "This might be a time when humans actually have the advantage." He turned to Áed, and then Erin. "What about magic?"

When neither Áed nor Erin replied immediately, he hurried on.

"Like Boudicca," he said. "She uses healing magic. And Áed, do you remember Ailbhe, from the Maze? Didn't they use some kind of truth magic or something?" He fidgeted with the quilt. "Fae might be more powerful, but humans don't have so many limits. What if somebody from here used magic to find the consort?" He was clearly attempting to suppress a degree of excitement. "That would work, wouldn't it?"

Áed frowned in thought. "Actually, Ronan, that's... a pretty clever idea." He turned to Erin. "Do you think that would work?"

Erin shrugged. "I don't know a thing about human magic. But if the plan is to send a human across the veil alone, I should tell you they won't last long."

"That wouldn't be the plan." Áed got up and started to pace. "What are the odds that a human could get an audience with a court leader?"

"Depends on the court leader, and how much fun they like to have."

That didn't sound good. Áed stopped pacing for a moment. "And what are the odds that *I* could get an audience with a court leader?"

Erin considered. "Better. At least you're fae. And nobody would know you're only half by looking at you."

"Okay." Áed bit at a cuticle, resuming his pacing. This was getting complicated. "We need to establish a diplomatic connection between the human realm and the faerie courts. Which means that someone from the human realm needs to cross the veil—and that person can't be human."

"So…" Ronan trailed off as if he thought he might be missing something. "That's just you."

Áed nodded helplessly. "And with some kind of diplomacy hopefully working as a stopgap, it would be excellent if we could end the war altogether. Which means finding the consort, which means at least one full human needs to come along so that they can perform the magic to *find* that consort." He pushed his hands into his hair. This all had to happen while the Gut was rebuilding itself.

"You'd need more than that," Erin said, and Áed looked to her. Her gaze had fallen to the bedspread. "You wouldn't last ten minutes." Her hands bunched the quilt. "You'd need a guide."

"Ah," Áed said quietly. His pacing slowed to a stop. "Of course."

Slowly, he walked back to the bed. Erin hadn't looked up. "Erin."

Her fists tightened on the blankets.

"You'd be saving lives." He lowered himself to a crouch by the side of the bed. "It's a lot to ask. I know that."

Erin let out a short, sharp breath. Her eyes were fixed on her lap. "I ran away because I didn't know what else to do." Her black nails dug into the quilt. "There was nothing I *could* do."

Áed opened his mouth but held his tongue when Erin's eyes flicked up to meet his. Her gaze was hot.

"That isn't the case anymore." She coughed a little humorless laugh. "And it isn't like you have other options. I'll be your guide, cross-blood." Her lip twitched up, sending wrinkles across the top of her nose. "Goddess knows you'll need all the help you can get."

⟫⟫

Éamon stood up from his seat on the floor as soon as Áed and Ronan stepped out of the room. "Áed!" He met them as Áed closed the door behind them. "How did it go?"

"Fine," Áed said. He really shouldn't be holding onto this nonexistent slight; it had to be obvious from his tone that he was irritated, and Éamon wouldn't know what he'd done wrong. Áed probably wasn't being fair.

But still. Éamon hadn't even wanted to *see* a faerie. He and Áed had been friends for years, and Áed had come close to telling him the truth on several occasions—usually when he was drunk—but he never had. And at moments like this, he had to wonder if all those years of friendship would make a difference if he ever *did* share.

He shook his head, starting deliberately down the hall. He wasn't being rational. Éamon had good reason to be afraid of faeries—hell, *Áed* had good reason to be afraid of faeries. That didn't change the fact that, irrational or not, it stung.

But that was a concern for a different time. The issue had waited for seven years, and it could wait for Áed to sort out the mess that was his kingdom. Priorities.

Éamon and his long legs easily fell into step next to Áed. "What's wrong?"

"Nothing." Áed looked up at his friend to find a worried periwinkle gaze looking back. "Sorry. It's nothing."

"We talked to Erin," Ronan supplied, and Áed was glad that the boy seemed willing to carry the conversation for a while. He had too many things to think about just then.

"Did she clear anything up?" Éamon asked.

Ronan began relaying what Erin had told them, and Áed tuned them both out.

If Erin's plan was going to work, he had preparations to make. His head was still spinning from everything she'd said; he couldn't quite wrap his mind around it. *Crossing the veil.* Risky. Downright dangerous, even. And that was just the *crossing* part. Was he actually considering *going* to the other side?

Part of him recoiled at the idea. He hadn't forgotten what it had cost him to get where he was. He was extremely nervous about leaving the kingdom that he'd worked for with blood and sweat to traipse through an unfamiliar land that held no guarantee of safe return—or return at all.

But he couldn't deny that he was hopeful. Terrified, yes. But hopeful.

"Áed?" Éamon and Ronan had stopped, noticing that Áed was no longer walking with them. "Everything all right?"

Áed shook himself and hurried to catch up. "Of course."

Éamon didn't look convinced, but he didn't press, and Ronan resumed his chatter.

CHAPTER EIGHT
ÁED

Éamon found Áed later that night.
Without making a fuss, he simply joined Áed sitting cross-legged on the ground.

Áed blinked at him, breaking out of the spiral of his thoughts. After speaking with Erin, Áed had gone straight to the Council of the King to arrange for the opening of the royal stores; they kept a portion of every year's harvest in the event of an emergency. He'd arranged for all the kingdom's healers to be dispersed through the cities and was trying to determine how palace funds could help with rebuilding. People had already fallen to looting. To Áed's surprise, the Maze was coping better than the White City. He supposed that centuries of neglect *would* enforce a mindset of self-reliance, but the gangs were using the disaster as an opportunity to hash out their turf wars. The August Guard could keep some order, but Áed thought it was more important to focus his energy on making sure that people could get the resources they needed.

The night wind drew cold fingers through his hair. He was huddled in his cloak, mindless of the chill. In front of him, a single, lonely tombstone was dull in the moonlight.

"I thought you might be here," Éamon said.

Áed glanced up. "You did?"

"No," Éamon said with a little smile. "Ronan told me." He sighed, looking toward the grave. His breath rose in little puffs. "Ah." He inclined his head respectfully. "He was a good man."

"Hmm."

Judoc's name had been engraved onto the stone three years earlier. It was getting weather-worn.

"Do you come here a lot?" Éamon asked quietly.

Áed shrugged. Judoc had been imprisoned with him, back in the darker days when Áed had first arrived in the White City from the Maze. After Áed escaped, the man had become a confidante. He had helped Áed work out his problems as Áed was struggling to wear the mantle of King. "When I need to think."

"It's quiet."

As if to accentuate the point, the wind died down. It was true. The little cemetery was as silent as snow.

"I need to talk to you," Éamon said softly. "Is it a bad time?"

Áed shook his head stiffly.

"All right. Well…" Éamon shivered. "Do you want to go inside?" He looked concerned. "Your lips are blue. And you hate being cold."

"I hadn't noticed that I was," Áed mumbled.

Warmth touched his shoulders, accompanied by weight, and he looked up to find Éamon draping his cloak over him.

Áed hugged it closer, smiling faintly. "You sure you want to trust me with one of your cloaks again?"

Éamon returned the smile. "Just this time. Come on." He offered Áed his hand and wrapped it around Áed's wrist when Áed took it. "Let's get somewhere warm."

They ended up settling on one of the benches that lined the hallway by the palace kitchens. The walls weren't marble here but brick, and at this hour, the corridors were still, save for the occasional scullery maid carrying hot water or dirty dishes. Most importantly, it was warm. The air was humid and smelled like cooking and smoke.

Áed could tell that Éamon was worried. The councilor tapped his heel, sending close echoes through the hallway. "You should see this," he said, once Áed had leaned back against the wall to absorb the warmth.

Áed accepted a small pamphlet from Éamon. "What is this?"

Éamon only nodded at the paper. His lips were pressed into a thin line.

Áed unfolded the pamphlet.

It was handwritten in a blocky script, and Áed read aloud under his breath. "The King consorts with faeries," he murmured, eyes skimming along the lines of text. "Allowed fae across the veil… city destroyed. Enemies hiding in our streets, King does nothing… families dying, King dines in palace." Unable to continue, Áed pressed the pamphlet closed. His breathing was uneven. "Is that what they're saying?"

Éamon took back the paper. "Those pamphlets were all over town this afternoon."

Áed propped his elbows on his knees to rest his forehead in his hands. "How many people do you think believe it?"

"They're desperate," Éamon said. "Some of them will."

"It doesn't change what I have to do." Áed lifted his head from his hands to fix Éamon with a stare. "The idea that this could—that this *will*—happen again… it isn't bearable. I have to stop it."

"So," Éamon started. Áed was still huddled under two

layers of cloaks. There was a seed of chill sitting behind his breastbone. *Gods*, he hated being cold. "That brings me to what I was thinking."

Áed looked at him curiously.

Éamon picked at his cuticles. "Ronan filled me in on your plan." His gaze flicked sideways to Áed. "It sounds dangerous." Éamon folded his hands and took a deep breath. "I want to come."

Áed blinked. "You what?"

Éamon didn't falter. "I want to come with you. Across the veil."

Áed leaned forward, narrowing his eyes to scrutinize Éamon's face. "Don't get me wrong, I *appreciate* it, but—"

"I know what I'd be getting into. Ronan told me everything." He shrugged helplessly. "You're my, um—my best friend." Suddenly, it didn't seem like he could keep eye contact. "I'm not going to let something as small as my own comfort get in the way of being there when you need me." He blinked, eyes flicking up. "I mean, *if* you need me. I'm sorry, I didn't mean to assume."

Áed couldn't help it. He chuckled, hand going to cover his mouth.

Éamon blushed. "What? What did I say?"

"Nothing." Áed waved a hand weakly. He was still laughing. All the stress had finally hit him, hadn't it? "Nothing at all." He wiped away a tear, unable to stop giggling.

"So, um." Éamon looked lost, fidgeting again. "Is—is that a yes?"

Áed took a deep breath and held it, trying to calm down. It *mostly* worked. "Are you sure you want to?"

Éamon nodded firmly. "Besides," he said, "after I heard about your plan, I talked to Boudicca. She knows just about every magic-user in the city."

"Of course, she does," Áed said. He should have thought of that. "Are there any who know tracking magic?"

"That's the problem," Éamon said. "She said she knows of exactly two."

Áed sat up straighter. "Why is that a problem? That's good news."

Éamon shook his head. "The problem is that according to Boudicca, you won't be able to find a single magic-user in the kingdom who will be willing to cross the veil." Áed slumped again, and Éamon leaned forward. "Magic-users are a wary bunch. They know better than anyone how strong the fae are. How dangerous."

Áed put his head back in his hands. *Dammit.* "What am I supposed to do, then?"

"Other than assert your royal power to make one of them come along?"

Áed rolled his eyes, even though, with his head in his hands, he knew Éamon couldn't see. "Yeah, that would go over *terribly* well."

Éamon chuckled drily. "Well, then I have a different suggestion." Áed lifted his head, and Éamon turned to face him more fully. "I imagine that you'll be much too busy with diplomacy and kingly nonsense to have much time to do it yourself, so…" Éamon shrugged. "Well, I'm human too. Maybe I could learn."

Áed stared at him for a moment. "You'd learn magic?"

Éamon looked away with a shrug. "I can't say it's something I ever *wanted* to do. But yes. I would if I needed to."

Éamon was making it hard to resist. He might not know that Áed learning human magic was likely not an option given his heritage, but he was offering a way to solve that problem anyway. It would be tricky. Áed didn't imagine it would be easy to hide his nature in a world where every person he met would see him as fae first, where everyone knew the truth except Éamon.

But potential for magic aside, Áed couldn't deny how much better he felt when he imagined Éamon coming with him.

"All right," he said finally. "You can join us."

Immediately, Éamon's face broke into a relieved grin, and Áed wondered what the hell he had just done.

"Gods," he mumbled, dragging a hand down his face. "This is such a mess."

Éamon dropped an arm over his shoulder, and Áed slouched against his side. It was comfortable. Familiar. Éamon radiated warmth. "It'll be okay."

"Yeah?"

Éamon gave him a light squeeze. "Yeah."

CHAPTER NINE
ÁED

The next week passed in a blur.

He talked to a healing Erin. Solidified plans. Collected supplies. Áed spent hours in the council chamber, preparing for every eventuality he could think of, which was depressing more often than not.

Depressing and terrifying.

"No," he told Ronan for what felt like the seven-hundredth time, "you are not coming."

At that moment, Ronan was standing with his arms crossed resolutely in the doorway of Áed's room. "I'm coming."

"You're *not.*"

Ronan's eyes were bright and rimmed faintly in red. "You can't just *go.*"

It felt like someone had squeezed Áed's lungs. "I'm going to be back."

"Let me come with you."

"I'm not going anywhere right now," Áed said, trying to keep his voice steady. "Just back to the council; there's something else I have to clear up." The word had gotten out that Áed was leaving, and tensions were running high outside the palace. Áed had assured the people again and again that he was not abandoning them, and now it seemed that he was having the same conversation with Ronan.

"I'm not talking about right now," Ronan said. He hadn't allowed his hair to get so messy in years. "I'm talking *to* you right now, though, because you've been so busy, and I don't know when I'm going to have time before—" He faltered.

The guilty pressure on Áed's chest increased a degree. "Gods, Ronan, it isn't like I'd just leave without telling you. We'll have time to talk."

Ronan didn't budge. "I want *more* time." His expression was hard, hiding turbulence behind it. "In fact, I want *all* the time. I'm coming with you."

"Ronan." Áed grimaced. "Someone needs to stay here and make sure that the kingdom is stable." He hadn't ever intended on making Ronan actually bear the burden of his title as Crown Prince. Not unless the worst happened. But he hadn't expected this, and he didn't know what else to do. "I need someone that I can trust. Someone smart, who's kind, and... and who I know will take care of the people while I'm gone." The Council of the King would back Ronan and provide any support he needed. Áed had made sure of it.

Ronan glowered. Áed's attempt at praise had only served to bring angry tears to his eyes. "Then *you* shouldn't go."

Áed stopped. "Aren't you the one who wanted me to help Erin?"

"I—I didn't—" He balled his hands at his sides. His mouth opened and closed a few times. When Ronan had been much younger, he had gone months on end without saying a syllable. Áed and Ninian had tried hard to help him, and he had found his voice over time, but on certain occasions, Áed noticed that speech still evaded him. Áed felt awful. It only happened when Ronan was *very* upset. Áed reached out instinctively, but Ronan stepped back. "Not like this," he managed, and getting the words out sounded like a struggle. "I didn't mean it like *this*."

Áed withdrew his hand like he'd been stung, drawing a deep, steadying breath. "Ronan, I *have* to." He realized he sounded a little pleading. Ronan was a *priority*. He always had been, and he always would be. Before anything else, Áed took care of Ronan. That was imperative.

But he didn't know what else to do.

"If this keeps happening—" He swallowed. "Ronan, people are going to die. A *lot* of people. Us, and them. The kingdom will never recover if it gets attacked every three months."

Ronan didn't seem to have a response for that, but a frustrated tear slipped down his cheek.

"Éamon will be with me," Áed said, trying to comfort him. "He'll be watching my back." The idea of Éamon having his back was strangely comforting. Perhaps Ronan would feel the same way. "I have every intention of coming back, *ceann beag*."

Áed hadn't called Ronan *ceann beag* since Ronan had gotten older and started looking embarrassed by the nickname, but the boy didn't combat it now. He simply held his stare. "That's not a promise."

"Do you want me to promise?"

"That's the thing," Ronan snapped. His hands were tight fists. "You can't."

§§§

The day came sooner than Áed was ready for.

The intention had been for the little party's departure to be a quiet affair. Ronan, as Crown Prince, was to rule in Áed's absence. The Council of the King had been thoroughly instructed on how to react in any emergency Áed had been able to think of. Packs of supplies for each party member had been gathered, following Erin's advice regarding what they would need. All that remained was to say their goodbyes and allow Áed's small detachment of guards to escort them out of the city.

But things were already deviating from the plan.

For starters, a crowd had gathered outside the palace doors.

It was not a calm crowd. Áed could hear their shouts through the great doors: *The King is leaving! The King is leaving us! The King is leaving with a faerie—King Áed allied with the faeries!*

"Do you want to address them, Your Majesty?" one of Áed's attendants asked nervously.

"I'd advise against it," one of Áed's guards interjected promptly. "Some of the crowd is armed."

Supporting the guard's point, a sharp impact on the doors made Áed jump. "They're throwing rocks?"

"Bricks, Your Majesty."

Áed closed his eyes. "Perfect."

He couldn't say he was particularly surprised. It wasn't as if he had a choice, but the fact remained that he was leaving the kingdom in a state of distress—another thing to worry about while he was gone. But he had done everything that he could, given as many explanatory addresses as he could have possibly given, and now, appreciated or not, he needed to take the next step. If his people were safe in the end, it would be worth it.

He just had to focus. Concentrate on the strategy.

Unfortunately, that brought Áed's mind to the other thing that had already gone wrong that day.

Ronan.

That morning, when Áed had gone to him to say goodbye, Ronan had locked himself in his room. Áed had said goodbye through the door, answered by nothing but Ronan's shaky breathing. It had almost been enough for Áed to back out. Postpone leaving, even just for a day. But Ronan had spat a choked-up "Go," muffled by the door, and… Áed had gone.

It hurt that Ronan wasn't there to see him off.

Badly.

He shook his head. He would be back, and everything would be fine. "Right," he said, wrestling his attention back to the present. "We'll just have to leave through the south door."

Éamon fell into step next to Áed, who was keeping pace with a grimacing but mobile Erin as they walked through the palace. The three of them were dressed in traveling clothes and carrying packs—Éamon in a dark sweater and sheepskin cape, Áed in a heavy tunic and coat, and Erin in the turtleneck, leather coat, and fingerless gloves she'd been wearing when she crossed the veil.

The south door, mercifully, was unhindered by crowds. It opened into a damp, drizzly morning, mist spitting from the heavy clouds that hung over a city notably worse for wear.

The August Guard flanked them as they climbed one at a time into the waiting carriage. Áed noticed that Éamon made sure to sit on the opposite side of Áed from Erin.

The dappled mare drawing the carriage nickered as the driver clambered into his seat, and then with a gentle jolt, they were off.

Erin leaned against the window. "I can't believe I'm going back," she murmured. "After all that effort to get away."

"I'm grateful that you are," Áed said, swaying with the movement of the carriage. The streets were largely empty, except for a few people hurrying down the alleys to seek shelter from the damp. The neighborhood through which they rode, Áed knew, was popular with former inhabitants of the Maze. It had become a place for people with similar experiences to find each other, and Áed was glad to see that it didn't seem to have been damaged too badly. Here and there, cracks ran up the walls of buildings, and there were a good number of scorch marks, but the integrity of the structures themselves seemed largely intact. Áed turned his attention back to Erin, tearing his eyes away from the window. "Thank you."

Erin only hummed. "I hope it's worth it."

CHAPTER TEN
ÁED

The western edge of the city was quiet. The perpetual gray patina over the white marble of the buildings, laid down from countless years of forge smoke, was complemented by stark black scorch marks. The soot seemed more at home in these districts than it did in the rest of the city, but the unsettled quiet did not.

The carriage stopped where the buildings met the cliff edge, and the driver slid the window open nervously. "Are you sure this is the right place, Your Majesty?" He glanced around. "Are you going over the cliff?"

Áed nodded. Just past the buildings, he knew, a narrow switchback stairway zigzagged down the cliff face. It was an old trail, weathered and hazardous enough for most people to avoid it—which was exactly why Áed had chosen it for their descent into No-Man's-Land. "We won't be disturbed."

Still looking skeptical, the driver swung down from his seat and walked around to open the carriage door. He helped Áed and Erin down, taking the faerie's gloved hand gingerly as if her touch would burn, and Éamon jumped down on his own.

Áed hitched his pack higher on his shoulder. "This way."

"No guards?" Éamon asked, looking around, and Áed shook his head.

"If anyone approaches, Erin can drive them off."

To illustrate Áed's point, Erin sent out a faint pulse of controlled emotion. Áed felt it distantly; Éamon flinched. "Not every faerie can project emotion like that," she explained. Her tone was clipped with nerves, but Áed thought he detected a hint of pride. "It's a lot easier to do when you're in contact with whoever you're trying to project on, but I've gotten good at doing it without. I'm best at fear, so we shouldn't have problems."

Áed frowned to himself. *Interesting.* He remembered the feeling of protectiveness flowing from himself to Éamon, and later to Cynwrig, like a defensive shield against the rest of the magic. Had he perhaps inadvertently done what Erin was describing?

If he had, he couldn't ask about it now.

With no more questions, the three of them turned down the alley that flanked the straight-backed, dirty buildings. There were no first-floor windows; iron scaffolding crawled up the walls, leading to rickety ladders beneath windows that were cracked and opaque with grime.

Éamon shivered, looking around warily and drawing his woolly cape a little closer. "Don't suppose we could have gone through a... nicer neighborhood?"

Áed shot him a look.

The councilor looked away awkwardly. "Sorry. It's just... there are other ways down the cliff that don't involve..." He glanced around, visibly on edge, and gave plenty of space to the bins along the alley. They were all overflowing with slag and broken wood crates, and a few of them bore the distinct marks of rodent teeth.

"This is the best way down," Áed said. "Not many people, and the stairs end close to where we need to be." He ducked under a drainpipe that had fallen away from its building and landed propped up against the opposite wall of the alley. "Besides, this isn't even a bad neighborhood."

Éamon blinked. "Isn't it?"

"It's industrial, that's all."

"Oh." Éamon didn't sound like he entirely knew what the difference was, but he chuckled nervously. "I guess I... wouldn't know."

Erin muttered something that sounded distinctly like "little aristocrat," and Éamon flushed pink and fell quiet. Áed chuckled to himself. Éamon had grown up with more privilege than Áed could have dreamed of, and sometimes, it did show. Áed didn't make judgments on the actual *quality* of Éamon's childhood—wealth aside, Áed knew that his friend's life had been far from perfect—but he didn't feel bad about laughing a little when Éamon was too obviously out of touch.

The sound of the wind announced their closeness to the cliff's edge.

As soon as they broke free of the buildings, Áed made straight for the edge, just a step away from the railing. The steady gusts blowing up the cliff face buffeted his hair back from his face, bringing tears to his eyes almost immediately. He felt, rather than saw, Éamon and Erin join him; his eyes were fixed, watering, on the faraway mountains. He could never get tired of this view. It wasn't as if it was a surprise anymore—he could see it whenever he liked if he just looked out the window in Ronan's room—but being there in person still took his breath away. The sheer height. The sprawling heath, the densely wooded foothills. The way the land buckled into peaks so far away that he still struggled to fathom the distance.

"Are *those* the stairs?" Erin's voice came over the sound of the wind. She sounded incredulous.

Áed tore his eyes from the horizon and looked over. In truth, he hadn't yet seen the stairs in person, only on a map. The railing ended, and the walkway dropped away. Over the precipice, he could see uneven steps trailing down. "Looks like it."

Erin's eyes widened. "Are you *serious*?"

The edges of the steps, carved into the cliff, were rounded with age and weather, each step no wider than the length of a hand. The handrail wasn't a rail at all but a rope bolted into the cliff face at intervals with rusted brackets. "Mm." Áed peered over the edge. "I suppose there's a good reason they're not used anymore."

"You do realize a fall from this height will kill us."

Éamon frowned at the faerie. "Even you?"

Making a face that Áed was a little too familiar with, Erin looked at Éamon like he was the stupidest person she'd ever had the displeasure to encounter. "I'm a faerie, not a bird. Do you see wings, here?"

Éamon looked rather affronted. "I don't think I like you very much."

"Feeling's mutual, *my lord*," Erin muttered.

Áed stepped between them, shooting each of them a chastising glance. "Focus, please."

"On the death stairs?" Erin grumped.

It was becoming easier and easier to see why Ronan liked this girl. "Yes, on the death stairs. I'll go first, and then..." He hesitated. "Who next?"

Éamon looked over the edge with trepidation, shuddered, and then shook his head. "No. I should go first." A touch of color filled his cheeks, and his eyes flicked to Áed. "If you fall, maybe I can catch you."

Before Áed could formulate a response, Erin raised her hand. "I support the blueblood going first."

Áed fidgeted with the strap of his knapsack. Swallowing anything he had been about to say—it wasn't like there was anything to defend, since Éamon *was* an aristocrat—he turned to his friend. "Éamon, this was my idea. You shouldn't have to—"

"I want to," Éamon interrupted. His hand found the railing and gripped it with a tightness that spoke both of nervousness and determination. "Please let me?"

Áed bit his lip. "*Please* be careful."

Flashing a tight smile, Éamon turned to the stairs.

"Try going down backward," Áed suggested. "That way, one hand can hold the rope and the other can hold the steps above you."

Éamon took a deep breath. Before he took the first step, though, he looked to Áed, a thought evidently just occurring to him. "How exactly are *you* going to do this?" He looked down, and Áed could feel his nervousness. "Can you even hold the rope?

"We'll find out."

"That is not the answer I hoped for," Éamon muttered. "All right. I'm glad I'm going first, then."

"I'll try not to fall and kill you."

When Éamon's head disappeared below the edge of the cliff, Áed started down. The wind was even stronger on the cliff face, and immediately, he felt his stomach drop. Éamon shouted something up to him, but even from just a few feet below, the councilor's voice was lost.

Áed leaned into the steps, trying to keep his body as close to the iron-red stone as he possibly could. The rope was taut with Éamon's grip—Áed reached for it experimentally but immediately put his hand back on the steps, feeling his stomach swirl. Nope. Even if he could get his fingers around the fat cord of wound hemp, he didn't trust the strength of his crooked hand to actually catch him if he fell. Best to just press himself to the rock as best he could.

Erin started down after him, and Áed could see her knuckles paling on the rope. She held herself stiffly, as if willing her body not to shake.

The descent was almost meditative, if meditation involved screaming wind, a constant bottomless hollow in the pit of Áed's stomach, and rough, rusty stone digging into the heels of his hands. Áed's entire concentration narrowed to the next step, so as not to think about the fathomless distance to the grassland below.

He slipped once, a little more than halfway down. He trusted his weight to his foot before he realized that the step itself sloped downward, and his boot skidded off. All the breath left him as his upper body hit the stairs hard, and he caught his weight on his elbows, heart racing so fast that his chest felt like it would split. Éamon called up to him, concern in his voice as a rain of dust and pebbles pelted the top of his head, but Áed was paralyzed for a few minutes before he could manage a shaky response. Above him, Erin swore and redoubled her grip on the rope.

It felt like it took a long time before the ground started looking closer when Áed glanced over his shoulder. It crept nearer and nearer until he started being able to make out separate plants and then individual stalks of long heath-grass.

Some ten feet from the bottom, a touch too eager to be on the ground, he got careless. In an attempt to move faster, he leaned away from the staircase—just slightly. He'd been holding onto each step with a forearm pressed to the stone, but on moving backward, he shifted his grip to solely his hands.

It wasn't much of a grip.

With a yelp, he felt his center of gravity shift. He scrabbled at the steps above as he tripped backward, and then he was falling.

Éamon grunted as Áed hit him, and he automatically released one of his hands from the rope to catch him. The grip of his other hand tore off the rope with the momentum of Áed's weight, and then they were falling. Éamon's back hit the ground, and Áed landed hard on his chest. "*Oof—*"

"Oh, my Gods, I'm sorry—" Áed gasped. He tried to push himself up, but his whole body was buzzing, and his arms shook too much to support him.

Éamon just wheezed, the breath knocked out of him, but he patted Áed's shoulder weakly.

Erin hopped off the bottom step gracefully and stood over both of them with her hands on her hips. Shading her eyes, she scanned the whispering grassland.

The wind was quieter here, Áed noticed as he caught his breath, still lying on top of Éamon. The sound of rustling plants, the occasional chirp of a songbird, and Éamon's pounding heartbeat were all that Áed could hear. "We made it," Áed murmured.

Éamon groaned, and Áed finally rolled off him. The pearly-haired councilor sat up and squinted up the cliff. A few leaves of grass were stuck in the fur of his cloak. "So we did," he managed.

"Damn," Erin said, bending over to look at Éamon more closely. His hair had blown away from his face. "That's a hell of a scar."

Éamon started with a jolt and hurried to finger-comb his curls back over his eye. He shot her a glare.

Áed dragged himself to his feet, using the cliff for support. Its base was thick with winter-dry wildflowers and the occasional dense, thorny shrub. "We still have good hours of light," he said. The tallest grasses reached his chest, and he stepped further into the little clearing that he and Éamon had flattened when they fell. "Erin?"

Erin's attention turned from Éamon. "The gate is in the woods," she said, adjusting the twine that held her own hair out of her face. "I've never tried to find it from here. But I should be able to sense it when we get close." She shot Áed a look, and Áed nodded minutely. Erin had already agreed not to divulge his secret to Éamon, but Áed got the message—he'd have to be alert to sensing the gate as well.

Áed helped Éamon up and brushed a few loose seed pods off his clothing. "Are you all right? I landed on you hard…"

Éamon laughed breathily, rubbing his ribs. "You don't weigh much." He shook his head, a glint of humor in his eye. "So much for me catching you, though, huh?"

Áed opened his mouth to reply, but Erin interrupted. "Come on, you two." She turned away, the copper studs lining the shoulder seam of her coat glinting in the clouded sun. "We should move."

CHAPTER ELEVEN
ÉAMON

Éamon had never been camping.

In fact, Éamon had never slept outside. Or anywhere but a bed.

Áed sidled up to him as he tried for the third time to arrange his bedroll flat on the tree-root-latticed forest floor. "Having fun?"

With a groan, Éamon dropped the edge of the bedroll. "Is this *supposed* to be fun?"

"Not really." Áed crouched down and started adjusting Éamon's sorry attempts. "Don't worry. I didn't know how to do this either for a long time."

Erin looked up from her own flawless little site. "You didn't?"

"Not before I had to go on a patrol of our borders a few years ago."

"Huh." Erin cocked her head. "I thought you grew up on your own in the wild."

Áed snorted, and Éamon felt his heart skip a beat. He didn't think Áed realized the exact way his nose scrunched up when he laughed. "Been listening to the servants gossip?" Áed asked, and Erin shrugged noncommittally.

Áed chuckled, shaking his head. "No, I grew up in—well, the slums, I guess." He gave Éamon's bedroll a final pat and stood. "And actually, I was never alone."

Éamon sank to a seat on his bedroll with a tired smile. "Thanks for the help, Áed." Gods, it felt good to sit. He was sore all over. Some of it, no doubt, was simply from working muscles he wasn't used to using—he'd climbed down a few hundred stairs, after all—but he also couldn't deny that some of it was from Áed falling on him. Áed really *wasn't* very heavy, but he also had fallen about ten feet and landed directly on Éamon's chest. He didn't suppose sleeping on the ground would help him be *less* sore. It was impossible to deny that he was ready for this part of the journey to be over. "So, Erin," he said, absently massaging his ribs. "Any idea how far we are from the gate?"

Erin had been collecting wood and propping it in a pile in the center of their campsite. For a moment, Éamon stupidly wondered how she was going to light it; he remembered the obvious just in time to startle as a sparking plume of fire manifested from her palms. "Well," Erin said, leaning back and brushing off her hands as the fire began to crackle. "I can feel it. I think we can make it by midday tomorrow if we rise with the sun."

Éamon took a deep breath, letting the night air, which smelled of smoke and icy forest things, center him.

The gate itself was supposed to be a bit tricky. It only went one way, and every person could only use it once—that was what Erin had explained. Which meant that after they crossed the veil, they would be trapped on the other side until the next seasonal festival in late winter.

With a sigh, Éamon dragged his knapsack into his lap and began digging around for the food he'd packed. His brows came together the more he searched. Hadn't he brought some meat buns? Boudicca had made them, along with a few mysterious herbal concoctions that she had promised weren't poisonous. He'd been looking forward to his sister's cooking. It wasn't that she was especially good—because she wasn't—but that everything she made tasted like home.

He looked up, frowning. "Has anyone seen my food?"

Áed blinked. "No. What did you bring?"

Éamon scowled, turning his attention to Erin. "It was you, wasn't it?"

The faerie was perched on her bedroll, picking through her own backpack and popping what looked like scraps of jerky into her mouth. She paused when he glared at her. "What?"

"My food." He glowered. "You took it."

Erin just scoffed. "What would I want with your food? I have my own." She jutted her chin at Áed. "Look at him. He's the one who helped you set up."

Áed's brow furrowed, ignoring Erin's allegation. "Éamon, I have some extra, if you want it. Maybe yours got lost when we fell?

Éamon shook his head. "No. I'd have noticed." He was more frustrated than perhaps he should have been, but something about the way Erin was just *looking* at him, like she was amused, was making his blood run hotter. "I swear to the Gods, faerie," he growled. He didn't have anything to finish the threat, but he didn't trust Erin. Not a bit.

"Oh, like your *Gods* have anything over me," Erin said scathingly. "I didn't eat your stupid food. I wouldn't want it, anyway. *Human.*"

Kneeling on his own bedding, Áed looked... cowed. A shiver of guilt slipped down Éamon's spine—why did it look like Áed wanted to be cringing away from *him*? "Please don't argue?" Áed offered. "Éamon, I have food. I don't think Erin took it."

"Damn right," Erin muttered, aggressively tearing another bite of her jerky.

Éamon shot her another glare for good measure before slouching over his backpack. "Sorry," he muttered to Áed.

Áed wordlessly handed him a bannock and turned his attention back to sorting through his own pack.

For a while, an uncomfortable silence hung over the camp, punctuated only by the popping of the fire.

Then Erin leaned back and swallowed a frankly impressive bite. "Gonna be cold tonight."

Éamon tugged his cape a little closer, glad for its thickness. "I didn't think that would be a problem since you can make fire."

Erin bristled. "I'm not your personal hearth."

"Could you two *please* stop," Áed said sharply. "Éamon, leave Erin alone." He flopped down on his side and drew his blankets over him. "I'm going to sleep," he muttered. "Wake me if you like death."

With a sigh, Éamon murmured a goodnight and picked at the rest of the bannock. What he didn't finish, he wrapped in the cloth that was meant to be holding his meat buns and tucked it in his knapsack. Then he lay down on his own bedroll and curled on his side to stare at the fire.

It really *had* been a long day.

It didn't take long for his eyes to droop, hypnotized by the dancing flame. The darkness was heavy around their little bubble of light, and it pressed him unerringly toward the edge of sleep.

The last thing he saw before drifting off was Erin standing from her bedroll and slipping away into the forest.

CHAPTER TWELVE
ÁED

Éamon and Erin were already fighting when Áed came around. He groaned, wishing he could just duck back under the blankets again, but the sound of their arguing was drilling into his head.

"Maybe you were dreaming!" Erin snapped.

"I *saw* you," Éamon insisted hotly. "You left the camp last night."

"So what if I did?" Erin demanded. "Maybe I had to—y'know, *relieve myself.* Did you think of that?"

"Tell me to my face that that's what happened."

Erin opened her mouth and then closed it in frustration. "Look—"

Áed sat up blearily, disappointed that he had to start the day being irritated. "What the hell is going on?"

Erin was standing on the remains of the fire, her fists balled at her sides and smoking slightly. Éamon looked equally combative if slightly more composed. "This *adult* is having a full fight with a sixteen-year-old," Erin fumed.

Éamon pressed his fingers into his eyes. "Áed, she left the camp last night. When I asked her why, she started throwing a tantrum." He shot the last three words at Erin deliberately.

Erin looked so riled that Áed half-expected her to unsheathe claws like a cat.

Áed groaned. "Erin, did you leave the camp?"

Erin scowled. "Maybe."

"Did you do anything to harm our plan?"

"No."

Áed stood stiffly, brushing himself off. "Then it doesn't matter, and I don't care. Éamon, a word?"

Smirking with satisfaction, Erin retreated to the far edge of the camp while Éamon slumped over to Áed, looking chastised. "I'm sorry," he said before Áed could say anything. "I got upset, that was out of line—"

Áed pressed a knuckle to the bridge of his nose. "Éamon, I'm glad you came on this mission with me. I really, really am." His eyes flicked over to Erin. "But we need her, okay? So…" He swallowed. "So I need you to either get along or go back home."

Éamon's eyes widened, and there was no mistaking the hurt that flickered over his face. "Áed—"

"I want you here," Áed said quietly. "I do. I want you to stay. But if you can't…"

"I can," Éamon said quickly. "I'm so sorry. I can, and I will." He glanced around, dropping his voice. "It's just… you are sure we can trust her, right?"

"She's a faerie. She can't lie." He shook his head. "I know she's fae, Éamon. I'm asking you to get over it. Please."

Éamon really did look contrite. "Yeah. I'm sorry." His eyes flicked to Áed's, and Áed sensed a hint of hesitation. "Áed, I know this isn't a good time, but…"

Áed cringed internally. "The festival?" he guessed.

Éamon nodded. "I'm sorry. If you don't know what happened, you don't know. But if you have any guesses…" He shrugged helplessly. "We're going to the fae side of the veil. It sounds like it could be important to know."

Áed let out a quiet breath. Éamon had been waiting for over two weeks for Áed to explain how he had shielded him at the festival—and no matter his patience, Éamon had to be feeling that he was missing something. He'd only grown more on edge as time had passed; maybe Áed shouldn't have been surprised that he'd snapped at Erin. "Yeah," he said, rubbing the back of his neck and feeling his gaze shift away. He didn't know what to say. The idea of telling Éamon that he was fae felt impossible. There was a reason the truth had never passed his lips. Boudicca knew, and Ronan knew, and somewhere deep in the Maze, the old shopkeeper Máel Máedóc knew. Two of those people had found out without Áed *telling* them anything, and Áed had told Ronan when he was still quite young. Áed had no idea how to actually talk about it. Besides, the fear of Éamon's reaction was potent. "I—I don't know yet. I'll figure it out."

"Right," Éamon said. He looked disappointed, and Áed knew that he had been hoping to hear something comforting.

"I'm sorry." Áed nudged his friend's side. "Let's pack up, all right? I want to get moving."

}}{

Erin led the party as the three of them trekked through the woods. It was impossible to deny the beauty of the dense trees; the wilderness on this side of the White City's plateau was healthier than the scraggly forest that separated the Maze's farmlands from the cliff. The underbrush was thick even as winter approached, and the trees were tall and sturdy. Áed spotted clumps of mistletoe hanging from some of the branches above them, catching pale sunlight through their yellow-green leaves.

Every now and then, Erin stopped as if scenting the air and then led them on a slightly different course.

Áed could feel the pull as well, and he only felt it more strongly the closer they got. It was like a resonance, buried somewhere behind his sternum; he felt it in his chest, his spine, his neck. It felt like buzzing in his molars. Not entirely pleasant, but strangely enticing all the same. He caught himself glancing to Éamon more and more frequently, checking to see if his friend noticed Áed's flinch each time the feeling grew powerful.

Every time Áed glanced back, though, Éamon seemed caught up in his own thoughts.

"So," Erin said, cutting into Áed's musings. She fell into step next to him. "What *is* the deal with the nobleman?"

Áed navigated a particularly gnarly tangle of roots, keeping his eyes on the ground. "What do you mean?"

"I mean, why is he here, out of all the other humans?" She glanced over her shoulder. "Is he your consort?"

Behind them, Áed heard Éamon choke. He decided to pretend he hadn't noticed, and let Éamon retain a little dignity. "No," he said, stifling a laugh. "No, he's my advisor. He's on my council."

Erin frowned. "You're clearly closer than that."

Áed rubbed at his mouth. "He's my friend."

"Lies," Erin whispered, perfectly voiceless and yet perfectly singsong.

Áed blinked, confused, and dropped his hand. "What? I'm not lying."

"Hmm. Liar." She clasped her hands behind her back, eyes glittering. "But he doesn't know about you?"

"Would you stop it?" Áed murmured sharply. "He'll hear you."

"He didn't." She cocked her head. "Interesting. I wonder how that'll go."

The resonant sensation in Áed's breast ratcheted up again, and he gasped. Erin flinched, too. "We're getting close?" he asked tightly, and Erin nodded. Her fingers found the ends of her dreadlocks and played with them anxiously.

"Tell your darling aristocrat to walk closer to us." She gave her hair a worried tug. "We'll be there in moments."

CHAPTER THIRTEEN
ÉAMON

"That… does not look like a gate."

"Nor do you look like—" Erin cut herself off. "Never mind. Just trust me. This is the gate."

Éamon held his tongue, reminding himself that, faerie or not, Erin *did* only have sixteen years. And Éamon could hold onto at least a shred of self-possession.

It was, however, gratifying when Áed sent a disapproving glare at Erin along with a little reprimanding noise from the back of his throat. It was a funny sound, actually, strangely animal and clearly instinctive. It made him uneasy, but Éamon had plenty to distract him from thinking on that for too long. While they had walked, Erin had told them more about the gate. Or really, more about gates in general. Nothing she had said made Éamon more comfortable. In the spirit of one telling a ghost story, she'd explained that gates big enough to walk through—like the one they would use—had once been very small, natural tears in the veil. Only if somebody died on the spot would the tear widen. The way Erin told it, a human's death would make a gate leading into the human realm. A faerie's death would make one that went the other way. Gates were so rare because they usually formed by accident. The odds of dying in just the right place were slim.

So when they stood in front of a cave, Éamon was profoundly aware that this was a grave. It was small, little more than a crack in a stony outcropping, shaded by a couple of trees. The cool breeze gusting from within however, insisted the crack was more than it looked. Erin—and Áed, too, actually—were staring at it like it was about to do a trick. Or burst into flames.

That thought gave him pause. Would it be completely foolish to wonder if the cave was going to burst into flames? It was a fae gate, after all.

"So…" Áed started uncertainly. "Do we just walk in?"

Erin nodded, but she didn't step closer. "One at a time." She fidgeted with her hair, rolling a dreadlock between her fingers. "You're ready?"

Éamon nodded, and so did Áed. It was a solemn, rather dreadful movement.

"Right," she said. She appeared to be steeling herself. "When you enter the gate, just walk. I hear it's very dark."

"Is it dangerous?" Éamon ventured.

Erin looked grim. "If you get lost, you'll be trapped inside the veil, floating in the eternal in-between where neither time nor death can save you."

"Lovely," Áed muttered. "Who's first?"

To Éamon's surprise, Erin raised her hand. "I'll go." She tugged on her hair again. "At least I know what the world is like on the other side."

Áed gave Erin's shoulder a supportive pat. "Good luck. We'll be right behind you."

Éamon echoed the sentiment more quietly.

With a healthy amount of trepidation, Erin walked to the cave. It was barely as tall as she was, and narrow.

Casting one last look back, she stepped into the gloom.

Áed and Éamon shared a look. "Is something supposed to... happen?" Éamon wondered. There hadn't been a flash of light or a noise, or anything to suggest that Erin had done more than step inside an ordinary cave. The gate hadn't even caught fire.

Áed leaned closer to the cave, peering inside. "Erin?"

Éamon heard his voice echo, but there was no reply.

"Well," Áed said tightly. His nervousness was obvious on his face. "My turn, I suppose?"

A spike of fear lanced through Éamon's heart. "Please be safe."

Áed gave him a crooked smile. "See you on the other side."

He barely had to duck to pass the opening.

And then Éamon was alone.

He approached the cave slowly. The crack loomed ominously, much larger up close than it had appeared from a few steps back; now that he stood in front of it, Éamon could see that he would barely have to squeeze to walk into the chilly maw of the earth. The cold wind that crept out sounded like whispers. He thought if he listened carefully, he might be able to hear what the ground itself was saying.

It almost sounded like his name.

Like music.

He turned back to the forest for just a moment, but the woods were curiously silent.

As if drawn by the strange whispers, he stepped into the cave.

Immediately, the darkness surrounded him.

He turned to look over his shoulder as cold blackness enveloped him, only to find that the mouth of the cave had never been there at all. He could feel his pupils widening, struggling to find even a glimmer of light, but the world had become empty.

So this is the in-between, he thought absently, and it

was a strangely peaceful thought. The world was so still. He couldn't hear his own heartbeat. His breaths made no sound. *This is the veil.*

He spread his arms and turned around, but his fingertips encountered nothing. No damp stone, no cave lichen. The air was the same temperature at his extremities as it was right beside him as if he had ceased to generate warmth.

Liminality eternal.

Already, he could feel the void pulling at him. An unraveling sort of force. If he spent long enough in this place that didn't exist, he would become it, wouldn't he? He would cease to feel, to think, to *be*. A creature that once had been Éamon, suspended in the vastness of forever.

He shook his head. It didn't feel like anything, but the habitual motion cleared his mind, and reminded him of the faint grain of fear he carried in his core. That was grounding. He took what he thought was a step forward.

Gods, it was so dark. He didn't think he'd ever experienced perfect lightlessness before. It didn't feel real. The silence around him resolved into soundless whispers, echoing without noise from everywhere at once.

The whispers split into indiscernible words, sounding like wind through dry leaves. A shudder passed over Éamon's skin, as if the air of the cave had suddenly become real, and ahead of him, the darkness seemed to crack. Splitting light traced over it like branching tree boughs, and then it was opening around him. It felt like being swallowed; he wasn't sure why he'd expected it to feel like being spat out.

He tripped on something that was suddenly very tangible, and landed on soft grass.

"Éamon!"

Éamon startled as someone knelt beside him. Blinking up, he found Áed looking at him worriedly.

"That took longer than—oh, Gods, that was scary. I was afraid you'd gotten lost in there."

Éamon shook his head, pressing himself to his knees. His mouth felt full of cotton. "I'm here."

Áed's hand was warm on his forearm. "Are you all right? You look pale—"

"I'm fine," Éamon said decisively. He inhaled deeply to find that the air smelled floral in a way he didn't think he'd ever smelled before. It was nearly intoxicating. "How about you?"

"I'm all right. A little disoriented, I think."

Suddenly, an echo sounded from the cave. And then a curse.

Éamon shot to his feet, mirrored by Áed. "What in—" Áed stepped back, raising his hands defensively. Éamon stepped in front of him without thinking, ready to protect, and felt Áed touch his back.

"What's going on?" Éamon stared at the cave with wide eyes. "Is someone else coming through?"

Erin, he noticed, hadn't budged from her seat. And it was satisfying when it wasn't Éamon but Áed who whirled on her suspiciously. "Erin, what's going on?" he demanded. Erin shrugged, and Áed growled deep in his chest. Éamon felt the vibration. "You know. Tell me."

"Can't," Erin said easily, lacing her fingers behind her head. "Promised I wouldn't."

Áed's lip curled in a snarl at her, and Éamon swung his knapsack off his shoulders to pull a knife from within. "We must have been followed."

A cough came from the darkness within the crevice and then stumbling footsteps.

Moments later, a black-haired figure tripped onto the grass. He caught himself on hands and knees, hair slipping down to screen his face, but Éamon would still recognize that short, red-cloaked figure anywhere.

Áed stepped around Éamon and gaped, aghast.

"*Ronan?*"

CHAPTER FOURTEEN
ÁED

Ronan groaned and flopped onto his back in the grass, his chest heaving. Beryl-green eyes blinked at the sky. "Ugh."

"*Ronan!*" Áed said, and perhaps 'snapped' was the better term, or maybe even 'shouted' because Ronan sat up bolt-straight immediately, looking around with wide eyes obscured by his hair. Áed crossed the clearing in two strides and gripped him by the shoulders. "What the *hell* are you doing here?"

The boy blinked, looking intimidated. "I—" A hint of stubbornness returned to his features. "I told you that I was coming."

Áed stared at him speechlessly.

Then he whirled on Erin. "You!"

Erin sat up straighter, pointing to herself as if there was somebody else Áed could have meant.

"You knew about this, didn't you?" Áed couldn't tell if he was more angry or more terrified. They were in the realm of the *fae*. Where, if that wasn't dangerous enough, there was a *war*. "You knew he was following us. Why didn't you say anything?"

Erin looked infuriatingly nonchalant. "All due respect, I'm

not one of your subjects. And even though I don't mind you, we're not even really friends." She shrugged. "Why *would* I say something? He wanted to come."

Ronan had the gall to look sheepish when Áed turned on him again. "You know what," Áed said furiously. "She's damn right. This is on you."

"I—I'm not sorry—"

The reality was sinking in. Ronan couldn't go back now. For three months, he was stuck on the fae side of the veil. Áed's breath caught. "Oh, Gods."

Ronan clambered to his feet, pushing his hair out of his face. Áed noticed that he'd brought a knapsack of his own and that he was wearing sturdy boots. Had this been why he'd refused to emerge from his room when Áed had been leaving? To hide that he'd been packing?

"Ronan," he managed helplessly. "What were you *thinking*?"

"It's okay," Ronan protested. "I prepared. I left General Cynwrig in charge, so the kingdom is still in good hands. I brought supplies of my own. The only thing I couldn't get was food, so…" He looked a touch sheepish. "Sorry about the meat buns, Éamon."

Éamon made a little noise of surprise. "That was *you*?"

"Well, Erin swiped them for me—"

Éamon turned on Erin. "You said you didn't take them!"

Erin snorted. "I said I didn't *eat* them. You're going to need to listen a little more carefully if you want to survive on this side of the veil."

"Can we concentrate?" Áed said sharply. "Ronan, you can't *be* here."

"I can't go back now." Ronan gripped the straps of his knapsack. "I can help. I know I can. And—and you know what?" He pointed at Áed. "For as much as you can't have me here, *I* can't sit at the palace and wait for you to maybe not come back."

"It's dangerous," Áed said. He knew the fight was leaving him. What was he supposed to do? Ronan couldn't use the gate to return. Áed couldn't watch Ronan get hurt. "If something happened to you, I'd never... I couldn't."

Ronan's face was set. "I can't go back. It's done."

"Áed?" Erin's voice slipped between them uncertainly.

"Just give us a moment," Áed said.

"No, really," Erin said, more assertively this time. "Áed."

"*What?*"

Erin pointed to her ears and then twirled a black-nailed finger as if encompassing the foreign forest around them. There was something imperative in her expression.

Áed fell silent and listened.

"What..." Ronan whispered. "What is that?"

The sound seemed to echo from the whole forest, directionless. A single, haunting tone, trailing off like a sigh before beginning again and sustaining a ringing pitch that sent prickles over Áed's skin. "Moon court," Erin said. She had gotten to her feet, gathering her backpack with distinct urgency. "Come on."

"Come on?" Éamon echoed. "To go where?"

"Anywhere but here." She waved them sharply to follow as she made for the edge of the clearing. "Come *on*."

Ronan hurried after her immediately. "Wait, why are we running?" He hiked up his pack. "Isn't Moon a low court?"

Áed and Éamon had no choice but to follow as Erin and Ronan plowed into the woods. "It's not that simple," Erin said tightly. "My court allied with Bone. Moon hates Bone. Beyond that, humans are *really fun* to play with, and I rather doubt that patrol has had any proper entertainment in a while." Ronan tripped, stumbling on the unfamiliar terrain;

Erin grabbed his hand and hauled him onward while Áed and Éamon ran to keep up. "We need to make it into another territory."

"How far is that?" Áed demanded, and to his chagrin, Erin grimaced.

"I don't know," she said, ducking under a golden-leafed bough. Her breath was coming faster with exertion. "I've never actually *been* here before."

"So we might just be running deeper into Moon," Éamon clarified.

"Well," Erin managed, "we might not be."

Áed swore. The chilling noise rang through the woods once again, this time joined by another. The tones were dissonant, making Áed's skin crawl. "Are those *horns*?"

"Hunting horns," Erin panted. "We need to run faster."

"What happens if they catch us?" Ronan asked breathlessly.

"To you, or to me?" Holding her hand flat, she cut a slicing movement through the air before her. The tightly knotted undergrowth before them fell away, smoldering. "Neither is good."

Áed whirled around at the sound of something whipping through the air. A split second later, there was a vicious *crack*, and Éamon cried out. He crashed forward through the brush, his pack slipping from his back, and his momentum sent him into Áed. They both went down hard, Éamon gasping painful, ragged swallows of air. "Éamon!" Áed sat up, trying to clear stars out of his eyes. "What happened?"

The hunting horns were getting closer. Erin cursed a stream of impressive profanity, skidding to a stop, and Ronan had already spun around, trying to see what had happened.

"Oh," Éamon gasped. His hand shook as he reached toward his legs. "Oh, no."

Áed scrambled to his knees, shifting Éamon's weight off

him. He was pinned, his side pressed against a fallen tree and his other side occupied by Éamon, but he shrugged his knapsack off his shoulders and freed himself enough to maneuver.

Éamon's skin was already beading with sweat. His face twisted in pain.

Áed's gaze, frantically scanning for injury over his friend's body, landed on Éamon's legs.

His throat went dry.

Éamon's shins were tangled in cord. Áed could see one of the cord's ends—it was a round, polished white stone the size of an egg, and it was stained with blood.

Erin landed on her knees on the other side of Éamon. "They found us," she said urgently. She quickly put her hands to use unwinding the cord from Éamon's legs. "They're close, this was—"

She was cut off by an arrow burying itself deep in the rotting wood of the fallen tree against which Áed had, until moments ago, been pinned.

Everyone froze, except for Éamon, whose eyes were growing glazed and whose breaths were coming short and uneven. His hands fisted and unclenched, scrabbling at the ground. There was bright, wet redness spreading across the fabric of his left pant leg.

Áed snapped out of it first. The hunting horns had fallen silent—in fact, everything had. He could hear no footsteps, no voices, nothing except Éamon's labored breaths, and somehow, that was almost more unnerving than the sound of those godsforsaken wailing tones. "One of you, help me," he demanded. "Roll up the leg of his trousers."

Ronan fell to his knees next to Éamon. His slender hands shook as he hastily began to do as Áed said.

Éamon let out a choking moan, biting down hard on the

meat of his hand to keep from shouting. Tears squeezed from his tightly closed eyes.

"Shit. Okay, stop touching his leg," Áed said. Ronan did. "Okay. Okay." He tried to concentrate on deep breathing, but it wasn't working.

Éamon dropped his hand from his face, still panting. "Broken," he managed. "Leg's broken."

From where Ronan had moved up Éamon's trouser leg, Áed could see the crater in Éamon's shin. Thin slivers of bone broke the skin, sticking up like thorns around the impact point where the stone had whipped around and smashed into Éamon's leg, and the entire limb was crooked. "Yeah," Áed breathed. Nausea lurched in his gut, uncomfortably warm as his throat closed. "Yeah, it is."

"It's quiet," Ronan said softly.

Erin nodded. Her crimson eyes were more luminous than Áed had ever seen them, practically glowing. She scanned the forest around them, crouched like a cat ready to attack. "They're here."

Áed heard Ronan's breath hitch. "Where?"

Erin didn't reply.

Áed slipped his hand into Éamon's and immediately winced when Éamon gripped it like a lifeline, sending sharp spines of pain through Áed's stiff joints. "You're going to be okay," he assured him tightly. "It's going to be fine."

"That's not your promise to make."

With a gasp, everyone but Éamon spun toward the voice.

The faerie was standing in one of the trees.

She wasn't carrying a weapon, but the danger of her presence impressed itself on Áed without one. Her pale tunic was belted around the waist with a silver chain, off which hung a horn; the horn was translucent, and its color shifted from milky blue to a strange coral in the light. A sheer veil hung from a silver circlet about her forehead, and her fingers, tipped with long nails, were girded with delicate rings. The only part of her that was not milky—for her skin was perfectly alabaster, and her hair an opalescent white even brighter than Éamon's—were her ruby eyes.

She walked along the branch without so much as shaking a leaf, one foot in front of the other. "State your courts."

Erin looked like she was fighting the urge to flee. Her hand fluttered to play with the ends of her hair. "Sand," she said, barely above a whisper.

The strange faerie's lip curled slightly. "Sand? I thought you lot fell in behind Bone. No reason for you to be here." She tilted her head toward Áed, her veil sliding over her shoulder like water. "And you?"

Áed's mouth was dry. This faerie couldn't be the only one around. She was unarmed as far as he could see, and he was sure that he'd heard multiple hunting horns playing over each other in marrow-chilling harmony. "I don't have a court," he said honestly. He still knelt close to Éamon's side, all too aware of the fact that Éamon's grip was no longer straining Áed's bones. The councilor's hand had gone limp, though he still blinked at Áed with eyes fogged with pain and confusion.

The faerie cocked her head. "You don't *have* a court?" Her eyes narrowed, and Áed realized that even her eyelashes were white. "Show me your fire. Now."

Erin stepped in front of Áed, holding up her hands. "He's not one of them."

The pearl-haired faerie looked skeptical, though she did seem to be taking Erin's word seriously—and why shouldn't she? Erin couldn't be lying. "He's not high court?"

"He's not."

Folding her arms behind her back, the strange faerie leaned forward suspiciously. "Can you explain the humans?"

"They're ours," Erin said quickly. "The black-haired one is

mine, and the other belongs to my companion." Her face slid into an impeccable mask of irritated disappointment. "You broke his."

The other faerie seemed unimpressed. "You're all trespassing."

"We have a good reason," Áed said, looking up from Éamon. There was too much blood pooling under Éamon's leg; it was soaking into the knees of Áed's pants from where he knelt beside his friend. Éamon's teeth were clenched, and his pupils were dilated so wide that only a thin sliver of periwinkle was visible around the edges. His skin was growing clammy under Áed's touch. "Please, we'll tell you, we'll explain everything, but Éamon needs help. Please."

The Moon faerie's expression didn't change. "There's no reason that we should help you." She seemed completely unmoved. "You aren't our allies."

"You're all in the same war," Áed pleaded. "Please, is it really so important?" He couldn't hold Éamon's hand any tighter. "Éamon is going to bleed out. I'm begging you." He pressed two crooked fingers to Éamon's pulse, only to find it weak and thready. Éamon squeezed Áed's hand weakly, and Áed growled—actually growled, fully feral and undeniably inhuman, at the faerie in the tree. It was a desperate sound. "Please."

Erin's fists were tight at her sides. "If you won't help us," she snarled, "then at least take us to Lachtna."

The faerie in the tree raised an eyebrow. "You sure you want to do that, sand flea?"

Erin's teeth came together with a click. "I'm sure."

With a sigh, the faerie raised a hand to her mouth and, pressing thumb and forefinger to her lip, blew a single shrill whistle. A couple of birds took flight.

At her cue, the forest moved.

Three other fae emerged from the woods as if they'd melted

from the wintering greenery. They all wore similar dress, but unlike the woman in the tree, every one of them was armed. Two of them carried longbows, and the third had three knives just that Áed could see. Every one of them had milk-white skin and pearlescent hair. "Take the trespassers to the cart. We're bringing this to Lachtna."

CHAPTER FIFTEEN
RONAN

Ronan was fairly certain that at least part of his mind had distanced itself from reality. Because that was the only explanation for how he could be sitting in the cart belonging to a faerie patrol, with his knapsack confiscated and his hands tied snugly behind his back, panicking about the fact that Éamon, lying still on the floor of the cart, had fainted and Ronan could *see his bone*... and yet Ronan was still marveling over the cart horses.

Because they weren't horses at all.

They looked like deer if deer had oddly sharp antlers and long, fluffy tails. The cart was pulled by two of them. One was dark brown, nearly black, and flecked with creamy spots around its eyes, neck, and belly. The other was fox-red. Ronan swore that their keen, liquid-black eyes were looking directly through him.

Áed had slid from his seat to kneel on the floor next to Éamon. It had been a clumsy operation since his hands were as immobilized as Ronan's—though with metal cuffs instead of flammable rope—but he had maneuvered the councilor's head into his lap so that it didn't bump the wooden floor of the cart every time they hit an obstacle on the unpaved forest road. His face was stamped with remorse and fear; Ronan was sure he felt responsible for allowing Éamon to come along.

Erin was the only one who looked composed, though if Ronan had to guess, it was a façade. "You look tired," he said. The words had come before he could stop them.

Erin's eyes flashed. "*That's* what you're thinking about right now?"

If he was honest with himself, Ronan wasn't sure what he was thinking about. He couldn't help feeling like this was somehow his fault, even though he didn't think his crossing had anything to do with the Moon fae finding them. At the very least, if he were back home in the palace, there would be one fewer thing for Áed to be worrying about. Ronan was exactly where he knew Áed hadn't wanted him to be: in danger.

Even if he couldn't bring himself to truly regret his choice, guilt still sat in his chest.

"Hey." One of the Moon fae, seated in the front of the cart and swaying with the movement of the deer-like animals' gait, nudged Áed's shoulder. "Get back in your seat."

Áed snarled at him. The fury of it, protective and feral, made even Ronan jump. He didn't think he'd ever seen Áed act that way before. He'd never heard him make a sound like that.

The faerie just growled back, the sound coming from somewhere deep and threatening in the cavity of his chest. Was this how fae communicated? Áed seemed to adopt the behavior without thinking. "Your crossling is in shock. Lower its head if you want it to live."

Ronan watched as Áed's defensiveness turned to fear, and he carefully edged his knees out from under Éamon's head. "I'm staying down here, though," he said firmly.

"Fine," the faerie sighed. "Don't try anything."

"Crossling?" Ronan wondered.

The faerie lifted an eyebrow. "Crosslings. Ashbloods. Mayflies." He smirked. "*Humans*."

One of the other fae, jogging alongside the transport, banged on the side of the cart. "Don't talk so much."

"Mm," the Moon faerie in the cart agreed. "Shouldn't be long now. Hopefully, we'll reach the mound before your Éamon bleeds out." He looked a little curious. "You care a lot."

Ronan actually heard Áed's teeth grit.

The faerie sighed nostalgically. "You must be young."

When Ronan could no longer look at the torment on Áed's face, the pool of blood spreading on the floor of the cart, or the white of Éamon's exposed bone, he stared into the forest. It wasn't as if Ronan had immense experience with any forest at all, but he supposed he'd expected the woods on this side of the veil to be more... strange. Without standing, Ronan had a view of the top halves of the trees over the opposite edge of the cart, but other than the deer-creatures and a few colorful flying things that may have been normal birds, Ronan hadn't seen anything in the woods that seemed particularly otherworldly. He wished there was *something* to look at to distract him from the sound of Éamon's faint breathing or the swirling of his own guilt.

Without warning, the cart jerked to a stop. The deer-creatures pranced in place, their tails swishing back and forth, and it took Ronan a moment to realize that odd little noises, sounding somewhere between a birdcall and a human voice, were coming from the creatures' mouths. The Moon faerie in the cart swore and stood up, leaning over the side. "What's going—" His voice fell into chagrin. "Ah."

Unable to stop himself, Ronan stood up for a better view.

Ahead of them, the land was scarred. Several trees had fallen, while others bore blackened starbursts of char that reminded Ronan of the damage in the White City. The ground was torn up in places as if people had dug out hurried, makeshift trenches. The path itself looked to have been hastily re-beaten, ash packed into deep grooves and craters in the earth.

"It's a few days old," one of the fae on the ground reported. "The hinds are just spooked." She clicked her tongue, stroking the darker deer-creature's neck. "It's all right. Come on, girl."

Slowly, the cart began to move again, though the creatures didn't stop crying nervously, and Ronan took a better look at the scene as they passed through it. He could see skidded footprints and indentations in the ash that marked where people had fallen. Here, a dark spot that could well be old blood. There, a half-burned glove.

He looked to Erin to find her sitting stiffly, looking straight ahead. He quickly dropped back into his seat. "Hey. Are you okay?"

She shook her head slightly. "This is what I was running from, Ronan."

Ronan didn't know how to answer that, so he kept quiet while the cart rolled on.

༄

The Moon court had a mound. A big mound. A deceptively large, incredibly impressive mound.

The patrol had heralded their arrival by a set of those chilling hunting-horn calls, and when the cart had reached the mouth of the grass-covered mound, there had been fae waiting for them. In a blur of action, they unhitched the cart, herded Áed, Erin, and Ronan off, and procured a stretcher for the unconscious Éamon. Áed had struggled against the faerie holding him as three people carried Éamon inside, but there was nothing any of them could do when they were brought into the mound itself. Four faeries roughly escorted the three of them down an arch-ceilinged hallway of black rock that sloped deeper into the earth, and Ronan stared in awe.

The subterranean complex was lit by chunks of milky-bluish crystal that seemed to grow from the ceiling and walls—rough, craggy stones that looked at odds with the finished appearance of the hall's smooth, unreflective stone walls and floor. Above them, painted stars in unfamiliar constellations glittered on the ceiling.

Their guides led them down a set of twisting stairs, and then into an empty room with a round door. One of them removed the bindings on their wrists while the other guides stood guard, and then he wordlessly moved to close the door.

"Wait!" Áed exclaimed. "What about Éamon? Where is he?"

The guide glanced to one of his companions, confusion flickering over his snowy features. "The human?"

"Yes!" Áed's knees were still bloody from where he'd knelt beside Éamon, and his eyes were haunted. "Where is he? Where did you take him?"

The guide just shrugged when his fellow escorts didn't offer any insights. "Not sure."

And then he closed the door. The lock clicked.

Áed immediately wrenched the door handle, but the door didn't so much as rattle in its frame. Fire lapped into his palms before Erin firmly took hold of his elbow. "We're in a fae court, Áed. You really think anything here is flammable?" She tugged at his arm, trying to get him to move. "Come on. Sit down."

"What are they doing to Éamon?"

"They carried him off on a stretcher. I doubt they're trying to hurt him." She managed to tug him away from the door; he sank against the wall instead. "Besides, it's in very poor form to hurt another faerie's crossling. We were trespassing and all, but they're not going to assume that was either humans' fault."

"They *did* hurt him."

"Eh." Erin shrugged. "They were probably aiming for you."

She dropped to a seat next to Áed, and Ronan sat next to her. "Could you explain this 'crossling' thing?" Ronan asked tentatively. He felt a slight flush of heat in his face. "Back in the woods, you said I was... yours?"

"And that Éamon was Áed's, yeah." She sighed, lacing her fingers behind her head. "Crosslings are humans who've come across the veil. And humans don't usually do that unless they've been brought across by a faerie." She looked a little uncomfortable, her eyes flicking to either side before fixing straight ahead. "Most of the time, the human is, uh... bewitched a little."

Ronan frowned. "So..."

Erin huffed. "Are you really going to make me spell it out?" She tipped her head against the wall. "I've never done it. I mean... I maybe danced with a few crosslings on festival nights—the festivals I didn't spend in your realm, anyway—but they weren't *mine*; they were just going around."

"What happened to them?" Ronan asked.

Erin's face turned a little guilty. "I didn't pay attention."

Ronan was sure he looked a little horrified. "You don't even know?"

Erin looked ashamed but defensive. "They looked like they were having a good time."

"They were enchanted!"

"This is our nature," Erin snapped tiredly. "This is what

fae *do*." She crossed her arms. "Do you have any idea how hard it is to care about something that's going to live for a *blink* of your lifespan? There's no human comparison. You talk, dance, fuck, we *like* you, but in the end, you die. So why should we care?" She was still staring dead ahead. "How *can* we care?"

Stricken, Ronan got to his feet and walked to the other side of the little chamber, then turned back. "I helped you."

"I know you did."

He ran a hand down his face, narrowing his eyes. "I—wait a minute." He put his hands on his hips. "You can't lie, can you?

Erin's eyes flicked away.

Ronan stared, a little smile playing humorlessly over his face. "You really can't."

The faerie pressed her lips together. "No," she said finally.

"Then…" Ronan stepped closer, scrutinizing her expression. "Then tell me. To my face. That you don't care."

Erin opened her mouth, then closed it again. A look of frustration passed over her face. "I shouldn't care."

"Not what I asked."

"I don't c—" Erin's brow scrunched down, and she scowled. "I don't—" Her hands clenched into fists, and she banged one on the ground. "Ugh!"

Ronan snorted and dropped back down to a seat next to her. "Yeah, keep trying." He sighed, propping his elbows on his knees, and leaned around Erin to look at Áed. He had his arms wrapped around his knees, staring at the floor. "Áed, how are you doing?"

Áed didn't glance up. "This wasn't supposed to happen."

Erin patted his shoulder awkwardly. "I'm sure Éamon's going to be fine," she said. "Our healers are better than your human ones."

"He shouldn't have gotten hurt in the first place."

"It was his choice to come, wasn't it?"

Áed fell quiet. He was tapping on one of the crystals, and Ronan observed that at his touch, every other crystal in the room grew half a degree brighter as if their glowing was connected. The room's walls were made of the same black stone as the hallway, making the whole place look unearthly in the crystalline light.

"I'm sure someone will be along soon," Ronan said. "We can explain everything. And find out how Éamon is doing."

Áed nodded, pressing his fingers through his already messy hair. "Yeah." He looked pointedly to Ronan. "Whatever happens, Ronan, you're not allowed to get hurt." His gaze moved to Erin. "If you've claimed him as your... your *crossling*—" He narrowed his eyes meaningfully. "You had better keep him safe."

Erin nodded, folding her hands in her lap. "Yeah," she said. "Yes, I will."

CHAPTER SIXTEEN
ÁED

*L*achtna.

Erin had been muttering that name darkly since she'd demanded an audience in the forest.

From what Áed understood, Erin's court was a small court, transient. Sand had no mound, no permanent home, very few stable resources. But war demanded warm bodies to turn cold, and Erin's court had some to provide. When things had started falling apart, every low court had allied with its friends first—Gold and Meadow. Garnet and Bone. Glass and Gold. Eventually, all of the courts that actually got along had formed into factions behind Moon and Bone, and despite the fact that every low court was fighting for the same purpose, it was clear that those factions were at each other's throats nearly as much as they were resisting the Queen's armies.

Except for Sand.

"It was just chaos," Erin said darkly. "Arguments between the court elders that lasted all night—because Moon had promised relief, but Bone promised vengeance. My mum thought that the Sand court deserved to have blood for blood. And in the end, the elders agreed. Sand fell in behind

Bone." She sighed, crossing her arms. "Lachtna's the leader of the Moon court. As soon as we allied with Bone, he withdrew every sliver of support he'd given us while he was trying to get us on his side. It was almost enough to send the whole court into collapse." She growled quietly. "And I'm going to *meet* this man."

"If we ever get out of this room," Ronan muttered.

For his part, Áed didn't like it here. It felt foreign in a way that was unwelcoming, clean and cold and oddly distant. It even *smelled* strange, as if he could detect the scent of unfamiliar magic and unknown fae. He was on edge and couldn't calm himself.

Erin broke the silence. "Moon court's nocturnal, you know. Like Sand."

Ronan looked at her in surprise. "You're nocturnal?"

"Normally. It's been a strange few weeks." She shrugged. "Anyway, I assume the patrol wouldn't have woken Lachtna for something as trivial as capturing trespassers. But I think it's nearly nightfall."

With a sigh, Áed leaned away from the wall. "Does that mean someone will finally come tell us what's happening?"

"I think so." She crossed her hands behind her head. "Soon."

⸎

'Soon,' it turned out, was a few hours later.

At the sound of footsteps outside, Áed was on his feet in an instant, and Erin shortly behind him. Ronan, who had drifted off, sat up blearily, looking disoriented.

The door swung open to reveal three pale, white-haired fae. The one in front wasn't dressed like the guards or the patrollers—if Áed had to guess, he'd say that her clothes were those of someone in charge. Or at least someone in *proximity* to someone in charge. That woman crossed her arms. "Do we need to tie your wrists again, or will you cooperate?"

"Depends," Áed said with a hint of warning growl in his throat. Erin put a hand on his shoulder, stepping in front.

"For as long as you and yours do us no harm, we will not act aggressively." She shot a glance at Áed and Ronan, and Áed understood: they'd take notes from her careful wording. It was never a good idea to agree to anything wholeheartedly. Nor to accept an affirmative answer as a complete 'yes.'

The woman seemed satisfied. "Come with us."

"Are we going to see Lachtna?" Erin asked at the same time Áed demanded, "Where's Éamon?"

The woman rolled her eyes. "You will see Lachtna. And the crossling is recovering in a quiet room."

"Is he all right?" Áed asked. He felt a bit desperate after so long without news. "His leg—"

"He will recover," the woman interrupted curtly. "Your devotion to him is… peculiar, but he is the crossling of another faerie. We treated him accordingly." She bowed stiffly at the waist. "The patrol, while unable to be present, extends their apologies for wounding him."

Áed knew he must look baffled. He didn't think he really understood the dynamic between crossling and fae.

"At any rate," the woman said, "I'm here to escort you an audience with Lachtna." She stepped aside. "Follow me."

〰

Lachtna was everything and nothing like Áed had expected. He had the same coldness in his eyes that Áed had imagined, but based on Erin's story, he'd been picturing a strict, weathered sort of person. So seeing such an unimposing man before him—shorter than he was, slightly soft around the middle, with loose, wavy white hair that nearly touched the floor—made him do a bit of a double-take.

The Moon leader folded his hands. "This is a rather unusual situation." He raised one pale eyebrow. He was still in his dressing-gown, an elegant white garment embroidered with a different shade of white. The Moon fae, apparently, liked adhering to an aesthetic. "A Sand faerie, a courtless faerie, and two crosslings." He looked at Áed curiously and sank into a cross-legged seat on a cushion on the floor. Uncertainly, Áed, Ronan, and Erin sat as well. "How does one come to be courtless? Are your parents from different courts?"

"Actually," Áed started. He glanced to Erin, hoping that she would have some kind of direction for him, but she was too busy glaring at Lachtna to meet his eye. Áed took a quick breath. Even if Erin didn't like Lachtna—and Áed's gut said that he didn't, either—Lachtna was still a court leader. Áed had come with diplomatic intentions, hadn't he? "Only my mother is fae."

The Moon leader looked at him with sharp interest. "And your father?"

"Human." Áed swallowed. He didn't know the proper form of address for a court leader. "Sir," he tried, "my name is Áed, and I speak for the human realm."

"This is an interesting place for you to be if that is so, *Áed*." Lachtna tilted his head. "Fae or otherwise, what is someone from the human realm doing here?"

"The human realm was badly damaged by fae who crossed over." Áed rested his hands on top of one another, trying to gather himself. The circumstances were very different, but he had been through plenty of negotiations before. Usually, his word was final, but in this case, he could adapt. "Perhaps, from one leader to another, we could arrive at some sort of arrangement to ensure that doesn't happen again."

Lachtna looked thoughtful. This came as a surprise; a part of Áed had definitely believed that he was about to be laughed at. "It is not by my hands that your people suffered." Lachtna shook his head before Áed could speak. "I'm afraid diplomacy will not serve you here. The low courts cannot promise to keep your realm safe; this is war. And the high court has neither allies nor friends."

"Surely, there must be something—"

"No," Lachtna said. His voice was quiet but final. "While it is cowardly that my people ran from this fight, I will not prevent it for the sake of yours. Mine are dying. If they wish to save themselves, I will not intervene."

Áed sat back. "And the other court leaders feel the same way?"

"None among us will be willing to sacrifice our own for yours. It is the high court that is at fault for attacking those who were only trying to flee, and you may reason with *them* at the cost of your own existence." He steepled his fingers. The conversation was over. "Now. I do not believe that the cross-blood's motivation belongs to all of you." He spread his hands with affected magnanimity. A flicker of calculation in his eyes ruined the effect. "What brings this unusual company to trespass on my court's territory?"

"We were just traveling," Erin said. Her voice was *just* on the right side of cutting.

Lachtna leaned back, that white eyebrow rising again. His expression had gone from faintly interested to faintly suspicious, but he hadn't lost that shrewd glint in his eye. He accepted a long, white pipe from an attendant, who bowed before moving off silently, and puffs of aromatic smoke began to fill the room when he sucked at it. "Traveling where?"

"Out of here," Erin said. "We don't want to be on your territory. We were trying to leave when your people caught us."

"Not heading to Glass, Gold, or Meadow, then?" Lachtna

asked. His voice sparkled with false innocence. It made Áed uncomfortable.

"We won't exactly be welcome there," Erin said acidly. "So, no, we hadn't planned on it."

"Hm." Lachtna looked at them. He took another puff of his pipe and nodded when a different attendant handed him a dainty plate with a cup of tea on it. He handed the attendant the pipe and took the tea without looking at them. He sipped it, looking over the rim of the cup with narrowed eyes. "Last I heard, Sand has split up into a number of groups. I couldn't tell you where they are."

"We could head to Bone," Erin muttered. "Get far away from here, at least."

Lachtna looked pleased by that. "Well, that would do nicely."

It seemed very much like Lachtna was saying one thing with the meaning of another, even though Áed couldn't discern any deception behind his words. "Is there anything else we should know?" he asked.

Lachtna frowned. The expression didn't put a single crease in his soft face. "That *you* should know from *me*?" He tapped the side of the teacup with the back of one fingernail. "That you are fortunate, perhaps. You interest me." A smile cut his face. "Not all who address me are so blessed with my patience."

Erin made a face. "Then is that all?"

Lachtna hummed. "I'm not the one who requested an audience. I have the information I want; I see no reason to prolong our little talk." He took another sip of tea. "You are free to leave. Until you do, my people will provide you accommodation." One of his attendants opened the door. It was a clear dismissal. "Best of luck in your travels."

CHAPTER SEVENTEEN
ÁED

The hallway was dim, reminding Áed that it was nighttime. Exhaustion was catching up with him, but the audience with Lachtna had left him feeling distinctly unsettled.

"Excuse me."

All three of them looked up. The well-dressed woman who had fetched them from their room was approaching from down the hall. She had no guards with her this time; apparently, the party had established themselves as nonthreatening.

"I have news from the healer who is treating the crossling's injury. You may see him now if you like."

"Yes," Áed answered immediately. The exhaustion he'd noted a moment before was quickly leaving him. "Yes, I want to see him."

"Will your companions accompany you?" She glanced over them. "If not, someone will escort them to a sleeping chamber. I believe your people sleep during these hours, yes?"

Ronan nodded, frowning. "I do want to see Éamon…"

Erin bit her lip, scrutinizing Áed, and then put her hand

on Ronan's shoulder. "Ronan, let's sleep. We don't want to crowd Éamon right now. We can see him in the morning, right?" She looked to the woman for affirmation.

The woman nodded. "If Áed permits. The crossling is his, after all."

Áed nodded, shooting Erin a grateful look. He almost felt guilty for being so relieved that he would see Éamon alone. He imagined his friend would be overwhelmed already without Ronan and Erin hovering—not that they would hover with anything but the best of intentions.

"Do you suppose we might have some food, too?" Ronan asked the woman nervously.

"Nothing prepared," Erin specified, and Ronan looked at her curiously. Erin shrugged at him apologetically. "If you eat faerie food, you'll get stuck on this side of the veil. We brought human rations for Éamon—Áed shouldn't need them—but our bags are gone."

Ronan groaned, and the fae woman looked confused. "Is he not already…" She shook her head. "Apologies. Not my business. Yes, of course, we'll deliver some food."

"I hope you don't mind raw vegetables," Erin murmured, and Ronan groaned again.

The woman snapped her fingers, and one of the guards at Lachtna's doorway stood at attention. "Take Erin and the crossling Ronan to a sleeping chamber," she ordered. "Bring them nourishment, as well."

The guard bowed. "This way."

Shooting glances behind them, Erin and Ronan followed the guard down the crystal-studded hall.

"Now," the woman said crisply. "Follow me, please, Áed."

※

"Can you tell me anything about his condition?" Áed asked as the woman stopped in front of a door. He was fidgeting nervously.

"I didn't see him. Just received word from the healer." The woman turned to face him. "I won't accompany you, but the healer is inside. She can answer your questions." She inclined her head politely. "Enter when you're ready."

With that, she set off down the hall, footsteps tapping neatly.

Áed steeled himself, but he wasn't about to hesitate for too long. With both hands on the doorknob, he stepped inside.

The room was even darker than the hallway, lit only by the faintest glow from those odd, bluish crystals. Áed blinked, waiting for his eyes to adjust.

A sound came from a shape against the dark. It grew taller, and Áed realized a person had just stood. "Good evening," the shadow said softly. "You must be Áed?"

Áed didn't recognize the voice. "Are you the healer?"

The figure nodded. As Áed's eyes adjusted, he saw that she had short, cropped hair that looked bluish in the crystals' luminance. He also saw the bed in the center of the room. The healer held out her hands as Áed started forward. "Wait, please."

"Is he all right?" Áed leaned to see around her.

The healer refrained from answering his question directly. "He's not conscious at the moment, but he's going to come around soon. We should talk before then." She herded him into a seat at the bedside, and Áed relaxed a degree when he finally saw Éamon's face. It was tranquil in sleep, his hair brushed back so that his scarred face was open and his curls splayed over the pillow. The blankets were tucked up to his chest, and Áed could see he was wearing a plain white tunic. Once Áed was seated, the healer let out a breath. "The injury was very serious." She interlaced her fingers. "When he arrived in my ward, his shin was in several pieces. The impact had not only broken it into two large pieces but had splintered off smaller ones, too. Some of the sharper fragments, as I'm sure you noticed, broke the skin. Ultimately, even his kneecap was compromised. The broken bone shifted and dislodged it."

Áed's stomach turned. He wished he was struggling to picture it, but his imagination was instead using what he'd already seen to create a painfully vivid visualization. "You *healed* that?"

At that, the healer pressed her lips together. "Actually, what I'm trying to say is that we didn't."

"You…" Áed stared, the words not processing. "You didn't."

The healer shook her head.

Áed leaned forward, eyes flicking urgently between Éamon and the healer. "Then what happened?"

"What I'm telling you," the healer said, running her palms down her tunic, "is that we did not save the leg."

It felt like the world had tipped. "You… amputated?"

The healer nodded.

Áed leaned over his knees, hands shoving forcefully through his hair. He'd allowed Éamon to come here. Yes, Éamon could make his own decisions, but Áed had known more clearly the kind of danger they'd be facing. And, selfishly, he had wanted a friend by his side. "You cut off his leg."

"It was the best option," the healer explained. "The damage was extensive. If we hadn't, he'd never have been able to walk again."

"And he will now?" Áed said, more cuttingly than he'd meant.

"That brings me to the second point," the healer said quietly, apparently unfazed by Áed's tone. She turned to the bed and began lifting the blankets by the foot. She rolled the blankets away, and Áed's breath caught.

There was more than just a bandaged stump.

It looked like it was made of moonstone. The smooth lines of the limb were almost disturbingly natural—not natural like the flesh-and-blood leg it was replacing, but natural in an otherworldly way, faintly luminous and bizarrely organic. In some places, Áed could have reached a finger straight through it; the shin was in three long, separate pieces that came together at ankle and knee, each rounded and almost bone-like. The prosthesis melded to Éamon's flesh, covering what once had been Éamon's kneecap but leaving much of the original knee joint intact. The pale material met his skin at the top of the knee and back of the calf, and only a thick line of rough, red scar around the joint indicated that the prosthesis had not simply grown there itself.

While Áed gaped, the healer explained. "It's not a flawless replacement. But it will suffice for our purposes." She looked down at Éamon. "It will take some getting used to. You should be ready for that."

Áed caught himself reaching out to touch the prosthesis and pulled his hand back. "What is it *made* of?"

"Moon crystal. The same material as the ones on the walls." If there was anything evasive about the healer's tone, Áed didn't dwell on it for long. "They have unique properties—intrinsic magic, you could say. One of these properties is the encouragement of healing."

"Encourages healing?" Áed's eyes caught on the scarring at the union between natural and unnatural body. Come to think of it, it was too early for scarring. Éamon's leg wasn't even *bandaged*. "How much, exactly?"

The healer, despite the somber mood of the room, appeared pleased. "It seems to depend. But it's been only hours, and your crossling's tissues are already repairing themselves around the new leg. He shouldn't put any weight on it for at least a week or so, and then he'll be taking it slow for a while longer, but I think that is significantly faster than humans usually heal. Isn't it?"

"Definitely." Under his shock, Áed could feel a distinct awe. "That's unbelievable."

"Well, not all magic is fire." The healer scratched the back of her head. "We control flames and feelings. Humans could do anything if they weren't limited by their own weakness, and the hinds that pull the carriages can run faster than wind. This world is *made* of magic. Just because we can't wield it ourselves doesn't mean we can't still use it for our own... ends." The healer straightened her tunic, letting out a breath. "Áed, I'm going to leave now. Your crossling is going to come around any minute now, and I think it would be best if you're the only one there when that happens." With a final look at Éamon, she lowered the blankets back over his new prosthesis. "Be gentle with him. He's going to be distressed."

On cue, Éamon's forehead furrowed, and he let out a woozy hum.

The healer made for the door. "I won't be far. Call if you need me."

⌇

The room was quieter without the healer's presence as if her heartbeat and breathing had really been so loud. Éamon moved again, the beginnings of sleepy agitation flickering over his face. Áed positioned himself closer to the head of the bed, right next to the mattress, and had to fight the impulse to brush a stray curl off Éamon's forehead. "Hey," he said quietly. "Are you waking up?"

Éamon mumbled something unintelligible.

"It's okay," Áed said, caving to the urge and using his

thumb to brush the hair off Éamon's face. "You can wake up. It's safe. You're safe." The blankets bunched as Éamon shifted, and Áed had to stop him by the shoulders so that he didn't roll onto the side of the new prosthesis. "Hey, lie still."

"Mmph." Éamon's eyelids scrunched, and then Áed was looking at a bleary, squinting glimpse of periwinkle iris. His friend's eyes looked uncannily silver in the dim light. Éamon blinked, seeming to focus. "Áed?"

Áed offered him a smile. "Yeah, it's me."

Éamon's attention drifted around the room, still foggy. "Oh." He frowned absently at the ceiling, studded as it was with those rough chunks of semi-opaque, luminous rock.

"It's a long story." Áed rubbed one crooked thumb with the other, his throat tight. "We're in the Moon court's mound. But we're safe, don't worry. We talked to their leader." He swallowed. "Right now, you're in one of their recovery wards."

"Recovery…" Éamon went still. Then his gaze flicked down to the end of the bed. "My leg," he said faintly. "What happened?"

Áed did his best to stop himself from chewing on his lip.

"It was bad," Éamon whispered. It wasn't a question.

Áed nodded. "Yeah." He couldn't meet Éamon's eyes. "It was pretty bad."

A look of concentration flickered over Éamon's face, and then one of anxiety. "I can't move it." He pushed himself to his elbows. "Áed, I can't move my foot."

"Éamon—"

"Why can't I—" Éamon's voice was growing agitated. "I can't feel it, Áed." He sat up and then held his head as a wave of dizziness seemed to overtake him.

"Éamon, you have to lie back down," Áed said, standing and trying to tamp down the urgent tightness that seemed to have lodged somewhere around his diaphragm. "Please, I'll explain—"

But Éamon was already pulling the covers aside and swinging his legs out of bed.

He froze.

Áed wasn't sure Éamon was breathing as he reached toward the prosthesis. His fingers hovered over the surface of the foreign material, not touching. "Áed," he breathed. "What is this?"

Áed hugged himself, wishing he could read Éamon's mind and know how to comfort him instead of simply drowning in the rapidly amplifying waves of Éamon's own panic.

Éamon looked up, wide-eyed. Behind the shocked blankness of his expression, it looked like he was trying to rationalize an explanation beyond the obvious. "Áed?"

"They couldn't save it," Áed said mutedly. He lowered himself to a seat on the edge of the bed, not taking his eyes off Éamon. "It's… it's a prosthesis."

"Prosthesis," Éamon echoed voicelessly.

"Éamon, please." Áed touched Éamon's arm, hoping to break his friend's shock before it spiraled. Éamon wasn't prone to panic, but Áed was pretty sure waking up in a strange place to discover that a limb had been removed and replaced—especially replaced with something so *alien*—would tip anyone over the edge. Áed could still feel Éamon's turbulent emotions, a hollow echo in his own head. "Lie back down. I don't think you should even be sitting up."

It didn't seem that Éamon was in a state of mind to argue. He leaned back, and Áed helped him carefully move his amputated leg back under the covers. Once settled, Éamon stared across the room without seeming to see the opposite wall.

Áed startled when Éamon slipped an arm out from under

the blankets and took hold of Áed's hand. When Áed looked back at Éamon's face, his friend's eyes were damp. The tears did not spill beyond his lashes, but his eyes shone more brightly in the odd light. "Hey," Áed said softly. "It's okay. It's going to be okay."

Éamon squeezed his eyes shut, curling against the pillow as if he could retreat into it. "Why did this happen?"

Áed's breath caught. "I think they were aiming for me." He put his other hand on top of Éamon's and held it as tightly as he could. "Éamon, I'm so sorry."

Now, a tear slipped free. It slid down Éamon's face until it melted into the pillow and left a trail for more to follow. It hadn't been long enough for him to begin calming down; in fact, it seemed like it was just starting to hit him. "What—" His breathing was beginning to speed up. "What do I *do*?"

Áed settled farther onto the edge of the bed and released one hand to brush it over Éamon's hair. He stroked it back, letting his crooked fingertips trail over Éamon's forehead before repeating the motion. "It's supposed to heal fast," he said quietly. "That's what they said." Éamon's hair was silky where it parted around his fingers. "You'll be able to walk."

Éamon couldn't seem to manage a reply beyond a quiet, choked-off sob. Áed's own eyes were growing damp. He had seen Éamon at some very low moments, but he had never felt this particular combination of emotions pour from him so strongly. Shock. Terror. Hurt. Grief. There was anger, too, layered deep in the whirlpool. Éamon was trembling; his breathing was slipping farther from his control. "Éamon," Áed said. "Éamon, hey. Take a deep breath."

Éamon opened his eyes, and Áed could see the panic in them. He didn't seem to have heard Áed's words. "Áed—it's my *leg*—"

"I know. Éamon, you're breathing too fast," Áed said. He

was trying to keep his voice stable. "Éamon. *Éamon*. You're breathing too fast."

Éamon's panic was only deepening as he began to hyperventilate. It had a life of its own now. "I don't know what to *do*."

"Just—" Áed was beginning to feel Éamon's panic seeping into his own emotion. "Well, you'll stay with us, and—I'll protect you." He swallowed hard. He hadn't done such a stellar job of that so far, and Éamon couldn't go home. Not until the veil opened just before spring. "I'll help you. We'll all help you."

Éamon didn't answer. His shaking had only gotten worse, and with the hand that didn't hold Áed's, he gripped the pillow like it was the only thing holding him over an abyss.

Áed's hand and Éamon's were still linked. He remembered what Erin had said about projecting emotion. For a moment, he hesitated. If he was successful, would that be a breach of trust? The first time he had done it, he hadn't known what he was doing. But now, if he managed to use magic to calm Éamon down...

He shook his head. Éamon was inhaling in choked, rapid breaths, panicking because his leg had been first broken, and then severed from his body and replaced without him knowing. If Áed could calm him down, artificially or otherwise, that would be a good thing.

He closed his eyes and tried to recall the feeling.

During the festival, he had felt protective. He had wanted Éamon to be protect*ed*. He didn't know how to manage a different feeling, but perhaps that one would work here, as well.

He allowed himself a steadying moment, and then he tried once again to press the feeling beyond his own body.

On the bed, Éamon's trembling began to weaken.

A weary smile turned the corners of Áed's lips. "There you go," he said softly. He hadn't stopped stroking Éamon's hair, and he kept the movement steady and rhythmic as Éamon began to breathe more slowly. "I'm so sorry." Áed maintained the connection he could feel between their hands. "This never should have happened to you. But I've got you now." He let Éamon's curls fall back from his face, twining between his fingers. "I've got you."

CHAPTER EIGHTEEEN
ÁED

Áed woke to the crystals' brightening glow and scrunched up his nose in sleepy irritation. He tried to roll over away from the light but was stopped by something solid and warm. He rubbed his eyes with the back of a hand, sitting up in confusion.

Oh.

Éamon was still sleeping, his cheek pressed into the pillows next to where Áed's face had been a moment before. Áed stretched, yawning, the past night coming back slowly. After Áed had gotten him down from the panic, Éamon had been exhausted—but he had asked Áed to stay. Áed must have fallen asleep.

It was disorienting that the crystals were the only indication of morning. With no windows, there could be no sunlight, no sound of waking birds. Áed reached out to touch the nearest crystal. It was smooth but not glossy, and his finger slid over it with a dry *whish*.

Such strange material. He wondered what other properties it had.

A knock at the door drew his attention, and he slid from under the covers. He didn't remember having gotten under the covers to begin with. Éamon must have tucked him in.

He slid the door open, rubbing his eyes again.

"Good morning," came the voice from beyond. Erin strode in without waiting for an invitation, immediately making herself comfortable in the chair while Ronan ambled in more slowly. "Ronan and I have been talking."

Ronan held up his hands. "Wait a moment. Is Éamon okay?"

Áed closed the door and sank to a seat back on the edge of the bed. "Good morning to you both, too." He kept his voice low for Éamon's sake, not sure how much it would matter if Erin and Ronan didn't speak a bit more quietly. "He's... he's okay. Needs more time to recover."

Ronan's shoulders relaxed. "I'm glad he's all right. I was worried."

"Mm." Áed ran a fold of the bedspread between his knuckles. "So. What were you and Erin talking about?"

Erin answered, spreading her hands out in front of her with an air of mystique. "Magic."

"Basically," Ronan said, filling in, "either Éamon or I could conceivably do it. But neither of us know how."

"We need to find somewhere they can learn," Erin finished. "Or maybe a book or something?"

Áed bit at his lip, checking on Éamon still sleeping next to him. "I might know somebody we could ask."

⸬

The healer looked concerned when Áed sought her out, finding her in a small personal room down the hall from Éamon's recovery chamber. "Áed!" she said, setting aside the document she'd been reading. "Is something wrong with your crossling?"

Áed shook his head. "No, it's not that." He leaned on the doorframe. "Actually, I had a question for you."

She folded her hands on her desk, narrowing her eyes. If Áed wasn't wrong, she immediately looked suspicious of him. Or perhaps Áed was too paranoid about Moon fae being shifty—after all, this woman had saved Éamon's life.

At any rate, the healer had spoken enough about magic the previous night that Áed hoped it might be an interest of hers. "Do you know where we—I mean, mine and Erin's crosslings—might learn a spell?"

The healer raised an eyebrow. "A spell? As in human sorcery?"

"Exactly." Áed fidgeted. "Neither of our crosslings have done any magic. But we want them to learn how."

The healer sighed, seeming to relax. "I see." She sat back in her chair, fanning herself with the document. "I don't know how much I can help you."

Áed felt his heart sink.

The healer went on. "I'm not an expert. Moon court doesn't have many resources on the subject; not many fae care to learn about humans." She ran a finger along the edge of her desk. Something about her body language was easing up. "Everything I know about magic comes from my own studies—not many humans, there—and records from other courts."

"Where did these other records come from?"

"Well, they're mostly captured items. So they're from courts that we've clashed with over the eons."

"Like Bone?"

The healer nodded. "Like Bone. In fact, if I had to guess, I'd say Bone probably has the best understanding of human magic out of any of us." Her lips pouted out in thought. "They're a big court, powerful. Lots of resources. And if I'm not mistaken, one of their leader's sons has a particular fascination with humans." She rubbed her chin. "Or at least, he has for the past couple decades."

Áed flashed her a smile. "Thanks so much for your help."

}}}

Éamon was just waking up when Áed returned to report what the healer had said. Áed hurried to his side. "Hey." He sat on the edge of the bed again, noticing Erin and Ronan share a glance. But then Éamon was blinking up at him sleepily; thoughts of Erin and Ronan went out the window. "How are you feeling?"

Éamon groaned and pushed himself up to a seat with his elbows. "Like I've been hit with a cart."

"Éamon." Ronan crossed to the side of the bed. "Thank the Gods you're okay. I swear, I was scared. I'd only ever seen so much blood one other time…"

Áed winced. That was right; the only other time Ronan would have seen so much blood was when Ninian had died seven years earlier.

"Hey." Éamon offered Ronan an exhausted half-smile. "I'm—yeah. I'm okay." He sighed, sinking against the pillows. "Still here, at least."

Ronan leaned over the bed to gingerly hug Éamon. He buried his head in Éamon's collar, and Éamon, looking faintly surprised, put his arm around the boy's back. Ronan spoke into Éamon's neck. "I'm so glad."

Éamon patted Ronan's back. "Are *you* okay, Ronan?"

Ronan stood up, discreetly brushing at his eye. He sniffed. "I'm fine. Didn't get hurt." He gave himself a little shake and stood up straight. "Just worried was all."

"Well, I'm—" Éamon swallowed. "I'm all right, Ronan. I didn't mean to make you worry." Before anyone could tell him that it was not his fault, Éamon cleared his throat uncertainly. "So, is there any good news? Because I could use some good news."

"I talked to the healer here," Áed said. "She told me that

if we want to learn magic, the Bone court is our best bet."

"Good." Erin sounded satisfied. "We were heading there anyway."

"Excuse me," Éamon broke in, raising a hand. "How far away is the Bone court, exactly?"

Erin pinched her lip. "Most of the low courts aren't horribly far apart. Maybe two day's walk? Three, at most."

"That's no good," Éamon said. "I'm missing a leg."

Both Ronan and Erin froze. Erin blinked. "You're what, now?"

Pushing himself up higher to lean on the headboard, Éamon dragged the blankets away. "Missing a leg." His voice was tight. "See for yourself."

Erin leaned forward with so much interest she nearly toppled off the chair. "Looks like you got two legs to me."

"This one isn't mine, moron." He flicked the hard material of the prosthesis. "Does this look like flesh and blood to you?"

"No?" Erin looked confused. "But it's definitely a leg. What's the problem?"

"The problem," Éamon said exasperatedly, "is that I just *lost* the leg that this thing is replacing. I can't walk yet."

Erin frowned, one hand going to play with her sea-green necklace. "Oh."

Ronan, at least, seemed to be showing a sympathetic amount of concern. "Gods, Éamon. Are you okay?"

Éamon slouched against the headboard. "At the moment?" He shoved his fingers through his hair, taking a deep breath. "I'm not sure."

Erin hopped off the chair. "I'm sure we can find a different way to travel. Áed, I nominate you to talk to Lachtna and see if he'll let us use a cart and a hind or two." Stretching, she leaned back and then folded forward to touch the floor. "I'd do it myself, but I really do hate him."

}}

Two days later, they found themselves loading a cart with fresh supplies and some rations that Lachtna had granted them for the trip. Áed had been surprised by the generosity. Instinctively, he distrusted it, but for as hard as he searched, he couldn't find a catch.

Erin stroked the nose of their hind, a tan-and-white-spotted creature whose antlers tapered to deadly little points, and Ronan sat in the cart, accepting the bags that Áed handed to him. Éamon, unsteady on crutches, leaned on the side of the cart and watched the forest suspiciously. "Erin," he said, "you do know where to go this time, right?"

Erin bristled. "Of course, I do."

"It's just that last time..."

"Well, I know now." She crossed her arms. "Lachtna gave me a map."

"All right," Áed announced. "Everyone in." He gave Éamon a hand, and Erin took her place in the front to wrap the hind's reins around her wrist. "Let's get to the Bone mound."

CHAPTER NINETEEN
ÁED

It looked like rain.

The clouds overhead were flat and textureless as the hind swiftly navigated the forest path, and their darkness made everything in the cart look dull. Even the fruits that Ronan had pulled out of the bags for lunch, coral-colored things with shockingly red insides and star-shaped seeds, looked bland.

In contrast to the grayness of the day, however, Áed's mood was hopeful. Éamon was quiet and clearly still processing everything, but Áed was beyond relieved that he was *alive*. Ronan was nibbling at a raw fruit and staring unabashedly at Erin, and Erin was… not currently too irritated with anyone, he supposed. He'd settle for that.

But best of all, they had a plan.

Áed couldn't say he was sad to leave the Moon court. The nocturnal cycle of its inhabitants had been disorienting, and he didn't enjoy not being able to see the sky. Not to mention he was tired of Erin's grouchiness there. The Bone court, she promised, was better.

The cart rattled along at a good clip, and the hind didn't seem to be growing tired. By the time the sun, peeking through the brooding clouds, began to sink below the tree line, Erin slowed the cart to a stop. The hind nibbled at some grass by the edge of the road, and Erin turned around to face the rest of the cart.

"Are we there?" Ronan asked, standing up to peer through the deepening gloom.

Erin, a silhouette against the cloudy orange sunset, shook her head. "Almost, but no. We crossed onto Bone territory about an hour ago, but it's their mound that we're heading for."

"Then what is it?" Ronan sank back down to a seat next to Éamon. "Why'd you stop?"

Erin sighed. "I need to tell you how this is going to work." She played with the hind's reins in her hands. "They already know we're here." With a flick of her wrist, she gestured to a nearby tree. Squinting through the dimness, Áed could make out nothing. He had almost opened his mouth to ask what she was pointing to before Erin started talking again. "That bunch of leaves on the right side of the trunk. Not natural. A camouflaged watch-post. I'm obviously Sand court, so they've been leaving us be, but that doesn't guarantee a warm welcome for the rest of you at the mound." She leveled a look at Áed, clearly addressing him. "I'm going to be vouching for you." She ran her tongue across her lips. "Whatever you do, don't say a word." Her gaze was intense. "Bone is not a welcoming court. Bone is not a *friendly* court. Bone is a court that will flay you first and ask questions never."

Áed blinked. "Now, I could have sworn you said they were better than Moon."

"Oh, they are." She shrugged. "They make sense. Straightforward. Don't mince words, don't play around with implications. When they say they'll kill you, it's not a threat; it's a warning. I like them." She crossed her arms sternly.

"But *I* am the only one who is protected when we step up to that mound."

"I take it that Ronan and I should keep quiet as well," Éamon said. His right eye, as usual, was hidden behind his hair, but his left was wide.

Erin nodded. "Yes. From what I've heard, the Bone leader doesn't like humans too well. Your best bet is to keep your heads down. Are we clear?"

Áed nodded. "I think I got it."

"For your sake, I hope so." Erin turned back around and gave the reins a snap, and then they were moving again.

Éamon rubbed at his knee, looking at Erin's back in alarm. "I can't tell whether she has a flair for the dramatic, or whether we're all about to die."

Áed groaned. "I'm so used to being stressed." He nudged Éamon's foot, the real one. "But this feels different."

Éamon nudged him back. "It's going to be all right."

It was incredible, Áed thought, if not downright unbelievable, that *Éamon* was comforting *him*. But he didn't argue, only sat back and watched the shadowed forest pass by.

⦚

Áed didn't need to wonder if they'd reached the mound.

Unlike the Moon court, which was little but a gentle swell of grass, mistakable for a simple hill if not for the doorways, the Bone mound was striking. Set back in a field, the front of the mound was a steep scarp face, exposed layers of rock open to the elements as if the earth had been pressed up from below. This rock was honeycombed with windows that made Áed think uncomfortably of eye sockets, except for the few windows out of which light glimmered warmly against the impending night. Atop the bluff, Áed could see fae standing at attention, with a few figures pacing back and forth along the edge. The main door was flanked by enormous brass bowl torches that illuminated not only impressive numbers of soldiers, passing the time by sparring with each other, but also the architectural tympanum over the door. At first, Áed thought it was sculpted, but as the cart drew nearer, he realized that what he was seeing were hundreds of animal skulls. He could identify the remains of horses, dogs, foxes, deer, and the gaps between the larger bones were filled in with the tiny, fragile skeletons of what he could only guess to be rabbits and birds. He shuddered.

"Damn," Ronan whispered. "They call it Bone for a reason, I guess."

"That's not the half of it," Erin said solemnly. "Everybody shut up. We're stopping here."

Following her lead, everyone clambered down from the cart. Éamon winced when he made contact with the ground, immediately taking pressure off his prosthesis and leaning on Áed until he could slide his crutches out of the cart. "That's eerie," he whispered, and Áed nodded. The empty hollows of the skulls' eyes seemed to track their movement.

"I said quiet," Erin said sharply. "I mean it."

The faerie walked in front as the group crossed the field to the mound. As they drew nearer, the soldiers at the door stopped their sparring and looked up at them with sharp, bright eyes. They relaxed slightly when they saw Erin, but two still stepped in front to bar the path. "Welcome, ally," one of them stated bluntly. His voice was rough, but if Áed had to guess, he didn't think it sounded hostile. "What brings you here?"

Erin nodded slightly, more respect than deference. "We want an audience with your leader."

The soldier's expression didn't change. "And who are your companions?"

Erin stepped aside to reveal Áed, Ronan, and Éamon.

She grabbed Áed by the upper arm and pulled him up next to her. "This is Áed. The tall human is his crossling; the younger one is mine."

The Bone soldier leaned closer, squinting. "Which court is he from?"

"He was born outside of a court."

The soldier leaned back, putting his hands on his hips. "He also wants to see Neasa?"

"He does."

"Why?"

"Same reason as me."

The soldier crossed his arms while his companion leaned on his spear. The position was casual, but Áed suspected how deadly it could turn in the blink of an eye. "Afraid that isn't good enough."

"We have an idea how to end the war," Erin said. Her stubbornness didn't decrease in the face of the Bone faerie's impenetrable stare. "But we need Neasa's help."

"And by 'end,'" the soldier asked shrewdly, "you mean 'win'?"

Erin grinned. It was a sharp smile, all edges. "I don't mean lose."

The soldier quirked an eyebrow, his gaze glancing over the party again. "You said the white-haired one was a crossling, right? A human?" When Erin nodded, he let out a little huff of a laugh. "That hair, thought he might be one of those Moon bastards."

"He's not fae, Moon or otherwise." Erin tilted her chin, and the inquisitive movement looked demanding. "So. Can we see Neasa?"

The soldier twirled his sword. It flashed in the light of the torches. "She's not here."

"That isn't an answer."

"I wasn't trying to answer you." The soldier stabbed the

point of his sword into the soft earth and leaned on it with crossed arms. "She'll be back soon. She can decide for herself whether she wants to talk to you."

"You're not a good guard," Erin sighed.

"My job isn't to vet supplicants. My job is to kill intruders." The sharpness of his smirk matched Erin's. "I'm damn good at that." He jerked a thumb to the side. "Just wait. It won't be long now."

When all four of them had settled off to the side, Éamon looking a bit uncomfortable with standing for so long, Erin sighed. "That went well. Keep it up."

"What was that about Áed?" Éamon said, sounding confused. "Born outside a court?"

Erin glanced at Áed uncomfortably, seeming to realize how close she'd come to revealing his secret. "Er." She shrugged. "It would be strange for one faerie to have three crosslings. Humans, I mean. So… better that they think he's fae."

"Huh." Éamon frowned. "You didn't tell me about that part of the plan."

Erin laughed, and Áed hoped he was the only one who could tell it sounded nervous. "It didn't come up."

Áed swept his eyes over the dark courtyard, the dramatic mound, the woods beyond, and hurried to change the subject. "How long do you think he meant by 'not long'?"

Erin seemed relieved by the diversion. "Haven't a clue. We can't lie, doesn't mean we have to be informative."

"I assume it's a short enough time that we can wait it out." Éamon winced and shifted his weight. "Hopefully."

The conversation ebbed as the night grew darker, and several fae emerged from the great mound doors to replenish the bowls of fire. Above them, the clouds remained dense enough to block out the stars.

Éamon sank to a seat within the first half-hour, and Ronan

followed shortly. Before too long, Ronan's head was resting on Éamon's shoulder, bobbing as he battled sleep.

That was when the horns sounded.

They sounded different from the Moon court's hunting horns. Those odd, translucent instruments had sounded ethereal, unnerving in a way that wasn't wholly natural, but these tones were something else altogether. The pitch was lower, but it was the quality of the note that made Áed's muscles seize. This horn sounded full. It held a rawness that was worlds away from the Moon court's unearthliness, something rich and haunting in a way that was not unsettling but truly terrifying. This wasn't the sound of a specter in the moonlight. This was the sound of war. In that moment, Áed had no doubt that whoever blew that horn had broken bones and sucked the marrow from within and that they would do so again.

The sound of the horns was quickly accompanied by the distant noise of voices and stamping footsteps. The soldiers in the yard, even the ones who had been sparring, righted their weapons and stood at attention. The effect was not starched, not the sort of disciplined rigidity that Áed had come to expect from his August Guard, but *eager*.

The tumult burst from the faraway tree line.

In front, a chariot was pulled by two sleek black horses, each tossing their heads as they galloped at full tilt toward the mound. Flanking the chariot, twin warriors likewise kept pace on horses, digging their heels into the steeds' flanks to encourage a breakneck pace, and behind, a small phalanx of soldiers ran. They pounded on their shields as they went, crying out over the clanking of steel. Several of them bore torches, and together, they looked like wildfire.

Áed took an instinctive step back.

When the group drew nearer, the one in the chariot

pulled hard on the reins. The black horses veered to the side, sending the chariot skidding out in a wide arc before it came to rest shrouded in the clouds of its own dust. The two warriors on horseback drew back their own mounts, one of which reared on its hind legs before its front hooves stomped back to the earth. Steam burst from its nostrils in the chilly night, catching the torchlight. The infantry behind caught up, maintaining their ruckus.

Now that they were closer, Áed could see more clearly. The soldiers on foot, all armed to different degrees, were stained with blood. The two riders alongside the chariot wore leather armor and helmets from under which thick, curly hair spilled to their waists, and each carried a longsword as easily as if the broad, stained steel were an extension of their arms. The figure in the chariot was easily the most intimidating—Neasa, Áed assumed, the Bone leader, clad in a steel breastplate and leather sleeve armor. She wore a ragged skirt of strips and cords, which parted about her long legs to reveal tall boots that ended above the knee. Her cheeks were painted in patterns beneath a vulpine skull mask that covered the top half of her face. Her hair was red and curly, cascading loose down her back, and her lips were as black as old blood.

She held up a fist, and her soldiers ceased their din.

In a motion so fluid that Áed nearly missed it, she vaulted out of her chariot, landing with wide legs and a palm to the ground. She looked up slowly, and a wide, wild grin began to crack her face. "My friends," she said, and her voice was as lyrical as it was gravelly. "We have much to celebrate."

Another raucous cheer roared from the soldiers behind her. She stood, turning to face the soldiers at the gate and spreading her arms wide as if conducting the shouts that concussed the night forest.

Still grinning, she swept toward the mound. In unison,

the two mounted warriors swung off their steeds. Neasa—Áed was still assuming the woman was Neasa—raised a beckoning hand. "Fionnlagh! Fionnuala! To me."

The warriors started after her, pulling off their helmets; one, Áed saw, was a man, and the other a woman, but the two shared the same shade of dark skin and sable tresses, the same movements in synchrony, and, if he looked hard enough through the fire-cut darkness, the same cheekbones and full lips. Each marched after Neasa without a word, heedless of the blood that stained their armor.

Before the three reached the mound door, it opened.

A smaller figure stepped out, keeping a hand on the door as if to ground himself. Áed hadn't ever seen a faerie that looked past their twenties, but this one didn't even look that; he was slight and not tall and didn't look older than a teenager. "They're back?"

One of the soldiers at the door looked over to the figure, raising an eyebrow. "Iarlaith?"

The person—Iarlaith—took a step away from the doorframe. He seemed to sniff the air. "I smell blood. And…" His brow furrowed, and in a swift motion, he pointed at Áed, Ronan, Éamon, and Erin. "Who are they?"

"Indeed," a gravelly voice asked, and Áed turned abruptly to find Neasa standing mere feet from them, her hands on her hips. Her expression was inscrutable beneath the fanged, bony mask. "Who *are* you?"

Erin stepped in front of the group once more, but this time, Áed could see that her expression had lost its confident set. Her eyes were wide, and her hands tight at her side. She did not bow, and Neasa didn't seem to expect her to. "I am Erin of the Sand court. This is my traveling companion and our human crosslings."

The leader's lip twitched. "Greetings, Erin of the Sand court. You are welcome here." She tilted her head, and the hollow eyes of her mask seemed to regard Áed much too deeply. "As for you, I cannot say the same."

The two warriors, Fionnlagh and Fionnuala, reached Neasa's side. "Mother?" Fionnuala's voice was low, rich as velvet.

Áed caught the barest flash of red behind Neasa's mask as the firelight caught just the right angle to illuminate her eye. "Nuala," the Bone leader said slowly, and the female warrior stepped forward. "Does this man look familiar to you?"

Frowning faintly, Fionnuala shook her head.

Her brother, however, remained still and silent. Áed noticed. Neasa didn't appear to. "I don't like him," she said. A grain of darkness rolled behind her words. One sharp-nailed finger reached up to absently tug at her lip; the tip came away black. "At all." In a flash faster than a blink, she'd flicked a blade from her sleeve, and then her arm was leveled easily at Áed's neck. The blade was no longer than a finger, but Áed felt a drop of blood roll down the column of his throat. He hadn't even felt the knife prick his skin. That edge was sharp enough to pass through his jugular like soft butter. "From which court do you come?" Neasa demanded calmly.

Áed swallowed, feeling his throat bob against the blade. "I have no court."

Out of the corner of his eye, he noticed the smaller person, Iarlaith, observing the exchange closely. He wasn't sure Iarlaith was *watching*, necessarily—something seemed unfocused about his eyes—but it was certain that he was under scrutiny.

"No court?" Neasa turned the blade thoughtfully. "Then allow me to rephrase." She leaned closer, so close that the empty nose of the fox skull mask nearly met Áed's own. "Where do you come from?"

He heard the truth on his lips before he could think of a

lie. "The human realm," he said and watched Iarlaith stiffen. The male warrior, Fionnlagh, looked stoic, but Áed was confident he hadn't imagined the stricken expression that flickered over his face.

Neasa leaned back suddenly. She glanced to the side, the first sign of uncertainty Áed had seen from her. "How interesting," she said after a moment. "I've never heard of a faerie hailing from beyond the veil."

"I was born there," Áed said, and immediately wondered if that was information he shouldn't have volunteered.

"Born?" Neasa echoed. Her voice had turned deadly, but Áed didn't miss the slight fear that pulsed behind the Bone leader's hardened exterior. The blade pressed more firmly against his throat. "Tell me," she said, and Áed got the distinct idea that she didn't want to hear the answer. "How old are you?"

Áed blinked. The question seemed odd. "I... I just turned twenty-four in the summer."

It was very difficult to tell beneath the mask, the red warpaint, and Neasa's rocky expression, but Áed could have sworn she looked shaken.

From his position in the shadows, Iarlaith took a step toward them. His step was tentative, but his face held determination, worry, and profound curiosity in equal measure. "Excuse me," he said, holding up a hand. His face, Áed saw, was patterned with lighter patches, pretty like cherry blossoms against the darker shade of the rest of his skin. "I have what might be an unlikely question." He inclined his head to Neasa. "Mother, if I may?"

Neasa didn't take her eyes off Áed, but she replied quietly: "if you must."

Iarlaith wetted his dry lips, turning his focus back in Áed's general direction. "To the human-born twenty-four-year-old," he said slowly. "Is your name Áed?"

For a second, Áed just stared at him. Perhaps he'd gotten word of Áed's mission from the Moon court? "Yes," he said finally. "That's my name." He frowned. Why would the Moon court have told their sworn enemy about a small group of travelers? Much less given their names? "I'm sorry, how did you know that?"

Several things happened at once, but none of them were an answer to Áed's question. Fionnlagh shot a pointed glance to his sister, whose eyes had flown wide. She stepped forward and then stopped at Fionnlagh's hand on her arm. Iarlaith didn't seem surprised, but he did seem *stunned*—as if the answer he'd expected wasn't the answer he'd truly been prepared for. And Neasa slowly lowered the blade from Áed's throat, her face entirely expressionless beneath her mask.

Áed looked to his friends, but each of them seemed equally as perplexed. "Is… am I missing something?"

It was Iarlaith who stepped forward. He reached out with a hand as he walked and stopped only when he bumped gently into Áed's shoulder. "I suppose you are," he said. His expression was complicated. "It's good to finally meet you." His eyes were deep in the torchlight, and his hand tightened slightly on Áed's arm. "Brother."

CHAPTER TWENTY
ÉAMON

Brother?

*B*It was almost a relief that Áed looked as lost as Éamon felt. Áed stepped back, breaking Iarlaith's touch. "I—I'm sorry?" he looked around, and Éamon realized that they had become the center of the entire courtyard's attention. The soldiers at the door were watching them intently, whispering to each other in confusion. The infantrymen still standing behind the Bone leader's chariot had fallen quiet, dulling their roars to listen. Éamon thought he even saw fae watching from the windows of the mound, peering out at the scene while that word echoed for far longer than it should have.

Brother.

Áed found Éamon's hand, and Éamon was startled to find that the ordinary rush of warmth he would have felt at being Áed's source of comfort was dulled by the sheer weight of the air. "I think there's been some confusion," Áed said, glancing around at the assembled faces. "I don't understand."

Iarlaith hadn't tried to follow when Áed stepped away, maintaining a respectful distance and crossing his arms. His face, Éamon thought, was sympathetic but unyielding, and he turned to Neasa. "Mother?"

Neasa was staring at Áed. "It can't…" She couldn't finish the sentence, her lips freezing around the words she seemed to want to say so badly. *It can't be.*

Fionnlagh dared a glance at his mother before approaching Áed and offering a short bow. "I have seen you before," he said curtly. "At festivals. But it is a pleasure to address you properly."

At that, Áed looked stricken, and Éamon remembered a story that he'd told one festival night: they'd both been deep in their cups, and Áed had spoken of shadows. He'd seen one at his very first Festival of Fire in the White City, a lithe figure that had melted away as quickly as he'd spotted it. "That was you?" Áed said shakily. "I saw you?"

"Ah…" The warrior frowned. "Perhaps I wasn't as cautious as I ought to have been."

Iarlaith shifted his weight from foot to foot. "Maybe it would be best if we continued this discussion somewhere more private?"

Fionnlagh looked up, seeming to notice their audience. "Indeed." He gestured toward the door. "Please. Come in."

Neasa's head snapped up. "Wait."

Iarlaith looked chagrined. "Mother…"

The Bone leader's voice was hard. "I said wait." She lifted a hand, fingers curling to point at the mound. "This," she said firmly, "is my mound. My home." With her other hand, she gestured to the two warriors and the short faerie with the cherry-blossom skin and the curly, dark hair. "These are my children. Mine." She swallowed, and her composure settled. "This is what I have built for myself. I need invite none into my home whom I do not wish to see." She took a deep breath, drawing herself up to her full height. "And I do not wish to see you." The roughness of her speech made the harsh words cutting. "Now that I do... you look just like him."

Éamon watched with horror as Áed's expression crumpled. "No," Áed breathed. He shook his head and stepped back. Closer to Éamon.

Neasa did not back down. "You have his hair," she said sharply. "And his face."

"He has your freckles," Fionnuala murmured, but Neasa ignored her.

"You look like him," she spat, "and I do not want to see you."

Tears were beading in Áed's eyes. He looked overwhelmed, still confused but now hurt, and Éamon couldn't shake the feeling that though he didn't know exactly what, *something* fundamental had just caved in over Áed's head. "I don't look like him," he whispered. "Don't say that. I don't look like him."

"Mother, *please*," Iarlaith insisted. "Let's take this inside. Please."

Neasa's face did not so much as twitch beneath the mask. "I will offer my hospitality to an ally of the Bone court," she said. "The Sand faerie and her crossling may stay."

"But not your son?" Fionnuala said softly.

Neasa's voice was rigid to the point of being brittle. "No," she said. "Not my son."

§

Áed sat against the side of the cart, his head buried in his arms. Though the cart blocked out the torchlight, Éamon could see him shaking—and even if he hadn't been able to, he could definitely hear Áed's quiet crying.

Hesitantly, he limped to Áed's side. When Áed didn't look up, Éamon sank to a seat beside him, leaning his crutches against the side of the cart. "Hey," he said softly.

Áed peeked over his arms, and Éamon saw that his face was flushed and blotchy with tears. His eyes were shining.

Éamon wanted to ask what was going on. He wanted to ask if what the Bone fae had said was true—that Áed was Neasa's son, that he was the warriors' brother, or if there had been some enormous confusion. But if it was just confusion, then why would Áed be crying? Éamon hadn't seen Áed cry in a long time.

"I don't know you at all," Éamon murmured, "do I?"

Pain twisted Áed's expression, and he hid his face again, tucking his knees tighter and leaning away from Éamon.

Part of Éamon wanted to demand a better explanation than what his own mind was frantically assembling. He thought back to the way Áed had been able to shield him at the festival. To the two fae with the child, the ones who had begged for directions to safety, who had spoken to Áed like one of their own. The Moon patrol had done the same thing, if Éamon remembered correctly; he'd been on the brink of unconsciousness at the time. Even Erin's odd phrasings seemed to point to one conclusion, but... well, for all of that, there could be some other explanation.

But the leader of the Bone court had just called Áed her son.

"You're fae," Éamon said softly.

There was a long silence.

And no denial.

"Damn," Éamon whispered.

Áed lifted his head for long enough to swipe the back of his hand under his eyes. His cheeks were soaked, wet with enough tears to sparkle even in the dimness. Those eyes— *red* eyes, eyes Éamon had never considered twice except for the passing thought that they were pretty—focused on nothing. "She hates me," he said hoarsely. His voice broke.

"You can, too. It's okay."

Ice filled Éamon's chest. What could he say to that? He looked away, casting his eyes over the inky woods. He wasn't sure what he was feeling. Betrayal? Sympathy? Dare he say... fear? But hatred... he shook his head. More feelings than he could identify were eddying around the maelstrom in his chest, but that emotion was not among them. "I don't hate you."

Áed hiccupped with another sob and pressed his hands to his face. "I'm sorry." His voice fractured, tears leaking between his fingers. "I've lied for so long."

It was very strange to look at Áed now. "You have, haven't you?"

"Are you afraid of me?" Áed managed. He wouldn't meet Éamon's eye.

"Yeah," Éamon admitted. "I am." He stretched his legs out in front of him. "I don't know *how* to feel about you right now. But..." He swallowed. "If that lady really is your mother, then *you* must feel kind of awful."

Áed let out a choked sob.

One part of Éamon desperately wanted to take Áed into his arms. He was *crying*, for Gods' sakes. The other part was still reeling. "Why didn't you tell me?"

Áed let out a soft whimper. "I wanted to." He wiped at his eyes. "I wanted to tell you everything, but I was scared." He sniffed. "You hate the fae. Everyone does. And you aren't even wrong to."

"They are pretty terrifying," Éamon said. "In a... steal-your-children, set-your-house-on-fire kind of way." He chuckled humorlessly. "A break-your-legs way."

Áed seemed to retreat further into himself. "Éamon, I—" He looked like he wanted to apologize for the fae as a whole, and also like he knew that he couldn't. "I'm not like that."

"I know." At least, he thought he did. *Did* he know Áed? Really? Truly? "Did you know Neasa was your mother?"

Áed shook his head. "I knew my mother was fae," he said. "That's all."

Éamon took a deep breath. When he released it, it ruffled Áed's hair. "I don't feel like I'm taking this very well."

"Better than I was afraid you would," Áed said quietly.

Éamon shivered. The wind was cold. "Áed, what your mother said…"

Áed stiffened slightly.

Éamon bit his lip. He knew the story Áed had told him, about his mother being a woman in the slums and a survivor of the King's violent lust, but to see it play out this way struck him with the forceful reality. "Maybe she didn't mean it?"

"She meant it," Áed murmured. "She can't lie, remember?" He shivered. "She meant it." He inhaled shakily. "I never assumed she'd love me. She left me a letter when I was a baby, detailing why she couldn't. And I… came to terms with it. I mean, my father *raped* her. I wouldn't want me, either." He let out the breath, just as unsteadily. "It just caught me off-guard." He swallowed. "And I really don't want to look like him."

"Well," Éamon said uncomfortably, "I don't think you do."

A noise made him look up, and he saw a figure approaching them. Immediately, he tensed; it was the young-looking faerie, Iarlaith. Iarlaith swung a slender cane in front of him, tapping at the uneven earth until it hit the wheel of the cart. The hind, still harnessed, snorted at his arrival, and Iarlaith found its nose with his hand for a pat before stepping further into the dimness. "Áed?"

Áed wiped his eyes. "Oh." His voice definitely sounded

like he'd been crying. "Iarlaith?"

Iarlaith tilted his head like he was listening. "Your crossling's here too, right?"

Éamon nodded and then realized the faerie probably couldn't see him. "Yes."

"Right." Iarlaith sighed, and it was a weighty sound. "I've come to bring you inside. It's cold out here. There's a room for you in the mound."

"I thought—" Áed sniffed. "I didn't think Neasa wanted that."

Iarlaith leaned his cane against his side and crossed his arms around it, shivering. "Mother is…" He pinched his lower lip with his teeth. "No. You're right. She doesn't." His face was unhappy. "The Fionns and I set up the room."

Áed looked down. "I don't want to force myself into her life," he said quietly. "That was never my intent."

"You aren't forcing anything," Iarlaith replied. "You're being invited." He adjusted his hold on his cane, letting out a breath. "I stopped aging at about seventeen, but I'm a lot older than I look. Fionnlagh and Fionnuala have been around for even longer. We were there twenty-four years ago when our mother went missing, and when she came back." He shook his head. "My point is that we think it would be good for her. To know you."

"She seemed fine before I turned up." Áed's eyes darted to the field where her bloody, cheering army had stood, where Neasa had leapt from her chariot with eyes blazing like victory.

"She is. Most of the time." Iarlaith tugged his cloak more tightly around his shoulders. "But it isn't just that, you know. The twins and I want to know our brother." He inclined his chin in Éamon's general direction, which was conveniently the same as Áed's general direction. "Your crossling is welcome as well, of course."

Áed looked to Éamon. "What do you think?"

Éamon honestly wasn't sure. Sleeping inside might be nice, but Éamon couldn't organize his thoughts enough to know if it would be worth it. "Your choice," he murmured.

Áed closed his eyes. "I'm just tired," he said heavily. "Gods, I'm so tired."

Iarlaith seemed interested. "Gods? Multiple? You really did grow up in the human realm, didn't you?" He blinked, seeming to realize his timing wasn't flawless. "Anyway. Will you come in?"

Áed hesitated for another moment and then nodded. He got to his feet slowly and helped Éamon up. "Yeah," he said as Éamon struggled to balance on his good leg and grab his crutches, wincing in pain. "Yeah, we will."

CHAPTER TWENTY-ONE
ÁED

"Does Neasa know I'm here?" Áed asked as Iarlaith led them into the mound. The air was warm, the hallway was smoky from the open torches that lined the walls, and the arched stone ceilings were stained with soot. At intervals, an alcove held some or another odd item—a cracked vase, painted in the bright shades of wildflowers, a sharp-toothed jawbone, a split breastplate that looked oddly like it was made of glass. *War trophies*, his instinct supplied. Mementos of victory.

Iarlaith shook his head. "No. But she will."

"Won't you get in trouble for bringing me in?"

"Perhaps."

Áed fell silent. The air smelled like tallow and something else, something familiar. Áed inhaled slowly and realized with a start that it was the scent that followed when he used his fire. He hadn't noticed that the magic had a *smell* before, but it was unmistakable; it clung to the walls themselves, warm and appealingly acrid. The Moon court hadn't smelled like this. It had smelled foreign, bright in a way that this place didn't.

Iarlaith turned to a stairwell, and Áed noticed that he was

barely using his cane now that he was inside the familiar mound. The stairs were carved directly out of the mound's stone, burrowing upward and hung with torch lanterns. Áed didn't look at the lanterns too closely; he had an uncomfortable feeling that they were made of bone. On the next floor, they turned into another hallway, airier than the last; this one had windows on one side, open to the outdoors, and the smoky odor was less powerful. Iarlaith opened a door for Áed and Éamon, stepping aside politely. "I'll let you rest for now," he said quietly. "You'll be safe here."

"Where are the other two?" Éamon asked. "Your siblings."

"The twins went to wash up. They both had to take care of some… gore."

"Are they hurt?" Áed asked, and Iarlaith shook his head.

"No. The viscera in question belonged to a regiment of high court soldiers who had been skirting the border of the Garnet court on their way to us."

Éamon looked alarmed. "On the way here? To this mound?"

Iarlaith raised a hand. "There's no reason to be alarmed."

Áed's mouth felt a little dry, and he knew he was looking at Iarlaith rather intensely. "Because now they're gore?"

Iarlaith's chin bobbed. "Indeed."

"That's what Neasa was pleased about," Áed guessed. "When she got back."

"Yes." Iarlaith brushed at his sleeves. "Our mother is an impressive fighter and a strong leader. Deserving of a great amount of respect."

At the words *our mother*, Áed's throat tightened. "Of course," he said quietly.

Iarlaith opened a hand to indicate the room outside of which they stood. "I'll leave you two for the night." He stepped away. "Rest well."

When the door closed, Áed turned to face it, rubbing his crooked fingers into his eyes. They were still puffy from crying.

"At least these fae aren't nocturnal," Éamon murmured.

Áed turned around to see the room properly. A wide bed was set against the far wall, and a table with two chairs was tucked neatly into the corner. The hearth was cold but stocked with wood, and through another doorway farther inside, Áed could see a washtub. The sound of trickling water came from that direction, and suddenly, Áed was aware of how filthy he felt.

Éamon crouched in front of the fireplace as Áed walked over to peer inside the bathroom. From a rectangular hole in the stone wall over the tub, water was leaking. Áed examined it to find that it was blocked by a slat of wood. A chain trailed down next to it; he tugged on it experimentally and jumped back when the slat lifted. Hot water sluiced out, drenching the front of his shirt. With a yelp, he tripped backward; as soon as he was out of the way, the water splashed merrily into the tub.

Éamon leaned into the bathroom, clearly tense. "Áed? What happened?"

Áed gestured to his wet shirt embarrassedly. "Figured out the bath."

Éamon relaxed. "Oh. I see." He exhaled. "I think I'm a little on edge."

Áed tried to wring out his shirt but gave up and peeled it over his head. He shivered at the chilly air against his wet skin. "Any chance you started a fire?"

Éamon shook his head. "There's nothing to start it with."

Oh. Well, that did make sense.

Áed brushed past Éamon in the door of the bathroom and knelt in front of the hearth. Éamon followed, frowning. "What are you—oh." His eyes widened. "*Oh.*"

Áed set his hands on top of the largest log and reached for the familiar ember in his chest. The heat tingled as it flowed down his arms, and then delicate tongues of fire began to lick their way between his crooked fingers.

He heard Éamon's sharp intake of breath. The fire leapt higher, shrouding his forearms, and woodsmoke began to curl up the chimney. He drew his hands away, pulling the fire inside again, and got to his feet as the wood began to crackle.

Áed heard Éamon take a step back. "You're really one of them." The words weren't harsh, but he couldn't disguise his instinctive fear. Áed could feel it.

"I'm sorry," he said.

He walked back into the bathroom and closed the door.

He stripped, crawling into the tub to let the stream of hot water pour over his head. It drowned out the world around him, reducing his senses to the roar of water past his ears, the warmth and pressure of it streaming through his hair.

It was time for this day to end.

❀

The mound looked different in the sunlight. It mirrored how Áed felt, what with its familiar unfamiliarity, everything oddly comfortable for a place where Áed felt like an outsider. Even his clothing felt *right* in a way he'd never felt, though still completely strange to him. The garments had been left at the door that morning, a set for both Áed and Éamon, and now Áed was wearing tall boots, simple black trousers, and a loose, comfortable ivory shirt that both rested off his shoulders and left his midriff exposed. That was the only part he wasn't particularly fond of; Éamon had needed to stop him from wearing the filthy shirt from the previous day instead. Áed had only given up when he found his old tunic still damp and freezing cold. At least Éamon was similarly outfitted: he was wearing a sleeveless tunic with an *entirely* open back. And that, Áed supposed, was at least a little distracting.

Iarlaith had come to fetch them early, and Áed had noticed the similarities in their garments. It felt incredibly odd to be dressed in the traditional garb of a Bone faerie. The sense of belonging put Áed on his heels, defensive for reasons he couldn't identify.

At that moment, Áed was tapping his foot impatiently, and the sound echoed through tall, close shelves. He and Éamon were sitting at a spindly-legged walnut table nestled between stacks of age-worn books in what Iarlaith had called his atheneum. Áed thought it looked like a library. Perhaps those two things were the same. He couldn't imagine it mattered one way or another, though, because whatever it was called, Áed was fighting the urge to stand up and pace between its dark, wooden shelves. Ronan and Erin were meant to be meeting them—or rather, Ronan and Erin were meant to have met them some ten minutes earlier. Iarlaith had promised that one of his siblings would escort the two teenagers to the atheneum as soon as they were dressed, and together, they could discuss the steps they intended to take. But Ronan and the Sand faerie were running late, and Áed was getting agitated.

"How do you read these?" Éamon asked Iarlaith, crumbling Áed's train of thought.

Iarlaith blinked. "Beg pardon?"

Éamon touched a thick, leather-bound tome on the nearest shelf. "These books. How do you read them?"

"Oh." Iarlaith traced a fingertip thoughtfully under one of his eyes. Ringed by the brilliant red of his iris, the pupil was an opaque, milky blue. "I have an assistant." He waved a hand. "I don't need her right now. I've already had her assemble the texts I think we'll need, given what your friends told Mother last night. I'm not going to disturb her on her day off; she has so few." He sat back, looking entirely at ease. "I imagine that you can read, yes?" At Áed and Éamon's affirmation, Iarlaith looked satisfied. "Then we won't have a problem."

At that moment, the round-topped door of the atheneum swung open, and Fionnuala strode in. Her hair was braided into a thick rope down the center of her back, and it was almost strange not to see her in armor. All the same, despite her civilian outfit, she moved like a fighter. Áed recognized the graceful confidence of her steps, the set of her chin—with a strange flash, he realized why it seemed familiar. Ninian had moved through the world the same way, as if it would shift to suit his path or be artfully destroyed. Fionnuala's eyes were falcon-sharp as they swept over the library, and Áed shivered despite the kindness in her gaze. It was not easy to believe he was related to this woman.

"I brought the Sand faerie and the other crossling," she said. At odds with her striking demeanor, her voice was easy.

Ronan and Erin peeked through the doorway at that, and Ronan hurried in when he saw Áed and Éamon at the table.

Erin slunk in more slowly. "Sorry we're late," she said. "Ronan overslept."

Ronan pulled out the chair next to Áed's and dropped to a seat. "Don't listen to her. She woke up after I did."

The Sand faerie shrugged as she sat down next to Iarlaith. "He still overslept."

Iarlaith pressed himself to standing, and the screech of his chair as it slid backward brought the room to attention. "Right. Now that we're all here—"

"Fionnlagh's not," Fionnuala interrupted. "Sorry, Iarlaith. He couldn't make it."

Iarlaith sighed, and Áed could sense his frustration. "Really?"

"He has training this morning."

"Goddess save us," Iarlaith muttered. "He's been training for three centuries. He can't put the sword down for an hour?"

Fionnuala grimaced. "Mother's orders."

"Well." Iarlaith leaned his palms on the table. "I suppose I'll fill him in later." He cleared his throat and started over. "Now that we're *mostly* all here, I would like to start with proper introductions." He held a hand to his chest. "I'm Iarlaith, Neasa's second son and the keeper of the archives. This," he continued, holding out a palm to Fionnuala, "is my older sister, Fionnuala. Call her Nuala and she'll cut you; only Mother and I can get away with that. She, along with my currently absent brother, is one of the Bone court's most successful generals." He turned to the rest of the table, sinking back down to a seat. "Your turn."

Erin spoke first, picking up where Iarlaith left off. "I'm Erin, of the Sand court. I crossed the veil with the refugees at the festival, but I came back to this side at the request of the human realm's King, who startled me by not being human at all."

"Not *fully*," Áed muttered.

Erin ignored him. "This short human with the soft hair is my crossling, Ronan. He's the human realm's Crown Prince, I think."

"You *think*?" Ronan complained. Then he blinked. "Wait, you think my hair is soft?"

"I couldn't help but notice," Erin griped. "It gets everywhere."

"Moving on," Áed interjected firmly. He stood, unable to

resist the urge to pace. "I'm Áed, King of the human realm, and Ronan is my ward. My friend is Éamon." He plucked uncomfortably at the hem of his shirt. The feeling of air touching his back was making him impossibly edgy, but to his surprise, he hadn't noticed a single faerie looking at his tattoos with more than absent observation. "We came here hoping to end the war." He turned down the table to Ronan and Erin. "You two talked to Neasa. What did she say?"

"She said that she didn't have many resources to spare," Ronan answered, "but that Iarlaith could maybe help Éamon or I learn the magic to find the consort. She said that if we found him, then we could discuss strategy." He winced. "She didn't sound too confident that we'd find him, though."

"That's because it's unlikely," Iarlaith said frankly. His hand found a thick journal next to him. "I've been studying humans and human magic for years now." He turned his head infinitesimally toward Áed, who remembered the Moon healer mentioning a Bone faerie who was fascinated with humans. He was willing to bet it was Iarlaith. "Even more so since I discovered I had a half-human sibling. The fact is, humans start learning magic *young*. Trying for the first time at an older age is much riskier. How old are both of you?"

"I've twenty-six," Éamon supplied.

"Fifteen," Ronan said.

Iarlaith sighed. "Ronan, you'll have a better chance."

"Wait," Áed interjected. "Why is it riskier? They'd only be learning a tracking spell. Nothing aggressive."

Iarlaith's fingers drummed on the cover of the tome. "It's nothing to do with the *kind* of magic." He seemed to catch himself tapping on the leather and stopped. "When human children siphon fae magic, they can't channel very much." He shrugged. "But the more humans mature, the more magic they're capable of using at once. If they try to handle a large quantity of power without those early years of developing control, the odds of something going wrong are a lot higher."

Next to Áed, Éamon swallowed. "And what exactly could go wrong?"

"Plenty," Iarlaith said grimly. "Our power is… how do I put this?" He steepled his fingers. "It's like fire, I suppose. To you, it's chaotic. When you channel, you're not just acting as a conduit for the energy to slide right through; you're using your *own* energy to force that shapeless magic into a very specific thing you want to achieve. I've heard it described as a battle: your energy against the fae power. Even if you win, it's possible to exhaust yourself dangerously with the effort. But if you lose, that power has to go somewhere." He was back to fidgeting with the journal. "And that *somewhere* is likely not where you wanted it to go."

Áed glanced sideways at Éamon. "Boudicca never told you about this?"

Éamon shook his head. "We never really talked about it. She knew I didn't like her, um…"

"Doing anything fae?" Áed finished, and Éamon nodded. "Well. I guess I can't blame you now." He frowned. "I always heard that when things went wrong with magic, it was because the fae found out humans were stealing power."

Iarlaith chuckled. "Well, I guess that's one way to encourage people not to channel beyond their limits." He shook his head. "There are some fae who resent humans using what they see as 'our' power, so I guess it's not *untrue*. Those are usually the same fae who burn human buildings on festival nights."

"Like crushing an anthill," Fionnuala chimed in with a quiet, scornful growl. "A power display for the insecure."

"At any rate," Iarlaith said, "those are the risks. I'll still do my best to help if you're set on this plan, but I wouldn't have you attempting it without knowing what danger you face."

Ronan looked nervous. "You said I had the best chance of succeeding?"

Iarlaith nodded. "You're still older than I'd like, but yes. Your odds are better."

Ronan's face set, and Áed could feel him steeling himself. "All right," he said decisively. "What do I have to do?"

CHAPTER TWENTY-TWO
RONAN

There was something eerie about Iarlaith's eyes. Not that they were sightless, but that they seemed to see through him anyway. The faerie felt around the table dexterously until he found a tome bound in black leather. He pushed it across the table to Ronan. "Here. My assistant marked the right page." He leaned back as Ronan opened the book. "Certain actions can help concentrate your energy to channel the magic, actions like speaking a verse. What you'd call a spell."

The page that had been bookmarked was inked in dark red, a color that reminded Ronan of old blood. "I don't know this language," he realized. "Or at least…" Some of it, he could read. *A Manner of Finding What You Seek*, announced the top of the page. But the majority of the words within the entry itself, arranged like a poem, were in a tongue he didn't know. "What is this?"

"Not a language at all," Iarlaith said. "They're just sounds. In a certain pattern to help guide a certain energy."

Experimentally, Ronan stumbled through the nonsensical writing out loud. Even despite his tripping over the pronunciation, he could tell it sounded musical, sharp in places, round and flowing in others. When he finished, he looked up. "Was something supposed to happen?"

Iarlaith shook his head. "No. Not yet. You have to deliberately draw on the magic for the spell to actually do anything." He held up a finger. "But before you try to do that, I want you to know this spell as well as your own name. The less you have to think about the spell itself, the more you can concentrate on moving the magic *through* it."

"That doesn't make sense."

"Just memorize the spell." Iarlaith sighed. "The hard part comes later."

Áed looked like he was trying to resist pulling the book away from Ronan. "Iarlaith," he said after a moment, and Ronan could hear the clipped tone in his voice. It nearly broke into something that sounded much less human. "Exactly how dangerous is this?"

Iarlaith let out a breath through his nose. "Well, it's not safe. I'm going to concentrate on simply teaching Ronan how to channel as little magic as possible; the spell shouldn't need much. That'll be less dangerous than trying to teach him control over larger amounts. But… it is still dangerous."

Áed turned to Ronan, intensity in his eyes. For the first time, seeing Áed in a room with his full-fae siblings, he struck Ronan as unearthly. Ronan shivered. He'd never seen Áed that way before. "Are you sure you want to do this?"

Swallowing, Ronan nodded. "I came across the veil with you because I wanted to help."

"Please be careful," Áed said quietly after a moment. "Do not get hurt. Please."

⟨⟩⟨⟩

Ronan spent the rest of the day in the atheneum with the book, practicing the words. By the end of the day, the lyrical nonsense was stuck in his head as surely as a song. It was dark when he and Erin returned to the room Neasa had granted them as a result of Erin's Sand court allegiance. He made directly for the bed and flopped onto his back. "I'm going to dream about those damn words," he groaned. "I can feel it."

"Maybe that's a good thing," Erin said. "Iarlaith said you needed to know them well."

"Oh, I know them." Ronan rolled over, smushing his face into the pillows. "Believe me."

Erin seemed to think on that for a moment and then exhaled with a soft trill. "I don't want you on the bed."

"Why?" Ronan patted it possessively. "It isn't *your* bed."

"It's more mine than yours. Neasa gave this room to *me*."

"You're nocturnal anyway."

"I'm sleeping at night to line up with *you* people."

"Well, then you can be on it at the same time as me." He looked up from the pillow. "That was fine last night."

Erin scowled. "You hogged the blankets."

Ronan raised an eyebrow. "You slept on *top* of me."

"I was cold." She pouted, looking away. "Because you stole the blankets."

Ronan rolled his eyes. He wasn't about to admit to the jolt of warmth that had shivered down the entire length of his body when he'd woken up to find Erin's face two inches away from his own and her body fitted against his. "Well, then I won't do that this time."

"You'll be sleeping on the floor," Erin mumbled. She turned away, but not before Ronan caught a glimpse of her hand moving to fidget with her necklace. She did that when she was flustered.

Ronan just grinned. "I don't plan on moving, actually."

Erin glared at him. "You had better."

"What'll you do if I don't?"

She fisted her hands at her sides. "You're such a brat!"

"I've been told." He spread out his arms, sprawling over the entire bed. "This is nice, though."

Growling, Erin kicked off her shoes. "You even didn't take your boots off. That's *gross*."

"They aren't touching the covers."

"Get off the bed, Ronan."

"Make me."

Erin didn't need much prompting. She pounced on him. Giggling, Ronan rolled over as she got her arms around his waist and started trying to drag him off the bed. He took her shoulders, and she yelped as he flipped her under him. "Agh! Get off!" She turned her head and managed to lick the inside of his wrist.

With a yelp, he released her. "Ew!"

Grinning wickedly, she got to her elbows and tackled him. He squeaked as she landed on top of him on the floor, all of the blankets from the bed *flump*ing after them. "Ronan! Look what you did!"

"I can't look at anything, actually," Ronan said, blinking at the darkness. There was a comforter over his face. "You've dumped the blankets on my head."

"That was your fault!" Erin was sitting somewhere on Ronan's midsection, squirming in an attempt to free them both from the tangle of quilts.

"How? You tackled me! You *licked* me!"

Erin managed to free herself from the blankets with a victorious huff. Then she looked down at Ronan and seemed to realize that she was straddling his body with her legs. Her pupils went wide, and she inhaled with a little hiccup. As collectedly as she seemed capable, she got to her feet and gathered the blankets back onto the bed. "You can sleep on the very edge, if you must," she said, tossing her head. "I suppose."

⑅

Ronan was surprised that he did not, in fact, dream about the spell. But that only meant that sleeping was the sole time he had free from the strange words for the next three days. From sunup to sundown, he read them, spoke them, wrote them. Once, he even caught himself singing them to himself, which would have been deeply embarrassing if anyone but Iarlaith had been in the atheneum at the time. As it was, the archivist faerie seemed pleased.

By the end of the third day, Ronan felt like his brain was melting. But after spending so much time with the verse, it almost felt like it meant something. Like he didn't speak its language, but it communicated something all the same. It was as if a thread ran through the sounds, through the shape of them, and it twisted into the form of a concept he could grasp.

When Ronan told Iarlaith this, the faerie had paused in his quiet discussion with his assistant—they had been arguing in an academic kind of way, something about where they'd organized old battle plans—and turned his head to Ronan. "That's good," he said. "Very good, actually. That shape is what the magic is going to flow along, so to speak. Keep working at it. See if you can get it to clarify."

So Ronan did. He was beginning to understand why most magic-users limited themselves to one genre of magic; out of curiosity, he'd flipped through the book. Other seeking spells—some for finding lost objects, one for finding true love, another for finding shelter—seemed familiar to him. Similar to the one he'd been working on. Curious, he tried speaking them and found that he got an immediate, if rough, understanding of their shape and how they worked. But other spells, like one he found for curing back pain, were entirely foreign. The words felt like nonsense. Given the way his head ached after working so hard at just one spell, he couldn't imagine trying to branch out beyond a couple of specialties.

It took until the seventh day in the Bone mound before it *clicked*. Ronan had taken to studying outside of the atheneum, preferring the colder but less-stifling air of one of the high balconies. He'd just taken a break to stare out over the tops of the surrounding forest; he could see all the way to the plateau from here. In the other direction, the forest spilled in rolling hills over the landscape. Sometimes he could see smoke rising from the trees. Every time he saw it, it encouraged his efforts, because beneath that gently curling smoke, wafting over the forest, he knew that there was blood.

When he looked back down at the open book on his lap, it happened.

One moment, the shape of the verse had been a fuzzy thing, understandable but undefined. The next, he *saw* it. Or rather… 'saw' was the wrong word. He *had* it. It was clear. Perfectly formed. The sensation was that of a lock clicking into place, that final snap of closure. If he performed this spell, he would know where to look for what he sought.

He jumped to his feet and then swore as he had to catch the book before he launched it from his lap over the balcony railing.

Iarlaith was, to no surprise, in the atheneum. Ronan had the feeling that the archivist didn't go outside much. He turned sharply from the shelves, startled, when Ronan burst in.

"Ronan?" he asked, sounding alarmed as he felt around for his cane, which had been knocked from its rest against a shelf. Iarlaith's assistant popped her head out of the shelves, looking offended by the noise.

"I got it," Ronan panted. "The spell. I got it."

Iarlaith located his cane and propped it up again. "Ah." He let out a little breath, still apparently recovering from being startled. "It's clear? You've gotten a grasp of it?"

"I did, yeah," Ronan said. He was out of breath from sprinting through the mound, high on his breakthrough. "Took me long enough, but I did. Just now."

Iarlaith looked intrigued. "That was quick, actually."

"*Quick?*" Ronan slumped to a seat at the table. "It's been a week!"

"Like I said." Iarlaith crossed the little space to join him at the table. "Quick."

Ronan put the spell tome on the table and slid it across to Iarlaith. "So now what?" He was jumpy from spending so much time being *still*. Out beyond the walls of the mound, people were dying. "Time to do magic?"

He half-expected Iarlaith to say no, but the faerie nodded. "Indeed."

Ronan blinked. "Whoa." He glanced around the now-familiar walls of the atheneum. "I'm... a little nervous, actually."

"That makes sense," Iarlaith reassured him. "Which doesn't sound comforting, of course, but for whatever it's worth, I do think you're being brave."

"Of course, I am." Ronan tossed his head, just a little bit. "All right, Iarlaith. Tell me how we're doing this."

CHAPTER TWENTY-THREE
ÁED

"Hm."

Áed looked up at Éamon, who was sitting in the chair in the corner of their chambers. He had taken to reading books borrowed from the atheneum. Áed had been lying on the bed, staring at the ceiling and feeling useless. Ronan was somewhere in the mound practicing his spell, and on the other side of the veil, his kingdom was struggling to recover from the fae attack without its King. He let his head hang off the edge of the bed to look at Éamon. "What is it?"

Éamon's eyes didn't lift from the book. "Did you know that a few thousand years ago, fae apothecaries used to sell human teeth as a cure for headache?"

Áed made a face. "That's grisly."

"And that some low fae have antlers, or tails, or claws and whatnot?"

"I had no idea."

Éamon chuckled drily. "At this rate, I'm going to know more about fae than *you* do."

Áed pressed his lips together. This topic made him a little nervous. "I see the irony." Since that first night at the mound, they had barely talked about Áed's fae blood. Áed hadn't wanted to bring it back up. "Er…" He swallowed, trying to sound casual. "Are we… okay? With that? And everything?" Immediately, he cringed. That had sounded ridiculous.

With a sigh, Éamon closed the book. For a moment, he just looked at it, and when he spoke, his eyes flicked up to meet Áed's. "Áed, you were entitled to your secrets. I can't be angry about that. But… you clearly weren't *comfortable* enough to tell me. That's what made me upset." He fidgeted with the edges of the book. "I really want to be someone you can trust. That's all."

Áed pushed himself to his elbows. "I did trust you. I *do*." He took a quick breath. "Just because I don't divulge my *actual deepest secret* doesn't mean that I don't trust you."

"I know." Éamon shook his head, looking frustrated. "It's just *that* and coming to terms with the fact that I've been taught to fear the fae for my whole life. And there's a good reason for that." His eyes were deep and earnest. "I'm working on it. Áed, you're—you're important to me. Very. This doesn't change that." He looked away, shamefaced. "I'm sorry if I've been an ass."

"And I'm sorry that you found out the way you did, instead of from me." He sat up and swung himself off the bed. He crossed to Éamon's chair and perched on the arm, leaning on Éamon's shoulder. "We're okay, right?"

Éamon closed his eyes and let out a breath with a small smile. "We're okay."

Áed breathed a sigh of relief. He hadn't realized how much the unspoken tension had been wearing at him. He poked Éamon's arm. "And how are *you*?"

Éamon grunted. "Now, *that* is a different question."

"That bad?"

Éamon stretched out his leg. "I'm all right. But *this*

thing…" He scowled at it. "What kind of prosthesis can you not *take off*?" He waved a hand irritably. "I understand that it has healing properties. That's nice. But it's not what I'd have chosen for myself." He leaned forward to rub his knee. "I've seen plenty of prostheses. None of them are like this. Why did I get the creepy prosthesis, Áed?"

Áed scratched his chin. "I knew someone in the Maze who had a false arm. She used to take it off and beat you with it if you looked at her funny."

Éamon looked amused. "See? I'm being deprived of an experience."

It was good to see Éamon smile. Áed settled more comfortably against his side. "Maybe when everything is over, we can find a way to get you a better one."

"I'd like that." Éamon sank back. "I have to live with this for the rest of my life." He shook his head with a bittersweet little laugh. "I'd better have a say in my own damn fake leg."

For a few minutes, both of them were quiet.

Then Éamon spoke up again. "Do you remember what it was like before your hands…" He hesitated. "Before they got to be how they are now?"

Áed let out a slow breath through his nose and held out a hand in front of him. "It was a long time ago." He opened his hand as far as it could go—it wasn't terribly far—and examined his crooked fingers. The backs of his hands were crooked, too, and his wrists were perpetually stiff. "But yeah, I do."

Éamon nipped at his own lower lip in thought. "How did you manage?" He inclined his head minutely toward Áed's hand. "Once it was done. How did you… deal with it?"

Áed let his hand fall back to his lap. "It was hard," he admitted. "There were things that I'd really liked to do that

I couldn't anymore." He rested his head against Éamon's shoulder. "I used to sew, did I ever tell you that?"

Éamon shook his head.

Áed sighed. "After I healed, I tried for a while to pick it back up. But needles are way too small for me to hold." He remembered his effort clearly: he'd had ten years and had been struggling to complete a patch that would have taken him seconds before his hands were ruined. He'd ended up throwing the fabric, thread, and needle all together across the room, and Ninian had held him while he cried out his frustration. "I had to let things go. And that was hard. But over time, I found workarounds, ways I could open doors, or hold things, or write—you know, I'll wrap a quill in fabric until it's big enough to grip. I'm still not *good* at writing, but I can *do* it." He shrugged. "And there are things that I still can't really manage. But for those, I know that first of all, I'm plenty good at other things, and second, that I don't have to do anything alone."

Éamon nodded. His gaze was hovering somewhere on the floor. "I see."

"I'm sorry." Áed nudged himself a little closer. "I wish I could tell you it'll be easy." He looked up at his friend's face. "But you can do it. You're not alone, either."

At that, a small smile came to Éamon's lips. He opened his mouth to reply but was interrupted by the door bursting open so hard that it nearly hit the opposite wall.

Áed yelped, automatically latching onto Éamon, who grabbed Áed's arm.

Ronan was standing in the doorway, grinning and out of breath. "Guys," he panted. Then he seemed to take in Áed and Éamon together in the armchair and raised an eyebrow. "On second thought, never mind. I'll be going." He grabbed the doorknob as he turned around, waving jauntily over his shoulder. "Get back to it!"

Áed felt himself flush red. "That little—"

Éamon was also blushing profusely as Áed hurried to clamber off him. Áed ran to the door and wrestled with the handle until, fuming, he could lean out into the hall. "Ronan! Get back here!"

Ronan turned to walk backward. "No, no! Carry on!"

"It's not—that isn't—ugh!" Áed pressed his forehead against the doorframe. "Just get back here! What did you want?"

"You sure?"

"*Yes!*"

The grin was back, wider than ever. "I'm going to try the spell." He waved at Éamon over Áed's shoulder. "You should come watch."

CHAPTER TWENTY-FOUR
RONAN

Ronan was still grinning to himself when Áed met him outside of the atheneum, telling him that Éamon needed to lie down for a while. That had stricken Ronan as odd since Éamon had definitely been awake when Ronan had come in, and it was an odd time to sleep anyway, but he hadn't argued. Maybe Ronan had embarrassed him too much.

Erin arrived a few minutes later. It was tricky to tell if she was worried for Ronan's safety, excited for the war's end to be a bit closer, or curious about seeing a disastrous magic show. Ronan didn't ask. He wasn't sure he wanted to know.

"We're going outside," Iarlaith informed them as soon as they were all there. "Less to damage if something explodes."

"Is explosion likely?" Ronan ventured.

"It's a possibility." Iarlaith took up his cane. "Follow me."

He led them out of the mound and into the fresh air, pausing only to grab them all some cloaks before they stepped into the cold air and made their way across the yard. The forest loomed before them, misty with the cold and damp; the shadow of the tall trees made the air silver-gray and almost murky, and the dying ferns clustered between the gargantuan trunks sparkled with moisture. "This forest looks ancient," Ronan said.

"It is," came Iarlaith's prompt reply. He maneuvered through the undergrown and fallen branches with enough ease to make Ronan reconsider his assessment of the archivist as an indoors-only type. "Come on, this way." Everywhere his cane brushed against the wintering brush, dew sprinkled to the forest floor.

Eventually, they reached a clearing. Looking back, Ronan couldn't see the mound through the trees. He supposed being far away was the idea. The clearing was edged on one side by a long, fallen log, bark worn away to expose the smooth, pale wood beneath. On the other side, a stream trickled. The water looked icy as it swept leaves over the stones along its bed.

"Right," Iarlaith ordered. "Áed and Erin, please sit. Ronan, come to the center." Ronan did so, shivering when he felt Iarlaith's warm hands adjust his posture. The slender faerie swept Ronan's hair off his shoulders, letting it fall down the center of his back, and nudged his shoulders down, his chin in. "Stand straight and neutral. Don't lock your knees."

Ronan obeyed, but it felt immensely awkward with an audience. "How come?"

"You want to consciously think about as few things as possible. Everything needs to be natural. Are you comfortable?"

"I guess."

"Good." Iarlaith stepped back. "Now, we aren't going to be starting by trying the spell." He slowly began to walk around Ronan. "Start by feeling the magic that you're going to be channeling. Don't call on it yet; just find it."

"How do I do that?"

Iarlaith seemed to think for a moment. "Here is where

my own teaching ability falls short. For as much as I study, I have not a single clue how a human experiences the world, or how they feel magic. For myself, I find that my magic seems to reside somewhere inside me—I often picture it in my chest, behind my breastbone, warm like a coal." He paused. "But for you, I'd imagine magic would feel more external." He circled back around to Ronan's front just as an idea seemed to occur to him. "You've lived with Áed for a long time, haven't you?"

Ronan nodded. "Since I can remember."

"Is there any feeling you associate with him that nobody else seems to carry?" Ronan looked to Áed as Iarlaith went on. "Perhaps something that felt familiar when you met other fae?"

Ronan swallowed. *Was* there? When Áed had told him what he was, Ronan had been young. It had happened not long after they both moved into the palace, Áed a seventeen-year-old recently crowned King and Ronan an eight-year-old who struggled to adjust more than he let on. At the time, he couldn't say he'd been surprised. Was that because he'd seen Áed's fire firsthand? Or on some level, had he always known Áed was something else? "It's hard to say," he said finally. "For a long time, Áed was like... like my older brother and father in one. And as I got older, it felt more like he was my brother, looking out for me, but there was always that *feeling*. I just mean..."

"No child can truly see their guardians as fully human," Iarlaith finished with a sigh.

"Exactly," Ronan mumbled. "He's *always* been on another level, for me."

"Ronan..." Áed said quietly from his seat on the log.

"Hush," Ronan grouched. "Don't get a big head over it." He swallowed, trying to concentrate. Beyond that, *was* there something different about Áed? A sensation in his presence, any gut feeling? It was hard to identify. Áed was so familiar. But… "Áed, would you come here, please?"

Áed looked to Iarlaith to make sure it was all right, and then he crossed to Ronan's side.

"Give me your hand," Ronan said. He accepted Áed's hand as Áed obliged, feeling the familiar shape of it in his palm. Then he turned to the other faerie. "Iarlaith, could I please have your hand as well?"

Looking curious, Iarlaith offered his hand, and Ronan took it.

"Now, I don't really know what I expect from this," Ronan mumbled, "but I'm just trying something."

He closed his eyes. He wasn't sure what magic *felt* like, but he imagined that Áed's and Iarlaith's would feel similar. They shared blood, didn't they? Maybe Áed's would be weaker since he was half-human, but… Ronan concentrated, trying to sense anything at all. It felt like trying to pick a single note out of a complex song, a note he knew was there but wasn't sure how to listen for.

"Ugh," he groaned. "I don't know what I'm doing."

From the log, Erin piped up. "What if one of us tried *using* magic?"

Iarlaith looked thoughtful. "Good idea." He held up his free hand, and Ronan watched as the faerie's skin began to glow faintly. It wasn't enough to make a flame, but Ronan still felt its warmth.

And also something else.

There was a *hum* hanging in the air. Like the sound of a river just out of sight, except that the sensation wasn't actually sound. The strangest thing, he realized, was that he'd *always* felt this around Iarlaith. The only difference was that now, it was strong enough to be distinct. And if he focused his attention on that feeling, isolated its frequency, he could notice it in Áed, too. It pulsed under Áed's skin where his palm made contact with Ronan's hand; it vibrated the air between them. Áed's was quieter than Iarlaith's, a softer version of the same feeling. Across the clearing, Ronan could feel Erin's power as well. Hers was unique from Áed and Iarlaith's, like a different instrument playing the same note. "Oh," Ronan breathed. "*That's* what that is?"

It was familiar. Painfully so. This was the feeling he associated with Áed, just as Iarlaith had hypothesized. It was warm, almost tingling, and the more he concentrated on it, the more clearly he could feel it: it reminded him of the energy that builds before a storm, of the crackling in a cozy hearth. It was comforting and yet untamed, surrounding him with shivering warmth. It was beautiful. It wasn't safe.

"You feel it?" Iarlaith asked.

Ronan nodded. "Could you stop your fire?"

Iarlaith did so. The intensity of the sensation diminished, but Ronan could still pick it out. "I still have it." He shook his head. "You have no idea how bizarre this is."

"I'm sure you're right." Iarlaith nodded to Áed. "Áed, it might be best if you back up again."

When Áed had, the archivist turned to Ronan. The mist of the woods swirled around his feet, seeming to rise directly from the soft moss of the forest floor.

"Ronan," Iarlaith directed. "You still remember the spell?"

"Of course." He had the feeling he'd remember it for the rest of his life.

"Good. Keep it in your head. I'm going to have you start channeling a little bit of magic, and even though I want to start small, you should have the spell ready. If you accidentally draw too much, which could easily happen, having that structure will help keep the magic from exploding without direction."

"What are the odds that I get this on my first try?"

"Low." Iarlaith spread his hands. "Now. When I say, I want you to take some of that magic you sensed and invite it to you. As small a quantity as you're capable."

It was getting a little bit easier to understand the vagueness of these instructions, given that with learning the spell and finding the magic to channel, he'd followed them twice. But that didn't make it easier to visualize. He felt for the magic, found it quickly. Perhaps that was another thing he was never going to forget how to do. Now to invite it in... He took a deep breath. If he was supposed to be a channel for the power, then maybe he should picture allowing the magic to move *through* him. Like, in one hand and out the other? He turned one of his palms skyward and imagined the magic gathering above it, melting through his skin.

Nothing happened.

"I feel stupid," he admitted.

"Keep trying."

Screwing his eyes closed, Ronan tried. He could *sense* the magic around him and wished Boudicca were here to tell him what it actually felt like to channel it. Iarlaith was being extremely helpful, but as the faerie had himself admitted, he couldn't use magic the way a human could. Everyone was bound by their natures, Ronan supposed.

He crunched down his eyebrows, trying to re-center. There was the magic; there was the spell in his head. He just needed to let a few drops of that magic flow through the structure of that spell, like water through a mill.

He felt warmth.

The feeling was that of submerging in a hot bath when he was numb with cold. It was very nearly painful as it washed over him, setting his nerves alight as it rolled over his body like a wave.

Despite the pointed, aching sharpness, Ronan found himself immediately pursuing the tingling magic, leaning into it. There really was a lot of it, wasn't there? Everywhere around him was a source to draw from, power to imbibe; the very air shimmered with energy. He couldn't tell how much he'd already called to himself, but given how much there was around him still, it couldn't have been that much, could it? And it felt… drunk. He felt drunk. He felt like he was floating on the magic, drinking it in, and it felt *incredible*.

"Ronan," a voice came urgently. "Ronan, stop."

Ronan opened his eyes. Iarlaith was in front of him, looking alarmed; on the log, Áed had sprung to his feet, and Erin's eyes had flown wide, her body tense. The warmth of the magic leaving his body made his knees weak. "What happened?"

"You're bleeding," Iarlaith said tensely. "I can smell it. Which means it's significant. Where?"

"I'm bleeding?" Ronan said numbly. The world turned around him, suddenly seeming very cold, and the next thing he knew, he was on the ground. Or rather, *almost* on the ground. Áed had hurriedly crossed the clearing and caught him before Ronan's knees gave. Ronan blinked, confused. There was red on his shirt.

"Your nose," Áed said tightly. "Oh, that's a lot."

Ronan reached up to his face, feeling wobbly. It was wet, and his fingers came away red. "Oh." He pinched the bridge of his nose, waiting for the world to stop rocking back and forth.

"Tilt your head," Áed directed, and Ronan was reminded of the many times, back in the Maze, when Ninian had come home from a fight with a bloody nose or Ronan had gotten one from being too reckless running around stealing things. Áed had patched them up over and over, each time with the same concentrated worry. Was that really so long ago? It didn't feel like it. "I think it's slowing down. Gods, Ronan, that was a lot of blood."

"I'm a little dizzy," Ronan mumbled.

Iarlaith crouched next to them. "You did well."

"Did I?" Ronan wiped his nose, streaking the back of his hand with blood. He could taste it in his mouth, coppery and repulsive. "I look like murder…"

Iarlaith chuckled. "Well. If all you got is a nosebleed—albeit a bad one—that's a very good start." He offered Ronan a handkerchief, which Ronan pressed to his nose. "You must truly be a natural."

"I think I'd have kept going if you hadn't stopped me," Ronan said. Gods, he was sticky with blood. How had he not noticed this happening? "It was so…" He hesitated, trying to find the right word. "Enticing."

"Did you try to channel it through the spell?"

Ronan shook his head. "No. I got lost."

Iarlaith pushed himself to his feet. "Well. I do think that you have great potential for magic, but that's enough for today." He played with the handle of his cane. "Rest. Drink plenty of water. Áed, could you help him back to his room?"

Áed nodded. "Ronan, can you stand?"

"I think so." He was dizzy, but the sweeping weakness had passed. Áed supported him to his feet.

"Are you sure you want to do this?" he asked Ronan tersely.

Ronan nodded. "I *can* do this."

"If you can't—"

"The other option is Éamon does it," Ronan said. He didn't think he could let go of Áed without toppling, but he tried to disguise how much he needed the help by grasping at the trees as Iarlaith began to lead them all back toward the mound. "He's too old. Iarlaith said so."

"We can find another way if we have to."

"If you were fully fae," Ronan said, "I don't think you'd be able to say that."

Áed pressed his lips together and let out a pained breath

through his nose. "Come on, Ronan. Let's just get you back home."

It took Ronan until much later to realize that Áed had called the Bone mound 'home.'

CHAPTER TWENTY-FIVE
ÁED

Something was bothering Éamon.

At first, Áed had thought it was the stress of crossing the veil and almost immediately losing his leg. That was the sort of thing that would take time to adjust to. Then he'd thought maybe it had to do with Áed's heritage finally being out in the open. Finding out that your close friend of seven years was actually not human was bound to create a couple of bumps, even after they'd talked about it.

But now, he was sure it was more than that.

"Éamon," he whispered sleepily. The room was dark; from what he could tell, he hadn't been sleeping for long. He had taken to drifting off on one side of the bed, and Éamon on the other. For the first few mornings, they'd woken together in the middle, Áed tucked against Éamon's chest. But over the past week, Éamon's sleep had grown troubled. He'd been sleeping a good deal more and, from what Áed could tell, a good deal more poorly. "What are you doing?"

Éamon didn't answer. He sat on the edge of the bed, eyes barely open. Áed crawled across the mattress to his side.

Before he got there, Éamon pushed himself to his feet.

Áed gasped as Éamon trusted his weight to his leg and

immediately staggered. His face didn't change as the leg gave out, and he crumpled to the floor. Áed accidentally took all of the blankets with him as he shoved himself off the edge of the bed to kneel by Éamon's side. "Éamon?" he said urgently. He rolled up the hem of Éamon's pants to find the silvery scarring intact; the prosthesis looked the same, and the healing wound itself looked undamaged. Áed looked to Éamon's face to find it tranquil and empty. His friend's eyes were closed.

Gently, he shook Éamon's shoulder. He wasn't sure if it would work, given that standing on his prosthesis—which Áed knew to be painful—and then falling over hadn't woken him, but he was rewarded with a bleary hum.

Slowly, Éamon blinked. His eyes slid from Áed to the bed. "What?" he mumbled.

Áed let out a relieved breath. "You were sleepwalking. Or trying, I guess."

Éamon's eyebrows came together. "Ow." He reached toward his prosthesis. "My leg."

"You put your weight on it," Áed said with chagrin. "I'm sorry, I didn't get there in time to stop you."

"Hurts," Éamon grunted. He sat up enough to rub at the thick scar. "Ow."

Áed helped him up, Éamon balancing on one leg with an arm on Áed's shoulder, and they both dropped wearily back into bed.

Áed frowned as Éamon's fingers traced back and forth over the near-opalescent scarring. "Is sleepwalking normal for you?"

Éamon shook his head. "Not that I know."

"It might be the stress." With a tired sigh, Áed dragged himself back over to his side of the bed. "Are you going to be all right?"

"I'm fine." Éamon swung his legs under the covers and settled back down. "Completely fine."

〰

The next morning came early and chaotically. Áed woke to the sound of footsteps falling hard down the hallway and was just blinking the sleep out of his eyes when the door opened with enough vehemence that it slammed against the wall.

Erin stood square in the doorway, panting as the door slowly creaked inward again. "He's got it," she managed.

Éamon, who had woken with surprising sluggishness given the *bang* of the door's violent opening, sat up confusedly while Áed tried to slow his racing heartbeat. *Why* did people keep barging in? "Who's got it? Got what?"

"The spell," Erin said. "Ronan got the spell."

Áed's eyes widened. "He *what*?"

"Don't make me repeat it," Erin gasped. "I can hardly breathe."

Áed was already sliding out of bed. "He wasn't supposed to work on any magic until he'd recovered!" He pulled on the shirt he'd worn the day before, simultaneously trying to shove his feet into his boots. "Where is he? Is he all right?"

Erin's gaze slipped to the floor, and her hand moved to scratch uncomfortably at the back of her neck. "Well... that's the thing."

〰

"I did not expect this." Iarlaith was rushing in the same direction as Áed, Éamon, and Erin peeled out of the bedroom. Iarlaith was also hurriedly dressed, his ordinarily neat vest unbuttoned over a crumpled tunic. "For him to succeed this quickly..."

"It must be from living with you for so long, Áed," Erin hypothesized breathlessly. "He's used to the energy. Could that be it?"

"I'm afraid answering that is a bit beyond my expertise,"

Iarlaith said. "The important thing is that it's done. What condition is he in?"

"*That's* the important thing," Áed snapped but then bit his tongue in anticipation of Erin's answer.

"He fainted." Erin led the way hurriedly down one of the stone-cut stairways. "That's all I know."

"More bleeding?"

"Not that I saw." She averted her eyes again. "He… may have been practicing the spell a little. After we got back from the woods."

Iarlaith turned to her sharply. "You didn't stop him?"

Erin held up her hands. "I'm not his keeper! Why do you assume he's my responsibility?"

"He's *your* crossling," Iarlaith said cuttingly. "And you should know better, Erin. You're fae. He's not."

"I don't know human magic!"

"You know that magic can *burn*." Iarlaith pushed past her none too gently and hurried on in front. "He's lucky he didn't blow up the mound. Or melt his own intestines." He touched the wall at intervals as he half-jogged down the corridor, leading the group behind him. "Did he tell you what the spell showed him before he fainted?"

Erin shook her head, a hint of guilt finally flashing over her face. "No. He just said that he got it, and then he was out."

They arrived at Ronan and Erin's room, and Iarlaith threw the door open and strode in. Erin went after, followed by Áed, who nearly pushed her over in his haste to get inside. Erin fidgeted by the edge of the room, her eyes hovering over Ronan and not breaking away. "He's still breathing and everything," she said defensively.

Áed dropped to his knees by Ronan's side. The black-haired boy lay sprawled on his back, his unbraided hair spilling out over the floor. His eyes were closed, and when Áed put a hand on his chest, he could feel Ronan's steady heartbeat. He let out a breath of relief.

Éamon, who had fallen behind on his crutches, reached the doorway. "What's happened? Is he all right?"

Iarlaith was feeling Ronan's forehead, lowering a finger beneath his nose to feel for breath, lifting Ronan's wrist to find his pulse with deft fingers. Iarlaith, too, seemed to sag with relief. "He's exhausted himself."

"Is that dangerous?" Áed swallowed. "You said that could be dangerous."

"It can be. It is. But he'll wake up in time." The archivist sat back on his heels. "He fought the magic through the spell." Iarlaith's red eyes stared into the middle distance. "He won."

Áed dropped his face into his hands and dragged his fingers into his hair. Every nerve in his body was buzzing.

Iarlaith found his knee. "Breathe, brother." He gave a reassuring squeeze. "Your ward will be all right."

"So…" Erin said tentatively. "What now?"

Iarlaith pushed himself to his feet, leaving Áed kneeling next to Ronan. "We wait for him to come around. And in the meantime—" He turned to the door with purpose. "We prepare to leave."

⟩⟩

It felt like everything was happening too fast.

As soon as Ronan was safe in bed and Iarlaith had ensured he was truly all right, the archivist faerie hurried Áed and Éamon back down the hall. "Pack your things," he directed. "We don't know where Ronan is going to say the consort is, but if he names someplace far, I want you to be ready. I'll have food and travel supplies sent up to you."

"Unprepared food?" Áed clarified.

"Of course."

"This seems rushed," Áed confessed. "Ronan hasn't even woken up yet. I don't understand why it's so urgent—"

"That," Iarlaith interrupted, not rudely, "is because you don't understand who the consort truly is." He stopped in the hallway, turning to face Áed and Éamon. "Perhaps I should have explained this to you sooner. There's a balance in this world. Fae magic is powerful but limited in its scope: our domain is fire, and to a lesser extent, the mind. Human magic is weak by comparison but can achieve any variety of ends." He clasped his hands behind his back. "For the Queen's dog, this balance is razed."

Éamon glanced to Áed, obvious concern on his face, before looking back to Iarlaith. "What exactly does that mean?"

Iarlaith opened his mouth to answer and then stopped himself. "Let's keep walking. I'll explain as we go." They set off down the stone hallway again, their footsteps echoing off the walls. "The Queen's consort is her right hand. Trusted advisor, court official, bedmate…" He shook his head. "Usually, they serve as a confidante. A settler of court disputes, at most. But not this one." They escaped the confines of the staircase. "*This* consort wields magic with the freedom of a human." They reached Áed and Éamon's room and stopped in front of the door. "Except that he wields it with the power of a faerie."

The weight of that sunk in slowly. "How?" Áed said finally. He couldn't truly grasp what that could mean. He had seen fae power, felt it in himself; it was a tide, a wildfire. It was *immense*. To be able to do *anything* with that power, unlimited by nature…

"It's complex," Iarlaith said. "High-court families vie to

have their members selected as consort when the choice-day comes. It's an honor. So they take steps." He shook his head, looking disgusted. "Families plan bloodlines for generations to raise a child with powerful magic, or extraordinary beauty, or something like that. But *this* consort's family went a step further." His expression of disgust didn't lessen. "Only human magic could have enabled the birth of the Cur. In other words, his family must have taken crosslings and made them create a way to break the limits which all fae are *supposed* to have." He crossed his arms. "It hasn't been achieved since, which is good. But the fact remains that this consort is no docile Queen's *pet*. He's her hunting hound and fighting dog, and he loves the taste of blood. If the Queen hadn't set her fury on all of us when he went missing, not a soul would mourn his loss."

A cold shiver ran down Áed's spine. "And we're going out to find this person."

Iarlaith nodded with chagrin. "Ronan, at least, needs to be in the party to direct it. I presumed that you would wish to accompany him."

"You presumed right." Áed shook his head. "What kind of backup is coming with us, exactly?"

"The twins, at the very least."

"Won't we know better what the right approach is when Ronan wakes up?" Éamon suggested.

"We will," Iarlaith agreed. "But I prepare for the most extreme eventuality." A faint smile flitted across his face. "I might not be built like the Fionns, but it's my head that's made sure the Bone court is a threat in this war. Preparation is what I do."

"I trust you," Áed said. "You won't make me regret it?"

Iarlaith laughed. "I'll try not to." He nodded toward the room. "Now, go. Pack. I'll send word when Ronan wakes."

CHAPTER TWENTY-SIX
ÁED

Éamon fell asleep again as soon as he'd gathered all of his clothing into his knapsack. The weariness seemed to hit him suddenly; one moment, he was hanging his sheepskin cloak on the rack by the door, and the next, he was swaying. He dropped into the bed, eyes already drooping as he mumbled an apology and something about a nap.

Then he was out.

Áed felt Éamon's forehead, a little worried. It wouldn't do at all for Éamon to get sick. He even rolled up the cuff of his friend's trouser leg again to make sure that there was still no sign of infection around the prosthesis, but Éamon's forehead was cool, and his scarred skin wasn't red or swollen.

"You really haven't been sleeping well, have you?" Áed said softly. As unobtrusively as he could, he pulled the blankets out from under Éamon and arranged them over his body. Éamon's face was smooth in sleep but not tranquil; something around his closed eyes looked troubled. Without thinking, Áed ran the tip of his thumb from the bridge of Éamon's nose up his forehead. It was something Ninian had used to do when Áed had trouble sleeping, even though that problem had much more often been the other way around.

He repeated the motion until the tension leached out of Éamon's face.

With a sigh, Áed turned away from the bed.

He clapped his hands over his mouth to stifle a yelp.

For a few pounding heartbeats, he just stared, trying to make sure he was actually seeing what he thought he was.

Her hair fell to her waist in wavy copper curls, parted down the center with a single thin braid hanging on either side of her face. That face was pale and freckled; her eyes were dark with the stains of washed-off war paint, and a single line of black pigment traced over her lower lip, down her chin. She wore the clothing that Áed had come to see as ordinary in the Bone court, but over the cropped tunic and hide trousers, she wore a simple leather breastplate, and slim leather gauntlets covered her hands and forearms.

Áed kept his eyes on hers, even as it felt like her gaze was boring through his pupils to the back of his skull. She leaned on the doorframe with her arms crossed, expressionless. "Neasa," Áed said softly.

Neasa did not acknowledge that he had spoken.

Áed glanced back at Éamon, who had curled into the pillows with a sleepy hum. "If you want to talk, maybe we could take this somewhere else," he suggested.

"No," Neasa said. Her voice was quiet but filled with authority. "This is a fine place."

Wetting his lips nervously, Áed nodded. "Do... do you have something you wanted to talk about?"

For a long moment, Neasa simply looked at him. Her expression told Áed nothing, nor could he feel any of her emotion. Looking back at her this way was powerfully odd. Not in the least because she scarcely looked older than he did—her face, though fierce, was still delicately featured and notably beautiful—but because he could see the resemblance between her face and what he saw when he looked in the mirror. It was something in the eyes, he thought, and the freckles.

He couldn't imagine her as his mother.

Neasa cleared her throat. "I heard that you would be leaving."

Áed nodded.

His words hadn't seemed to ruffle a single one of the Bone leader's feathers, but his silence clearly unsettled her. She shifted in her position against the wall, looking away for the first time.

Áed sat down slowly on the edge of the bed, trying not to disturb Éamon. Neasa didn't move.

"Why did you come?" Áed asked finally. He did his best not to imbue his words with any of the faint bitterness he couldn't seem to talk himself out of.

Neasa bit the tip of her tongue between her teeth with a short exhalation.

Áed found himself crumpling the bed's quilt by his sides in his stiff hands. "Do you even know?"

Neasa didn't answer. Her eyes scrutinized Áed's face as if her gaze could pierce the thoughts that swirled silently behind his expression. "Do you hate me?" she asked.

"Do—" Áed blinked. That hadn't been what he'd expected, if he had expected anything. He stilled himself. "No," he said after a pause. "I don't hate you." Neasa's shoulders relaxed just a fraction, so slight he scarcely noticed it. "I don't blame you for leaving me, either. For some time, I did, but… I don't, now."

Neasa nodded, a wave of hair slipping over one shoulder. Her voice was carefully controlled. "Do you wish I had stayed?"

Áed stared at her for a long moment. "What do you think you'll get out of asking?" he said, hoping it didn't sound unkind. "Are you looking for forgiveness, or do you want me to say I mourned you?" He swallowed. "You made your choice, and I understand it. But..." He disengaged his hands from the bedclothes and folded them in his lap. "Yes," he said softly. "If you couldn't take me with you, of course, I wish you had stayed."

Neasa's crimson gaze took in Áed's mangled hands. She said nothing.

"Even so," Áed went on, and Neasa's eyes flicked up again. "Because of your choice, I've experienced things that I wouldn't give up for the world." The memory of violet eyes and green, only one pair still bright, rose in his mind. "It's too late to change anything now."

"You've done well for yourself," Neasa said. "I did hope for that."

Áed tracked her movement as she stepped into the room to lean on the wall just inside the door. "Why?"

"Hmm." Neasa pondered that, arms still crossed. "It's a complicated thing, what I feel for you." Her hand absently traced the hilt of a knife strapped to her side, its pommel a bird's miniature skull, and her expression was thoughtful. "You never felt like my son. You were always *his*."

"Not anymore," Áed said. "I killed him."

"Oh?" If that information changed anything, Neasa's face didn't show it. "Well. That was deserved, I suppose." She sighed. "The fact remained that you were never *mine*. Some in my position would have claimed you, I think. And maybe they're strong, for doing that." She shook her head.

"You couldn't," Áed finished. "I know. I read your letter."

"Then you know," Neasa said simply. "That I do resent you."

Despite years of accumulated armor against that blow, those words still rattled Áed enough to make him let out a breath.

Neasa's gaze softened somewhat. "But that was never your fault."

"So." Áed shook his head, finding himself grabbing at the

bedding again. "Why *did* you come here?"

Neasa lowered her head, almost resigned. "Because I heard you were leaving." She reached as if to scratch the back of her neck. "And I don't wish to see you dead." In a fluid movement, she grasped something behind her back and drew it over her shoulder. Her hair parted as she lifted something that had been hidden on her back and held it up straight in front of her body with a warrior's practice. Áed saw it as barely more than a rod until Neasa turned it, and he realized she'd been holding it perfectly aligned along the blade. Once the flat of the weapon faced him, he took it in with wide eyes.

It was an axe, wrapped in loose fabric. It had a head the size of an open hand, hooking to a wicked point at the top and bottom of its hammered curve. Like so many things in the Bone court, something about it looked raw. It had a beauty to it, but that beauty was born not of elegance but unyielding, deadly function.

Twirling it expertly, she offered it to Áed handle-first.

It took two hands for him to support without it falling through fingers that refused to properly flex around it. Neasa stepped back, clasping her hands behind her as Áed held up the weapon. The rest of the wrapping was falling away. "The head is iron," she said, eyes running appreciatively up and down the edge. "Salted and rubbed with rowan." Her eyes flashed. "Do you understand what this means?"

Iron. Salt. Rowan. "I... I think so."

"This blade is death," Neasa said frankly. "It is hard to kill a faerie. We are strong." She pressed the pad of her forefinger to the head and then held it up for Áed to see. She hadn't so much as flinched, but where her skin had made contact with the iron, it was blackened. Áed's mouth fell open slightly as a drop of brilliant blood oozed from a raw crack in Neasa's charred flesh. "This is stronger."

Áed lowered the axe, letting its own not-insignificant weight draw it to the floor. It slipped out of his uncertain grasp at the last moment, and in an unusual instant of shyness, he hoped that Neasa hadn't seen. He wasn't sure he could actually wield this weapon, but he didn't want to ruin the moment. It felt like it meant something. "What am I supposed to do with this?"

Neasa's expression changed only to quirk one eyebrow. "If someone tries to kill you," she said simply, "kill them first."

CHAPTER TWENTY-SEVEN
ÉAMON

Éamon had strange dreams.

In them, everything was dark, save for glowing lights embedded in the formless blackness that surrounded him. After a while, he realized that they looked like the crystals from the Moon court's mound. They pulsed in unison as if they all belonged to the same strange, luminescent organism.

Confused, he tried to stand. Pain shocked through his leg. When he looked down, he found that his prosthesis wasn't a prosthesis at all; instead, a large, jagged shard of crystal stabbed through his calf, protruding through the top of his knee. He tried to detach himself, but the moonlight shard had barbs deep in his flesh. Blood poured from his wounds. The crystals, scattered and leading away through the darkness, began pulsing faster. With every bright pulse of the crystal in his leg, pain fired through Éamon's body.

He woke up sweating.

His leg really was throbbing—it was what had woken him. In fact, it hurt so badly that he had to bite down on his fist to keep from crying out.

When he did, he tasted… dirt?

Still biting back a sob—oh, his leg *hurt*, and on top of

that, he was *freezing*—he pushed himself to his elbows and looked around.

"Oh, that's bad," he murmured.

When he had gone to sleep, he'd been surrounded by pillows and blankets.

Now, he was surrounded by dying ferns, leaf litter lying quiet between wide trees, and snowflakes drifting from a slate-gray sky.

Trembling, he reached toward his bad leg. His fingers were numb as he clumsily rolled up the cuff of his pants, acting on a half-manic impulse to make sure the dream hadn't been real.

His leg looked bruised but otherwise completely fine. Other than the obvious fact that there was foreign, pearly material where his lower leg should have been, everything looked the way he thought it should. It just *hurt*. Which... he looked around again, his breath coming faster. If he had somehow walked all the way into the woods, of *course*, it hurt. He'd just barely begun to allow weight on it.

How had this happened? He'd never been a sleepwalker. How had he suddenly sleepwalked into the middle of the woods? And where exactly *was* he? He needed to figure that out, and fast; his teeth were already chattering, and the foot he still had was almost senseless with the cold. He was lucky it was still the beginning of winter, or he'd have frozen before he had a chance to wake up at all.

He couldn't entirely hold back a cry when he struggled to his feet. As he did, something in his pocket *crunched*.

He reached into his pocket, confused. *Papers?* They were crumpled over themselves, and he unfolded them shakily. Right away, he frowned. "Attack plans?" He turned the pages, perplexed. He was certain he'd never seen these papers before in his life, but they seemed to depict battle setups, as well as jotted strategy notes. He hadn't a single clue how they had gotten into his pocket. Had he accidentally nicked them from the atheneum last time he was there to borrow a book? He wasn't sure how he'd have managed that without noticing.

He folded them again and put them back in his pocket. He'd have to return them when he got back.

Keeping his weight on his good leg as much as he could, he limped over to the closest tree. He leaned against the damp bark, shivering with pain and cold. He couldn't have gotten far, could he? For all he knew, the Bone mound was just out of sight past the trees. The problem was, he didn't know which direction that might be. And on top of that, the sun was setting. What if he ended up walking in the opposite direction of where he needed to go? What if he crossed into another court's territory—it wasn't like he had any idea where the borders were—and got killed on sight? What if he was *already* on another court's territory?

Maybe the best thing to do would be to head away from the sun. If he sleepwalked out of the front of the Bone mound, then that faced west. Assuming he'd stumbled in about the same direction, then he'd need to go east to head back.

That made sense.

Gritting his teeth, he set his sights on the closest tree to the east of him. When he reached it, he let his fingers dig into the deeply grooved bark, keeping him standing. Then he set off for the next. And the next.

The sun set. Now, the woods were even colder; the snow hadn't stopped, and where before there had been dampness, now there was soft ice. The cold *was* helping to numb the pain of his leg, but it was also numbing everything else. He was still wearing the loose, cropped top and soft trousers he'd fallen asleep in, and the cold leached through the thin fabric as if it wasn't there at all. A while ago, he had stopped shivering. Distantly, he thought that was a bad thing.

He'd been walking for too long. If he'd chosen the right direction, he should have hit the mound by now. The trees looked the same in every direction, blue in the silvered moonlight, and the snow drifting down was making him dizzy.

He sank to a seat against a tree. The bark was freezing against his spine, and he hugged his knees to his chest in an attempt to preserve warmth.

Someone had to have noticed he was gone. With Ronan having fallen unconscious after completing the spell, and everyone rushing around and preparing to leave as soon as Ronan told them where to go, Éamon could understand why noticing his disappearance might take a while, but surely, Áed would see that he was gone. If anyone was looking for him, he might have already made their job harder by walking in the wrong direction; maybe it was best to stay in one place.

The night was still, but the leaves still rustled. Sometimes, their whispering resolved into imagined voices, and Éamon curled around himself more tightly. It was hard to convince himself that he shouldn't still be trying to get back to the mound, but he couldn't see in the dark, and he had no idea which way to walk even if he could.

The woods were eerie without the light. He heard birdsong through the shadowed, ancient trees. He didn't think he'd ever heard a bird cry with such a dancing, haunting melody. And owl hooted, mournfully keening a call that echoed directionlessly off the accumulating snow. There were other noises that he didn't recognize either: an odd, trilling song that sounded like faraway laughter. A growling bark that could have come from a deer or some fey creature looking to hunt. A shriek from somewhere chilling and deep that sounded very much like a human scream, and which came thrice as he sat, each time sending spines of ice deep into his bones.

The cold was creeping in. The longer he sat still, the deeper it sank. And the deeper it sank, the less he could tell what was real. His ears were playing tricks on him. The forest was calling his name.

After a few minutes, Éamon shifted. *Was* that the forest? He heard his name; he was almost sure. Could he trust his ears to discern whispering leaves from voices?

"Hello?" he called. His voice broke to nothing halfway through the word, and he tried again. If he was on unfriendly territory, he might be dooming himself. But the cold was settled inside him, and the forest was singing anyway, and he didn't know what else to do.

"*Éamon?*"

That was definitely a voice. He was sure of it. He stiffly pushed himself to his feet, feeling like his joints were frozen. He couldn't feel his extremities. "Who's there?"

There were lights through the trees. They bobbed, flickering through the branches and wide trunks, orange like warm candlelight. It was from that direction that someone was calling his name.

"I'm here," Éamon shouted hoarsely.

There came a cry from the direction of the lights, and then they began to come nearer. "Éamon?" the call came again.

"Áed?" Éamon responded. It sounded like his voice, and warmth swelled in Éamon's chest. "Is that you?"

"It's me!" The light was getting closer, enough for Éamon to see that it was a lantern hanging on a pole. Its glow glanced off the snow-glazed ferns as its bearer ran closer, and then Áed broke through the undergrowth. His cheeks were rosy with the chill, and he wore a fur-lined red cape that fell to his waist. He held the lantern pole ahead of him, illuminating the forest around him in a sphere of warmth.

When he saw Éamon, he rushed over. He stuck the lantern pole into the forest floor and then hurried to swing his cape off his shoulders. He pulled it around Éamon, his breath misting in the air between them. He turned to call over his shoulder. "I've found him!"

There were footsteps crunching closer, but Áed turned back to Éamon. Éamon gripped the thick cape with uncooperative fingers.

"You're freezing," Áed said, his eyes searching Éamon's form as if to make sure he was still in one piece. "Hell, your lips are blue." He held up his hands, and in the next moment, Éamon felt heat radiating from them. A shiver wracked his body. "Why did you leave?" Áed asked. His voice sounded a little frantic. "Are you all right? What happened?"

"I don't know," Éamon managed. His teeth were chattering hard. "I woke up in the forest, and I didn't know where I was."

"On your way to the Moon court," another voice came, and Éamon squinted past the lanternlight to see Fionnlagh stepping through the ferns. "If your tracks are any indication."

"Moon court?" Éamon said faintly. He shook his head. "I must have been sleepwalking. I don't even know how to get to the Moon court from here."

"It doesn't matter," Áed interjected firmly, shooting Fionnlagh a look and a quiet, warning growl. He stepped close to press himself against Éamon's side, and Éamon shuddered again at the sheer warmth of his body. "We're going back."

Éamon leaned on Áed as they turned in the direction

Áed had come. Fionnlagh plucked Áed's lantern out of the ground and propped it over his shoulder, carrying his own in front of them.

"I'm sorry we didn't come sooner," Áed said. "I left our room when I heard that Ronan had woken up, and I didn't come back for a few hours. That's when I noticed you were missing."

Éamon was reveling in Áed's warmth, so much that he barely noticed what Áed had actually said. "Wait. Ronan woke up?"

Áed nodded. "He's awake and all right. A bit tired, but fine."

"We're leaving in the morning," Fionnlagh said. "The boy did well. We know where to go."

Éamon blinked. He hadn't actually had any doubts about Ronan's capabilities, but the speed of everything still surprised him. "In the morning?"

"It's quick," Áed sighed. "But the sooner we finish this, the better for everyone."

Éamon couldn't argue with that. "Well. I guess I'd better warm up and get some proper sleep." He shivered. "The kind that doesn't have me hiking into the middle of nowhere on a leg that barely works."

"About that..." Áed said. He glanced to Fionnlagh as if for affirmation, and his half-brother nodded. "You and Erin are staying at the Bone mound." He gestured with his chin to Fionnlagh. "I'm going with Ronan, Fionnlagh and Fionnuala. But I want you and Erin to stay here."

"What?" Éamon demanded, stunned. "Why?"

"It's safer," Áed said. "Erin's decent at playing with emotions—better than most, from what I understand—but she still only has sixteen years. And you're human."

"Then what about Ronan?" Éamon asked. "And what about *you*?" He looked down to Áed, who was staring straight ahead. "Don't take this the wrong way, but you aren't a warrior."

"We need Ronan to navigate," Áed said with chagrin. "And I'm not letting him go alone."

"Wouldn't he be with the Fionns?"

"I'm not letting him go without me," Áed rephrased. His face was hard. "I can't."

Ahead of them, Fionnlagh held up a hand, and Áed, still supporting Éamon, froze. Somewhere in the forest to their right, the sound of crackling twigs and shuffling was moving between the trees. Éamon felt his blood run even colder than it already was. "What is it?" Éamon whispered.

"Nothing you want to hear about while we're still out here," Fionnlagh replied softly. His broad frame was silhouetted against the lanterns. "And nothing I can't handle."

After a few minutes, the shuffling sounds passed, and Fionnlagh began to move forward again. Éamon bit his lip, gripping Áed's shoulder to keep on his feet. "Áed," he said quietly, his voice nearly lost under the winter chorus of the woods. "Let me come with you."

"I can't, Éamon."

"I crossed the veil so that I could help," Éamon said. "This is my fight, too. You're the King, but it's still my city that got damaged in the festival." He could tell his voice was sounding more stubborn. "And you're my—my friend. I know I can't do magic or anything like that, but..." He let out a short breath through his nose. "Please let me stay with you. If it gets messy, I'll wait behind. But I want to be there for you."

"If you got hurt," Áed said tightly, "I'd never forgive myself."

"I've already been hurt," Éamon reminded him. "And it

wasn't yours to forgive then, either. *I* chose to cross the veil, to come with you. I knew it would be dangerous." He suppressed a wince as he was forced to put his entire weight on his prosthesis to step over a log. "I want to choose again now."

Áed stopped, nearly making Éamon trip. Still letting Éamon lean on him, he turned to face him. "Why?"

Éamon blinked. "What do you mean? I just told you."

Áed's expression was inscrutable, but his eyes darted back and forth between Éamon's like he was searching for something. "Why do you *care* so much, Éamon?" He shook his head, and Éamon realized he was genuinely confused. "You lost your *leg* following me. Why in the world would you want to keep doing that?"

Éamon frowned. "Is it bothering you that I'm here?"

Áed shook his head. "No. I just don't understand." Fionnlagh had paused ahead, waiting for them, and the golden lamplight he bore made Áed's eyes deep and unfathomable. "Why do you do this for me?"

Éamon let his eyes drop. With the hand not holding himself up on Áed's shoulder, he drew the red capelet closer about his throat. A little, breathy laugh pressed its way past his lips. The words were out before he could stop them. "I don't know how I can be more obvious."

For a moment, Áed tilted his head, confusion passing over his features. "Obvious?"

"Can't you tell?" Éamon said quietly. He was in too deep, now. "For me, it's always been you."

The words hung in the dimness, and Áed went entirely still. Then, to Éamon's horror, he took half a step backward. "Oh." Even in the dark, Éamon could see the color flood Áed's face. His eyes were stunned. "I—didn't realize—" He looked away, apparently unable to make eye contact.

"Dammit," he whispered. The word was so quiet the wind nearly took it away.

Ice twisted inside Éamon's ribcage. "'Dammit?'" he echoed faintly.

Áed looked up at him, horrified, and covered his mouth. "Éamon, I—"

"I never expected anything from you that way," Éamon said, and his voice sounded just a little bit choked. "I still don't. But I can't help feeling this way, can I?"

"I—" Áed couldn't back away any farther without removing his support and sending Éamon to the ground, but it was clear that distance was his instinct. "I can't—"

If Éamon had ever imagined it as more than a dream, this was not how he had pictured his confession to occur. Not standing in the snowy woods, fey creatures lurking in the darkness and held at bay only by the glow of lanternlight, while Áed struggled to hide his shock.

And his dismay.

Éamon couldn't look at him any longer. Not when Áed was now looking anywhere but Éamon. "I'm sorry," Éamon whispered, and he was. Sorry that he had spoken. Sorry that Áed was unhappy now, and sorry because his chest was tight and painful in a way that made his eyes feel hot.

"Let's…" Áed said quietly, and he swallowed, still staring pointedly at the frozen ground. "Let's just go home."

CHAPTER TWENTY-EIGHT
RONAN

Ronan felt like shit.

He was reminded of the fateful winter, some two years back, when he had come down with a fever and needed to stay in bed for almost two weeks. Right at that moment, he felt much the same. Faintly nauseous. Achy. His head pounding.

But he'd done it.

Completing the spell had felt like wrestling a river through a drain-spout—a very twisty, narrow-mouthed drain-spout riddled with leaks sealed with nothing but soft tar. But he had kept the spell in his head, forcing the drainpipe to stay together, and when the magic had flowed through the shape, he felt it. The information had poured into his awareness at first in scenes, bright as vision: he saw a wood-front building, adorned with sprouts of leaves as if the walls themselves were growing branches. There were shelves of bread, and somehow, Ronan knew that the loaves were fresh. A crooked staircase wobbled upward. There were shadows on the floor, shadows in the shapes of leaves, and they danced in golden light He caught a flash of shoulder-length dark brown hair, a long-fingered hand.

Then came the pull behind his breastbone.

Of course, he had fainted. But since he'd woken, that pull hadn't ebbed. It was as if a line were connected to his sternum, drawing him into the distance, and he knew that all he needed to do was follow it.

All in all, he was pretty proud of himself.

He moved stiffly as he packed his bags and Erin's. He knew that Áed had told her to stay behind, but she didn't take orders from Áed. It seemed a safe assumption that she'd be coming along.

At the sound of a knock on the door, Ronan pushed Erin's half-packed knapsack under the bed. On the bed, Erin mumbled something in her sleep and rolled over. "Yes?" Ronan called softly.

The door opened a crack. Éamon leaned inside.

Immediately, Ronan blinked. "Wow. You look worse than I do."

Éamon stepped inside, noticed Erin snoring on the bed, and closed the door behind him quietly. "Well. Thanks."

"It's true, though," Ronan said, and it was less teasing than genuine concern. Éamon's eyes were shadowed with violet circles, as though he was missing at least a few nights' good sleep. He leaned on a crutch, but even with it, Ronan could tell his limp had somehow become even more pronounced. There were a few scratches on his cheeks as if he'd run through the forest with twigs whipping at his face. But more than all of that was the heavy *despondence* that entered the room with him. Even as he offered Ronan a smile, the sadness didn't leave his eyes.

Éamon waved an exhausted hand. "I'm fine. Don't worry about it." He gestured to the chair in the corner of the room. "Can I sit?" At Ronan's nod, he did, letting out a heavy sigh of relief as he got off his feet. "I wanted to talk to you. And Erin, actually."

Ronan took a seat on the edge of the bed, scrutinizing Éamon's face. *Something* had definitely happened. "What is it?"

Éamon rubbed at his knee. "I assume that Erin will be following the party that's going after the consort."

Guiltily, Ronan shrugged. "How would I know?"

"You can tell me."

With a little sigh, Ronan reached under the bed with his toe and dragged Erin's bag out by the strap. "Yeah. She's probably coming along."

Éamon nodded. "How?"

"What do you mean?"

There came an annoyed, sleepy groan from under the covers. "Why are you so loud?" Erin groaned. "It's the middle of the night. Isn't your lot *supposed* to be sleeping at this hour?"

"Sorry," Ronan whispered apologetically. "Go back to sleep. We'll be quieter."

"No, wait," Éamon cut in. "It'll be good to have you awake."

Erin propped herself up on an elbow to glare at Éamon with irritated, woozy eyes. "Not good for *you*."

"Yeah, well, it really hasn't been my night. What's one more thing?" Éamon leaned forward. "How are you tagging along tomorrow?"

Yawning, the faerie rubbed at her eye with a fist. "You assume I am."

"Don't play coy." Ronan was almost taken aback by the intensity of Éamon's stare. He didn't think he'd ever seen the councilor look so *done*. "You have a stake in this, too. You wouldn't miss this chance."

Erin sighed, plucking at her dreadlocks. "Fine. Yes, I'm going." She scooted up, taking the blankets with her, to lean against the headboard. "The hind from the Moon court is still in the stables here. I was just going to ride it after them. I'd join up once we were far enough away that they couldn't send me back in good conscience."

"I'm coming with you."

Erin scoffed. "That hind won't carry both of us."

Éamon shook his head. "No. But it's in the stables, isn't it?" His eyes flashed. "I'll just steal a horse."

Ronan laughed nervously. "Éamon, is everything all right?" He played with the ends of his hair nervously. "You seem, uh... tense."

"He's upset about *something*," Erin supplied helpfully. "His emotions are all over the place." She raised an eyebrow. "Is that heartbreak I smell?"

Ronan felt his eyebrows lift. "Heartbreak?" He leaned forward so fast that he nearly fell off the bed. "Wait, what happened? Did Áed—did you—"

"That," Éamon said, "isn't your business."

If anything, that just made Ronan more desperate to know. "Did you finally tell him how you feel?"

"Wait, wait," Erin interjected. "Tell Áed how he feels? What do you mean?"

Ronan rolled his eyes. "Erin! And here I thought you could sense emotion!" He gestured to Éamon with an open palm. "Our dear friend has been head over heels for the King since he met him! Even *I* could tell that!"

Erin shook her head. "No, no. I knew *that*." She just looked baffled. "I just mean, why would you need to tell Áed how you feel? Aren't you already—you know." She shrugged. "Together?"

"No," Éamon said tightly. "We're not. And never will be."

"That doesn't make any sense." Erin seemed properly interested now. "Couldn't Áed tell how you feel? He can sense emotions too, can't he?"

"Maybe he's in denial," Ronan suggested.

Erin pointed at Éamon. "To be clear. You and Áed are *not* a couple."

"No."

"And he didn't actually know how you feel."

"No!"

She threw up her hands. "That doesn't make any sense!"

"And why *not*?" Éamon snapped. "I don't see what's confusing about it. We were friends, I wanted more, he doesn't. Simple as that. Now, can we *drop it*?"

"No, no!" Tucking the blanket up to her knees, Erin waved a hand. "No, it's not as simple as that!"

"What do you mean?" Ronan asked. He was following the exchange with fascination.

Erin looked exasperated. "Éamon, he feels the same way for you!"

Éamon leaned back in his chair, looking like Erin had just thrown something at him. "What?"

"It's why I assumed you were together!" Erin sank back into the pillows. "Goddess, what a mess."

"Éamon," Ronan said carefully, "what *exactly* did Áed say to you when you confessed to him?"

Éamon swallowed. "Well, he said… he said 'dammit,' and then 'I can't.' And then said we should go home. He hasn't spoken to me since."

Ronan cringed. "That's rough."

"Thanks, I couldn't tell." He turned to Erin. "You must be wrong about him feeling the same way."

She shook her head. "I'm not, though."

"Then he just must not know he feels that way," Ronan reasoned. "Or maybe…" He winced as a thought occurred to him. "Gods. It's been seven years, but…"

"Ninian," Éamon said heavily.

Ronan nodded, while Erin looked confused. "Ninian? Who's that?"

"Áed's old partner," Ronan explained. Thinking of him still sent a dull pang of grief through his chest, but years had dulled the sharp edge to a quieter thing. Mostly, it brought back memories. "He died seven years ago."

"Is seven years a long time or not?"

Ronan snorted a little. Since Erin's youth was as real as his own, it was easy to forget that the future stretched out for her limitlessly. That had to blur her sense of scale a bit. "Well, it's… kind of both, I guess." He sighed. "It's a long time because so much has happened since then. It's time to move on. But the thing is, if Ninian were alive, I'm absolutely certain they'd still be together." He shrugged sadly. "It's hard, I think, knowing that. They were each other's… soulmate sounds sappy, I guess. But I don't know that it's far from the truth."

"I can't compete with that," Éamon said. "Not even with the *memory* of that. And I don't even know if I should. It feels cruel." He pressed his palms to his forehead, and Ronan truly took in how exhausted he looked. "I just don't want to lose him. Not as a friend, at the very least." He shook his head. "And I'm unloading to a pair of fifteen-year-olds. Gods." He moved to stand, but Ronan held out a hand.

"I've sixteen," Erin muttered as Ronan jumped to his feet.

"Éamon, wait." Ronan took a step closer. "Áed might still be holding on to Ninian, but he definitely has feelings for you. I'm sure of it."

"That isn't why I'm here," Éamon said, voice clipped. "The point is that I'm not staying behind." A hint of anger seeped into his voice. "After everything I've been through on this trip, I think I have a right to be a part of this. Áed doesn't get to decide that for me." He fixed his gaze on Erin. "So when you go to the stables to take the hind, I'll be going with you."

Erin looked faintly impressed. "Well, it isn't like I'll stop you."

⧘

The morning dawned cold and fresh. Even inside the mound, which was usually warm enough to justify the loose clothing of its inhabitants, Ronan felt like his breath was about to puff into mist as he shook Erin awake. He'd been up for a good part of the night, buzzing with anticipation. When the sun rose, he'd already spent several hours wound up enough to leave.

Erin mumbled something blearily and turned to him, blinking. Ronan couldn't tell if she was actually alert, but he spoke to her anyway. "I'm leaving now. If you're following, you should get ready."

The faerie stared at him for a moment and then nodded and rolled back over.

Well.

She would figure it out.

Ronan hurriedly pulled on his clothes and cloak, grabbed his knapsack, and slipped out of the room.

He met Iarlaith coming down the hall. "Good morning!" he greeted, hiking his bag higher. "Were you coming to get me?"

Iarlaith looked surprised. "Ronan. You're up early." He seemed to appraise Ronan without his eyes. "You're feeling well enough?"

"Definitely." If anything, the constant tug of the spell, showing him the way, was putting him on edge. He was more than ready to go.

"Good." Iarlaith sounded pleased. "I had encouraged the party to let you rest a while longer, but it seems that won't be necessary. They're waiting outside of the mound."

Ronan started. "Already?" There were no windows in the hall, but he had just stepped out of his own scarcely sunlit room. "It's barely dawn!"

"Everyone is eager to see this war done. There's no use in delaying."

Iarlaith walked with Ronan down the stairs, through the winding, anthill-like hallways that burrowed through the stone. "I won't be accompanying you," Iarlaith said as they walked. "I'm needed here." They approached the great doors of the mound, which rested slightly ajar and allowed the entrance of frigid air and the sounds of shouting. Iarlaith put a hand on Ronan's shoulder. "I had never truly spent time with a human before you. I confess that I was surprised by what a pleasure it turned out to be." He held out a hand, and Ronan shook it automatically. "It was good to get to know you."

"And you," Ronan said. He searched Iarlaith's face. "That sounds a little final for a goodbye, don't you think?"

A flicker of shadow passed over the archivist's features. "You never know which goodbye will be the last," he said, and something in his tone informed Ronan that he was speaking from experience. The hand on Ronan's shoulder squeezed, and Ronan was surprised by how much the gesture felt familial. "I hope we meet again."

"Me too." Ronan swallowed. "It was good to get to know you, too, Iarlaith."

Iarlaith chuckled faintly. "It'll take you another century to get to know me, young one." His smile was bittersweet. "I've already said my goodbyes to my siblings. Including Áed. So this is where we part." He dropped his hand from Ronan's shoulder. "Be safe."

"I will."

Iarlaith sighed. "The easy promises of humans." He folded his hands. "I hope you mean it."

"I do." Ronan drew back one of the great wooden doors and stepped outside. "Goodbye, Iarlaith."

}}}

The field before the mound was busy, even in the early morning. Already, warriors were training at the forest's edge, swinging their swords in unison through an elaborate pattern of positions as a tall, blond faerie shouted orders. A unit of lookouts, usually housed in the camouflaged outposts in the trees, was chatting with the guards at the door while at the far end of the field, a detachment of warriors followed a leader out of the snowy woods. The last group looked worse for wear—Ronan spotted a number of stretchers and plenty of limps. A couple of fae supported each other as they hobbled into the field, and Ronan thought perhaps, though the distance was great, he saw blood.

"Ronan!"

Ronan tore his eyes away from the sight to see Áed jogging toward him. He was dressed warmly in a fur-lined hide cloak, and his breath was white in the air.

Áed looked tired, but Ronan recognized the determination on his face. On his back was slung a wicked-looking axe that Ronan hadn't seen before. "Are you ready to go?"

Behind him, Fionnuala stomped through the snow. Her hair was pulled back into a bountiful, curly knot on the nape of her neck. She smiled when she saw him. "Good, you're here," she said. "Come on. We've been waiting for you."

Ronan followed both of them along the scarp face. Sheltering together in a shallow hollow in the rock, Fionnlagh held the reins of two horses. Behind him, the reins of two more mounts were tied to a temporary stake in the ground, and the horses nosed at the thin snow in search of grass. Ronan frowned. "I thought there'd be… more."

Fionnlagh shook his head. "The vision you described is clearly in the high court."

That wasn't something, apparently, that anyone had seen fit to let Ronan know. "Doesn't that mean we should have more people?"

It was Fionnuala who answered. "It means we can't invade like an army. Stealth is on our side."

Fionnlagh handed his sister the reins of one of the horses, and Áed led Ronan to the horses behind. He kicked the stake until it came loose and untangled the reins. He handed the reins of a beautiful, dappled-gray mare to Ronan. "I hope you didn't run off for too many of your riding lessons."

Ronan laughed awkwardly. "'Course not." He looked up at the horse nervously. "I *had* hoped there'd be a cart."

"Not maneuverable enough," Fionnlagh said. "Goddess, please tell me you can ride."

"Of course, I can ride." To prove it, he stepped into the stirrup and swung himself into the saddle. "No problem at all." The mare snorted, stepping to the side and shaking her neck. Ronan patted her neck, trying to get her to stop moving so much. "Um… good girl."

Áed mounted his own horse, and the Fionns exchanged a glance before doing the same. "Fionnuala will take the lead," Fionnlagh said as his twin nudged her horse's sides with her heels. "I'll be in the back. Ronan and Áed, stay between us."

They set across the field toward the forest, heading in the direction of the wounded detachment of soldiers. Ronan couldn't help but stare as they got closer. He had thought he'd seen brutal injury, what with Áed's gruesome tattoos and Éamon's smashed leg. But the sheer extent and variety of the damage he saw... his stomach turned at the sight of a faerie on a stretcher. Their hair had burned away, along with the better part of their face and right side. If they hadn't been moaning quietly, Ronan wouldn't have believed them to be alive beneath the cracked, bloody soot of their remaining skin. Another was missing a chunk out of her side. One, supported on the shoulder of a fellow soldier, had no fewer than three arrows lodged deep in his back.

The warriors looked up at their passing. A halfhearted cheer went through their numbers, and Ronan heard both of the Fionns' names. Fionnuala bent to offer supportive handshakes to the fighters who could still reach up to clasp her hands, and Fionnlagh exchanged a few words with each of the soldiers they passed. Suddenly, Ronan felt rather out of his depth. The feeling was late-coming, perhaps, but seeing the battle-wounded receiving encouragement from their generals stirred something in Ronan's chest.

He couldn't tell whether he was relieved or chagrined when they finally led their horses into the woods.

The trail was narrow, but the horses maneuvered it with ease. Ronan did his best to relax into the rhythm of his mare's gait; they were moving in the right direction, according to the tugging in his chest. Until they reached their quarry, there was nothing to do but ride.

CHAPTER TWENTY-NINE
ÉAMON

Erin was already in the stables by the time Éamon limped down. After the previous night's sleepwalking hike and the walk up the stairs to the atheneum to return those papers, his leg felt positively hellish. It was incredible that he could put any weight on it at all.

At his approach, Erin put down the brush she'd been using to groom the hind's soft pelt. "You made it."

Éamon nodded, leaning on the door to one of the stalls and lifting his prosthesis off the ground with a wince. "Thanks for waiting."

"If you'd taken much longer, I'd have left."

Éamon sighed. "Well, I'm here now." He eyed the horses waiting in the stalls. "Any ideas which one would be best for me to take?"

Erin stroked the hind's head, reaching up to scratch behind its ears and antlers. The strange animal was already saddled, and Erin's bags were fastened to the back. "How much riding experience do you have?"

"Plenty." He wasn't sure how different it would be with his leg, but he was nobility. He'd been riding horses since boyhood.

"Then just choose one that you think can keep up with

the hind. I trust you can handle it."

Éamon bit his lip in thought and crossed to the stall of a sleek-looking black stallion. The horse tossed his head and huffed at Éamon, stamping a hoof. "You look like you want to kill me," Éamon said affectionately. He leaned back to look at the name painted on the door of the stall. "Echdían?" He looked back up at the horse. "Is that your name?"

The horse snorted.

"Well, Echdían," Éamon said, and without taking his eyes off the horse, he slid back the bolt to the stall door. "You look pretty quick."

As if to say *yes, in fact, I am*, Echdían shook his inky mane and butted his nose against Éamon's chest. Éamon stumbled backward, catching himself on the open door of the stall.

"It's nice meeting you, too." He cast about for the proper equipment and located a row of saddles hanging on the opposite wall. Ordinarily, when he rode, the grooms had already tacked up the horse for him, but he knew how to do it. He grunted as he lifted a saddle down from its place and began readying Echdían to ride.

"So, Éamon," Erin said. Even without looking, Éamon could tell she was watching him intently. "About last night…"

Éamon clenched his teeth, redoubling his attention to the buckle in front of him. "What about it?"

"I'm not talking about Áed," Erin said. "I'm talking about how you ended up in the woods."

"Hm." Éamon stroked Echdían's nose before he began fastening the bridle. "I just woke up there."

"So you sleepwalked?"

"Apparently."

Erin stared at him shamelessly. "Is that normal for you?"

Éamon closed his eyes and took a deep breath. "Look.

Erin. I appreciate your concern, but I would actually rather pretend that last night didn't happen, so if you don't mind—"

"I'm not con—" Erin started, but her voice cut out, and she turned away, grumbling. "Never mind."

Éamon sighed under his breath. "You aren't so bad." He finished with Echdían's tack and turned to face her. "I suppose I might owe you an apology for being standoffish at first."

"You don't owe me anything," Erin grouched. "I still think you're annoying."

Éamon rolled his eyes. He stepped into the stirrup with his good leg and pushed himself into Echdían's saddle. "You ready?"

A hint of a grin flickered over Erin's face. "Are *you*?"

⟩⟩⟩

For the first time since crossing the veil, Éamon felt *good*.

Echdían ran through the winter trees with nimble ease, leaping over fallen logs and weaving after Erin's hind without so much as slipping a hoof in the wet snow. On the horse's back, Éamon rode low, feeling fine twigs whip at his face and the falling snow buffet him with icy dampness. The wind cut sharply; around his wrists, where his gloves left a centimeter before his heavy sleeves, his skin was freezing.

He was *alive*.

Ahead of him, Erin was laughing. The sound carried back to Éamon on the wind, and he couldn't help his smile. Finally, it felt like he was *doing* something.

They rode until Erin's hind began to flag. The sun was high in the sky when they stopped on the banks of a stream, and Éamon carefully dismounted. The horse was lathered, breathing hard, but if Éamon wasn't mistaken, the stallion had a spark of excitement in his eye that mirrored the one in Éamon's. Holding the trunk of a tree for support, Éamon used his good foot to punch a hole through the thin layer of ice that shielded the surface of the stream. Echdían drank greedily.

Erin walked in a circle around the hind, who was nosing around the hole in the ice as well. "This is fine," she said, stretching. "The animals need to rest, and we're moving faster than Ronan, Áed, and the Fionns. We shouldn't catch up just yet."

"When should we?"

"Closer to the high court," Erin answered. There was something delightfully wicked in her expression. "The closer we get, the more patrols there'll be. I don't think they'll try to send us back when it's so dangerous to travel without trained protection." She patted the hind's side. "But that means that when we near the border, we're going to have to follow the group more closely. The Fionns know the patrols better than I do. We're going to want to follow their lead."

"We'll be careful," Éamon said firmly, and Erin looked at him approvingly.

"We'll certainly try."

When they set off again after letting the hind—which Erin refused to name—and Echdían rest for a while, their pace was slower. They rode side by side while the trees dropped snow off their windblown boughs.

"What's it like?" Erin asked after a while, and Éamon looked away from the frosted ferns to find her watching him.

"What's what like?"

"Being you." Her gaze skated back to the woods before them. "Being human."

Éamon let out a short, amused breath. "I don't have any idea how to answer that. Could you tell me what it's like *not* to be?"

"To be fae is to be… forever," Erin said after a moment. "When we die, it's a tragedy. We aren't supposed to do that."

"It's tragic when humans die, too."

Erin shook her head. "That's different. You're already dying. You were *born* dying."

Éamon hummed thoughtfully. "It isn't so different, I don't think." He glanced at her. "You might die someday. You might get killed. The only difference is that for you, the question is *if*, while for me, it's *when*." He shrugged. "It's the uncertainty that matters."

Erin's lips were pursed. "What is it like to fall in love?"

Éamon raised his eyebrows. "Do fae not do that?"

"We do," Erin said grumpily. "But… I haven't yet. I don't *think*."

"You do only have sixteen years." Éamon shrugged. "I hadn't fallen in love by sixteen, either."

"How did you know when you did?" She frowned intently. "Was it… nice to look at him? Or—or maybe you wanted to slap him but also play with his hair?"

Éamon shot her another look, raising an eyebrow in amusement. "Is there a *reason* you're asking me this?"

"Because you're here," Erin muttered. "And you'll die someday, so it won't matter that I asked you embarrassing questions."

Éamon laughed. He reached up a hand to brush aside a pine bough that would have otherwise hit him in the face. "I might not be the best person to ask. It's been so long since I *wasn't* in love that I barely remember what it was like." He let out a little breath. "It was bleaker, I think."

Erin looked curious. "You're still in love with Áed, even though you don't think he loves you back?"

Éamon sighed. "Yeah."

"Doesn't that hurt?"

"It does," Éamon said. If he were honest, he felt rather

raw. And he wasn't sure it was the sort of feeling he could get used to. "But more than anything, I want Áed to be happy. And if reciprocating my feelings won't make him happy, then I don't want him to do it."

"And you love him even though he isn't human?"

Éamon bit his lip, taking a deep breath. "Yeah," he said finally. "Yeah, I do." He shook his head. "I was hurt that he hadn't told me, but I understand why he didn't. It's just that…"

"You hate the fae."

"I don't think I do, actually." Éamon had been doing a lot of thinking on this since that fateful night of Áed crying in the dark. "But they—you—do scare me." He shrugged. "Children go missing every festival night, and they don't come back. People go mad. Buildings burn. Your kind treats mine like either playthings or pets. And don't think I don't understand what *crossling* really means."

Erin cringed.

"So, yes," Éamon went on. "When I realized that half of the man I love is *that*—literally the monster in the dark that parents tell their children about…" He shook his head, swallowing the end of that sentence. "But he's never acted like that. I can tell he has instincts that aren't like mine, but he's *Áed*. He hasn't changed. He's still the person I fell in love with."

"I see," Erin said quietly. "Fascinating."

"I do have a question for you," Éamon said after a few moments. "You just made me think of it." He kept his eyes deliberately on the snowy woods. "Do you have any idea how long a half-faerie might live?"

He heard Erin suck in a breath through her teeth. "I don't know, exactly," she said. "But, Éamon?" He looked at her askance to find the faerie looking solemn. "That might be something it's better for you not to think about."

CHAPTER THIRTY
RONAN

The day was waning, and Ronan wasn't sure he'd ever walk again. He wasn't too confident in his ability to even remove himself from his horse. He'd never felt so stiff in his life.

Around the little party, the forest was beginning to change. Ronan couldn't tell how much of that change was geographical and how much temporal; as the sun dipped lower, everything looked different. The woods were changing their song from trilling birdcalls and the rustling of small animals in the undergrowth, adopting a deeper, *older* voice. Ronan shivered at an echoing cry from somewhere deep in the trees, a screeching bark that sounded just dissimilar enough from a human scream to be unnerving. "It's a fox," Fionnlagh said quietly from behind him, and Ronan swallowed. The faerie must have sensed his unease.

"Right," Ronan said, tugging his cloak tighter around him. His horse shifted under him. "Of course."

"Are we going to keep moving through the night?" Áed asked. The still air made his voice sound cold, and Ronan shivered again. He kept imagining the sound of branches breaking some distance behind them, snapping with a noise like splitting ice. Especially as darkness filled the interstitial spaces of the trees, he couldn't stop his ears playing tricks on him.

"We'll stop soon," Fionnuala answered. Like her brother, she kept her voice low. "Right now, we're threading between high court patrols. We have to keep moving."

"Patrols?" Ronan said softly. "Are we in the high court, then?"

"Still in Garnet," Fionnuala said. "But we're far enough on the outskirts that it's hard to enforce borders. The Queen's armies have been encroaching."

The fox screamed again, and Ronan shuddered. "Is someone *murdering* that fox?"

"It's just a warning call," Fionnlagh said. "Even carnivores have to be wary. There are much bigger animals than foxes in these woods."

"That doesn't feel great to know," Ronan murmured.

"The patrols are more dangerous than the wildlife," Fionnuala put in. "But we're avoiding both. Just stay close."

❱❱

Ronan couldn't shake the feeling that they were being followed, but he was certain it was paranoia. He tried not to focus on the sounds of the woods—noises he couldn't identify became terrifying, the heavy breathing and footfalls of creatures whose teeth would snap his bones—and instead concentrated on trying not to shiver.

They had made camp in the shelter of a stone outcropping, where rock protruded from the ground like a giant's finger reaching out of the earth. Ronan couldn't tell if, once, the giant stone had been a monument. Now, it was damp and weatherworn, listing as if the centuries were intent on toppling it. They tied the horses nearby before laying their bedrolls in the raw shelter of the rock. "It's too risky to build a fire," Fionnuala said, "but if you'd rather eat something hot, Ronan, I'm sure one of us could warm up your food for you. That shouldn't count as preparing it, so you won't get stuck here."

That sounded like a good idea, so Ronan dug his travel rations out of his pack and handed them to Áed. Everything was raw—he had some fruit and some flax bran that he'd soaked in water to make a runny meal—but he decided that he'd rather eat baked apples and hot cereal than frozen fruit and cold porridge. Áed handed the rations back steaming, and Ronan ate while leaning back against the rock. He did his best not to be jealous of the Fionns sharing a raisin bannock and some thick stew out of a canteen, and Áed eating his own meal of bread, cheese, and sausage. It wasn't like Ronan regretted coming along, but he was looking forward to returning to the human side of the veil if only because he'd be able to eat proper food again.

"You should sleep," Fionnlagh said, wrapping the remains of his bannock in a cloth. "We're going to move again at first light."

Ronan groaned. "My legs can't take much more of this riding."

Fionnuala chuckled. "Please bear it. If we succeed in this, you'll have played a part in saving hundreds of lives."

"I do like the sound of that." Ronan slouched down into the marginally warmer enclosure of his bedroll and blankets. "What do you suppose will happen to the consort once we turn him in?"

Fionnlagh shrugged. "He'll go back to the Queen. Things will return to normal, I expect."

"Huh." Ronan yawned. From what he'd heard of the Queen's dog, 'normal' still might not be ideal for the lower courts, but... "I guess that's all we can ask."

〰

It was harder to get to sleep than Ronan would have anticipated. Physically, he was exhausted; he wasn't sure he'd be less tired if he'd foregone riding altogether and just walked to the high court. Mentally, though, he couldn't slow down.

Maybe it was the unfamiliar woods, ever shifting and hazy in the nighttime mist and falling snow. Maybe it was anticipation of the coming encounter with a consort who had earned the moniker 'The Cur.' Ronan's vision hadn't shown him much, so his brain was filling in the gaps: he'd never seen any fae that looked old, so he imagined that the consort was probably youthful, and beautiful in the way that wildfire and disaster are beautiful. The sort of beauty that's hard to look at.

He wasn't that cold, but he shivered.

Maybe the forest was just playing with his head. The sound of the horses shifting now and then, snapping twigs, made him jolt. The hoot of an owl, or an owl-like creature, sent chills running under his skin. He was on edge even in the relative shelter of the tipping stone.

And he kept thinking that he heard footsteps.

The harder he listened, the more he convinced himself. There were soft cracks as damp, frozen wood broke, as if underfoot. The leaflitter crunched. Even the wind itself sounded like soft voices.

Ronan froze.

Wind?

The night was still. The snow drifted straight down. There was no wind.

Suddenly, Fionnuala's hand went to her weapon. Ronan's breath seized in his throat as the Bone warrior slowly, silently got to her feet. She nudged her sleeping brother with her toe, and wordlessly, he also rose. She gestured something to him, bringing the faintest amount of heat to her hands so that they glowed enough for Fionnlagh to see the gesture clearly. He nodded, and without so much as rustling a fern, they set off in opposite directions around the stone.

Ronan could barely breathe. He wished his heart would beat more quietly so that he could *hear*—

A yelp split the darkness. "Goddess! Stand down!"

Ronan sat bolt upright. He knew that voice.

There was some quiet cursing and louder footsteps coming back to the stone. An animal nearby made a soft, trilling sound. Ronan thought it sounded like a hind.

He cast off the blankets. Áed was waking up as well, and he looked at Ronan in disoriented alarm. "What's going on?"

In response, Fionnuala marched back around the stone to the camp. Her brother followed her, holding a slight, annoyed-looking figure by the arm. Behind him, Éamon looked somehow both smug and chastened. Fionnuala stopped in front of Ronan and crossed her arms. "Really?"

Ronan blinked. "Why are you looking at me?"

The warrior just glared. "Don't give me that. You knew they were coming, didn't you?"

Still in Fionnlagh's grasp, Erin squirmed. "Let me go," she complained. "You're hurting me."

"*Hurting* you?" Fionnlagh hissed. "Are you *mad*?" He released her with a little push that sent her stumbling to right herself against the stone. In the same motion, he bent down and began rolling up his bedroll. "We need to move."

"What?" Ronan blinked at the warrior. "Why?"

"This area is swarming with patrols," Fionnuala said. Her voice was kinder than her brother's but clipped nonetheless.

"If we were followed, the odds are good that our location is compromised."

"But we were careful!" Erin protested. "We did everything you did—"

Fionnlagh turned on her, eyes blazing. "I'll say this once and not again. Fionnuala and I threaded between those patrols with about two minutes to spare. You were more than two minutes behind us because if you were any closer, we'd have known. Which means you missed the safe window, which means you were probably seen. Which *means*—" he threw his packed bedroll over his shoulder— "that we need to leave. Now."

Having finished with his own bedroll, he moved on to his sister's while she began tacking up the horses with expert speed. Ronan was reeling. *Two minutes.* The twins had kept so calm, he had had no idea they were so close to danger.

"Ronan," Áed said firmly. "You heard him. Pack up."

Shaking his head firmly, Ronan dropped to his bedroll and began folding it to fit on his saddle again.

"I'm sorry," he heard Éamon say. "We never meant to endanger—"

"It's not your fault," Fionnuala cut him off with a sigh. "You're not even from this side of the veil." She moved on to fasten the saddle onto Ronan's horse. "Erin, however, should have known better."

The horses seemed grouchy about having to move out again so quickly, or perhaps Ronan was projecting. Whatever the case, they did at least seem used to the workload; once saddled again, they moved without complaint as if aware of the urgency of the situation. Ronan found himself sticking close to Erin, who kept glancing over her shoulder at him as Fionnuala led the now-longer train of horses and riders through the trees.

"Won't we leave a trail?" Ronan whispered. Whispering felt like the thing to do.

In the lead, Fionnuala's silhouette nodded. She was maneuvering her horse as quickly as Ronan imagined she could, but the ground was gnarled with roots, and the horse could only risk so much without twisting an ankle. "We will. Fionnlagh's going to do his best to melt the tracks out of the snow behind us, but don't count on it working."

Ronan fell silent, his heart in his throat. Just in front of him, Erin was worrying at her lip. "We're… we're going to be okay, right?"

Fionnuala sighed. "I'm sorry, Erin. I don't make promises like that."

Erin's shoulder hunched just slightly. "That makes sense." Ronan watched her with a degree of worry—worry that had little to do with the pressing, potentially fatal darkness of the woods around them. He had seen her look scared, which she clearly was now, but he didn't think he'd ever seen her look *guilty*. "I didn't mean to put you in danger," she said quietly. She fidgeted indiscriminately with her hair and her necklace. "I'm sorry."

Ronan's eyes widened. He had never heard Erin *apologize*.

Fionnuala looked back at Erin, her thick curls shifting with the movement. "I know you didn't." She lifted an ice-shrouded branch with her hand. "I have more important things to do than be angry, Erin. I'm concentrating."

Seeming to take the gentle chastisement, Erin fell silent. She was tense and slumped in the saddle.

Ronan nudged his horse with his heels, catching up to her. She looked over at his approach, and he offered a nervous smile. "I know you didn't mean any harm," he whispered. "It's okay."

Erin's gaze slid away. "It won't be okay if I get us all killed."

"That won't happen." He cast around for something

comforting to say. "I'm glad you brought Éamon here," he offered. He glanced around to make sure that his voice wouldn't carry. "Áed was pining."

The faintest hint of amusement passed over Erin's face. "Was he really?"

"Maybe not *pining*," Ronan admitted. He cast another look over his shoulder. Áed and Éamon were a few yards behind them, backed by Fionnlagh, and Fionnuala forged a path ahead. Ronan kept his voice low. "But Áed worries a lot. About losing people, I think. He wants everyone he loves to be safe, but when that means they aren't close to him, he gets nervous."

Erin looked at Ronan strangely. "That's very insightful for a human."

Ronan scoffed. "I don't have to be able to read emotions to have figured that out. Trust me, I've lived with him my whole life."

"So he's overprotective?"

"He can't help it," Ronan said with a sigh. It seemed he'd been at least marginally successful in distracting Erin, and it was helping to distract him, too. Even if the falling snow kept registering as motion in the corners of his vision, making him turn his head with a bolt of nerves. "His last partner, Ninian... he died right in front of us. In Áed's arms."

Erin sucked in a little gasp. "Oh, Goddess." One hand covered her mouth. "I didn't know that. You just said he died."

"Well, he did." Ronan played with the leather of the reins in his hands. "So Áed lost Ninian. And then I got separated from him while he was in prison, and I was fine, but he had no way of knowing that..." He shuddered. He could remember that horrible scene almost more clearly than Ninian's death: the sight of Áed, faint after his escape from the dungeons, bloodstained and crying at the sight of Ronan's face. "So. Overprotective."

It didn't seem like Erin knew how to respond. Which Ronan supposed was fair. They were, after all, discussing Áed's complicated emotional state in an attempt to ignore the fact that they all might die. He wasn't sure how he'd have reacted if it had been Erin who started analyzing her family.

"My mothers are a little like that," Erin said. "My mum lost her sister. And ma's father is the Sand court's best fighter, so he's gone all the time."

Ronan had been right. He didn't have any idea what to say. "I see."

"This is a terrible thing to talk about." Erin laughed quietly. "When we might be attacked any minute."

"I don't think there are *good* things to talk about."

Just then, from the trees floated an eerie, hollow call, like the sound of breath whistling through folded hands. As if in reaction, Fionnuala swore quietly. The hair bristled on the back of Ronan's neck.

"What was that?" He strained his eyes uselessly at the snowy darkness around them. "Was that one of the creatures you were talking about?"

"Worse," the warrior said seriously. Her hand migrated to the sword at her side. "That was Fionnlagh." Ronan frowned, but before he could ask how Fionnlagh could be worse than a monster, Fionnuala drew her long blade deliberately from its sheath. "The patrol is here."

CHAPTER THIRTY-ONE
RONAN

With a grace as natural as breathing, Fionnuala wheeled her horse around in the narrow space between the trees. Ronan hurriedly tugged on his own reins, hurrying to get out of the way as she maneuvered back toward her brother. "Where are you going?"

Fionnuala didn't answer. Instead, she addressed all of them, and Ronan was struck by her presence: he had always *known* she was powerful, but he realized he'd mostly seen her as little more than the friendlier twin. Now, though... well.

"Follow Ronan," she said. Her voice was dangerous but not harsh. "He knows the way to go. You'll reach a lake. Stop there and wait for us. Understand?"

Áed steered his horse closer. "You're going to hold them back? Alone?"

Fionnuala made a little sound in the back of her throat, and Ronan looked to Áed for a reaction. Áed looked slightly mollified, so Ronan assumed the noise had been reassuring. "Not alone," Fionnuala said. "Fionnlagh and I can handle this." She swept her gaze over them and then to the encircling woods. "Now, go."

And with that, she was riding past back into the darkness.

It took Ronan a couple of seconds to collect himself, but then he was digging his heels into his horse's sides, moving past Erin to the lead. "Come on!"

Behind him, he heard Erin, Áed, and Éamon following; a few moments later, further back in the woods, he heard a shout from an unfamiliar voice. A pulse of ice-white fire briefly illuminated the woods more starkly than daylight, followed by a whooping battle cry that sounded like Fionnuala. With dazzled eyes, Ronan rode as quickly as he could without risking his horse's safety on the uneven forest floor. Overhead, the moon flickered through the barren branches, adding to the strobe of light that crescendoed at their backs.

The tug behind Ronan's breastbone was as clear as ever. He let it lead him, drawing him forward even as he fled from the battle behind. The clang of metal on metal echoed through the trees, accompanied by the smell of damp wood burning.

He had no idea how far away the lake might be, only that it was apparently in their way. So he ignored his riding-sore legs, and sped his horse through the woods.

⅏

Both steeds and riders were sweat-soaked and windburnt when Ronan suddenly tugged hard at his horse's reins. The horse reared up, making Ronan hold on for dear life as the animal skidded to a stop.

Erin's hind stopped more gracefully, and Ronan heard Áed and Éamon rush to bring their mounts to a standstill. The horses' breath misted hot in the air; they were steaming too. "What is it?" Áed demanded from somewhere shrouded in the brush behind.

Ronan's horse snorted, sidestepping and swishing her tail

as if irritated that Ronan had nearly driven her directly onto the ice.

"The lake," Erin said softly. "We're at the lake."

Ahead of them, the vast, clear expanse stretched until it met the blurry forms of trees on the distant bank. Near the shore, the surface was frozen, trapping white bubbles beneath the ice; farther out, black ripples glinted and shifted under the starlight, hazy with mist. "I almost rode right into it," Ronan said. His voice was raw from breathing hard, and the damp air scraped at his lungs. "We'd have gone right through the ice."

The sound of footsteps hit the ground behind him, and then Áed pushed through the scraggly brush with his horse's reins in hand. He looked out over the expanse of the lake, eyes faintly luminescent. "It feels wrong to just wait here."

"It feels wrong to keep going." Ronan swung out of his own saddle, wincing at his stiff body. "Fionnuala said to stay put."

Áed hesitated for a moment, still staring over the lake. His expression was faintly unsettled. "Yeah," he acquiesced finally. "All right."

There was little bank to speak of. The frozen waters of the lake crept right up to the forest, so close that Ronan could see tree roots wending their way beneath the ice. He sank to an exhausted seat against a tree while Áed, avoiding the councilor's eye, wordlessly helped Éamon from his saddle. With quiet thanks, Éamon hobbled to a tree and leaned against it with a soft curse.

"You know," he said after a few moments. Ronan looked over, a little startled by his tone of voice. Éamon didn't sound apologetic. If anything, he sounded a bit vindictive. "If I'd been allowed to come along, this wouldn't have happened."

Áed didn't say anything. Ronan could tell he wanted to,

but he just looked frustrated and held his tongue.

"I mean," Erin piped up. "He's not wrong."

Áed crossed his arms. "It was dangerous. What if the Fionns get hurt?"

"Then I'll feel bad," Éamon retorted. "But Bone's two top Generals aren't going to be beaten by a *patrol*." He shook his head. "Until that happens, I'm not sorry, Áed. I made my choice. I'm not apologizing."

"Éamon—"

"Áed." Éamon fixed him with a stare, and Áed pressed his lips together. Ronan was pretty sure he didn't imagine the darkness that colored Áed's cheeks.

"For whatever it's worth," Ronan ventured. His words rolled over the surface of the lake, sounding frighteningly open even though he hadn't spoken loudly. He lowered his voice. "I'm glad you're here now."

Silently, Erin sat down next to Ronan. She offered him her hand without a word, and Ronan took it; a moment later, warmth filled the faerie's palm, and Ronan shivered, cupping his hands around it to conserve the heat.

"I don't like this lake," Áed muttered after a while, breaking the tension. The horses were nosing at the grass, and the hind had folded its slender legs to rest on the ground. Áed was the only one still standing.

Ronan frowned over the expanse of the water. "It's a little eerie, I guess?" Fog hung over it in the cold, holding the moonlight in ghostly forms. "It's just a lake."

At Ronan's side, Erin hummed. "I don't love it," she said tiredly. She'd begun to doze off against Ronan's shoulder, sharing body heat. "Just don't touch the water."

Áed blinked. "Seriously?"

Erin opened one eye with a hint of annoyance.

"I didn't think you'd agree with me," Áed admitted.

"No, something is off. But these are the wildlands. There's always something." She closed her eye again. "Whatever it is, I think it's keeping animals—and worse things—away from the lake."

Ronan frowned at her, ignoring the fact that she couldn't see that with her eyes closed. "Might the animals have the right idea?"

"Fionnuala told us to wait here." She leaned into him, her hair pressing against his cheek. "And I don't know that this is more dangerous than anywhere else so long as we aren't stupid." She cracked her eyes again to glance at Áed and Éamon. "Think you can manage not being stupid?"

Áed looked skeptical, but Éamon just shrugged. "I'm not mobile enough to be stupid."

Áed looked like he wanted to contest that, but Ronan interrupted quickly. "Do you think skipping stones is a bad idea?"

That was enough to get Áed to turn to him, exasperated. "Yes, Ronan. That is a bad idea."

The moon painted their faces and clothes in shades of silver and jet, and the sound of the lake—the *pings* and *cracks* as the ice shifted, combined with the quiet lapping of waves in the unfrozen center—was oddly soothing. That, and the quiet noises of his companions, were all Ronan could hear. He could feel Erin's heartbeat against his side.

He didn't trust this quiet.

⟩⟩

Despite the perfect stillness, not one of them heard the Fionns approach.

The twins slipped through the trees like phantoms, not snapping a single icy twig in their passage to the narrow bank of the lake. Ronan, Erin, Áed, and Éamon all started as the two fae broke through the woods into their midst. "Hello," Fionnuala said quietly.

Ronan clambered hurriedly to his feet, trying to still his racing heart. "You're back! Are you okay? Where are your horses?"

Fionnuala held up her hands. "Slow down. We're fine." She touched the hilt of the longsword slung over her back, and Ronan noticed that the blade was dark. "We took care of the patrol. It wasn't even a fight."

"And the horses?"

"Let them loose," Fionnlagh answered. His voice wasn't as warm as his sister's, but it wasn't gruff. If anything, he seemed energized. "They'll find their way back." He stepped to the horse nearest him—Ronan's mare, who looked like she was sleeping—and began unfastening Ronan's bags. "The horses can't follow the rest of the way."

"Just one can," Fionnuala clarified. "In case we need to send a message quickly. But the barge won't hold more than that."

"We'll keep Echdían," Fionnlagh said. "He's the fastest. And Éamon needs to ride."

Éamon was struggling to his feet. "Echdían? My horse?"

Fionnlagh snorted. "One of my *mother's* horses, actually. You have high taste when you steal, crossling."

"Ah." Éamon rubbed the back of his neck sheepishly. "Sorry."

"Can we back up a moment?" Ronan interrupted. "Did Fionnuala say 'barge'?"

Fionnuala nodded. "This lake lies on the boundary between the Garnet court and the high court. It's longer than it is wide. Much faster to cross over water than to go around."

Erin looked uneasy at that. "Are you sure?" she said, and there was a hint of nervousness in her tone. She looked at the water with much more distrust now that the possibility of crossing it was in the open.

Fionnlagh nodded. "Quite."

"Where's the barge?"

While her twin unburdened Áed's horse and Erin's hind, Fionnuala stepped to the bank. Frost crunched under the soles of her shoes.

She extended one hand over the water and opened her palm to the sky. As Ronan watched, a single tongue of flame, no bigger than a candlewick, fluttered to life in the center of her open hand.

And then she whistled.

It was a low note, long and hollow. It rolled over the lake, and the fog seemed to ripple at its passage.

Ronan shivered.

Twice more, Fionnuala repeated the haunting sound.

Gooseflesh had prickled up on Ronan's arms, and without thinking, he took a step closer to Erin. For a few moments, nothing seemed to happen; Erin stared, wide-eyed, over the water, and Áed startled at Fionnlagh behind him. Nothing moved.

Until the flame began to rise from Fionnuala's palm.

It floated over her hand and then drifted toward the lake. Moving slowly, fluttering in the faint night breeze, it sank down toward the frozen surface.

Ronan didn't notice that he was holding his breath. The tiny fire hovered through the chilly haze, moving steadily toward the open water, and without a sound, the mist parted around it. Ronan couldn't tear his eyes from the miniature orange light. He hadn't realized that fae could command fire so far from their bodies. "How are you doing that?" he whispered.

"Shh," Fionnuala replied. She sounded unusually tense. "Don't speak."

Behind the light's passage, the lake's mist had closed again.

By now, the tiny flame was in the center of the lake, a golden flicker in the silvery moonlight. Ronan squinted at it.

It was getting bigger.

He frowned, shaking his head. It wasn't getting bigger—it was coming back. Fionnuala's expression hadn't changed, but Ronan thought he began to hear a noise, coming closer through the mist, just a whisper above silence. It sounded like water lapping against something, soft and insistent.

Then a shape slipped from the fog like a phantom.

From the prow hung a single, cloudy lantern. Behind the glass, Fionnuala's tiny flame flickered without oil or wax.

The vessel itself was dark, beams of oak that looked mossy with age in the fluttering dark, damp with the lake they belonged to. The boat drifted nearer, propelled not by so much as a breath of wind, and the water smoothly parted as it drifted toward the shore. Along its sides, bells hung silent.

It seemed to encounter no resistance when it met the ice near the banks. The mist seemed to follow it, and Ronan couldn't see where barge met frozen water; he didn't hear the ice break, but the boat approached as smoothly as if it was sailing on a placid pond.

Unguided, it stopped at the shore.

Fionnuala beckoned them forward. "Come on," she said softly. "Get in."

Ronan balked. "Really?"

The faerie nodded. "Come on. Hurry, now."

There was something profoundly unsettling about the silent craft. It didn't rock as it waited at the banks, and its wood seemed to absorb more light than it should, glistening only where wet moss caught the moonlight.

"Fionnlagh, go first," Fionnuala whispered.

With a nod, her brother led Éamon's horse to the boat. The animal hesitated, obviously wary, but under Fionnlagh's guidance, it stepped onto the barge. The vessel, Ronan noted, sank no lower in the water.

"Now the rest of you," Fionnuala prompted. She was still speaking under her breath as if she risked being overheard. "Go on. Don't wait, please."

Erin looked to Ronan with wide eyes. The fear in her expression was plain, and she looked at Ronan with wide doe eyes. "Are you really going to make me go before you?"

Ronan made a face. "That's manipulative."

"I'm fae." She glanced to the waiting boat. "Well?"

With a sigh, Ronan took a step toward the boat. Fionnlagh, already on board, extended his hand and helped Ronan over the side. Immediately, Ronan hugged himself. The air, already cold, was now both freezing and oppressively, stiflingly damp.

Erin boarded, and then Éamon. Áed followed, clambering on with a look of extreme trepidation, and Fionnuala gracefully jumped on last.

As soon as her feet touched the wooden boards, lashed together as they were with thick, fraying ropes, the boat ceased its stillness.

Ronan stumbled into Erin as the vessel began to glide away from the shore.

"This is the creepiest thing I've ever done," Ronan whispered to her, and she nodded fervently. Ronan grinned. "Oh, you agree? I thought this might be normal for you."

Erin just shook her head. "There are plenty of scary things out here. I'm not *surprised*; I'm just…"

"Unnerved?" Ronan suggested. That was how he was feeling, anyway.

Erin nodded. "Unnerved."

Quietly, Fionnuala shushed them. "Keep your voices down until we're across."

On the boat, the lake felt wider. Ronan seemed to remember being able to see trees on the opposite shore when he'd stood on the bank, but as the barge sailed into open water, he lost sight of any land at all. Before long, his sense of direction was spinning. A few times, he could even have convinced himself that they'd stopped moving entirely.

And then something bumped the boat.

Immediately Ronan looked to the horse. Perhaps it had shifted its weight, dropping a hoof or bumping its nose against the side. But the animal was still, ears pinned and nostrils wide. A shiver cut down Ronan's spine as he realized that both of the Fionns were also holding perfectly motionless.

Bump.

That had definitely not been the horse. Everyone on board exchanged a glance as if to confirm that yes, they had felt it too.

Bump.

Slowly, Fionnlagh raised a finger to his lips.

Bump.

The boat rocked, sending ripples silently over the surface of the black water. Ronan's heart was in his throat, thundering, and, squeezing Erin's hand, he peeked over the side of the boat.

A long face stared back up at him.

The scream was out of Ronan's mouth before he could stop it. He shoved back from the edge, toppling Erin as he landed hard on his back in the bottom of the boat. The vessel tipped, splashing as it tilted with his weight and then regained its balance, and Ronan was left gripping Erin while his heart beat wildly out of his chest. The bells along the gunwale rang hollowly.

The Fionns were already in motion. They took up positions on opposite sides of the boat, legs wide for balance, and drew their weapons in tandem.

Ronan was still catching his breath as Áed dropped to his side, face pale. "What was it? What did you see?"

"I—I don't know." Ronan could barely get the words past his lips. He wasn't sure what had been there, waiting just below the surface of the water. The shape had been shadowed from the moonlight, but he knew he had seen a long, oblong face, as black as the night itself and framed with pitch-colored hair that floated eerily in the water around it. "I don't—I don't know." He pressed a palm tight over his mouth, trying to slow down his breathing.

"It knows we're here," Fionnuala said tersely.

"I'm sorry," Ronan whispered. "I didn't mean to scream, it just—"

"I didn't warn you not to look in the water. I can take the blame for that. But I need you to be very still and very quiet." The moonlight gathered along the wicked edge of her blade. "Keep your body low to the boat, and do not move."

Ronan was already low in the boat since he'd fallen, but at Fionnuala's command, Erin, Áed, and Éamon also carefully brought themselves down.

The boat glided onward.

And then it stopped.

Ronan's heart skipped a terrified beat. They were nowhere near the opposite shore; last he'd seen, land had still been invisible, somewhere far out in the fog. Which meant they had stopped in the middle of the lake. Which was inhabited by *something*.

Fionnlagh cursed under his breath.

A wave of lake water crested over the vessel, immediately soaking Ronan to the bone. He sucked in a gasp at the icy water and blinked the spray out of his eyes to see Erin looking stunned. There was algae in her hair. On Ronan's other side,

Éamon was coughing, clearly trying his best to muffle it, and the horse, on some instinct, had lowered itself to its knees for stability. Its eyes were wide. Áed, with nowhere else to go, was stuck by the edge of the vessel, holding onto the side as best as he could.

"Áed!" Fionnuala exclaimed. "Get away from the edge!"

The boat rocked violently in the wake of whatever had made the splash, but there wasn't time for it to settle again before something collided hard with the port side. It tipped violently; Ronan tumbled, landing on the side of the boat precariously close to the water. The floor of the boat was too slick for him to crawl back to the center until the port side dropped again, tossing him. The air left his lungs painfully when he hit the solid, mossy wood.

Once again, the barge's passengers got little respite. This time, the blow came from the starboard side, even more powerfully than before. Erin let out a yelp as they all were pitched again. The twins were somehow keeping their footing, but they staggered at the impact. The lantern at the boat's prow swung wildly, casting its light in disorienting, moving shades, and the bells clamored in empty tones.

"It's trying to tip us!" Erin choked. "What does it want?"

Fionnlagh growled. "It's hungry."

Ronan choked. "It wants to *eat* us?"

Another blow to the boat sent Fionnuala to her knees, and Fionnlagh gripping the side. A scream from Ronan's left made him look, and he felt all of the air leave his lungs.

Áed had been thrown against the side of the boat, but that wasn't what had made him scream.

What had made him scream were the long, too-white teeth, set in mossy gums and framed by loose black lips, that had sunk into the neck of his cloak.

Éamon was gripping Áed's wrists with both hands and

had, in an impressively reactive move, braced his feet on the side of the boat to keep them both from being pulled overboard, but the creature affixed to Áed's clothing was not letting go. It was big. It was big, and it was night-black, and its hair poured over its oblong head and thick neck to completely obscure its form.

"Take off your cloak!" Éamon shouted, but it was immediately obvious that there was no way for Áed to do that.

"Fionnlagh," Ronan cried. "Cut his cloak! It's hide, it won't tear, Fionnlagh, *cut it*!"

"Or stab the monster!" Éamon managed through gritted teeth.

Before Fionnlagh moved, the beast gave one last brutal wrench.

Áed's wrists slipped out of Éamon's grasp.

With a terrified cry, Áed went overboard.

"No!" Éamon screamed. He was at the side of the boat in a second, looking desperately over the dark water. "Áed!"

Fionnlagh looked wild. "That wasn't how this was supposed to go," he managed.

Éamon turned on him. "*No, really.*" He began shucking off his outerwear, stripping to his shirt and trousers. Áed's axe was sitting at the bottom of the boat. "I have to go after him."

Fionnlagh seemed to be in a sort of shock. "It's too late."

Fionnuala, though, gripped her brother by the shoulder, so tightly that her knuckles went pale. "Let him," she growled.

Fionnlagh looked at her in surprise. Éamon, for his part, wasn't waiting for the conclusion of their exchange. He threw the last of his cloaks to the ground and tripped to the side of the boat.

Fionnuala grabbed his arm. Her eyes were burning bright

as she pressed a dagger into his hand. "If it's a choice between him living or you," she said, and her words raked fiercely over Ronan's skin. "*Choose him.*"

Éamon gripped the dagger tightly. He did not flinch. "I will."

And with that, he dove off the side of the boat.

CHAPTER THIRTY-TWO
ÉAMON

The water hit Éamon like a shock.

Immediately, he felt every muscle seize up, and lightning cold fired through every inch of his skin. The urge to suck in a desperate gasp was overwhelming, and he stopped it only when he choked on lake water. It tasted green and murky on his tongue.

The lake was dark and very, very still.

Above him, the glimmer of the boat's lantern shimmered faintly. It illuminated little, leaving Éamon with the panicky feeling that the darkness below him was bottomless.

Well, well, little one.

Éamon let out an involuntary cry. Bubbles rolled upward, sparkling barely.

The water shifted around him, leaving Éamon with the feeling that he was spinning as something large swam silently past. Its voice echoed like a song. *The Goddess sends me interesting meals tonight.*

He pressed his palms over his mouth. His lungs were already starting to burn.

He needed to find Áed.

He kicked experimentally downward, half in the hope

that he would see Áed in the gloom and half to find out if the beast would eat him immediately. As he did, the leg of his trousers floated up at the ankle. A bluish-white glow permeated the water.

Oh? The voice sang. Éamon began to make out a shadow, hovering just at the edge of the light. The glow was coming from his prosthesis, he realized. The entire moon-crystal limb was fluorescing in the icy water. *That's unusual.*

Éamon's lungs felt like they were going to burst. He needed to find Áed, and he couldn't do that if he couldn't *breathe*—so with a kick, he propelled himself to the surface. His head broke the water with a splash, and the frigid air felt warm on his face. He gasped. Distantly, he heard his name being called.

But then something had his good leg, and he was going back under.

Don't flee now, the voice said darkly. *I've grown used to eating well.*

Thinking fast, Éamon bent double in the water. The dagger that Fionnuala had thrust on him felt heavy in his hand, and, without hesitating, he took it to the fabric of his pants. As the leg of his trouser fell away below the knee, the shine of the prosthesis illuminated the water in an eerie shade. Éamon saw a dark shape below him. It looked like a horse, if horses had reflective eyes and teeth as long as a hand. Its hooves were hooked, spurred, and pointed, and where its inky mane parted, billowing in the water, a long, bony fin followed the crest of its spine. The sight of it made Éamon's blood run colder than the water of the lake.

He turned on it without thinking.

The creature showed no expression on its elongated face, but Éamon could have sworn it was surprised as he slashed at it with the blade.

What are you doing? It released his leg and backed up,

seeking the dark and cold. *You can't be here for the other one.* Its lips parted over its mossy teeth, a horrible charade of a smile. *That one was part of the bargain.*

"What bargain?" Éamon said before he could stop himself. His words bubbled away past his lips, but the water horse made a sound like a high, whinnying laugh.

The bargain with the faerie folk. To cross my lake.

Éamon blinked, but there was no time to process the implication of the words. "Give him back," he demanded, trying to exhale as little as possible.

That isn't how this works. The water horse cocked its head, staying just outside of Éamon's reach. If he didn't know better, he'd say it looked thoughtful. *You wouldn't be a full meal,* it mused. It drifted around Éamon, making him turn clumsily in the water as it glided without effort. *Missing a part. Netted with magic. Not good to eat.* Its eyes, still reflecting the light like a cat's, narrowed slightly. *But the faeryling looks… toothsome.*

It moved faster than Éamon could have prepared himself for. In a black flash, it was before him, crooked and enormous teeth a finger's-width from Éamon's nose.

And he smells sweet.

Éamon's teeth gritted, and his grip tightened on the knife. "You'd better not have hurt him."

Why shouldn't I? The horse looked like it was leering. *He belongs to me, now.*

Éamon was barely aware of his own body lurching into motion. He had no plan; all he knew was that Áed was running out of time and that the horse's words incensed him. The water hindered his movements, so instead of swinging the knife, he thrust it forward.

The water horse clearly hadn't expected him to go on the offensive. It drew back, moving easily through the water, which dragged at Éamon's limbs. Still, Éamon cut it. He felt the edge of the blade slide through something that resisted its passage, and the horse let out a guttural shriek.

Fine, then, it hissed, and then Éamon was tumbling through the water, head over heels as it sped past. *I'll simply eat you as well.*

The next thing Éamon knew, the horse's teeth closed around his foot again. He was wearing leather boots, so its fangs didn't break the skin, but in the next moment, he knew that they didn't need to. With a powerful jerk, the horse started downward, and Éamon felt the pressure of the water beginning to build.

His air was running out.

Frantically, he slashed at the horse's body. He felt the blade cleave the horse's hide, and he could taste murky blood on the water, but the horse only responded by tightening its bite on Éamon's foot. Éamon winced, fighting back the urge to cry out and waste more breath: if the horse didn't clearly prefer drowning him to maiming him, he knew it could crush his bones easily. Éamon had had enough of crushed bones.

He pulled his leg toward him, hard.

The horse didn't release him. Instead, the motion had only pulled Éamon's body closer to the horse's gigantic, mossy head.

That was what he needed.

Aiming by the milky light of his prosthesis, he found the glint of the water horse's eye.

He slammed the point of his blade directly into it.

The horse bucked him free with a vicious, reactive whip of its head. It released Éamon's foot, sending him tumbling upward, and in the next moment, he broke the surface. Sucking in a few deep gasps, he dove back down underwater.

The horse was screaming, ripping the lake with dreadful screeching. Its eye was now somehow blacker than the rest of its head, and Éamon realized with a start that there *was* no eye anymore. Or, at least, if there *was*, it was ruined so thoroughly that he couldn't distinguish it. The horse's screams were agonized, sending icy shards raking over Éamon's body that had nothing to do with the temperature of the water.

"Let me pass," Éamon snarled, "or I'll come back for the other one."

The horse only screamed louder. Éamon decided that was enough for him.

He kicked down toward the fathomless lake bottom. There had to be a bottom, didn't there? And somewhere on that bottom, there had to be Áed.

Above him, the boat's lanternlight was fading from his view, and the pressure of the water increased with every stroke he took. His ears popped, but—there was algae. Long, still ropes of slimy, black algae.

That meant he had to be close.

He swam desperately, relying on the strange glow of his leg to see. Áed had to be here. He had to be here somewhere.

Among the black, hairy weeds, Éamon spotted something fair.

He kicked toward it, and then his light was landing on weightless sandy hair and a placid, empty face.

Áed's lips were just parted. His eyes were slightly open, but the sliver of red iris that Éamon could see beneath his lids did not move at Éamon's approach. Gritting his teeth, Éamon scooped an arm under Áed's narrow shoulders and another under his knees. The lake bottom was soft, almost silky with silt, and as Éamon planted his feet, they sank into the quiet sediment up to the ankle.

He pushed off.

Áed's weight worked against him as, without the use of his arms, he kicked madly for the surface. His bad leg ached. The light drew nearer at a snail's pace, and his muscles burned; for a moment, he had to wait, treading water beneath the surface as the horse thrashed madly above them, but then it passed, and Éamon was once more fighting toward the air.

He broke the surface just as the blackness began to close over his vision. His hair trailed in his eyes, pouring lake water over his face, and he coughed, sucking in air in desperate gulps. His body protested, but still, he fought to keep Áed's head above the water. "Here!" he cried. He couldn't see much through his hair and the water in his eyes, but the boat had to be close. "I got him, come help!"

He managed to shove his hair back in time to see the boat drawing closer. Fionnuala was kneeling, reaching out over the side, and Éamon did his best to press Áed into her arms. She bundled him on board, and then Ronan and Erin were each reaching a hand out for Éamon. They grabbed hold of his wrists and hauled him onto the barge.

The urge to collapse onto the bottom of the boat was overwhelming, but Éamon fought it. Áed was lying on his back, unmoving. His freckled skin was chalk-pale, and his chest neither rose nor fell.

Éamon crawled over, his wet clothes and cold, stiff limbs doing their best to hinder his movement. "He isn't breathing."

Ronan had his hands clasped over his mouth. "He's not..."

Erin finished the sentence in a whisper. "...dead?"

Éamon shook his head. Áed couldn't be dead. He couldn't be. With shaking hands, Éamon turned Áed's head to the side. Water ran out of his mouth.

Áed had told Éamon stories about his life before the White City. He'd confessed that much of his early memory was hazy, but Éamon knew that he had grown up on the Fisher's Shore. Even after moving farther from the coast, he had still spent more than half his life in a city surrounded by water.

Once upon a time, he had told Éamon how to do this.

Moving as deliberately as he could, Éamon tipped back Áed's chin and pressed his mouth to Áed's.

He barely registered Erin's surprised gasp as he exhaled, feeling Áed's chest rise with his breath.

"What's he *doing*?" Erin whispered to Ronan. She sounded stunned. "Is now really the time?"

Ronan made a helpless, terrified noise. It sounded like perhaps he wanted to speak but couldn't get the words out.

Éamon moved back and set the heels of his hands low on Áed's breastbone. He let his weight fall behind each stroke, trying to force life into Áed with every push into his chest. Then he leaned over again to press his mouth on Áed's again.

It went on for too long. Nobody spoke a word as Éamon repeated his ritual—breathe air into Áed's lungs, force his blood to move in his veins, do it again, do it again. After three rounds, the sound of water lapping against the side of the boat seemed to have amplified, as if the lake itself was pointing out the stillness within the tiny vessel. Áed had not moved. He made no sound.

Éamon didn't stop. He didn't feel Ronan's hand on his shoulder. He didn't see Fionnuala gripping the hilt of her broadsword with gritted teeth as if she wished this were an enemy she could fight.

Éamon drove his weight into Áed's chest.

Áed gasped.

Éamon tripped backward immediately, eyes flying wide. "Áed?"

Áed's chest heaved weakly, his eyes fluttering, and he coughed. This time, water dribbled from his lips, and then he was rolling onto his side and hacking as the rest came up from his lungs.

"Áed!" Éamon managed. He couldn't get another word

out before he was gathering Áed into his arms, desperate to prove to himself that he lived. Áed felt shaky in his hold.

"Éamon?" he rasped. His own hands came up to touch Éamon's back, unsteadily holding him close. "You—what—"

"He kissed you," Erin said. She still sounded dumbfounded. "He kissed you and brought you back."

Éamon felt his cheeks flood with cold blush. "No, I—that's not—"

His stammering was interrupted by Áed coughing again, and this time, the attack devolved into violent shivers. Éamon held him close. "You need to warm up." Éamon hesitated when he realized that he, too, was trembling. "*I* need to warm up." At least Éamon had had the chance to strip some of his dry clothes before diving into the lake. Áed had had no such fortune; his cloak was saturated, clinging to him in a stiff way that it suggested it would soon start growing icicles. Éamon grabbed his own dry cloak. "Take yours off, put this on."

"Áed," Ronan urged. His voice was shaky. "Áed, fire. Warm up."

Éamon glanced at Áed, but Áed was too busy trying to unclasp his own cloak with uncooperative, blue-tipped fingers. "Let me," Éamon said, and Áed allowed him to brush his hands aside and undo the clasp. Once Áed's cloak was off, lying in a puddle in the bottom of the barge, Éamon pulled his own dry cloak over both of them. Trembling, Áed called heat to his hands, and Éamon found himself huddling close. He wished that Áed's fire could dry them completely, but Áed seemed to be struggling to maintain the warmth as it was; perhaps Erin or the twins could help.

The twins.

With a frown, Éamon looked up.

Neither Fionnuala or Fionnlagh had spoken since he and

Áed had gotten back on board. As he looked between Áed's half-siblings' faces, the water horse's words flashed back through his mind.

The bargain.

"Did you let this happen on purpose?" he asked quietly. His teeth were chattering, but his words were clear. "The horse said something about a bargain." Éamon narrowed his eyes. "For us to cross safely, it would take somebody." He held Áed closer without thinking. "Did you know about that?"

Fionnlagh shot a glance at Fionnuala, who had crossed her arms. She only looked back at him mulishly. "I'm sorry," Fionnlagh said, looking back at Áed. "We've never encountered the creature of this lake before."

"But you knew how to call the boat."

Fionnlagh hesitated. "Mother told us how."

Éamon narrowed his eyes at them both. "So you didn't know it was going to come for Áed?"

Fionnlagh shook his head indignantly. "Of course not! Áed is our *brother*."

Éamon stared at them. It was true that both of them looked immensely relieved; Fionnuala looked near tears. Still, he got the feeling that they weren't saying something. Neither of them seemed likely to respond to his searching glare, however, so he let out a breath and huddled closer to Áed's warmth. "Let's just get off this lake."

CHAPTER THIRTY-THREE
RONAN

Ronan didn't think he could take any more stress. Not for a good, long while.

He also didn't think things were going to get less stressful anytime soon.

Watching Áed tumble into the water—and then watching Éamon dive in after him—Ronan felt like his guts had tied themselves into knots. He had wanted to scream after them and then plead for someone to help them, but distress had blocked his words. He hadn't been robbed of speech that way in weeks, and the feeling of it still left him shaken. Now that Áed and Éamon were sitting against the side of the boat, slouched together under Áed's cloak, Ronan could feel the terror slowly leaving his system. He slumped against Erin without a second thought.

Erin, however, did not slump back. She was stiff beside him, her eyes narrow, and he glanced up at her worriedly. "What is it?"

There was a frown on her full lips, and she was fidgeting with her necklace. "Nothing that the Fionns said just now *meant* anything," she murmured, just loud enough for him to hear.

"Huh?" Ronan sat up a little to look at her better. "What do you mean?"

"I mean they didn't answer the questions."

Ronan thought for a moment. Come to think of it, he couldn't remember the twins actually saying that they didn't know about this apparent bargain with the monster that lived in the lake. They *had* said that they didn't know it was going to come for Áed. Did that mean they expected it to take someone else? "What are you saying?"

Erin just shook her head. "I'm saying they're not telling us everything." She worried at her lip. "I don't like it."

"Should we do something?"

Slowly, Erin shook her head. "We don't know anything. My hunch could be wrong, anyway. Just stay alert, all right?"

Ronan nodded. He was still shaken by how close he'd come to possibly losing Áed. He had absolutely no idea what he'd have done. If he'd have been able to do anything at all.

He flinched as his imagination carried him deeper into the possibility and shook his head hard to banish the images and all-numbing grief he knew would fall over him if it ever became real. That's what had happened when Ninian had died.

But it didn't bear thinking about. Áed was fine. Éamon, too—he was murmuring something to Áed about *aren't you glad I came along after all*, and Áed was chuckling between attacks of shivers. It was going to be all right. The tug behind Ronan's breastbone was still strong, and once they were done, he, Áed, and Éamon could go *home*. Ronan couldn't regret crossing the veil, but home sounded better all the time.

}}{{

Reaching the opposite shore brought blessed reprieve. They set up another camp, Áed and Éamon got dry, and they'd all managed some sleep before the sun came up. But the next midday saw them still moving—walking, now, as Éamon was the only one with a horse—and Ronan felt like his feet were going to fall off.

The sun was dropping again by the time Ronan felt it. He'd already gathered that they were getting close by the increased frequency with which they'd needed to avoid patrols, but when the tug in Ronan's chest suddenly amplified its intensity, he *knew*.

"Where are we?" he demanded.

Fionnuala looked back at him over her shoulder. "Not far from the court proper. Can you feel the spell?"

Ronan nodded. "We're really close."

"Good." Fionnlagh, who had been bringing up the rear, closed the space, herding everyone together. Éamon's horse snorted. "Can you tell *how* close?"

"Maybe an hour's walk? Maybe less."

"It will be easier to decide how to approach once we're near enough to see what we're getting into," Fionnuala said. "The plan doesn't involve fighting; we would lose. That means surprise will be our weapon, and we need to learn the terrain. But to get closer, we're going to need to blend in more." She bent to touch her toes, seeming to enjoy the brief reprieve from walking. "Fionnlagh and I are, unfortunately, recognizable by anyone who's fought us in the past, but hopefully, that's not most people. Still, we'll do what we can." She teased her hair, letting its volume hang around her face in side bangs before tying the back up into twin buns. Fionnlagh snorted, and Fionnuala sighed. "Your turn, brother, dear."

"Touch my hair and perish, sister."

Fionnuala crossed her arms, fixing Fionnlagh with an unfazed stare and cocking an eyebrow. "Do it yourself, then."

Grumbling, Fionnlagh began to braid his own tight curls into a thick plait in the back. He left enough loose in the front to arrange around his face, obscuring his high, distinctive cheekbones.

Seemingly satisfied, Fionnuala turned to Áed. "You have freckles."

"Not sure how to hide that."

Fionnuala bent down and wordlessly scooped a handful of dirt from the ground. "We already look like travelers—we just need to make sure we look like *high-court* travelers. Dirty but flawless. Get to work."

While Áed set to that, Fionnuala turned to Ronan. "You." She looked thoughtful. "I can't say I know much about the high-court attitude toward crosslings."

"Oh," Fionnlagh groaned. "I do." He finished with his hair, looking annoyed, and crossed his arms. "Before the war, maybe... a hundred years ago? I went to one of the festivals here."

"Oh, Goddess, I remember that," Fionnuala murmured. "I'd never seen you so drunk in my *life*."

"The wine was strong," Fionnlagh groused. "Anyway. There were plenty of crosslings there. Wearing silk and ermine or nothing at all. All enchanted." He sighed, waving a hand. "The high-courters treat crosslings like being taken is a blessing."

"So I have to look, like, really happy to be here?" Ronan said.

"Just stick to us, and don't talk. Nobody who looks closer will be fooled since they'll be able to feel that you're not enchanted, but we just need to be overlooked for a while." He frowned thoughtfully. "The party should be as small as possible. Ronan, we need you to navigate. Áed, I imagine that means you'll be coming."

"He's my ward." Áed's voice was still a little bit rough from his near-drowning. "Try to stop me."

"I wasn't going to." Fionnlagh adjusted his hair, looking irritated. "Fionnuala and I will be coming for protection. Éamon and Erin, you stay behind with the horse. Be ready to run—we'll find a way to send you word if something goes wrong, and it'll be on you to bring the message back to the mound."

Erin scowled. "Are you trying to keep us out of the way?"

Fionnlagh rolled his eyes. "A group of four is already going to stand out. A group of six would just be ridiculous. The only reason I'm not making *Áed* stay behind too is because of Ronan." He crossed his arms. "You have a job. If something goes wrong, bring reinforcements. Understand?"

Éamon nodded as if the motion pained him. Clearly, he wanted to come, but in this case, he seemed to agree that he and Erin shouldn't. "You had better stay safe."

Áed looked like he wanted to give him a parting hug but wasn't sure he should. "You, too."

"Excellent," Fionnlagh interrupted. "Then it's settled." He looked around. The land was not flat; in places, rock broke from the surface of the earth in natural monoliths as high as a horse, and in others, the forest floor fell away in small scarp faces. "You two, find a shelter and stay alert." His gaze was sharp as he looked over the rest of the group. "Everyone else," he said, "with me."

§§

Half an hour later, the magic in Ronan's chest felt like it was *humming*.

Around them, the forest hadn't changed. Ronan was keeping a careful eye out for any signs of civilization, but so far, he'd seen nothing. The trees were covered in a light scrim of snow, and the rough forest floor was undisturbed by footprints. And yet, they were close. Ronan was sure of it.

"Where is everyone?" he said quietly.

Fionnlagh fell into step next to him. "They're in the trees."

Automatically, Ronan looked up. Against the slate, cloud-blanketed sky, he saw nothing but whispering branches. "I don't see anything."

"They're there," Fionnlagh assured him. "*In* the trees. Look." He gestured with his chin to a darkened hollow in the wide trunk of one of the larger trees—not the largest but so large that Ronan was certain that all four of them holding hands couldn't encircle even a quarter of the trunk. At first, the hollow appeared as nothing but a darkened indentation, but as Ronan gave it closer attention, he realized that it led into the trunk of the tree itself.

Suddenly, the knowledge that they had been walking among unseen high fae hit Ronan like a slap, and he shivered. "Oh."

He focused on the tugging in his chest and pointed to a tree some twenty paces away. "I think it's over there."

"We'll get closer," Fionnuala said. "To be certain. We don't want to make mistakes."

They approached the tree cautiously, and Ronan tentatively laid a hand on its deep, rough bark. "Yeah," he whispered. "This is the one."

"All right," Fionnuala said. Her hand absently felt for the hilt of the knife at her belt. "We go in, speak to no one. Ronan, don't make it obvious you're leading; you're a crossling, and that would look conspicuous. We don't have much information, so if we find that it's too dangerous to engage, we retreat and regroup. Understood?"

"What do you mean by 'engage'?" Áed asked.

Fionnuala's fingers stopped moving over her sword. "Depends," she said. "We can't fight him. He's powerful enough to take us out with a blink." Her eyes narrowed. "I'm not trying to scare you. I just want you to know who we're dealing with. This is the man who rotted every edible crop in Glass's territory when their leader insulted the Queen. When the Queen takes prisoners, he's the one who tortures them. He has pulled the lungs from faeries' chests while they still lived, without even touching them. He is the last kind of person who you'd ever want to wield the power he does. So." Her face was set and stony. "Combat is not an option."

"We'll see if there's any way to use an element of surprise," Fionnlagh said, taking over while Fionnuala nodded. "The goal is to incapacitate him before he realizes he's in danger. If that isn't possible, we retreat."

Ronan nodded. "Clear."

"Good." Fionnuala stepped around to the dark opening in the trunk of the tree and peered inside. "Follow close."

Inside the tree, the light was dim and warm, as if lit by unseen candles, and Ronan immediately felt chills creep over his skin. Never had he felt so exposed and yet so trapped. The entire inside of the tree seemed to have been hollowed out, to the extent that Ronan didn't understand how the gigantic plant still lived. Along the edge, a staircase, hewn of the tree's own wood, spiraled upward. In the space around it, the tree had been carved into apartments, little shopfronts, vendors' booths. On higher levels, they connected to the staircase by catwalks, woody sinews holding the place together.

Something bright moved near Ronan's face, and he startled, almost jumping into Áed. As he watched, it floated as aimlessly as if it were being drawn by nothing but the air currents.

"It's pollen," Fionnuala said, as Ronan stared after the little, glowing orb. "From the tree."

Now that Ronan had seen one, he began to notice more of the little sprites. They seemed to be the primary light source, hanging suspended in the air, drifting tranquilly. Some of the shopfronts had glass lanterns full of them; a few levels above, Ronan watched a faerie in a long skirt shoo a couple out of her hair. "Wow."

"Focus," Fionnuala chided gently. "And keep your head down. Where are we going?"

"Up," Ronan answered immediately. He nodded toward the stairs. "A few levels, I think."

Nobody looked at them twice as they made their way to the staircase and began to ascend. Áed was looking around suspiciously. "If it's this easy to get into high-court territory," he said in a hushed voice, "I mean, relatively, then why haven't you already tried?"

"It's easy to get into places like *this*," Fionnlagh answered, equally quietly. "There's nothing special about this tree. Nobody important lives here—or so we thought, anyway." He shook his head. "Getting into anywhere royal is a different story."

"I wonder why the consort came here, of all places," Fionnuala wondered. "It's so…"

"Peaceful?" Ronan provided, and Fionnuala nodded. He let out a little breath. "I don't know. But he's here. Close." Just as he said it, he stopped short on the stairs, and his eyes slid over the narrow catwalk intersecting it. "Really close."

Across the catwalk, carved into the opposite wall of the tree, a narrow two-story structure was settled. It was quaint, with yellow-painted shutters and shingles graven into the sloped roof, and the door was propped open with a round, moss-blanketed stone.

Fionnlagh, Fionnuala, and Áed all stared at it.

"Ronan," Fionnuala said after a few moments. "I hate to question you but…"

"Are you *certain* you got the spell right?" Fionnlagh finished.

Ronan bit his lip. "The pull is coming from in there," he said. "I'm certain of it."

"I think it's a bakery," Fionnuala said. She sounded skeptical. "So our plan of attack is… what?"

"Go in and buy some bread?" Ronan suggested helplessly. "Scope it out?"

"That could go poorly," Fionnlagh mused.

"It could also go well," Fionnuala put in. "Besides, look at it." She opened a palm to the structure as if to encompass its charming front, complete with a little round window just below the crook of the roof. "It isn't exactly guarded. Or defensible at all. I'm sorry, Ronan, but I'm not convinced the consort is even *there*." She shrugged. "At the very least, we could get out easily."

Fionnlagh let out a little breath. "All right. But we aren't going in as a group. That's too suspicious."

"I'll go in," Fionnuala volunteered. "I'll take Áed—he's not so recognizable as you, Fionnlagh."

"Fine." Fionnlagh crossed his arms. "I'll stay out here with Ronan." His face was stern and worried. "Try not to take too long."

CHAPTER THIRTY-FOUR
ÁED

On some level, it was impossible to see the bakery as capable of hiding someone so threatening. On another, Áed could see how something so unequivocally *cute* could provide the perfect front.

After leaving his axe with Fionnlagh, he followed Fionnuala across the catwalk, making a point not to look down over the railing-less sides. He stuck close when, hesitating only a moment, she pressed open the door.

A little bell heralded their arrival, and it tinkled softly as they stepped into the shop. It seemed that Fionnuala had guessed correctly: fresh bread lined the shelves, and the air was heavy with the warm smell of yeast and baked goods. A counter took up half of the space, shadowed in the dimness but softly lit by pollen lamps in every corner, and behind it, a doorway led to another room, where Áed guessed the actual baking was done. At their arrival, a voice called from the other room. "Be with you in a second!"

Fionnuala and Áed exchanged a look. The voice hadn't *sounded* particularly threatening. In fact, the voice hadn't even sounded like a man's. "I think Ronan got the wrong place," Fionnuala muttered.

A few seconds later, a woman bustled out of the doorway,

brushing flour off her hands and onto her apron. She smiled at them. "What can I get for you?"

Áed swallowed. "Actually," he ventured, "we're, um… we're new around here." He glanced to Fionnuala, who nodded slightly, and went on. "Just trying to look around a bit. Meet people. You know."

The baker propped her elbows on the counter. "That's nice. We don't have many new faces—I think everyone hunkered down once the war started. Where are you from?"

Thankfully, Fionnuala answered. "Dún Darach," she said.

The baker looked surprised. "I thought Dún Darach was destroyed."

"It was," Áed said quickly. "That's why we moved."

"Oh! I'm sorry." The baker offered a conciliatory smile. "Well. I'm glad to meet new people, and I hope you can find a place here. I'm Róise."

"I'm Áed." He figured it was probably safe enough to use his real name; nobody would recognize it. "And this is my sister, Niamh."

"Do you live here on your own?" Fionnuala asked. Her tone was a perfect imitation of neighborly curiosity.

"Usually," Róise said, and Áed thought her voice might have been *just* too casual. "My brother is visiting at the moment, but he ordinarily has a place somewhere else."

Fionnuala shot Áed a meaningful look, and then she pulled out her coin purse and counted a few into her palm. "While we're here, could we perhaps buy a few loaves?"

The baker's demeanor changed, brightening immediately. "Of course. Let me get that for you."

While she turned, busying herself with fresh-baked bread, Áed leaned closer to Fionnuala. "Dún Darach?" he whispered.

Fionnuala let out a tight breath. "Fionnlagh and I were

born there," she muttered under her breath. "Mother was on a diplomatic trip at the time. Thank Goddess, too. Do you know a single place name in the high court?"

"Er…" He shrugged. "No, but is that my fault?"

"Here you are!" Róise said, interrupting them by turning around and passing three warm loaves in a paper bag to Fionnuala. "Nice meeting you two. Perhaps I'll see you around."

"I hope so," Áed responded with a smile. "Have a nice day."

Once they were outside again, Áed slumped. "Gods, that was stressful."

Fionnlagh and Ronan were still waiting on the stairs. Ronan seemed to have collected a handful of the floating pollen lights, and Fionnlagh was trying very hard to look casual while holding a traveler's pack, his own weapons, and Áed's battle axe. "It went all right, though," Fionnuala said. They started crossing the catwalk, and she tore off a chunk of the bread, offered it to Áed, and then took another herself. "That brother of hers… that's interesting. She's hiding him, I'd put money on it."

"You think he's the consort, then?"

"Could be. Did Róise look nervous to you?"

Áed frowned around his bite of bread. "A bit, yeah."

"He might be keeping her there to act as a front for him. Poor woman's probably terrified."

"Would the consort really hurt his own *sister*?"

Fionnuala pursed her lips. "When she said 'brother,' she might not have meant by blood. It's a loose enough term that sometimes it can extend to friends or people who grew up together, without being a lie." Her eyes were dark. "But whether they're childhood friends or actual siblings, the answer is yes. I have no doubt that he would."

They reached the end of the catwalk, and Ronan's gaze immediately darted to the bread. "Oh, hell," Áed sighed. "I forgot you couldn't eat this."

Ronan groaned. "It smells *great*."

Fionnlagh stepped forward. "Do we have enough information to make a plan?"

"We should go somewhere else," Fionnuala said. "It was already foolish to say so much here. Go on, down the stairs."

They ended up convening in the chill, hazy air outside, on the opposite side of the tree from the door. Áed leaned against the rocky bark of the trunk, and the others circled around. It felt like there were strangely few of them, without Éamon and Erin.

"I'm confident that someone is sheltering in that place who does not want to be found," Fionnuala began. "And given Ronan's directions, it doesn't seem so unlikely that it might be the consort."

Ronan looked a little smug. "So you believe me now."

Fionnuala sighed. "I'm just trying to be logical."

"It seems reasonable to assume that the consort is on the second floor, right?" Fionnlagh asked, and both Áed and Fionnuala nodded.

"It looked like there was just the shop floor and the kitchen downstairs," Áed said. "Granted, we couldn't see the whole kitchen, but I think upstairs would make more sense."

"Ronan?" Fionnuala asked. "Can you narrow down the location any further?"

Ronan pinched his lip between forefinger and thumb. "In the vision," he said, "right as the spell succeeded, I saw stairs." He nodded at the loaves still in Fionnuala's arms. "Also bread. But I think the stairs are more important right now. They led upward."

Fionnlagh nodded. "Assume he's on the second floor,

then. We're going to have to get there at a time he's not expecting."

"Tonight," Fionnuala suggested, and she swept her eyes over the group. "We go tonight."

CHAPTER THIRTY-FIVE
ÁED

The plan was simple. They would break in through the front door. The Fionns would head upstairs while Áed—and Ronan, who everyone thought it was best not to leave behind alone—kept watch on the ground floor. And at first, that plan had gone well. Fionnuala had dealt with the lock in no time, and Fionnlagh had reached up to wrap his hand around the little shop bell before it could chime to announce their entrance. They'd slipped into the dark room, and the floor, carved directly of the tree, had no boards to creak as they moved. The pollen lights had all faded, leaving them in the obscurity of shadow.

It was perfect.

Until, of course, something cold and sharp pressed against Áed's throat.

Whoever was behind him pressed a hand between his shoulder blades, steering him forward and keeping the knife against his throat. "Nobody move."

Áed recognized the voice. "Róise?" he said. In response, the blade was pulled harder against his throat, and Áed raised both of his hands in surrender. "Okay. Okay."

"Who are you?" Róise growled. "*Really?*"

Fionnlagh and Fionnuala had drawn their weapons, but neither seemed prepared to attack when Áed had a blade to his neck. Ronan, it seemed, could only gape, eyes full of fear.

Áed took a deep breath. The woman was digging the edge of the knife into his skin. Behind him, he could feel her: the hand that didn't hold the knife was pressed to the back of his neck, and one of her feet was planted by Áed's own.

He really hoped that his old skills weren't too rusty.

In one motion, he grabbed Róise's knife arm as best as he could, one hand at her wrist, the other at her elbow. The knife pointed left, and, drawing back as much as he could to avoid being cut, Áed yanked her arm in that direction.

With a yelp, she lost her balance, tripping as she pivoted with the force of Áed's pull. She stumbled into the center of the room, nearly falling.

Áed took a moment to thank whoever was listening that the skills he'd learned in the Maze had not deserted him.

"Well," Fionnuala muttered. She sounded a little impressed. "All right."

Róise hadn't dropped the knife, but that didn't last. Fionnlagh took her wrist firmly, and with a flick of his hand, she gasped. The knife fell, skittering across the floor. Seemingly by instinct, she brought fire to her hand, and Fionnlagh released her, eyes widening as snow-white flames licked up over his palm. Róise gasped at his reaction. "You're… low-court?"

Fionnlagh backed off, cradling his burned palm.

In the middle of the room, Róise held her stance. Her fear was obvious, but she didn't give. "Who are you?" she spat again. "What do you want?" She dove for the fallen knife and scooped it up to hold out in front of her. She was shaking slightly. "Is this about my brother?" She turned as if she might be able to point the knife at all of them at once.

Fionnuala held up her hands. "We're not here to hurt you."

"No, you're here to hurt *him*," she retorted.

"Your brother," Fionnlagh said. "The Queen's consort, yes?"

Róise's face was flushed with fear and anger, and she set her jaw, evidently refusing to respond.

"Whether it means hurting him or not, he needs to be returned to the Queen." Fionnlagh's face held no pity. "The low courts have been *decimated* since he ran off. I know who I blame."

Róise looked furious, but tears had pricked into her eyes. "That isn't *fair*—"

From the stairs, a voice cut over the woman's words. It was a low voice, and rough—rough like it had been damaged, the sound flowing over cracked gravel. "Róise?"

Áed immediately looked over, tensing—whether to fight or run, he didn't know. Everyone else did the same, both Fionnlagh and Fionnuala instinctively raising their weapons.

The man on the stairs was about as tall as Áed. His hair, a shiny burnt-hazel brown, fell in messy waves to his shoulders, and the hand on the banister was fair and almost delicate. His face was finely-boned—beautiful, actually— and his eyes were graceful.

He looked like hell.

There were purplish circles under his dark-lashed eyes, standing out against the paleness of his skin even in the half-light. When he took another step down the stairs, he moved stiffly.

Ronan sucked in a gasp, his hands flying to his chest. "That's him." He rubbed at his sternum as if he could physically feel the magic. "I'm certain. It's the consort."

If Áed wasn't entirely mistaken, he thought he saw a flicker of a wince pass over the man's face.

Róise had blanched. "Rian," she said breathlessly. "Rian, I'm so sorry, I don't know how they found you—"

Rian.

Somehow, being able to assign a name to the Queen's dog made the whole endeavor seem more real.

Fionnlagh and Fionnuala stood shoulder to shoulder, facing the consort. "*You.*"

"Wait," he said quickly. That voice, even in one word, sent shivers over Áed's skin. It was broken without being harsh, and around its ruined edges, something about it was soft. He held up his hands, and the twins flinched like they expected power to roll forth at the simple motion.

"Don't try anything," Fionnuala growled.

"You couldn't stop me if I did," Rian said. His torn-silk voice sounded tired, but there was fear in it. Áed had not expected the consort to sound afraid. "But if you leave my sister out of this, I won't."

Fionnlagh lowered his sword by a centimeter. "Why would we hurt your sister?"

The consort's fingers were tight on the banister. "It's me you want, isn't it? To bring me back." He swallowed hard. "I'll go with you if you leave her alone." He looked to Róise. "I'm so sorry. I should never have brought you into this." Áed thought he saw the faintest shake in the consort's clenched hands. "I knew they'd come sooner or later."

"Rian, just *go*," Róise said helplessly. "They can't stop you, right? Just go, please—get away, *please.*"

As Áed watched the exchange, he found himself lowering his hands. He was getting the feeling that he was missing something.

Rian turned to them again. "You won't hurt her if I come

quietly, right? Will you swear?"

Fionnuala was blinking. "We were never going to hurt an innocent civilian." She was looking just a little lost. "That's the Queen's job. That's *your* job."

It was the consort's turn to look confused. "You're not with the Queen?"

Fionnuala shook her head.

"They're low-court, Rian," Róise interjected. "But they're here for you; they want to bring you back."

"Hold on a moment," Áed interrupted. He was taking in the consort with narrowed eyes. "Everyone."

To his surprise, the room fell quiet.

"Something isn't right." He shook his head minutely. "This isn't what we expected."

"What *did* you expect, Áed?" Fionnlagh said harshly. While Fionnuala had lowered her guard somewhat, Fionnlagh hadn't backed down a centimeter. "Did you expect the Cur to be less *polite*?"

"I expected him to be less *scared*," Áed retorted. He held out a hand, gesturing to the man on the stairs. "He's terrified, can't you tell?"

Fionnlagh was practically growling. "Maybe he should be." He leveled his sword at the consort's face. "Áed, you don't know what this mutt has done. He's lucky I want this war over more than I want his head on a pike because trust me, I want that *badly*." He took a step forward, keeping his sword pointed at the consort's chest, and addressed him directly. "If threatening your sister is what it takes for you to cooperate, then I'm not so opposed. You're going back to the Queen one way or another. You've let my people die for far too long."

"He can't go back there," Róise pleaded. "Please, Goddess, if you have a soul, don't make him go back there."

"Fionnlagh, please," Áed said. "Stand down." He looked to the consort and then to his sister. "Can we talk? No magic, no weapons. Just talking."

Fionnlagh looked about to retort, but Fionnuala put a hand on his arm.

The consort took a shallow breath, and then he nodded. "We can talk."

"Agree to it all," Fionnuala said warningly. "No magic, no weapons. We won't use them if you won't."

He swallowed. "I won't move to harm you if you don't move to harm my sister or me."

Róise echoed his promise.

Fionnuala nodded, looking warily satisfied. Moving slowly, she set her sword on the ground and straightened slowly. Fionnlagh was growling quietly, a low, constant rumble that set the entire space on edge, but when Fionnuala nudged him, he reluctantly parted with his weapon as well. Áed slung the axe off his back and rested it on the floor.

Róise had backed warily toward the stairs. She nodded at Ronan. "What about him? Whose is he?"

Ronan crossed his arms. "Mine, actually."

The baker looked startled. "Oh. You're—oh, I didn't notice." She glanced at the rest of the party. "He's not enchanted?"

Ronan huffed, answering her himself. "No. And anyway, I'm not armed. I'm sure that's what you were going to ask."

"But you can't promise not to hurt anyone," Róise said worriedly. "Since you're human, your word's not binding."

"I already said I was unarmed. And I only know a little magic—just the spell that led me to him." He pointed to Rian. "As much as I like to think I could be a threat, I'm not actually stupid enough to believe it."

"Let's go upstairs," the consort suggested, breaking in. He

didn't sound much less wary. "Please."

With one last distrustful glance, Róise nodded. She crossed to the stairs and brushed past her brother. "Fine," she muttered.

Fionnuala followed her first, and then Fionnlagh and Ronan. Áed lingered last and paused as he passed the consort. *Rian.* His sister had called him Rian. "Hey," Áed said. Rian had been chewing his lip as everyone had nervously trouped past him, and when he'd turned to return up the stairs, he'd winced at the movement. "Are you all right?"

In response, Rian just chuckled dryly. "I'm not injured, if that's what you mean." His gaze hovered for a moment on Áed's face. "You look…" His brow creased faintly. "Have we met?"

Áed frowned. "No, I don't think so." He'd definitely have remembered meeting someone who looked like Rian.

Rian's eyes flicked between Áed's for a moment longer, and then he was looking away. "Never mind. I thought you looked familiar."

The second floor of the building seemed to be one room, divided down the center by a sheet that had been tacked to the ceiling. One half, nearest the stairs, had a bed, a little desk, and a chair that looked rickety. The other side had nothing to show but a few blankets and a pillow on the floor, tucked into the corner under the steep slant of the ceiling. Rian made his way over to the blankets on the floor and stiffly folded himself into a cross-legged seat.

"I told him he could take the bed," Róise muttered as if someone had accused her of being a bad sister. "But he insisted."

"I don't want to be more trouble than I already am," Rian said. His face was almost lost in the dark, but he pinched the wick of a candle on the floor beside his bedding, and warm light enveloped the space. He settled back onto the sheets and propped his elbows on his knees. "You wanted to talk."

The whole space held an air of uncertainty, with the fluttering candlelight and the glances that flitted between everyone except Rian, with whom none but his sister seemed willing to make eye contact. Áed snuck another glance at him in the nervous silence. He had closed his eyes, holding his hands neatly in his lap, and he held his back straight despite the weariness on his face. It was a breathtakingly attractive face, somehow walking the line between pretty and handsome. Áed knew that even if he'd met Rian on the other side of the veil—even if he hadn't seen his eyes the color of poppies in the sun—he would never have mistaken him for human.

"The war," Fionnlagh said then, breaking the tension. "You know about it."

Rian did not open his eyes. "I know about it."

Áed heard Fionnlagh's teeth grit. "Then what *is* your excuse?"

Rian took a deep breath, his closed eyes tightening just slightly. "I never wanted it to happen this way."

Fionnlagh's fists clenched. He was still standing, his long shadow in the candlelight reaching all the way back to the stairs. "You could stop this, and you haven't."

"I didn't make the Queen's choices." Rian's voice had grown no louder, but it was tight.

Fionnlagh scoffed. "At the very least, don't pretend you disagree with her. You've never had a problem with ruining us before."

It was Rian's turn to clench his fists. "If this is the '*talk*' you wanted," he said, "then I think I would rather not have it after all."

"Wait," Áed interjected. "Fionnlagh, sit down. Please."

"You weren't there, Áed," Fionnlagh said bitterly. He shook his head. "You don't know what there is to be angry at."

"All the same." Áed turned to Rian. "Could we start with why you're here, of all places?"

Rian licked his lips and opened his eyes just a sliver. "I needed somewhere to go. And I didn't think anyone knew about Róise."

"We're half-siblings," Róise said. "But my mother didn't marry his father until a century after he'd become consort, and I wasn't born for another thirty years." She perched on the edge of her bed. "Nobody was paying any attention to our family anymore."

"A century," Áed echoed, marveling a little. It was still strange to fathom the length of so many years. "How long have you been consort?"

Rian sucked in a breath. "One hundred and seventy-two years," he answered. "Six months, and eighteen days." He looked up a little more, and the barest flicker of a smile crossed his lips. "But I stopped counting when I left."

Fionnuala frowned thoughtfully. "That's interesting, though. I remember when the Queen chose you." She tilted her head. "It wasn't always so bad. In the beginning, I mean, you weren't so…" She trailed off.

"Bloodthirsty?" Rian supplied. "Evil?"

"Rian," Róise said chidingly.

"He said it," Fionnlagh muttered.

Fionnuala looked resigned. "I was going to say corrupt." She looked at him with sadness in her face. "You became a cruel man, Your Elegance."

Rian's eyes snapped open, fixing on her immediately. "Don't call me that."

Fionnuala blinked. "What, cruel?"

"'Your Elegance,'" Rian said, biting the end off each word

as if it left a foul taste on his tongue. "I left that title. Don't use it." He took a deep breath, closing his eyes again. "My name is Rian. Please."

Fionnlagh looked thoughtful. "In any case, she makes a good point, Your Elegance." He didn't stop at Rian's subtle flinch but carried on. "I remember you from the choice-day revel. Dressed all in white, I remember. A flirty drunk, and happy. I didn't speak to you, but you seemed decent." He scrutinized Rian, and from his expression, he judged harshly. "Was it the power that turned you? Or the wealth?" He scoffed. "Or is the Queen truly so base that you were ruined by sharing her bed?"

"Fionnlagh," Áed said sharply. "Please."

"Stop, Áed," Fionnlagh snapped. "Why are you taking his side?"

"I'm not," Áed argued hotly. "But you're not being helpful. We have a chance to talk, which we didn't expect. Insulting him isn't going to achieve anything."

Fionnlagh growled softly. Rian didn't flinch.

Fionnuala leaned forward. Her expression was patient. "Your El—*Rian*—" Her eyebrows came together. "I do remember the choice-day revel. All the courts had been invited." Her voice was quiet. "You were smiling, all in white. You danced with half the crowd. I remember *worrying* for you—you looked young and cheerful, and the Queen had gone through a dozen consorts before you, but you looked happy when she kissed you on the dais." She shook her head. "I thought that you seemed lovely, actually. And then, years later, I thought I must have been wrong." Her gaze was searching. "Was I?"

The image that the twins' words painted in Áed's head— that of a young consort who laughed and danced, genuinely delighted to be at the revel held in his honor—did not match the reality of the man with the shadows under his beautiful eyes.

Rian met Fionnuala's gaze. "I don't know," he said softly. "Maybe you were."

CHAPTER THIRTY-SIX
ÁED

In the end, Rian had fallen quiet, and Róise grudgingly seemed to accept that nobody was going to leave. Ronan had started nodding off first, and after that, Fionnlagh had dictated that they would stay the night. Róise had protested, and Rian had watched the proceedings with exhausted eyes. In the end, Áed and Fionnuala ended up sharing the floor upstairs while Fionnlagh and Ronan, under solemn oath not to touch a thing, were sent to sleep downstairs.

All that done, it was impossible to actually sleep. Áed lay on his back with his eyes closed, but he wasn't sure if he even wanted to drift off. So much had happened that he felt the need to sort, to turn events over and over until they made *sense*. Until whatever piece he was missing fell into place, and he could figure out what was going on.

He had prepared himself to confront a monster. A beautiful monster, maybe, but a monster all the same. And maybe Rian was one. Fionnlagh certainly seemed to think so.

But Áed wasn't sure.

You can't be biased because he's beautiful, Áed told himself sternly. If that was what was happening, that wouldn't do at all. That was probably part of the consort's danger, after all.

But it wasn't just that he was beautiful, was it?

Áed turned his head to glance at him, peeking through the dark. Rian was staring at the ceiling, his arms folded over his stomach. For someone who looked as tired as he did, Áed was surprised that he hadn't fallen asleep as soon as the candle went out.

As Áed watched, Rian brought his hands up and covered his face, and Áed thought he heard him sigh. Then he was sitting up, slouching over his knees as he dragged his hands back through his hair. He glanced over at the others in the room—Áed quickly closed his eyes to peek through his lashes—and then, apparently satisfied, he got to his feet. He stepped over his bedding to the window and pushed the pane open. For a few moments, he just propped his elbows on the sill, looking out over the drop to the bottom of the hollowed-out tree.

Then he threw a leg over the bottom of the window and began to climb outside.

Áed's eyes flew wide, and he nearly bolted upright. Was Rian *jumping*? Faerie or not, a fall from this height would break him, if not kill him immediately. But Rian appeared to grab hold of something on the outer wall of the building because the next thing Áed knew, he was outside the window and climbing upward.

Was he running away? Quickly, Áed clambered to his feet and hurried to the window. He looked out hesitantly, and then confidently when he didn't see Rian. Poking his head fully outside, he craned his neck to look upward.

Rian wasn't in sight, but a ladder had been bolted to the side of the house.

Áed eyed it thoughtfully.

This is stupid. You're being stupid. You should at least wake up Fionnuala.

But he already knew what he was about to do.

The ladder creaked quietly as he hooked a wrist over one of the rungs, praying that it would hold him. Biting his lip hard, he managed to get a leg out of the window.

Immediately, his stomach dropped out from under him, and he squeezed his eyes shut. This wasn't the same as descending the stairs on the cliff face. At least there, he'd been able to grip the steps with his forearms while his legs held his weight. Here, though, he *really* wished his crooked, uncooperative hands could properly hold the rungs while he got his feet under him. Even without that, he wasn't as graceful as Rian, and it was all he could do to move quietly enough that Fionnuala didn't wake.

Taking a deep breath, he swung his legs over.

For half of a terrifying second, he was convinced he was falling, but then he felt the bottoms of his feet meet the rungs solidly, and he hooked both elbows over the higher rungs with a gasp while he waited for his heart to slow.

And then, making a point not to look down, he climbed.

When he reached the roof, he peeked over the edge.

Rian was sitting next the chimney that channeled smoke to the outside of the tree itself. He was visible as nothing but a silhouette resting his forearms on his knees. He looked out over the strange, nighttime colony.

Making up his mind, Áed climbed onto the slope of the roof.

Rian didn't look at him, but he didn't pretend to not notice Áed's intrusion. "Áed," he said quietly. "Right?"

Áed wasn't sure what exactly he'd planned to do once he got to the roof, but it was too late to turn back now. He stepped uncertainly toward Rian, moving carefully on the sloped surface. "Yeah."

When Rian didn't reply, Áed lowered himself to a seat a few feet away. For a while, neither of them spoke.

Rian broke the stillness. "What do you want?"

Áed didn't quite know, but he wasn't sure if he should admit to that. Instead, he asked, "Why are you up here?"

Rian shrugged. "I like the view." With a little sigh, he leaned against the chimney. "Night is the only time I can come out of the house, anyway." He fell quiet for a few minutes, and Áed didn't disturb the silence. Then: "I didn't know you were awake."

"I couldn't sleep."

"Áed," Rian said suddenly, and Áed looked to him. His face looked deadly stunning, even weary in the darkness. "Do you know why the Queen is still attacking the lower courts?"

Áed frowned. "To find you?"

Rian shook his head. "No. She knows they don't have me."

"Then..." Áed knew his confusion was plain. "Why would she?"

"It's for me," Rian said. His hands moved to rest on each opposite shoulder, subtly defensive. "She thinks that, eventually, if she hurts enough people, I'll come back. To make her stop."

Áed stared at him. That had never occurred to him. And it said something about Rian's character, that the Queen thought he would want to stop people being hurt, didn't it? But... he studied Rian's face, and reality sank into his chest. "But you won't, will you?" Rian was staring over the edge of the roof to the drop below. "You won't go back."

Once again, Rian shook his head. "No. I won't."

Áed wasn't sure why hearing that hurt. It wasn't anything he hadn't already known. "I see."

"Do you?"

Áed hesitated. "If I don't," he said carefully, "could you tell me what I'm missing?"

For a moment, Rian seemed to pause. Then he looked

away. His eyes were dark, shadowed further under long, black eyelashes. "People are dying, and I've done nothing. And I will continue to do nothing. I will not stop it, even though I can." His eyes slid to Áed and then away again. "Do you truly think I can justify that?"

Áed took a long breath. The night was chilly. "Maybe you don't have good excuses," he said after a minute, "but you do have excuses, right?" It was easier to look over the roof's edge, like Rian, than to look at Rian directly. "Maybe you could tell me one of those."

"Why?" A glossy strand of Rian's dark hair slipped out from behind his ear. "It won't change anything."

Áed looked at him curiously. "You have a chance to defend yourself, and you're not taking it?"

Rian didn't answer.

"Look," Áed said finally. "I know there's something else going on here. You're not who they say you are."

The consort's voice was low and cutting. "You're naïve."

Áed shrugged. "Maybe."

After a long pause, Rian glanced over. "Can I ask *you* a question?"

Áed quirked an eyebrow and held up his hands. "Is it about this?"

Rian nodded. "Forgive me. I was curious."

"I don't mind." Áed held out his hands in front of him, propping his elbows on his knees. "They were smashed when I was younger. Never healed right. With the way they broke, I don't think they ever could have."

It was with very little expression that Rian looked at Áed's hands, but Áed could feel a suppressed flutter of *something* just beneath the shields that masked the rest of Rian's emotion. "Do they still hurt?"

"Sometimes." He folded his arms again, and then paused, wondering if he should ask what he wanted to ask. He wasn't sure how Rian would take it, but he did want to know. "*You're* in pain, aren't you?"

That seemed to elicit a reaction, however muted. Rian blinked and held his knees a little more closely to his chest. "What makes you say that?"

"It's just a guess." In truth, Áed was thinking back to Rian standing on the stairs, ascending each one like his body was fighting him.

Rian let out a little breath. "Yes," he admitted. He was gripping each opposite wrist, and his fingers tightened slightly at the word. "But it's nothing I can't manage."

"What happened?"

Rian made a frustrated face. "Are you always so… talkative?"

Áed laughed dryly. "This isn't much talking, you know."

"Invasive, then."

"It's not like I'm forcing you to answer me."

The look on Rian's face was somewhere between incredulity and annoyance. "Unbelievable." He shook his head wearily. "Fine. You could probably guess, anyway." He waved a slender hand, obviously trying to dismiss it. "I'm ironbound. And like I said, it's nothing I can't handle."

Áed cocked his head. "Ironbound?"

Rian looked faintly surprised. "You don't know what it is?" He frowned. "How?"

"I'm not from here," Áed said lamely, with a half-smile. "Er… sheltered upbringing."

Rian's face didn't lose all of its skepticism, but he let out a short sigh. "There's iron in my system."

Right away, Áed's eyes widened. "Iron in your system? Like, in your body?"

Rian nodded minutely.

"Like… like from eating it?"

Rian looked away. "It can happen many ways." He let

out a breath, resting his chin on his folded arms. "It aches. Makes you tired. Stiff."

"Does it pass?"

"Not that I can tell."

"Damn," Áed murmured when the silence had stretched on for too long. "That sounds awful."

"I didn't tell you so that you could feel sympathy." Rian closed his eyes. "Please save it."

"Oh, of course," Áed sighed. Somehow, he truly didn't believe that Rian was as terrible as he was making himself out to be. "I couldn't *possibly* feel sympathy with someone like you."

Rian winced, and immediately, a stone dropped into Áed's stomach.

"Wait—" He put a hand over his mouth. "That's not—"

But Rian, if he permitted any expression at all, looked dejected. "Of course," he murmured. Any openness that had crept unwillingly to his face was gone, replaced by cold closure.

Áed waved his hands as if he could erase what he'd said. "I'm sorry," he stammered. "I didn't actually mean that—"

"You did," Rian said. His voice was once more distant, exhausted, and void of emotion. "You couldn't have said it otherwise."

Áed opened his mouth and then closed it. "Well," he started, and then hesitated. "Actually, I wouldn't have been able to say, 'I didn't mean it,' either."

Rian blinked, looking at him more fully. "Wait a moment."

"It was sarcasm," Áed said, feeling that on some level, he was only digging himself deeper. "I didn't mean it literally—"

Rian interrupted him sharply. "You can lie."

Ah, hell. "Yeah," Áed said, letting all his breath out with the word. He slumped. "It's not a big secret, really, but Fionnlagh will be angry I told you." At that, a thought struck him, and he sat up straight. "I'm still going to honor the agreement, though! I'm not going to try and hurt you or Róise. Not that I could anyway."

Rian looked stunned. "How can you lie?"

Áed moved to a cross-legged seat, now facing Rian fully. "Here's the thing," he said, pressing his crooked hands together. "When I said I wasn't from here, I really meant it." He huffed a little laugh. "I'm not even from this side of the veil. The two warriors are my half-siblings. But..." He hesitated and then shrugged. "I only traveled here a few *weeks* ago."

"You're... you're *human?*" Rian still sounded disbelieving. Suddenly, his eyes fluttered open wide. "Wait a moment." He pointed to Áed as if he had just recognized him. "You! I *knew* I had seen you before." He looked shocked. "You're the human King!"

"Half-human," Áed said slowly. "Wait a minute, how did you know that?"

Rian drew back as if Áed had struck him. "Ah." He looked away. "I'm sorry. I... spied on you. For the Queen. She likes to keep tabs on what's happening across the veil." He shook his head. "I apologize."

Áed wasn't really sure what to do with that. "Er... see anything embarrassing?"

Rian looked startled that Áed hadn't started shouting at him. "No," he said, sounding a little baffled. "No, I tried to avoid private moments if I could..." He smiled uncertainly. "But you sing to yourself while you're doing paperwork."

Áed blushed. "That's embarrassing."

"I thought it was sweet."

Áed shook his head with a short sigh. "I'm sorry about what I said. About not being able to feel sympathy for you." He pressed a hand to his chest. "I want to stop the war. I *need* to stop the war. But I don't actually hate you the way the others do." He shrugged helplessly. "I just haven't been here long enough. Everything's new. Every*one* is new. And you don't *seem* so bad, so I think part of me wants everyone to be wrong."

This time, Rian just chuckled. His tone had grown a little bitter. "You *are* naïve."

"You already said that."

Rian looked at Áed with guarded curiosity. "You said you've been here for a few *weeks?*"

"Just about."

"Goddess." Rian looked stunned. "You seemed so collected, but you must be overwhelmed."

"I'm good at being both."

"No wonder you actually followed me." He shook his head. "You don't know how terrified you should be."

"You promised not to hurt any of us."

Rian let out a soft, crippled laugh. "Do you know how easy that promise is to break? No, of course, you don't." He dragged his hands through his hair. "All I need to do is interpret something one of you does as 'harm.' I mean, you could *sneeze* on me, and I'd be able to retaliate. That goes both ways. For creatures who can't lie, we're remarkably adept at deceiving, and your siblings know it full well."

It was Áed's turn to blink in surprise. "What was the point, then?"

"It's just—it's what we *do*." Rian ran a finger under one of his shadowed eyes. "Áed, you're playing games in a world where nobody's given you the barest idea of the rules."

"Right," Áed said slowly. "Okay." He narrowed his eyes. "But I'm not *so* stupid." He leveled his stare at Rian, calculating. "Right now, you're distracting me."

Rian's eyebrows lifted a degree.

Áed crossed his arms. It was chilly. "I'm going back to my point. I'm not from here. I don't come with memories of things you've done. I don't assume I know who you are." He crossed his arms. "I want the whole story."

If Áed wasn't wrong, a degree of respect edged into Rian's eyes. At the same time, though, the shadows there deepened. "And what will change if you know it?"

"I'll talk to Fionnuala," Áed replied, thinking on the spot. "My sister. She'd listen more than Fionnlagh. And then she'd talk to Fionnlagh. We'd work from there."

"That doesn't answer my question."

Áed took a quick breath. "What would change?" he echoed. "I don't *know*. I don't know anything yet."

In the dark, Rian's eyes were the dusky blood-red of a marsh cinquefoil, and they didn't break from Áed's face. "You're very different," he said eventually. Once again, he settled with his arms resting atop his knees, holding them to his chest. "Not many people, I think, would want to talk with someone who's done what you know I've done."

"Maybe."

Rian exhaled another chuckle, no less disbelieving than the first. "All right, Áed," he said. His voice was resigned, in the worn-out way of someone who was too tired and too stunned to argue any longer. "What do you want to know?"

CHAPTER THIRTY-SEVEN
ÁED

Rian leaned on the chimney, ankles crossed and knees still tucked up to his chest. Faint wind—from where, Áed couldn't say, if not the breath of the great hollow tree itself—made strands of dark hazel hair flutter into his face, and with a look of faint annoyance, he blew them away. When that didn't work, he captured his hair in a sloppy ponytail at the nape of his neck. Something about the gesture muted the *otherness* of his beauty. He didn't seem quite so unknowable with his hair up, hands tucked into his sleeves, and the hem of his sweater snagged on the rough wood of the chimney.

"What do I want to know?" Áed echoed. Truly, he hadn't thought that Rian would allow him his curiosity. "Oh. Well, actually, a lot." He rubbed his chin. "Why did you run away? And why don't you want to go back to the Queen?"

Rian let out a breath of a dark laugh. "Any question you'd have asked would likely have ended up at that. Excellent job cutting to the pith." He pressed a little further against the chimney. "She's a bad person."

"That was never in doubt," Áed said. His eyes were fixed

on Rian's face, watching carefully for emotion even as Rian didn't meet his gaze.

"She's worse than you know," Rian muttered. He pulled his hands deeper into his sleeves. "And I helped her." He managed eye contact for a brief moment before his gaze darted away like a bird. "Little things, at first. I spied on people. Reported on highborn gossip that she could use for blackmail. But at some point, the things she started asking me to do got worse." He shook his head. "I didn't stop doing them."

"The twins have told me a little of what you did," Áed said.

"It's all true, I'd expect," Rian said. He was staring at his knees. "I came of age at fifteen. My parents had raised me—no, had *birthed* me to be the Queen's consort. Since I was a child, I'd been training in courtly mores and... you know, everything else." He swallowed. "Nobody was surprised when I became a candidate as soon as I came of age." He took a deep breath. "That's *young*."

"Ronan has fifteen," Áed murmured. He couldn't imagine allowing Ronan to even be *considered* for a position like Rian's, much less raising him specifically for the purpose. It made him feel sick.

"It's a good age, I think," Rian said distantly. "At least, it ought to be." A lock of hair slipped out of its tie. "At eighteen, she chose me as her consort. With what I can do, it wasn't a surprise." His gaze was somewhere far away. "At twenty, she asked me to kill."

A chill slipped down Áed's spine. "And did you?"

Slowly, Rian's chin lowered in a minute nod. "I said no at first. I'd never killed anybody before." The quiet weight in his voice would have told Áed, even if he hadn't heard Fionnlagh's accusations, that the first kill had not been

Rian's last. The consort worried at his lip. "But my lady was, uh… persuasive." His face was troubled. "She has a way of getting into people's heads." He trailed off. "Anyway. I did it."

"You killed the person."

Rian nodded again. "I did."

Something was bothering Áed. "Why did *you* have to do it?"

"What do you mean?"

Áed's brow furrowed. "I mean that you were her consort, not her executioner."

"Ah." Rian rubbed his hands together as if his fingers were cold or going numb from being still so long. It wasn't warm on the roof, but it wasn't frigid either, and Áed wondered if being ironbound affected the circulation of Rian's blood. "Well, that's a fair question, but it's one I didn't ask at the time." His eyes were distant. "I was still new to being important. Far away from my old friends, my family. The Queen was all I had. I never wanted to do anything that would make her disappointed in me." He chuckled tightly. "That's pathetic, said out loud." He shivered again. "I killed a faerie because I was afraid she would be disappointed in me."

The nape of Áed's neck was tingling as if sensing danger in Rian's words. Something was wrong here. "What would happen if she was disappointed in you?"

"Oh." Rian looked away. "Back then, nothing, really. But she'd ignore me." He licked his lips. "The royal consort is… exalted. There's no better word for it. Nobody of lower status—so, nobody but the Queen—is permitted to speak to them directly." His face was tight. "It's lonely."

Áed let out a breath. "So what I'm hearing," he said, "is that the Queen cut you off from everyone who might have supported you and then made sure that she was your only source of contact." He blinked. "That's twisted, Rian."

"It wasn't so bad as all that," Rian muttered. "In those days, I loved her."

"Still."

"It doesn't justify murder," Rian said firmly. "The man I killed was a criminal, but his blood is still on my hands. Mine, and nobody else's." He cleared his throat quietly. "After I killed him, I was sick for three days. Didn't get out of bed. Refused to see the Queen. When I finally came out, it was like nothing had happened at all."

"But she asked again," Áed guessed.

Rian nodded. "This time, I really did say no. Stubbornly." He tucked his hands even further into his sleeves. "She actually backed off. After that, she moved onto bigger things that were less direct. Asking me to use my magic to rot low court crops. Or break dams. Things like that. She framed it as court involvement, that I was helping, being a part of things. But I think part of me knew that people were still being hurt—I just couldn't see it happening." He rubbed his eyes with a sleeve-covered hand. "In hindsight, going along with it was the wrong choice."

Áed could only listen, enthralled and horrified.

"She started escalating that, too. It was like she was relying on my relief that I wasn't killing outright to convince me into other atrocities—I could tell myself 'at least it isn't murder.' I was afraid that she'd return to that if I stopped doing as she said." He shook his head. "After a while, it was clear that the things she had me do were playing into some grander scheme, and around that time, I started hearing whispers that the low courts were getting uneasy." He shifted. "This little balancing act—me helping the Queen slowly gain control over the low courts, strategy by strategy, and squashing any rebellion that came—lasted over a century." He looked disgusted with himself. "I got used to it."

"She was using you for your power," Áed said.

"Of course, she was." Rian's voice was bitter. "I knew it from the beginning, from when she first chose me from among the others who'd been presented when we came of age. But I didn't want to see it. Apparently, we can still lie to *ourselves*." He cupped his hands behind his neck, curling over his knees. "But I stopped being able to do that when the first low court pushed back."

"What happened?"

Rian's hands turned to fists. "I had rerouted one of their rivers, and they were being forced to trade through the high court for the resources they lacked. They sent the Queen a formal appeal, requesting that she cease hostilities, and she—Goddess, I remember it so clearly. She turned to me and said, 'They don't know a thing about hostilities.'"

"That doesn't sound good," Áed murmured.

"It wasn't." His entire face was shadowed. "She told me to set their mound on fire."

Áed gasped.

"I didn't do it," he said quickly. "At least, not then. But—" He swallowed and tried again. "But that was when—well, things started…" It seemed he was having trouble getting the words past his lips. "Things started crumbling."

"What does that mean?"

"I really wouldn't do it," he said. "It was too much. Too big. Too many people would die. I'm high court. My fire hurts low court fae. I—I couldn't do it." His eyes were growing bright. "It was the beginning of the end, I think. That moment."

"Rian," Áed said. His eyes were wide and worried in the

darkness, and he resisted the urge to creep closer. "What did she do?"

Rian's breath hitched. "Well. First, she hit me." One hand migrated unconsciously to the side of his head, where his hair was pulled back. "She had a scepter with an iron length. Just for intimidation—mostly. She hit me with it." His slender fingers loosed his hair from its tie, and, letting it fall through his fingers, he lifted a section from the side of his head. "Here."

Áed's hands flew to his mouth.

The scar cut across Rian's scalp like a burned whip-slash. From its beginning just behind the top of his ear to its end near the base of his skull, the pale mark sliced brutally.

Áed heard his own low, horrified sound—another one of those peculiarly inhuman noises that seemed to come on instinct—and Rian hummed quietly in response.

He let his hair down again and re-fastened it into its tie. "Apparently," he said, "burning the Meadow mound was important to her plan. A show of dominance, maybe. I never learned. She closed me in my chambers and told me in no uncertain terms to do as she said."

"Did you do it?"

"Sort of." Rian laced his fingers neatly together, looking ashamed. "The mound burned, but I tried to warn the Meadow fae first. Hopefully, they got out."

Áed closed his eyes, holding out a hand as if he could pause the conversation. "How is it that you could set fire to a mound from your *bedchamber*?"

"I had something to look at, to aim. Something from there. It was a leaf of grass, I believe. That's all I needed." Rian's eyes were downcast, and his voice was muted. "I am fairly powerful."

That sounded like an understatement. "I'm sorry if this

is an awful question," Áed said hesitantly, "but if you're so strong…"

Rian seemed to guess quickly where the question was leading, for his eyes darkened. "Why didn't I just overpower the Queen?" he finished.

Áed nodded.

Rian slumped. "I… I need you to understand," he said. "I had spent over a *century* speaking to nobody else. What I felt for her, I thought was love." He sounded miserable. "She'd… she'd done well with me, you know." A faint tremor shook him. "They call me her dog. I'm sure you've heard. And it was a deserved title." He held himself tightly. "She could sic me on anybody, and I wouldn't bite her hand."

"Rian," Áed said quietly. The consort's agitation was breaking through his careful shields. Áed could feel it rolling over him, tumultuous and dark.

Rian seemed to make an effort to steady his breathing. "I think, though, that she did wonder the same thing that you did. When I would snap. Turn on her. And at the same time, I believe she realized it would be much easier to *make* me do what she wanted than carefully press against my limits."

"Oh no," Áed whispered. He didn't want to know what happened next.

It was with hands that slightly shook that Rian tugged at his sleeves. "There was one servant," he said. "We never spoke, of course. But he would leave little things for me— flowers, pretty stones, that sort of thing—and I'd leave him things too, for him to find when he came by to do his chores. Drawings, mostly." He pressed his face into his sleeve-covered hands. "The Queen noticed."

"Was she angry?"

Rian shook his head. "No. She was *pleased*. And that was worse." He grimaced. "The next time I checked the spot where we left our little gifts, there was a note there from the Queen. My friend's life was dependent on my cooperation." He sounded slightly choked. "That evening, I tried to warn him. I went to the servant's quarters, asking after him. I wanted to tell him to run, if he could." He curled himself tighter. "Nobody would talk to me. And finally, one of the castle guards spotted me, and—" he broke off raggedly, wiping at his eyes. "I'm sorry," he managed. "This is pathetic."

Tentatively, Áed moved so that he sat nearer. "It's not pathetic," he said quietly. "This is just... this is more complicated than I'd imagined." He nearly made to stand, to close the distance between them, but then thought better of it. "Are you all right?"

A crooked, tearful smile crept over Rian's face. "Good question."

"Maybe a stupid question. I'm sorry."

"You don't have to be kind," Rian said, wiping once more at his eyes. His hair was slipping into his face again. "When the guard reported what I was doing to the Queen, she came within minutes. And then she found my friend and brought him to the middle of the room and just—" He wavered. "She made eye contact with me the entire time she flogged him."

Áed's breath caught in his throat.

"I could have done something," Rian said. "I had the same power then as I do now. The Queen was in my line of sight; I could have *made* her stop. But I didn't." He shook his head bitterly. "I just... I couldn't imagine harming her any more than I could imagine cutting off my own hands. Looking back, I don't know if that was something she did— she has more astute control over emotions than any faerie I've met—or just my own weakness." A tear traced down his cheek. "One of my many flaws," he said, "is that I can't *heal*. I have no control over creating life, even on the scale of new skin in a wound—that's too close to the Goddess's domain. I couldn't even speed up my friend's recovery. I tried to take away his pain, but... I don't know if it worked."

Stiffly, Rian pushed himself more firmly against the chimney as if seeking something stable.

"After that, my lady dragged me away. Back to my own chamber. She still didn't even seem angry, which was... unnerving." He gave a strangled laugh. "Not that I had many nerves to spare, at that point." He composed himself, more or less, reigning in the choked laughter. "I spent the next fifty years there."

Áed drew back. "Wait, you what?"

Rian found the cuff of his trousers and began to roll it up. "The next fifty years. In that room." He swallowed. "Already, she had stopped coming to me for... you know. What I offered. As her consort. It had been years already—since the incident with the Meadow mound. I'd have been willing, but she didn't come." He ran his tongue over his lips. "In hindsight, that was for the best. She never hurt me *that* way. But it was at this point I realized that in everything but name, I'd stopped being her consort." He finished with his cuff and extended his leg with a wince. "I still don't know quite what I was."

Curious and half-appalled, Áed leaned over to look at Rian's leg.

When he did, he gasped. "Rian." He looked up from the scar, so similar in texture to the one on Rian's head and so, so much worse. "What made that?"

"An iron shackle." Rian's voice was carefully flat. "It was connected to an iron chain, connected to an iron weight. Not complicated."

"But—" Áed managed. "But it's *iron*. You—you had an iron shackle for *fifty years*?"

"Give or take." Rian still spoke with deliberate steadiness.

"That's why," Áed said. He couldn't stop gaping at the reddish, rippled scar tissue that encircled Rian's ankle as if the cuff was still there. It looked healed but fresher than his other injury. "That's why you're ironbound."

Rian nodded. "It never healed while the shackle was on. How could it? The cuff rusted, rubbed into an open wound... you know." He shrugged stiffly. "After fifty years, there was enough iron in my blood to make it painful to move at all."

"That's *horrible*."

"It hurt," Rian said simply.

"What did the Queen *gain* from that?" Áed still couldn't tear his eyes away from the scar. He had never seen one so bad. It looked like someone had tried to cut off Rian's foot with a white-hot snare.

"Safety," Rian said. "From me. And control." He wouldn't meet Áed's eyes. "I don't know what you've heard about my magic, but it probably isn't entirely correct. I have a lot of flexibility, true, but there are three real restrictions. I already told you I can't create life. Second, I can't cast anything on the veil, on iron, or on myself. And third, I can't cast on something without having a connection to that thing." He looked frustrated. "I couldn't cast on the Queen so long as I couldn't see her or get my hands on anything she'd touched." He huffed. "Not counting myself, of course. I tried that. Didn't work." He drew his leg back toward him and set about rolling his pants back down. "After a while, hurting me couldn't make me do what she wanted anymore." A shudder that looked quite involuntary wracked him from head to toe. "I mean, she didn't *stop*. Like I said, she has power over emotions like no faerie I've ever met. I'd have chosen physical pain if I could. Every time." He clasped his hands tightly. "Anyway. She took to sending all of my orders by way of the servant who'd once been my friend. That way, if I ever refused to do as she said, I could see the ways she hurt him." His hands fisted the fabric of his trouser leg. "I learned my lesson quickly. She cut out one of his eyes." His own eyes were bright, still looking somewhere out into the distance. "I didn't argue after that. And I did terrible, terrible things."

There was an element of Rian's story that felt... desperate. As if no matter how little he wanted to speak of it, the past had been pressing at him for so long that the words came on their own.

Áed couldn't help it any longer. He got to his feet and crossed to the chimney. Rian looked at him, blinking out of the well of his own misery, as Áed lowered himself to a seat next to him. He didn't brush against Rian's shoulder, but he was close enough to feel the other man's warmth through the chilly night air. Rian looked absolutely confused. "What are you doing?"

Áed shrugged.

Rian laughed humorlessly. "Why aren't you moving *farther away*?"

"Are you going to hurt me?"

"No."

"Then why should I move away?"

Rian stared at him blankly. "Did you not hear what I've been saying?"

Áed nodded. He leaned against the chimney, crossing his arms over his middle. "How did you get out?"

Rian glanced at him, then looked away, then back. He didn't seem to know what to do with Áed being so close. It looked very much like part of him wanted to close the little space, and the rest wanted to run. "I—well." His eyes were dark, but they still shone. "It had been fifty years. And everything hurt, all the time. And my being *alive* wasn't really…" He swallowed. "People were suffering because I was alive," he said softly. "I was so tired."

Áed's heart stuttered. "You didn't."

Rian's voice barely broke the silence. "I did." He exhaled tremulously. "High fae are hard to kill. But my old friend, he—he helped me." One hand traveled unconsciously to his throat. "One nail," he said. "And one pinch of salt. I had rowan, because it was in all my meals to keep me docile, and…" His fingers tightened slightly around the column of his neck. "I swallowed it."

"You… swallowed a nail." Áed knew he sounded exactly as horrified as he felt.

Rian's chin bobbed in affirmation. Suddenly, his ruined voice—so clearly once velvet—made sense. "I didn't imagine it would take much. There was already so much iron in me." He rubbed his fingertips under his eyes, as if he could work away the dark circles there. "But instead of dying, I came around in some healer's cell."

"You sound disappointed," Áed said softly.

Rian was looking down, but his eyes slid over to Áed anyway. "I was." His breath slipped out in a mirthless chuckle. "Devastated, actually."

"Rian," Áed murmured. Tentatively, he let his shoulder touch Rian's. Rian shivered hard, eyes squeezing closed, but he didn't move away.

For at least a minute, neither of them said anything else. Rian was stiff next to Áed, and only the quiet sound of his breathing broke the stillness.

"They'd taken the shackle off," he said eventually. "And the healer's cell wasn't so guarded as my own chambers." His shoulders rose and fell. "If I couldn't die, at least I could run." He stared into the middle distance. "I barely remember it, actually. Running. I wasn't all right."

"I'd imagine not." Áed didn't think he could entirely wrap his head around what Rian was telling him. "That's when you came here?"

"It must have been." Rian ran a palm over the roof's surface. "Like I said. The memory is choppy." He turned toward Áed but didn't break the minimal contact with his shoulder. "I want to help. I swear it. I can't undo the damage I did, but I don't want to be…" His ragged voice faltered. "I don't want to be so dark."

"But you can't go back."

Rian's eyes were helpless. "I can't. I'm so sorry."

Áed shook his head. "No. No, I understand better now." He pressed gently against Rian's shoulder.

"I haven't been doing anything since I got here, though," Rian said unhappily. "I tried to get my hands on something low-court, so maybe I could cast some kind of protection, but I couldn't get anything without leaving, and my sister doesn't have many connections. She's a *baker*. I don't want her involved with this, anyway. I want there to be more *I* can do." He pressed his palms into his eyes. "But instead, I do nothing."

"Well," Áed said. He didn't know the right thing to say. If there *was* a right thing to say. "We're here, now. At the least, we can give you something to cast from. And maybe we can help make a plan." He examined Rian's face, taking in the lines of it, broken and breathtaking in one. "Maybe we can help you, too."

Rian met his eyes, searching, like he expected to find deception there.

Áed extended a hand. "Friends?" The word came out uncertainly.

Rian eyed his hand skeptically. "I don't feel right letting

myself be your friend," he admitted. "I'm sorry. I just... I don't know if I can."

Áed lowered his hand a degree. "Okay. That's okay." He offered it again. "Then... allies?"

At that, Rian held his breath. Then hesitantly—gently, like he wasn't sure how best to touch it—he accepted Áed's hand. "Allies." He pronounced it as if the word felt odd in his mouth. "All right."

CHAPTER THIRTY-EIGHT
RONAN

Ronan could have cut the tension with a bread knife.

In the window of the bakery door, the sign was flipped to 'Closed,' and at the table in the kitchen, everyone sat without speaking. The only noise was the sound of the slate ovens, which filled the air with the smell of fresh bread.

It was *intensely* awkward.

Áed was the only one not seated. He stood at the head of the table with his hands braced on it, staring at Fionnlagh specifically. Fionnlagh, for his part, stared at the edge of the table as if perhaps the answers to everything were written on it, and beside him, Fionnuala stared blatantly at Rian, her mouth slightly open. Rian stared resolutely at his hands folded on the table, and his sister stared at the twins with her arms crossed righteously over her chest.

Everything was in the open.

Róise broke the silence. "I told you so."

"This is…" Fionnuala braced her elbows on the table and shoved her fingers into her hair. "This is so much more than I realized." She looked up to glance around. "More than any of us realized."

"Can we think objectively?" Fionnlagh tried. He sounded

rather stunned. "This is new information. We need to process this."

"What's there to think about?" Róise said, crossing her arms even harder. "It's obvious now, isn't it? That he can't go back there?"

Rian himself didn't respond, only nudged his sister. "Róise, the bread's done."

"Thank you." Róise sent one last glare over the table before sweeping up to take the loaves out of the ovens. "That's right, though, isn't it? You won't try anything, now?"

Fionnlagh opened his mouth, but before he'd even planned on saying anything, Ronan had interrupted. "We can't." He sat up in his chair, feeling everyone's attention suddenly on him. "I mean, even if we ignored the fact that he was being abused, he's *way* too powerful to just hand over for the Queen's use." He winced apologetically. "That sounded horrible."

"It's fine," Rian murmured. "I take your meaning."

"It's a fair point," Fionnlagh said. He shook his head decisively, his gaze focusing. "But ultimately, it is irrelevant."

Rian looked up sharply, clearly anticipating the worst.

Fionnlagh went on, sighing heavily through the words. "The royal consort is meant to be treasured. Loved. Not badly mistreated." His expression was dark. "Even if it weren't for your power, it wouldn't be right to force you back. That isn't a level to which we can stoop."

Rian slumped again, apparently in relief. "Oh. Good." He nodded. "That's good."

Fionnlagh steepled his fingers, pressing their tips against the bridge of his nose. "Unfortunately, that leaves us with no plan."

"That," Áed cut in, and a smile began to steal over his features, "is where I had a couple of ideas."

〰〰

"I'll fix it, I'll fix it." Rian put an arm over his sister's shoulders. "Promise, all right?"

"You had better," Róise said indignantly. "But next time, use parchment, for the sake of the Goddess."

"You don't have any," Rian responded. "But I promise, I'll put your table back in order as soon as we're finished."

Ronan leaned over the table, tracing the glittering black lines that had manifested in the wood at Rian's touch. They didn't feel any different from the rest of the surface—just smooth, unvarnished wood—but they sprawled over the table in a complex map, complete with place names marked in a delicate hand. "You really are magic," Ronan said in awe. He paused his examination of the table. "Do you use spells?"

"Not really," Rian said. He crossed from his sister to the table, and Ronan observed absently that he limped. "Humans use them because their nature struggles to channel raw magic on its own. Fae don't have that problem."

"Not that any of them could do *this*."

Rian chuckled quietly. "No," he agreed. "Not that they could."

"Anyway," Fionnlagh put in deliberately. He stood over the table on the opposite side, looking very much like the warrior he was, with his shoulders wide and his demeanor imposing. "Could we please—?"

"Right." Rian extended a hand. "If I could have something of yours, please."

Fionnlagh tugged at the hem of his shirt and twisted it deftly. The material tore. He ripped off a thin strip and dropped it into Rian's hand.

"Thank you." Rian's fingers closed around the fabric.

"Will that protect the low courts?" Ronan asked.

Haltingly, Rian shook his head. "Not as a whole. With a focus like this—" he held up the fabric—"I can't extend a casting over such a large domain. But I can defend the Bone mound, at the least."

"Better than nothing," Fionnuala murmured.

Rian closed his eyes, and for a moment, seemed to concentrate. When he opened them again, and his hand with them, the scrap of fabric slid to the table, charred. "There."

That hadn't looked like much, and Ronan examined the fabric scrap curiously. "What did you do, exactly?"

"I made a barrier. None who wish it harm can enter the mound." He shook his head. "I wish I could do more, but even I have limits. Besides—" He looked suddenly chagrined. "In magic, as in life, it's much easier to destroy than to defend."

That settled over the room for a number of heartbeats.

"Well," Fionnuala said thoughtfully. "Speaking of destruction, I would be very interested in talking about whatever other options we might have." She inclined her head to Rian. "If you ask me, I'd much rather have an ally than a bargaining chip. With him on our side, I'm sure this war will end sooner in our favor."

"I'll help," Rian said. If Ronan wasn't mistaken, there was more life in his rough voice that morning than there had been the previous night, but still, he approached his next words almost tentatively. "I only request that you don't ask me to kill."

"You won't kill?" Fionnlagh leaned forward, and Ronan didn't need to sense emotions to detect his surprised disapproval. "Not even the people who held you chained in iron for half of a century?"

"I—" Rian faltered, looking a little cowed. "I've done enough harm."

"There are ways to help without killing," Áed interjected

hurriedly. He stepped forward to gesture at the table and tapped the lines upon it. "Rian, maybe you could…?"

"Of course." Rian brushed a palm over the marked wood, and Fionnlagh and Fionnuala leaned closer to see. "This is a map of the Queen's grounds. If we get some paper, I can copy it for you so that Róise can have her table back, but until then…" He tapped the table. The lines he indicated flushed glimmering crimson at his touch, and Ronan made out what looked like the outline of a castle floor—a simple, crooked square structure with rounded protrusions at each corner that looked like the footprints of towers, encircled by a wall. Another odd polygon nested within the uneven square, indicating a courtyard. "This is the castle." He let his fingertip drag between the lines of the walls. "It's the oldest construction on this side of the veil, which likely means it's the oldest in the world. It was ancient when the eldest living faerie was born, which means it's stood for more than eight thousand years." His eyes flicked up to glance at the surrounding people. "This is where the Queen lives. Where I lived."

"If it's old, is it fragile?" Ronan asked thoughtfully.

Rian shook his head. "The opposite. This castle has survived earthquakes, sieges, and once, someone detonating an explosive in the vaults. It's not fragile because it's old—it's old because it isn't fragile."

"So destroying the castle won't work."

"Well—no. But destroying the castle shouldn't be your goal, anyway." Rian said. He looked to Fionnlagh and Fionnuala. "What you need to do is seize it."

Ronan let that sink in for a moment and then turned back to the table-turned-map. The castle itself was surrounded by outbuildings, a wide moat like one plucked from a story, and a single narrow bridge. He couldn't claim to be an expert at this sort of thing, but between the thick walls and the moat, it was already looking extremely hard to assault. And that wasn't even factoring in any internal defenses that didn't appear on the map. "Seize it?" he repeated distantly.

Rian nodded. "The citadel hasn't ever fallen to an invading army. But if you take the castle—" He shrugged one shoulder. "The war's as good as won. The Queen might be powerful without her castle, but her *forces* aren't. Eliminate the power of her followers, and she's on her own. Even she can't stand up against all the low courts alone."

"We've considered storming the castle," Fionnuala said with a frown. "But we've dismissed those plans. As you said, it's never been done."

"Wouldn't it be nice to be the first?" Rian pointed to the map again, where the bridge began to cross the moat. "Guard towers here are the first line of defense, and the bridge itself can be raised. The moat, incidentally, has a water horse in it."

Áed scowled. "I hate that."

Rian dragged his finger over the bridge, to where two towers stood guard on either side of the outer wall. "This is the second defense. The curtain wall itself is around two meters thick." Again, his finger moved. "Here. The third defense." He tapped it twice. "To get into the keep, you pass through here. Three gatehouses on each side, full of soldiers. Three portcullises—solid iron. And before each one, a trapdoor above."

"Above?" Ronan said, frowning. "Wouldn't a trapdoor be more useful *below* you?"

"Not so much," Rian said. "From below, nobody can pour molten lead over your head."

"Ah." Ronan looked at the little gateway with new appreciation. "I see."

"It goes without saying," Rian went on, "that any army within range will be taking fire from all along the walls, and there are arrow slits in the walls of every entrance passage." He leaned back. "Are you with me so far?"

Fionnuala bent at the waist, propping her elbows on the table. "All you've described is more or less what we already knew. We didn't have the details, but..." She looked to Fionnlagh for affirmation, and she got it with his displeased nod. "It still sounds like we don't have much of a chance."

"That's just the thing, though," Rian said. He sounded almost excited, his rusty voice brighter than Ronan had heard it before. "Those are *siege* defenses."

Ronan studied the map thoughtfully. "All right," he said slowly. "They're prepared for an army." He looked up, eyes narrowed. "So what *aren't* they prepared for?"

Rian's mouth actually twitched into the barest hint of a smile. "That," he said softly, "is the right question."

}}}

Darkness had fallen, and candles burned quietly in the room when Róise finally interrupted the conversation around the table. She dropped a stack of parchment onto the marred surface and put her hands on her hips as everyone, startled from their planning, looked up at her. She pointed to the parchment imperiously. "There. Unhand my table, Rian."

Rian took the parchment with a muted chuckle. He pressed the stack flat to the surface of the table, and as Ronan watched, the lines in the wood seemed to slither into the creamy paper. Rian handed a leaf to each of them, the parchment now impressed with the map that had a moment ago marred the table's surface.

Both of the twins accepted their maps, clearly still deep in thought, and turned to each other, conversing quietly. Áed sidled next to Rian.

"Hey," Áed said, and Rian inclined his head slightly to acknowledge his presence, not looking away from his own map. "Are you going to be all right with this?"

"I don't know what you mean."

"I mean going back to the castle." Áed's face was concerned, cast in gold and black shadow where the candlelight flickered. "After everything."

Rian's expression didn't change. "I'll manage," he said, and the words, though not unkind, were short. "Thank you for your concern."

"If you change your mind—"

"I won't."

Áed appraised him, worried and impressed in equal measure. Then he turned away, brushing Rian's shoulder in what *could* have been an accident if Ronan hadn't been quite certain that it wasn't. He made his way across the room to Ronan. "And what about you?" he said, easily dropping an arm over Ronan's shoulders. The motion was familiar, and Ronan didn't shrug it off. He might have, he realized, back in the palace. Back home, where all he wanted was the freedom to go somewhere else. Now that he *was* somewhere else, the impulse to resist Áed's protective affection was much dampened. He understood it better, perhaps. "Are you up for this?"

Ronan nodded. "I couldn't say no, could I?"

"I'm sure we could sort it out if you did."

"No." Ronan stood up straighter, which really only served to remind him that Áed, who wasn't particularly tall, stood over him by six inches even when Ronan's posture was perfect. He slumped again, conceding to live in denial. "No, I can do it. I *want* to do it."

"It's dangerous."

"You're worrying."

"Of course, I am." Áed cuffed him on the back of the head, not hard. "*Amadán.*"

Ronan breathed a chuckle. It *was* dangerous. They had

arranged a good plan, poring over the table as the evening waxed—or at least, Ronan thought so. But it was a dangerous one. There wouldn't be one of them who didn't risk their life.

As Áed and Ronan talked, Fionnlagh was donning his cloak. He was off, Ronan knew, to meet Éamon and Erin and travel with word back to the Bone mound.

"Wait!" Rian said hurriedly. He cast about quickly, and with cupped hands, captured a dimmed, floating pollen sphere. Fionnlagh, and indeed the rest of them, watched curiously as he opened his hands to let the pollen float in the cage of his fingers. Closing his eyes, he blew on it, and the pollen tumbled confusedly about before landing on Rian's palm. Once it had settled, Rian pinched it gently, and with a twist, began to wind from it a thread, much like plucking at an old sweater. He worked the thread into a loop, opening it with his fingertips until the little pollen was a bead on a circle of luminous yarn. He held it flat in his palm, and as he did so, it glowed faintly. The room pulsed with quiet light as the other spheres glowed in tandem.

He offered it to Fionnlagh. "Wear this on your wrist."

Fionnlagh accepted it. "Why?"

"Communication." Rian plucked another pollen from the air and quickly repeated what he had done to the first. He held it up and tapped it purposefully with the pad of his finger. The one in Fionnlagh's hand glowed happily. "See?"

Ronan's eyes were wide. "Is that magic?"

"It is, but not mine." He tapped an absentminded pattern on his own pollen bracelet, making Fionnlagh's flutter with light. "The pollen is already all connected—that's its own magic. As natural to the tree as fire is to any of us."

A thought struck Ronan suddenly. "Like the crystals at the Moon mound!" he said. "They glowed too, actually."

"Oh, that's an example. Yes." Rian nodded. "It isn't so uncommon. Fae tend to live in places with a lot of natural magic." He looped his pollen bracelet around his wrist. "It's useful. You can exploit the connectivity of things like the pollen or the moon crystals—if you know how, you can make the connection to do lots of things." He held up his wrist. "If I had more time, I could use these to connect our voices, so that I could speak to you, or even speak *through* you, using your mouth. Or I could link our minds, though that's an invasion of privacy in my eyes. The possibilities go on." He tapped his bracelet again. "We won't need that, though. It'd take weeks for a connection of that complexity to mature. Just signal us when you're at the Bone mound and again when you're ready."

Fionnlagh nodded and experimentally touched his own bracelet. Rian's glowed. "I'll tap three times," he said, and demonstrated the pattern. "So you know it isn't an accident."

"Very good." Rian was already busying himself with making more little communicators, and passing them out among the rest of the group. Ronan drummed a little rhythm onto his, and it flickered on the wrists of each other person. "Don't lose those."

Fionnuala crossed the room to give her brother a parting hug, and Fionnlagh, after she released him, offered his hand to Áed. When Áed accepted it, his half-brother pulled him into a brief embrace. "Fionnuala will be with you," Fionnlagh said, "but mind yourself." He put a hand on Áed's shoulder and held him back. "Be safe, Áed."

"You too." It sounded like there was emotion behind Áed's words.

Fionnlagh shook Ronan's hand, offered a slight, formal bow to Róise and nodded to Rian with an unreadable expression on his face.

Then he left.

And the plan was in motion.

CHAPTER THIRTY-NINE
ÉAMON

At first, the waiting hadn't been too unpleasant. When Áed, Ronan, and the Fionns had left, the quiet had sunk in quickly, settling around the undergrowth like a second layer of fog. It was easy to feel small among the giant trees. He and Erin had made a makeshift camp with the supplies they had. Neither of them knew how long they were expected to wait, and at first, they had talked to pass the time. Erin was interesting to talk to—the Sand court, where she'd grown up, was apparently one of the only nomadic courts, and she had been to places from the coast of some great Sea that Éamon had never heard of to a desert that spanned farther than could be walked in a month.

Eventually, though, even the chatting had died out.

It hadn't been too long, he didn't think. A day, a night, another day—and now night was falling again. He hoped that nothing bad had happened. Surely, they would be coming back soon.

He was fairly certain that made sense, but it was difficult to tell. His head, like the forest around them, felt a bit misty. Erin had noticed his fogginess, he was sure. She'd found a sheltered, stony hollow half a day earlier and told him he could sleep there when night fell. She kept watch; she was still most comfortable being awake after the sun went down. When he'd drifted off, though, feeling as if he was being pulled underwater, his dreams had been full of dull pain and the pulsating light of a thousand pale, jagged stones. He had managed, with nauseating effort, to claw himself back to consciousness, where he woke sweating and sick. He hadn't let himself sleep again, even though the mist in his mind seemed to be calling him louder all the time.

Erin said maybe he'd caught something from the icy lake water and his fight with the water horse. Éamon had told her he didn't want to talk about icy lake water and his fight with the water horse.

So now they both sat quietly, and the wait dragged on.

Noises came from the undergrowth behind them.

Erin was on her feet in a heartbeat, moving without a sound. She produced a knife from somewhere while Éamon used the stone wall of the outcropping to help himself up. Echdían snorted.

"Hold," came a familiar voice from the brush. "It's Fionnlagh."

Éamon relaxed in relief, and Erin lowered her blade. "Just Fionnlagh?" she said as he moved into the clearing. He disturbed ferns at his passing, whose brittle fronds sent whorls silently through the mist. "Where's everyone else?"

"With the consort," Fionnlagh said. "It's a long story."

"They're safe?" Éamon demanded.

"Yes," Fionnlagh said. "No need to worry."

"And the consort?" Erin said, hurrying around Fionnlagh as he crossed the clearing to take stock of their shabby camp. "What happened?"

"It's a long story, and I'll tell it as we move."

"Move? Are we meeting Áed and the rest?"

The warrior shook his head. "We're going back to the Bone mound. We have a message to deliver."

Éamon looked at the sky. "Right now? It's almost nightfall."

"It's an important message." Fionnlagh unwound Echdían's reins from the tree they'd tied him to and offered them to Éamon. "I told you, I'll explain on the way."

"I have my eye on you," Erin said darkly, and Fionnlagh blinked at her.

Fionnlagh looked at her blankly. "You… what? Why?"

Erin only stared him down with crossed arms. "We're not going back across that lake, right?"

Fionnlagh sighed heavily. "We are." He held up a finger, keeping Erin from protesting as Éamon was certain she was about to. "But only because Éamon said that the water horse is no longer a threat."

"I'll stab it again if it is," Éamon muttered. The bravado was mostly false, but it did feel good.

Fionnlagh rolled his eyes. "Come on," he said. "We don't have time to waste."

⟨⟨⟩⟩

It was a hard trip. They crossed the lake without molestation, but unlike the previous time, they did not stop to rest for more than a couple of hours for the entirety of the trip. Fionnlagh, unsurprisingly, held up the best, but Erin needed to take some time riding in front of Éamon on the horse, who was flagging as well. Éamon didn't think horses were supposed to work so hard for so long, but Echdían stepped on as if encouraged by pure stubbornness.

Several times, Éamon caught himself drifting. It made sense, he thought, given the strain of travel, but he caught himself each time just before he slipped out of the saddle. Erin noticed. "Are you always this tired?" Her eyes narrowed thoughtfully. "You were like this back at the mound, too."

He shook his head. "It's just the stress."

"You get sleepy when you're stressed?"

Éamon shrugged. "Maybe."

"Huh." Erin frowned. "Weird. I always get really jumpy when I'm stressed." She grinned at Fionnlagh. "Jumpy and inclined to violence."

"Contain yourself," Fionnlagh muttered. He had been looking at Éamon sideways now and then, when he thought Éamon wouldn't notice. "Éamon, how *have* you been feeling?"

That was such a strange question coming from Fionnlagh that Éamon only blinked. "What do you mean?"

"Have you been feeling well?" Fionnlagh tried again. "Anything unusual?"

Éamon looked at him skeptically. "Are you concerned for my well-being, or is there something else going on here?"

Fionnlagh huffed. "Oh, forget I asked."

That, as it chanced, was not easy to do.

It happened when Éamon reached to accept a waterskin that Erin passed to him. The feeling was sudden, bowling him over; it cut him off in the middle of his 'thank you.' It was exhaustion if exhaustion were *forceful*. It rolled over his mind like a blanket had been pulled over his awareness. His vision blurred as his muscles went weak.

This time, he couldn't stop himself from keeling out of the saddle. He thought maybe Fionnlagh caught him because he couldn't feel himself hit the ground.

Piercing pain shot through his head like a bolt from a bow. He gasped, jerking a hand up weakly to his eyes only to have it fall back by his side. The powerful exhaustion seemed to rob his body from his control. His vision sharpened without his permission, and he found himself focusing on Erin's worried face before his eyes flicked involuntarily to

Fionnlagh. "My head—" he managed. His voice came out strangled, barely audible. In fact, he wasn't sure he *did* hear it. Had he spoken? "My *eyes*—"

Something covered his eyes. A hand, maybe, or a cloth, he didn't know, because for just a moment, the stabbing pain increased enough for him to choke on an agonized cry. And then it was gone.

The exhaustion rolled back, lifting its grip from his mind, and he was immediately aware of his chest heaving.

Without a moment to hesitate, he rolled to the side just in time to vomit onto the forest floor.

Erin was swearing. "What the—Goddess, *what?* What just happened? Éamon?"

"I'm okay," Éamon panted. As soon as the words left his mouth, he wasn't sure how true they were. Aside from the hot nausea rolling in his gut, the weakness of his body and the fact that his mind felt almost *bruised*, he felt... violated.

"Here," Erin said, and she pressed the waterskin into his hand. "Drink."

Éamon did. Whatever was covering his eyes slipped, and warm, rough fingers brushed it back up. "Keep your eyes covered," Fionnlagh's voice came. The warrior's tone was hard enough to make Éamon flinch.

"Why?" Erin asked, voicing the question Éamon had been about to ask.

"I think it'll help," Fionnlagh's answer came. Éamon was getting better at recognizing faerie non-answers, and he touched the cloth with a shaking hand.

"What's happening?" he said. His throat felt dry despite the water. "Do you know something about this?"

"Has this happened before?" Fionnlagh's voice had lost none of its harshness.

Éamon shook his head. "No. No, never like this." Being in the dark felt somehow soothing to his head, but it didn't do any favors for the panic rising in a jagged lump in his throat. "Fionnlagh, do you know what's happening to me?"

Fionnlagh only sighed, and then there was a heavy hand on Éamon's shoulder. "Nothing that's your fault," he said. He sounded sorry in a way that Éamon couldn't understand.

"What does that mean?" he asked and wasn't embarrassed to hear the tremble of fear that leached into his voice. It was honest.

"Don't move the blindfold," was all Fionnlagh said. "I'll help you back onto your horse." His voice was once again grim. "We need to get back to the mound."

⟩⟩⟩

Iarlaith was the first to greet them. Éamon recognized the sound of his cane on the damp earth and then his voice as he hurried across the field to meet them. "Fionnlagh?" Iarlaith demanded, and Éamon lifted the blindfold just a sliver so he could see what was going on. "It's you, isn't it? I heard the lookouts say that you were back, but—where's everyone else?" Iarlaith pulled up short in front of them, looking worried. "Who's here?"

Fionnlagh answered. "Me, Erin, and Éamon."

Iarlaith's eyes widened. "That's all?"

"The rest are safe," Fionnlagh said. "We're only here with a message." He crossed to clasp his brother affirmingly on the shoulder, making Iarlaith jump. "But…" he leaned in close to Iarlaith's side to say something softly in his ear. Éamon couldn't make it out, but Iarlaith's face shifted fast into horror.

Fionnlagh leaned back, seemingly letting Iarlaith process whatever he'd just said. The archivist faerie looked aghast, but he collected himself with a slightly frantic air. "All right. All right, we'll get it sorted."

Fionnlagh turned back to Éamon, who quickly dropped

the blindfold again. "Éamon," the warrior said, and his footsteps crossed to the horse's side. "I'm going to help you down. After that, can you walk?"

"Yeah." Éamon reached down to rub gently at the juncture between flesh and crystal. "Yeah, I can walk."

"It hurts?"

Éamon nodded.

"I'll support you, then." Fionnlagh's hand tapped Éamon's knee, letting him know to begin dismounting, and Éamon carefully swung himself out of the saddle. Fionnlagh guided him to the ground and then looped one of Éamon's arms over his shoulders. "Come on."

"Can I take off the blindfold now?"

"No."

He heard Erin following them toward the mound and Iarlaith taking up his place beside them. "Éamon," Iarlaith said, "we're going to show you to your room. I'll make sure the fire is lit and that you have clean clothes. All right?"

This was even more unsettling than Fionnlagh's earlier harshness. "What is going *on*?"

There was a moment of pause, and Éamon wondered if Iarlaith was debating what to tell him. Then the archivist exhaled shortly. "First things first. I'm going to need you to just cooperate for a little while."

Éamon felt a draft of warm air and realized that they must be near the entrance to the mound. A bolt of pain shot through his left leg as soon as he crossed the threshold, and he let out a cry.

"What happened?" Fionnlagh demanded.

"I don't know." Éamon hadn't gotten past the door. "My leg hurt. I don't know."

There was a pause, and then Fionnlagh's hand tightened around Éamon's shoulders. "Come on."

Again, as soon as they passed the doorway, frigid pain slammed through Éamon's leg. He choked on his shout and bit his tongue before forcing himself to take another step. It felt like he was struggling through an invisible defense, and for some reason, his leg in particular was protesting. But then he was past the doorway, and all at once, the pain evaporated.

He was led to the stairs and guided up to the next floor. He heard a door open and recognized that he'd been led to the room he'd shared with Áed.

Fionnlagh helped Éamon to the bed. He sat gingerly on the edge and stretched out his leg. He could hear Iarlaith by the hearth, starting a fire. "Should I stay with him?" the archivist asked quietly, and Fionnlagh hummed in thought.

"Maybe for now. But don't be careless."

"It's like you don't know me." Iarlaith's footsteps crossed to the bed. "Right. Éamon?"

Éamon nodded. It was hard to track Iarlaith when he wasn't actively moving around anymore.

"You're going to have to stay in this room," Iarlaith said. His voice was patient and not unkind. "Fionnlagh is going to lock it from the outside. I know this is confusing, and you're probably alarmed, but I have to ask you to trust us."

"How can I trust you when you won't tell me anything?"

There was a moment's pause, and then slender fingers were removing Éamon's blindfold. He blinked in the sudden light, even dim as it was. Iarlaith, in front of him, leaned back, taking the strip of fabric with him. "I'm sorry, Éamon," he said. "If we're right in this suspicion, it would be unwise to tell you more." He folded the blindfold on the side of the bed. "I'll stay with you. If that feeling comes back—like what happened in the forest—putting the blindfold back on might help."

"It helped then." Éamon rubbed at one eye, feeling the

familiar scars and remembering the pain that had lanced through his head just a few hours ago. It had hurt worse than being hit with a candlestick. "Why?"

Iarlaith pressed his lips together.

"You can't answer."

"I won't answer. I'm sorry."

Fionnlagh stood. "Iarlaith," he said seriously. "If it comes down to it…"

"Yes, yes." Iarlaith waved a hand. "Go on. Speak to Mother; I know you need to."

The warrior crossed to the door. "You won't be able to get out either, Iarlaith."

"Just have someone bring us my deck of cards later." He rubbed his fingers together. "You know the ones, with the imprints that you can feel."

"I know the ones."

"And clean clothes. And food. And don't forget to send unprepared food, for Éamon."

Fionnlagh rolled his eyes. "All right, I got it."

Iarlaith smiled at him. "Thanks, Fionnlagh."

Fionnlagh closed the door, and moments later, Éamon heard the sound of the lock turning from without.

"Has this door always locked from the outside?" Éamon said numbly.

"There are two locks. One from the inside, one from the outside. Most of the doors here are like that." Iarlaith sighed. "I caused a lot of mischief with that, when I was younger."

Imagining the bookish and reserved Iarlaith causing mischief was surprisingly easy. Éamon adjusted his seat on the bed and began working at his shoelaces. "So we're stuck here, now?"

"Unfortunately. I'm sorry, I know it must be stressful."

"How long?"

Iarlaith exhaled. "I'm not sure. Hopefully, we can find a

solution to this soon." His face grew thoughtful. "I should have my assistant look through some books for me…"

Éamon got his shoes off and brought his feet up onto the bed with a little groan. He was almost getting used to being so exhausted all the time, which wasn't something he liked. "If I'm going to be here for long," he said, "then I'm going to rest for a bit."

"All right." Iarlaith slipped off the edge of the bed and crossed to the fireplace. "I'll be quiet."

"If I…" Éamon hesitated. "If I sleepwalk…"

A flicker of worry passed over Iarlaith's face, but it didn't reach his voice, which remained perfectly composed. "I'll try to wake you before you hurt yourself." He sat back, seeming to get comfortable. "Sweet dreams, Éamon."

Somehow, Éamon didn't think that he was going to have sweet dreams.

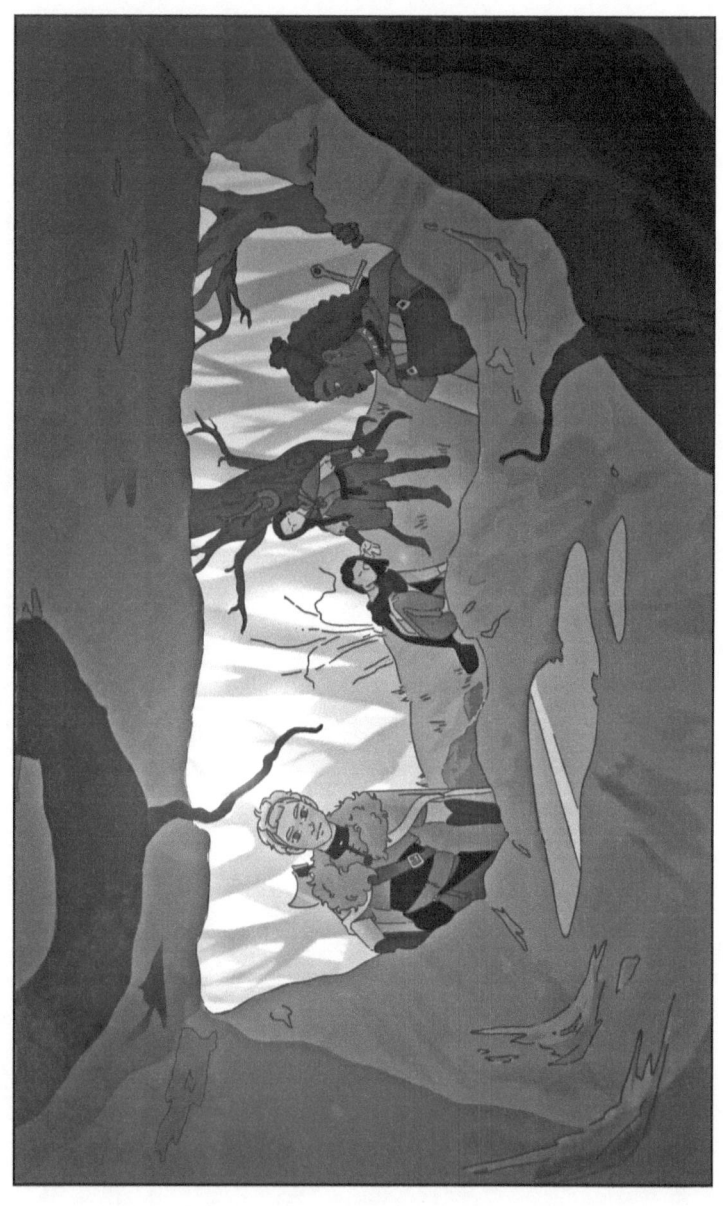

CHAPTER FORTY
ÁED

The flicker of pale golden light through his eyelids brought Áed into wakefulness.

He sat up woozily, looking to his wrist, where the pollen bracelet was flickering deliberately. "Oh," he murmured and hurried to push himself to his feet. Fionnuala was closest to him, so he woke her with a little shake. She blinked at him until he held up his wrist. "It's Fionnlagh."

Fionnuala rose quickly, just as Rian emerged from upstairs, looking disheveled with sleep. Ronan, who had taken to helping Róise in the kitchen when she prepared goods for the bakery in the wee hours of the morning, stepped out and waved his wrist. "It's Fionnlagh," he announced in a loud whisper. "That means it's time, right?"

Rian made his way down the stairs. "Three days," he said. One hand gripped the banister. "That's how much time we can expect to have."

"That's not much." Áed had rallied fast now that he felt urgent about something.

Rian was already tapping back, affirming receipt of Fionnlagh's signal and making the whole dim room flicker with the light of their combined bracelets. "It's enough." He looked up, and his eyes were sharp. "It's enough."

⑅

The afternoon sun spilled through the forest like sage honey. In its light, the world looked fair and alive.

Rian led the way, a sturdy, twisting branch serving as a walking stick. The path was thin and uneven, and Rian apologized tightly each time he needed to pause and gather himself. "We have time," he always made certain to assure the party as he leaned on some or another tree, fighting hard to keep the pain off his face, but adequate time or otherwise, he apologized nonetheless. When he wasn't apologizing, he was wordless. He guided Áed, Ronan, and Fionnuala through the woodlands as surely as if he followed the wind for direction.

If anybody else noticed his silence, they said nothing. Áed had hovered at Rian's side for a while, wondering whether he should say something, but Rian hadn't seemed interested in talking. Áed couldn't exactly blame him. He wasn't sure that if he were in Rian's shoes, he'd be able to return to the castle at all.

The castle was not overly far to travel—about a day to walk, Rian had told them, in good health and good weather—but the pace had been slow. They couldn't safely travel on main roads. Áed tried hard not to be frustrated by the delay, but it was taxing.

It was on that honey-sun afternoon, however, that the wait ended.

They had been making their way through thinning woods when Rian held up a hand, and the group came to a stop. "We're nearly there," he said quietly. "Just past these trees. Do you remember the map of the castle?"

Everyone nodded.

"Good." Rian poked a thumb over his shoulder. "You're

about to see it in person."

One by one, Áed, Fionnuala, and Ronan all crossed to the twiggy net of trees and peeked over the short bluff.

"Damn," Ronan murmured. "That's incredible."

The castle, seated on the plain some quarter-mile away, was built of earthy-gray stone, patched with green where plants had found root in the ancient mortar. The keep seemed almost to sprout like a shipwreck from a greenish, stagnant sea, for the moat around it was wide enough to be a lake. Dotting the plain, stone watchtowers looked over the surrounding land of fields and scraggly orchards, some of which looked as old as the castle itself. One watchtower seemed to have fallen in some long-ago siege; its southern face was missing, crumbled away so that the light fell onto the half-collapsed stone staircase and rotting rooms. A window-frame arched from the side of the ruin, supported by nothing at all.

The castle, on the other hand, looked untouched by anything but time. Even at something of a distance, the weathered stone looked stubborn and staunch.

"We're going to capture that?" Ronan said incredulously.

Fionnuala was staring at it intently. "We're going to try."

"First, we have to get there," Rian said. His eyes were still fixed on the castle, and they burned with something that looked a lot like hate. He began to pick his way through the woods again. "Come on, follow me."

"Are we getting in the same way you got out?" Ronan asked. He tore his eyes away from the castle reluctantly to trail after Rian.

Rian shook his head. "No. I just ran until I got to the battlements, and then I jumped."

Ronan's eyes widened, and Áed felt his heart seize a little. "But—" Ronan looked over his shoulder to where the castle was once again hidden behind a screen of dead branches.

"That's so high! How did you know you'd live?"

Rian waved a hand, and Ronan yelped and stumbled backward as he seemed to bounce off the air in front of him. He felt in front of him frantically, his hands clearly meeting some obstacle before, with a small smirk, Rian flicked his hand again. "I cushioned the fall," he said, and Ronan felt around suspiciously at the normal air in front of him before hurrying to walk at Rian's side once more. "But at the time, I wasn't really thinking about—" He cut himself off, glancing at Ronan as if wondering whether he should hold his tongue. But Ronan seemed to pick up on the unsaid, for his face fell.

"You weren't thinking about living," he finished.

His eyes fixed on the path, Rian nodded resignedly. "I wanted to be free. Whatever that meant." Quiet fell for a moment, and then he sucked in a sharp breath. "But then I was falling, outside the walls for the first time in almost two hundred years, and it was a bit heady. Catching myself was an impulse." He offered a half-smile to the rest of the group as if suddenly afraid of how they saw him. "I'm not in that mindset so much anymore. You don't have to worry."

"Good," Fionnuala said firmly. "Because when we're done, things will be better for everyone."

"Well," Rian said. His mouth twitched up, just at the corner. "Not for the Queen."

"Not for her," Áed agreed. Suddenly, he looked at Rian curiously. "Hang on a moment."

Rian looked back over his shoulder. "What?"

"The Queen." Áed frowned. "Does she have a *name*?"

"Ah." A faint expression of distaste crossed over Rian's face. "She does. It's quite illegal to use it, though." He sighed, waving a hand. "Even to me, even at the nicest points of our relationship, she was only ever 'my lady.'" He looked a bit satisfied. "But her name is Líadan."

Áed repeated the name quietly to himself. Somehow, it fit his mental image of the Queen while at the same time feeling too human. "Why is it illegal?"

Rian sighed with a shrug. "Because she's a controlling bitch."

Ronan snorted quietly.

"Here we are," Rian said presently. He poked at the ground with his toe. "It's around here somewhere."

Áed dropped to a squat and brushed at the ground. It felt good to squat, actually; his axe was heavy, and he was tired. "What will it look like?"

"You'll know it when you see it." Rian, with a grunt, got to his knees. "It should be very big and probably flat."

Ronan and Fionnuala joined the search, scraping away the dirt and leaves over the forest floor. What they were looking for, Rian had explained earlier, was the mouth of an old siege tunnel. The tunnel itself dated back some two thousand years, and when the siege had failed, the castle had simply flooded the tunnel and blocked it with an enormous granite stone. The tunnel itself led to the castle foundations, where the attackers had attempted to burrow their way underneath the defenses. They had been thwarted by the depth of the foundation and the thickness of the stone. Nobody had used the tunnel since; after all, it led to a six-meter-thick stone wall, was full of ancient water, and was blocked by an immovable stone.

Rian had assured them this wouldn't be a problem.

"Here," Fionnuala said, brushing her palms more firmly over the ground. "I think I found something."

They all gathered around, and Rian nodded with satisfaction. "I think that's it."

The stone under Fionnuala's hands was dark with lichen

and settled into the ground. Tree roots, as wide as a torso, laced over it in a protective cage, and in places, the stone looked like it was fused into them.

Áed looked to Rian. "You can move that?"

Rian studied it with narrowed, thoughtful eyes. "I don't know if that would be the best course of action."

Ronan looked immediately alarmed. "What do you mean?" He got to his feet. "We don't have a backup plan for this part."

"No, no." Rian shook his head. "It's all right. We're still going to use the tunnel. I'm just not going to move the stone." At everyone's obvious confusion, he let out a little laugh. He pointed to the other side of the stone, which was higher. "All right. Everyone, go stand over there."

When Áed, Ronan, and Fionnuala did so, Rian moved to kneel directly in front of the stone. He closed his eyes and took a slow breath.

Áed didn't think a single one of them blinked as Rian raised one hand in front of him. He turned it sideways and deliberately raised it to a point just above his head. Then he held his other hand out in front of him.

"See, that looks like a spell," Ronan whispered. "He said he didn't use any, but I think the motions are helping him focus."

Áed shushed him. "Then let him focus."

Rian exhaled firmly and turned his extended hand back to face him. As he did so, the ground gave a shudder. Áed caught himself on a tree, and Ronan caught himself on Fionnuala.

Rian's face was tight with concentration. Áed stared, wide-eyed, as crumbs of earth began to float off the stone. They stopped before they touched Rian, changing direction in the air as if sliding against an invisible shield.

Before long, more than just dust was rising from the rock. Gravel, pebbles, and sand all fell away, crumbling from the ancient granite, and they parted around Rian to fall to the ground again some meters back.

"He's disintegrating it," Fionnuala murmured. It sounded like she was in awe.

The rock flowed around Rian's graceful, kneeling form like it had turned to water. It fell away from the roots, leaving them suspended in air, and a hole began to form in the forest floor. Soon, the hole was deep enough for a person to stand in.

Then came the water.

Rian stiffened as if fighting against a physical force. He quickly flipped the hand of his extended arm, no longer pulling away but pushing back, and in a moment, Áed saw why. The second that Rian reached the other side of the stone, water burst out in a spray. It smelled earthy, stagnant, and alive, and Rian gritted his teeth against its outpouring. It cleaved around his shield, pouring in a discolored tide into the forest on either side.

Soon, its flow ebbed. Rian began to tug at it again, coaxing the water out of the tunnel and into the open air. It wetted the piles of sand and gravel, turning them back to earth.

And then, finally, everything was still.

Rian slumped, catching himself with straight arms. He was breathing hard. When he was sure everything seemed stable, Áed hurried over. The ground was wet, except for the patch where Rian knelt. "Rian!" Áed exclaimed. "Are you all right?"

Rian looked up. His chest was still heaving as if he'd been running, but he was smiling. He nodded, a bead of sweat rolling down his temple.

Ronan hurried down next, and then Fionnuala, more

carefully. Ronan dashed to Rian immediately. "That was *amazing!*" His emerald eyes glinted with enthusiasm. "You—that rock—it's *sand*—"

Rian pushed himself to his feet with a breathy chuckle. "I'm glad you're impressed."

Fionnuala crouched next to what had once been a two-thousand-year-old stone. She let the grains run through her fingers. "Incredible."

Áed picked his way over the wet ground to the mouth of the tunnel. It smelled a bit foul, in the way a lake does when it's covered entirely with algae, and he couldn't see more than a few meters. He brought flame to one hand and held it out experimentally, squinting to the edges of the firelight. "Is this stable?"

"Good question." Rian joined Áed, looking into the dark mouth of the earth. "I imagine it had supports originally. They might have rotted by now."

"You can make sure it doesn't collapse on us, right?"

"As we go. It does lead under the moat, so we'll proceed carefully." Rian took the first step in. His left hand flickered with icy sparks, and then his palm was engulfed with white fire. He held his hand up, examining the ceiling. His flames shone more brightly than Áed's, and whiter than daylight. It was odd to see since Áed had grown so used to the natural, warm-colored fire of himself and the low court. Rian looked back at the rest of them waiting in the entrance. "Come on."

One by one, everyone trouped after him.

Periodically, Rian paused to press his hand to the wall, stabilizing the millennia-old tunnel, but beyond that, nobody wanted to stop for long. Even illuminated by Rian's brilliant fire, the darkness was eerie. In places, water still pooled on the ground, reflecting the light as mirrors, and tree roots often penetrated the walls, grasping like petrified fingers. Áed once made the mistake of holding his own light too close to the wall and had to stifle a cry. As it was, he jumped back, knocking into Fionnuala, who was fortunately sturdy enough to prevent them both from tumbling to the soggy ground. When she'd demanded what the matter was, he'd only had to point to the side of the tunnel for her eyes to widen as well.

"I told you it was a siege tunnel," Rian said quietly. "I never said it was empty when they flooded it."

"Good *Gods*, Rian!" Áed gasped. He stared at what had startled him. It lay crumpled against the wall of the tunnel, half pulled-apart. The skull, which stared hollowly at Áed, was separated from its spine, and Áed spotted the pelvis a ways off, devoid of flesh and pocked with decay. The water had likely swept the skeleton along as Rian cleared the tunnel. "You could have warned us."

"Sorry." Rian lifted his hand higher, letting the light reach deeper into the blackness. "There are more. For warning."

Áed shuddered.

Ronan made a noise of disbelief. "They *drowned* here?"

Rian nodded. "That's what I gather." He touched the wall again, adding another point of stability. "I read every history I could get my hand on. That's what they said."

"That's awful."

"Think of it like we're avenging them," Rian suggested. He didn't seem overly affected by the bones. At this point, Áed supposed, they *were* more archeological than anything else. "We're trying more or less the same thing, after all."

Ronan nodded firmly. "Right. We'll succeed where they didn't."

"Good attitude," Áed said softly.

Their footsteps echoed. For a long while, nobody spoke. They passed more bones, but the shocking effect diminished after a while. And really, it wasn't a very long while at all. Within ten minutes, Rian's firelight fell on a wall ahead of them, and they all came to a stop.

"Well," Áed said. The rock was soft with the sort of life that grows in the lightless damp. "That looks sturdy."

"So did the stone over the tunnel," Fionnuala reminded him.

Rian pressed a palm to the castle foundations. "Someone else, take over the light. I don't know that I can do both things at once."

"You dissolved the stone *and* made a shield for yourself," Ronan said thoughtfully.

The corner of Rian's mouth twitched up as he looked over his shoulder at Ronan. "You're clever. I suppose I did." He turned his attention back to the wall. "Still. Just as backup, maybe?"

Áed and Fionnuala both responded with their own fires, and with his free hand, Áed tugged Ronan off to the side as Rian assumed his position before the wall. Once again, Rian closed his eyes, but this time, no dust flowed from his target. Instead, with a shiver, one of the great foundation stones began to slide from its precise fit amongst its brethren. Rian seemed to hold his breath as the stone slipped free, and it floated a few inches above the ground as he moved it behind him.

"That looks heavy," Ronan murmured.

With a grunt, Rian released it to the ground, opening his hands as if physically freeing the magic. "It is." He stared at the wall with narrowed eyes. "Only about twenty more of those."

The tunnel behind them began to fill as Rian moved stone after stone, until he was sweating and winded. After about ten, he braced his hands on his knees, catching his breath.

"Sorry," he panted. "I just need a moment."

"Don't apologize," Fionnuala put her hands on her hips, surveying the stone that Rian had already moved. "We'd never have made this progress without you."

"You'd also never have been in this situation without me," Rian reminded her. "The war and all."

Fionnuala sighed heavily. "If you hadn't removed yourself, I'm sure the Queen would have only used your power for worse and worse. And then we wouldn't have been able to fight back at all." She let her gaze fall on Rian's, and she didn't blink when it met his. "Maybe this way is better. If there's a war, at least we're *in* it."

Rian broke eye contact first. "I never thought of it that way."

"I'm not saying that I absolve you of everything," Fionnuala said. She leaned against the wall. "There is blood on your hands. But you're not wicked, Rian." She let out a little chuff. "You might even be good."

For a while, Rian said nothing. Then, he turned back to the wall with a little smile and raised his hands once more. "I'd like that."

After another ten stones, Rian stopped again. The castle foundation was truly wide; the tunnel now continued at least five meters into the stone, and the tunnel behind was lined with gigantic, eight-thousand-year-old blocks. Rian walked into the hole in the foundation, and Áed peered after him. "Are we close?"

Rian pressed his hand to the end of the tunnel. "We should be."

Ronan took a few steps into the tunnel after him. "We're going to come out in the vaults, right?"

"Right." Rian looked thoughtful. "There shouldn't be anyone there. But we should be quiet all the same."

Áed pursed his lips. When Rian pulled out the stones, it did result in a deep, grinding rumble. Now and then, an imperfection would catch, and the stones passed over each other with horrid screeches. "Can you silence the blocks as they come out?"

"I probably could. But we're so close to the end that I think it would be easier to just…" He touched a fingertip to the block in front of him and covered his mouth and nose with the other hand. Just like the gargantuan stone covering the tunnel entrance, the block fell away into sand. When it settled, Rian dared another breath. "There should only be a few more."

When the final brick crumbled away, Áed didn't notice that they had reached the end. He knew that Rian had said the tunnel would end in the vaults, but on some level, he'd still expected light to spill free when Rian removed the final stone.

Instead, there was nothing but a faint gust of stale air.

Ronan stepped forward, just out of range of Áed's firelight. "It smells like dust." The sound of his voice had changed; now, instead of close whispers, it echoed until, as softly as a gust of night breeze, it faded to nothing. He clapped his hands over his mouth immediately. The little *slap* echoed as well.

"Well," Rian murmured. The word reverberated around the invisible space, a chorus of voices. *Well. Well. Well.* "We made it."

He held up a hand, and white fire danced to his fingers.

As soon as it did, Áed gasped.

The space was enormous. The ceiling, far above them, was still drowned in blackness, and in all directions, shelves rose upward until they were out of sight. And on those shelves…

Áed could do nothing but gape. In the warm light of his

own fire and the sun-white glow of Rian's, the contents of the shelves somehow looked even more foreign. Immediately in front of him, a round mirror, cracked and gilded with gold in the shape of oak leaves, flashed in the light and yet showed Áed no reflection. A complete skeleton, standing against the edge of a shelf, had two citrine earrings carefully placed to hang from each side of its skull; the rest of it was clothed in a samite gown whose train snaked under the shelf and into dusty obscurity. A gemstone, as big as Áed's head and as clear as glass, sat on a pillow of brittle, woven reeds.

Fionnuala let out a soft cry. "This is ours!"

Áed turned to look to find her holding a skull helmet, much like he had seen Neasa wear. Set in the bony forehead, a bloodred ruby glinted, and the skull's fangs were as long as a finger.

Fionnuala ran a hand over it, almost reverently. "This belonged to the leader before my mother. It was stolen in a raid by the Moon court and never seen since."

Rian looked thoughtful. "About sixty years ago, the Queen stole a lot of bounty from Moon when they wouldn't pay festival tithes." He grimaced. "I, ah… had something to do with the stealing. But maybe that's why it's here."

Fionnuala put it back down gently. "What else is here?"

"Spoils of war, much of it." Rian ran a hand over a shield that was scarred with deep grooves. "But nothing that should delay us."

Áed shook his head, trying to banish the distraction. It wasn't easy. He'd never been in a place like this.

Rian beckoned over his shoulder. "This way."

They wound their way in single file through the shelves. Finally, their footsteps quieted, and the light began to reach the ceiling as it grew lower. They must truly have been far underground. "Stairs here," Rian whispered. "We go up; I check for anyone nearby. As soon as we're clear…"

"Time for the plan," Áed said.

Rian nodded. "Ready?"

In turn, Áed, Ronan, and Fionnuala nodded their heads.

Rian replied with a curt bob of his own chin, and then he was climbing the stairs. It was rather impressive that someone who moved so stiffly could make so little sound. A few moments later, he reappeared. "Clear."

Áed's heart thrummed against his ribs as he climbed the steep stairs after Rian. He felt Ronan's presence behind him, and as they reached the top of the stairs, he turned and quickly drew the boy into a hug. Ronan stiffened in surprise, but not for long. Áed held him close while Rian waited patiently to open the door. "Be safe."

Ronan nodded against Áed's shoulder. "You too."

"I mean it, okay?"

"So do I." Ronan squeezed back. "I'll see you when it's over."

It was hard to pull away. Now that it was time, stress was pumping through Áed's blood. But it *was* time. "All right," he murmured. He looked up at Rian. "Let's go."

CHAPTER FORTY-ONE
ÉAMON

Éamon wasn't sure why he'd expected anything different, but sleep brought nothing except nightmares. He had woken from dreams of flickering, crystalline pain to find Iarlaith shaking him, and when he'd come around fully, Iarlaith had looked almost as relieved as Éamon himself.

But that had been hours ago. Without sleep to pass the time, Éamon was getting mind-numbingly bored. He had bathed and changed his clothes. Iarlaith's assistant had dropped off a deck of cards and some food earlier, but Éamon couldn't sit still. The room only felt smaller as time dragged on.

Reprieve came a few hours before nightfall.

Éamon had been trying hard not to sleep again, and Iarlaith had been doing his best to help by teaching him a new card game. The complexity of it was not *fun*, but it was something to think about. Still, when a loud crash sounded from somewhere deep in the mound, Éamon's first response was gladness at the diversion. Worry came a split second later when Iarlaith stiffened. "What was that?"

"It sounded like it came from outside."

"It did," Iarlaith agreed.

"Maybe somebody dropped something?"

Iarlaith worried at the cards in his hand, creasing the corners.

"Hey, stop that," Éamon complained. "Now, when those go in the pile, you'll know which ones they are."

"Oh." Iarlaith flattened the corners again. "I didn't notice." He shook his head. "Anyway. When the next person draws…"

He didn't finish the thought because from down the hallway came the sound of flying footsteps.

With a frown, Iarlaith put down his cards. "Sorry. Hold on a moment." He slid off the bed and crossed to the door, pressing his ear to the wood.

Immediately, he jumped back as three loud raps sounded from the other side of the door. "Hello?" a voice called. "Iarlaith? Are you in there?"

Iarlaith, rubbing his ear and wincing, called back through the door. "What happened? Who is it?"

"It's Síofra. There's been a mishap," the voice said frantically.

"Síofra? A mishap?" Iarlaith's brow creased. "What mishap?"

Síofra's footsteps danced agitatedly outside the door. "A pipe burst over the atheneum."

Iarlaith's face fell into alarm immediately. "A pipe?" He braced a hand on either side of the door. "The books! Are the books safe?"

"There are so many—I moved the ones that were right in the way, but the water's spreading."

"Can anyone help you?" Iarlaith started pacing back and forth before the door.

"Everyone's running about! Please, Iarlaith, you've got to come; the whole place is going to be *ruined*." Síofra, who Éamon identified as Iarlaith's assistant, sounded genuinely distraught. "I just finished sorting those old poetry manuscripts, too, and you know they can't stand the humidity—"

"Right," Iarlaith said, still pacing. "Right. Okay." He pressed both palms to the door. "Síofra, there's a key on the frame." He turned to Éamon. "I'll be back, all right? I'm sorry, I've—I've really got to handle this." He looked a little panicked.

"It sounds important," Éamon said. "Don't worry about me. Go."

Iarlaith shot him a grateful look, and then there came the sound of a key biting into the lock. The door swung open to reveal a slight, pretty girl with sable skin and an even darker halo of hair, looking positively frantic. "Thank Goddess. Now come on, we've got to hurry. It's coming through the ceiling."

"Wait—wait—" Iarlaith shot an apologetic look through the door to Éamon, and then he was closing it. The lock turned again, and Éamon heard him through the door. "Take my hand; we're running."

With that, their footsteps pattered away down the hall.

Éamon slumped back against the pillows and vaguely considered using the opportunity to peek at Iarlaith's cards. It wasn't like it would help him win, anyway. He hoped the atheneum would be all right.

Suddenly, the sound of a key came again in the lock. Éamon sat up, staring at the door. "Iarlaith?"

The door swung open. A short, lithe figure leaned one hip on the doorframe, twirling the key around her finger with a self-satisfied smirk. "Guess again."

"Erin!" Éamon pushed himself to his good leg, one hand on the bed for stability as he stood. "What are you doing here?"

"What does it look like?" She reached around the outside of the door and brought back a crutch, presenting it with a flourish. "I'm getting you out, obviously." She tossed the crutch, which Éamon caught with surprise. "Why are you in here, anyway?"

"I don't know, actually." Éamon tested his weight to the crutch. "Nobody will tell me anything." He shook his head to clear it. "Did you flood the atheneum?"

"Only a little. Might have accidentally ruined some old poetry, but everything else is fine." She turned away from the door. "Come on; we've got to hurry."

Éamon hesitated. "Are you sure it's a good idea?"

Erin turned back, looking confused. "What do you mean?"

"I just mean…" Éamon fidgeted with the crutch. "Fionnlagh and Iarlaith seemed to have a reason for me to stay here."

"What reason?" Erin crossed her arms. "They didn't give me a reason. Didn't give you a reason." She shrugged, both hands to the ceiling. "Way I see it, you don't have any obligation to be stuck in a room for who knows how long. Besides—" She looked over her shoulder, and her mouth pressed into a line. "I don't think you're going to want to miss this."

Curious, Éamon limped over to the door. "Miss what?"

Erin stepped out of the way and poked a finger over her shoulder at one of the hall windows. "See for yourself."

Éamon crossed the hallway and peered over the field. Right away, his eyes widened. "What the…"

Erin crossed to his side to lean on the edge of the window. "This must have been Fionnlagh's message." She rolled her eyes. "You know, that one he wouldn't tell us."

In the field, soldiers were forming ranks. Around the lines of armored fae—spear-wielding, sword-wielding, chariot warriors and infantry—faeries rode on horseback, standing in the stirrups and shouting orders. The chaos was muffled by the distance, but close to the window, Éamon could hear the shouting, the clanking of weaponry. "Where are they *going?*"

Erin's face sobered. "That's why I thought I should get you," she said. She nodded out the window. "Because wherever they're going, I think that Áed is there too."

⏃

Erin really did know how to get Éamon moving.

"Hello, Echdían," Éamon murmured, stroking the horse's velvety nose. "I know you're tired, but I guess we're doing this again."

Echdían snorted but stayed compliant while Éamon readied him for travel. He'd taken the spare clothes from his room, and Erin had procured him a sword and breastplate from somewhere; that, along with a blade and light shield for herself, was the best they could manage at short notice. "Troops are moving out fast," Erin said as she fastened her hind's bridle. "And frankly, I don't trust the Fionns. Fionnlagh especially. He's on our side, but he might not be on *your* side, so watch your back."

"What does that mean?"

Erin shook her head. "*Someone* was meant to go overboard on that lake. It just wasn't supposed to be Áed. Which means it was either supposed to be you or me. And I'm pretty cute, so I'm betting it was you." She patted her mount firmly and swung herself onto its back. "Instead, you decided *nobody* was going to die. Think you can decide that again?"

"Doubt it." This was war; he held no delusions about that. Not after seeing the army amassed in the field. Éamon pushed himself into Echdían's saddle. "But I can decide that Áed won't."

Erin grinned. "I like it."

Suddenly, there was a clatter from the door of the stable.

"Stop! Who goes—" The faerie who had burst in looked shocked. "You!" She stepped back, her hand going to her weapon, and leaned out the door.

Before the soldier could cry for backup, Erin had dug her heels into the flanks of her hind and charged directly at her. Startled, the soldier stumbled backward out of the way, and as Erin flew by, she knocked the soldier hard on the head with the butt of her sword. Erin called back over her shoulder to Éamon. "Come on!"

Éamon had always expected an army to look organized, and perhaps the battle lines did. The chariots and vanguard, far ahead, held bone-white banners high, each emblazoned with a sharp-toothed skull, and the infantry marched in steps that shook the earth in rhythm, driving a beat deep into Éamon's chest. But between the rows of marching fae, where carts of supplies and support troops trundled along among faeries hurrying on foot or riding two to a horse, it was extremely easy to blend in with the chaos.

When the lines narrowed to enter the forest road, Erin and Éamon kept pace, avoiding eye contact with everybody and hanging near the bulky, canvas-covered carts.

Éamon drew near to Erin and leaned over. "I can't believe this is working."

"Don't jinx it." Erin held the hind's reins loosely. "Everyone has business to attend to. They rallied this army faster than I've ever seen." She looked up at him, her red eyes narrowed against the fading sun. "They've sent out messengers to every other low court, too." She looked a bit self-satisfied. "I was eavesdropping, I admit. But there hasn't been such a concentrated low-court effort in thousands of years."

That was a bit unnerving. Éamon wrapped Echdían's reins around his wrist. "All of these soldiers are going to the high court?"

"It sure seems like it." Erin looked impressed. "This battle

is going to be one for the histories. Whatever the outcome…
that is a certainty."

CHAPTER FORTY-TWO
RONAN

I have the easiest job. This is the easiest possible job.

Ronan repeated it to himself like a mantra as he and Fionnuala walked through the halls. Fionnuala was doing a better job at maintaining her composure: if Ronan hadn't known better, he'd have said she belonged here, in this strange and gigantic high court stronghold. Ronan, on the other hand, could feel himself sweating.

Along the hallways, lamps burned brightly. Now and again, the lamps would flare in a complicated series of flashes, and Ronan wished he'd had time to memorize what each series meant. Each one had *some* effect, for Ronan could see people rushing about. They paid him and Fionnuala no mind—clearly, something urgent was going on.

Ronan knew what it must be.

This is the easiest job.

Their destination was the gatehouses. Ronan still had the layout solidly in his head; what time he hadn't been able to spend memorizing the torch signaling system, he had spent mentally rehearsing every detail of the map Rian had drawn.

The inside of the castle, at least where it lacked windows to the outside or the courtyard, was dim and close, full of winding side passages. Ronan and Fionnuala followed the primary hallways only, moving quickly but not *too* quickly.

"We're going to have to cross the yard," Fionnuala murmured to Ronan. It was a good thing nobody was around just then because their height difference made subtle murmuring a bit difficult.

Ronan nodded. "I know."

In the middle of the castle, a courtyard was nestled. According to the map, it held the stables, a few goat and chicken pens, and a vegetable garden, but Ronan imagined that it wouldn't be peaceful just at that moment. If they'd gotten the timing right, it should be bustling with soldiers preparing the castle defenses.

Sure enough, as soon as Fionnuala opened the door to the yard, the sounds of chaos assaulted Ronan's ears. Fionnuala gave him a nudge, and then they were wading through a cacophony of stablehands trying to calm horses as guards shouted orders from the battlements. Foot soldiers crossed this way and that, forming lines and reforming them at the burning signals of the torches.

They managed a straight path across the open space, and it was almost a relief to reach stone walls again.

There were the portcullises. Each was closed, which was no surprise. Through the iron lattices, far off on the edge of the plain, Ronan could see a dark line converging.

"Hurry," Fionnuala said sharply, breaking his attention from the glimpse outside. The door to the guardhouse was situated next to the innermost portcullis, deeply set into the stone wall. The Bone warrior didn't so much as hesitate before she grabbed Ronan by the collar and dragged him over to the door.

Two hard, efficient raps rang out as her knuckles hit the door.

There came the heavy sound of a lock bolt turning, and

then a guard opened it, looking harried. Her red-blond hair was drawn into a long braid; strands had come free and were stuck to her lips. "What do you want?" From somewhere deeper inside the guardhouse, someone yelled at her about arrow inventory. She *tch*ed.

"Sorry to bother," Fionnuala said. For someone so powerful, she performed flustered very well. She held Ronan forward. "This mayfly was going around without a keeper. Where should I bring it?"

A look of annoyance crossed the guard's face. "What do I care?"

Fionnuala wrung her hands apologetically. "It's just, I didn't think it should be wandering, what with everything happening."

The guard frowned and looked at Ronan more closely. "Hey. It's not enchanted?"

"Oh." Fionnuala laughed, and Ronan thought the nervous pitch in it might be at least a little genuine. "Isn't it?"

The guard rolled her eyes and grabbed Ronan's wrist. She dragged him inside, making him stumble over the doorframe. "I'll handle it. The alert ones always manage to get in the way of things."

Fionnuala stepped forward. "I'll tell you what." She looked over the guard's shoulder to where one of her compatriots was fuming with a handful of arrows. "I'll take care of it. You look like you need to go."

The guard scrutinized Fionnuala with pursed lips. "Who are you, again?"

"Oh," Fionnuala laughed, and Ronan's heart tripped. *A direct question.* But Fionnuala sidestepped. "I'm new here. From Dún Darach. Sorry, it's probably obvious."

Ronan let out a relieved breath as the guard rolled her eyes. "Yeah," she muttered. Then she jerked a thumb over her shoulder. "Enchant him, then stick him in one of the holding cells. I don't have time to deal with this."

Fionnuala nodded a few times, still perfectly flustered. "Of course."

When the guard turned away, growling at her fellow guard about whatever was happening with the arrows, Fionnuala steered Ronan toward the cells.

"The young ones," she muttered, sounding a little triumphant. "So cocky."

"Young?"

Fionnuala pushed him into a cell, closing the door without locking it. "That guard has no more than fifty, mark my words." She gave Ronan's shoulder a bracing pat through the bars. "You know what to do?"

Ronan could only nod.

Fionnuala grinned tightly. "Then I'll see you soon."

"Hopefully," Ronan murmured.

"Don't be negative," Fionnuala chided. "Good luck."

Ronan swallowed hard. "You too."

And then she was gone, slipping past the cells.

Right. Ronan had no doubt that whatever happened, Fionnuala would accomplish her task. Ronan's job was just as important. He had to be reliable.

He waited almost ten minutes for an opportunity to slip out of his unlocked cell. The guard room—or rather, *rooms*—were divided into several smaller chambers. Gatehouses, storeroom, stairs leading upward to where Fionnuala was currently incapacitating the murder holes. He chewed his lip as he peered around the corner into the first gatehouse. Currently, two guards inside were working together to move a sack of what looked like beads. Ronan glanced down the narrow hallway to see that nobody was coming before staring more intently at the guards. Both of them, he noticed, were wearing gloves. And the sack of beads looked very heavy.

Iron pellets.

Awful. How clever. He could only imagine that they were destined for the murder holes, or perhaps they were meant to be launched as projectiles from some catapult on the battlements.

Ronan narrowed his eyes. Behind the struggling guards—they really needed another person to lift a sack that big—was a winch.

Ronan needed a way to get the guards out of the way without drawing attention. And more importantly, he needed to time this right. His job was to open the portcullises for the approaching armies. Too early, and he risked being exposed and having his work reversed. Too late, and the low court forces would suffer under the barrage of arrows, stones, and apparently iron pellets from the battlements and castle defenses. Which meant that he needed to be in position to receive the signal from his softly glowing pollen bracelet. And then he needed to run to the next gatehouse to lift the second portcullis and repeat the process for the third. Ideally, the arrival of a hostile army would draw attention from one human scampering through the chaos.

But before he could do any of that, Ronan needed to clear out this gatehouse.

He drew back from the doorway again and looked around down the hall. It was lined with supplies: spears leaning against the walls, barrels stacked on crates of crossbow bolts.

Hmm. A risk, maybe…

Oh, well. Nothing for it.

With a quiet grunt, Ronan picked up one of the barrels. It was as big as his torso, and heavy. Something inside sloshed, thicker than water.

Staggering, Ronan brought it to the door. He squatted with difficulty and dropped the barrel on its side. As both guards looked up at the impact, he gave it a kick and darted back around the corner.

A moment later, the sound of a crash and furious swearing reached his ears. Both guards stormed out. One had a hand clapped over his eye, and the other just looked livid. "Who stacked those barrels?" he bellowed, marching with purpose down the hall. Ronan hurried to crouch in the shadow of one of the crates. "Don't have *time* for this."

As soon as they were out of sight, Ronan darted into the gatehouse.

The sack of pellets had been dropped, and iron beads had rolled to every corner of the room. The barrel had cracked, and liquid had begun to leak onto the floor in a wide, dark circle. It smelled like lamp oil. Acting on an inspiration, Ronan bent to scoop a handful of pellets into his pocket.

He crossed to the winch. He hadn't received a signal yet, but it couldn't be long now. He heard horns blowing through the castle's dense stone walls, and from somewhere in the castle itself, people were shouting. The rhythmic, wild noise of drums echoed.

Ronan examined the winch. It was a large drum, around which a thick iron chain wrapped several times. The lever of the handle was as long as his arm. Experimentally, he gave the handle a push, just to see how easily it would turn. It resisted but gave when he applied more pressure.

This was going to be an exercise.

Suddenly, Ronan's wrist flickered with soft, golden light. His heart rate spiked.

No time to waste. Hopefully, Fionnuala had already dealt with the murder holes between the first and second gates. Ronan threw his weight against the winch and watched as the chain began to draw through a hole in the stone wall. As the chain wound around the drum, the sound of metal grating on stone rumbled through the room as the great portcullis slowly lifted.

Shouts were coming from outside the gatehouse. It wouldn't be long before high fae realized that there was foul play afoot, and the gatehouse was the first place they'd check. Gritting his teeth, Ronan strained against the heavy windlass.

He had broken a sweat by the time the chain had been wound all the way in. This task was definitely better suited to several adult men working together, not one short fifteen-year-old, but Ronan knew that it was his job for a reason—if only by the sheer amount of rust building up under his palms. It was an extra security measure, Rian had explained. The portcullises could be *lowered* with one pull of a wood-handled lever, but they could only be *raised* again with great difficulty. This prevented invaders from manually raising the gates from within; a faerie would need very thick gloves, probably of leather, to touch the handle. When they had been planning their invasion, there had been discussion of trying to get their hands on some, but Ronan was glad, ultimately, that they'd simply decided to use the human at their disposal.

Or perhaps 'glad' was the wrong word. He didn't think he'd ever been so stressed in his life, and his life had had its fair share of stressful events. He leaned on the winch for half of a moment, gathering his breath, before pushing himself up and heading for the door.

As soon as he did, he heard footsteps round the corner. In the next second, the doorway filled with armored fae. With a yelp, Ronan jumped behind the winch just in time to avoid a rolling wave of brilliant white fire. It singed the end of his braid, and he batted at it frantically.

"Come out," a voice ordered authoritatively.

"No!" Ronan pressed his back against the winch, trying to shield as much of his body as he could. His heart was *flying*. "Burning to death sounds miserable!"

The footsteps advanced into the room, and Ronan could hear one set of them heading for the lever to lower the portcullis. Acting on terrified instinct, he grabbed a handful of iron pellets from his pocket.

He hurled them at the approaching faerie with everything he had.

The faerie let out a garbled scream, clutching his face and doubling over, and Ronan crouched to scrabble at more pellets on the floor. Without emerging from his pathetic shelter behind the winch, he lobbed another handful toward the doorway and was rewarded with more curses. Unfortunately, they seemed to have been ready for it because in the next moment, more fire was filling the air. Ronan curled into a ball on the ground as searing heat poured around the winch. He couldn't keep in a cry as he felt the skin of his arms blister.

And then the flames stopped.

Shakily, Ronan dared a peek. Blood was roaring so loudly in his ears that he could only see, rather than hear, a tall, dark-haired warrior swing a punch at the nearest soldier. Relief melted over him as he watched Fionnuala draw her great sword and swing it in a precise, shining arc.

Relief turned to horrified disgust as hot blood spattered Ronan's face.

Still, he vaulted over the windlass as the last guard crumpled to the ground. "Fionnuala!"

The Bone warrior turned to him, pushing aside a corpse with her toe. "Ronan! You're safe, thank Goddess." Her own face and armor were already adorned with other people's blood, but her smile was white behind that macabre blush.

"Two more gates. I got the drawbridge down; I'll cover you." She stepped aside, letting him hurry out the door. The hallway was already filling with more soldiers.

"You can take that?" Ronan managed breathlessly. It had not yet caught up to him just how close he had come to dying.

"Who do you think I am?" Fionnuala's sword flashed red as she twirled it easily. "Now, go!"

Ronan went.

When he skidded around the doorway to the next gatehouse, he had to choke back a gasp at the sight of two bodies—one of which was *only* a body, its head quite separated—greeting him. The floor was slick with blood. Fionnuala must have visited before rescuing Ronan. Tamping down nausea, he strode purposefully to the winch. Somehow, it turned more easily. Ronan suspected it had something to do with the frantic buzz in his core that was making his hands shake.

He shot a glance down the hall at Fionnuala when he darted out toward the final gatehouse. She was holding her own, using the narrowness of the hallway to her advantage, but Ronan saw a new cut on her arm. It looked deep, but if it hindered her, she didn't show it.

Ronan clenched his teeth and hurried on.

This time, he wasn't surprised by the bodies.

He made straight for the winch and threw his weight against it without hesitation. It turned with screeching complaint, and Ronan grinned mirthlessly at the sound of the portcullis rising on the other side of the wall.

In another minute, the final gate was up. Arms burning, Ronan took a moment to listen through the wall to the horns and battle cries as low-court forces poured into the formerly unbreachable citadel.

CHAPTER FORTY-THREE
ÁED

Far away, Áed could hear the violent mayhem that meant Ronan and Fionnuala had succeeded. In the next moment, his and Rian's bracelets flickered.

"Right," Rian said. "Better hurry."

He and Rian had been capitalizing on the distraction of the attacking armies to navigate the hallways unnoticed. It was absurdly hard to concentrate knowing that Ronan was, at that moment, in the center of said distraction. As soon as the gates were up, he was supposed to retreat to a safe location, but knowing Ronan, he wouldn't be so eager to get out of the action.

If he got hurt—if he *died*—

No. No, Áed could not think about that. In fact… "Rian," he said. "Can you tell if Ronan is all right?"

Rian bit his lip. "Do you have anything of his?"

Automatically Áed looked down. After a moment, he found a single long, black hair and plucked it off his sleeve. Apparently, Ronan had been shedding. "Will this do?"

With a nod, Rian took Ronan's hair and seemed to concentrate for a moment. "He's not badly injured. He's moving in the direction of the courtyard. Fine, for now."

Áed released a breath. "Useful skill set you have."

"I've been told."

Áed glanced at him sideways as they turned down another hall. "And how are you doing?"

Rian hummed, keeping his eyes ahead. "Achy, but no worse than usual."

"That's not what I meant."

"I know." He fell quiet, pausing to touch one of the signal lamps on the wall. After a few moments, he started moving again, and Áed followed. Rian sighed shortly. "I'm fine."

Áed was starting to suspect that 'fine' was a word vague enough for Rian to say without properly lying.

They moved through the hallways like ghosts, Áed following Rian's lead. Throughout their journey, they encountered a number of people, many in the black masks of high-court soldiers that Áed recognized from the festival attack in the White City. If any looked too closely, Rian made a flicking movement with his fingers, and their eyes turned away.

It was impossible not to feel like a spare. Ronan was a human and could touch iron to raise the gates. Fionnuala was strong and could fight a squadron of soldiers all on her own. Rian, of course, was an arsenal.

Áed couldn't do anything that the three of them couldn't. He swallowed hard.

"We're nearly there," Rian said quietly. "If the Queen is there, we double back."

"Can't you take her?" Áed worried at the hems of his sleeves. "You don't even have to hurt her if you still don't want to. Just knock her out, maybe?"

Rian looked away, clearly uncomfortable. "While I could," he said, "I'm afraid that the theory and the practice would not align."

"You don't think you would do it."

"I'm afraid I might not." Rian sounded ashamed, but he determinedly regrouped. "And failing would be much worse than not trying."

}}}

The rest of the walk was quiet and tense. The hallways they walked were unadorned with anything that could make them feel homey, and Rian led the way without lifting his eyes from the path ahead.

Finally, they stopped.

"We're there."

The words left a shiver in Áed's spine. He'd never heard Rian sound so reserved, and never before had something as simple as reservation been so frightening.

The hallway ended in a tall, arched door of midnight-black wood, and Áed slowed to a stop. "The Queen's chambers."

Rian nodded. "Stay put."

He crossed to the doors and raised his hands in front of the door. He was removing his own magic, Áed knew; as consort, Rian had placed charms on the room to warn the Queen of invasion or notify her of his coming. Now, he was simply undoing what he'd wrought. A moment later, he pressed his palm directly to the door.

His shoulders sagged in relief. "She isn't inside."

Áed jogged to be next to him. "Right. Let's hurry."

This was a very important part of the plan. The signaling system of lamps around the castle meant that wherever the Queen and her commanders were, they could communicate with their soldiers. The first step to setting them at a disadvantage was to prevent them from talking to each other.

Rian pushed through the door with purpose. "I set this system up," he said. He didn't even look at the room, striding straight across it to what looked like a font of fire against the far wall. "I can take it down."

Áed walked into the room more slowly. It had a high-posted bed made of dark wood and a rich fur rug on a floor made of countless, colorful glass tiles. Besides that, the room was as bare as the halls. A desk sat beside a tall, narrow window, where a beam of cloudy sunlight fell across a mess of papers, pens, and ink pots. Curious, Áed wandered over to look at it. What did a sadistic faerie queen write about, anyway?

At first, he simply leaned over the papers, not wanting to touch anything he shouldn't. Farther into the room, Rian muttered to himself as he worked on the core of the signaling system. Most of the papers were scratched in a peculiar hand; it changed from illegible scratchings to smooth, languid script. Áed frowned, trying to read the script. The words were interspersed with rough drawings; it looked like ink had been scraped onto the paper with a knife.

He heard a little huff from Rian and looked up. "Are you done?" Rian nodded, and Áed beckoned him over. "Come look at this."

Frowning, Rian joined Áed at the desk. "What's this?"

"I don't know." Áed pointed one gnarled finger to one of the lines that he couldn't read. "Any idea what this says?"

Right away, he could tell Rian hadn't heard him.

The faerie's gaze had sharpened and without hesitation, he scooped a couple of the pages off the desk. "No," he whispered.

Áed got the distinct feeling that response was not an answer to his question. "What is it?"

Rian was still shuffling through the papers, but now, the intensity was turning to fear. "No," he said again, hushed. "No, she c—" The word seemed to catch in his throat.

"Oh, no. She could. She *would*." He looked up, staring at the wall as if looking through it. "She *did*."

"Rian," Áed said sharply, and Rian looked at him with wide, frantic eyes. Seeing such a fear response from someone as powerful as Rian was positively chilling. "What *is* it?" He grabbed a paper but couldn't make sense of much beyond the occasional legible word. "What did she do?"

But Rian was already moving. With a sheaf of papers crunched in his fist, he made for the door.

Áed was after him in a heartbeat, slipping through the great, blackwood door before it closed, and he hurried around in front of Rian as the faerie limped down the hall again. Rian actually growled, an inhuman, impatient sound, putting Áed's hair on end. "Get out of the way," he snapped. He didn't sound angry, but he did sound urgent.

"Okay." Áed raised his hands and moved aside. Immediately, he found himself hurrying after Rian again. "But tell me what's wrong."

Without a word, Rian pressed the papers forcefully against Áed's chest. Áed flipped through them again, frowning. "I can't read most of this. It's scribbles."

"It's Old Seelie."

"A language?" Áed guessed, and Rian nodded.

"She used it when she didn't want the servants to see what she was working on."

"But you can read it?" Áed tore his eyes from the papers. "What does it say?"

"We need to find the Queen."

Áed balked. "I thought we were trying to *avoid* that."

"We can't." Rian turned down a hallway and stopped in the shadow of an alcove. He held out his palm. "Give me those." When Áed handed him the papers, Rian flipped through the pages. "Áed, do you know how gateways are made?"

"Gateways across the veil?" He had a memory of Erin explaining it before the crossing. "Doesn't someone have to die?"

"Some are natural," Rian said, nodding. "Little anomalies. Only big enough for rodents, sometimes tiny fey creatures." He flipped a couple more pages. "Not this one." Rian extended one hand, holding a leaf of paper by the top for Áed to look at. It was one of the illustrated ones, scratched in rough ink, like a schematic.

Áed had to stare at the drawing for a long moment before he understood what he was seeing. When he did, he felt his mouth fall open.

Rian nodded grimly. "It doesn't even *matter* if the castle falls. She's already been planning her exodus." His expression darkened. "Or rather, the expansion of her empire."

Áed snatched the paper as if by staring at it from another angle, the truth would change. The illustration was stark. What would become the gateway was pressed onto the page in jet-black, a half-moon against the parchment; in front of it, a single figure lay on his back. Áed would have thought he was sleeping if not for the jagged line of ink— ink that pooled on the page like blood—that slashed across his throat. "She's doing *this* to get to the human realm?"

"A long-term, steady connection," Rian said quietly. "She wouldn't need an army against a kingdom of humans. With her power, your world would fall in days."

"Who is she killing?" The vicious image seared into Áed's mind.

Rian had stopped shuffling the pages and was reading one intently. "Well, she would need a human to get to the human side." He looked up, face falling into horror. "We *brought* one here."

Áed's blood turned to ice.

Ronan.

"It could be some random crossling," Rian said. He didn't sound convinced. "She might have had someone collect one for her at the festival, or she might have stolen another faerie's…"

"We need to find her." Áed knew he sounded desperate. "Rian, we need to *go*."

CHAPTER FORTY-FOUR
ÉAMON

It went without saying that Éamon had never been in a siege. He and Erin hadn't breached the castle walls; when the portcullises raised as if welcoming them inside, about half of the army had charged in like the tide. The other half had swarmed around the base of the castle, pouring over the drawbridge onto the narrow strip of land at the foot of those ancient, towering walls. They were armed with ladders. More than once, Éamon saw one of those ladders, ablaze with white flames, topple backward and land wholly in the moat, but as soon as the flames were extinguished, those same ladders began to pivot upward again as the forces at the bottom raised them from the water. Arrows fell like rain from the battlements.

Éamon shielded his eyes with a hand as he squinted to the tops of the walls, where the silhouettes of faeries stood stark and small against the bright gray sky.

Áed had to be somewhere in that castle. He wondered if Ronan was, too.

The vanguard of the armies had charged into the castle without hesitation, and even from where he was—still closer to the supply wagons than the fighting—Éamon could hear the clash and scream of battle.

He turned to Erin. "We're going in, right?"

She wrapped the hind's reins around the saddle horn as an arrow whistled into the ground not ten feet ahead of them. Her eyes ranged over the battle, which was spreading into the field as high court fae emerged from the castle like ants from a nest. "We actually might die if we get closer."

"Don't tell me you're backing out." Something about the sound of battle was getting into his blood. "You're supposed to be the one I do stupid, dangerous things with."

"And you're supposed to be a one-legged aristocrat who's never swung a sword," Erin pointed out.

"You don't know if I've used a sword before."

"Have you?"

Éamon glared at her.

Erin groaned, slumping over her hind's back with an air of melodrama. "I do want to help," she said into the hind's neck. "But I guess I didn't expect you to actually want to charge into battle. Do you know you look like you haven't slept in a week?"

The truth that, in all, Éamon hadn't slept more than eight hours over the past three or four days wasn't something he needed to mention. "Are you *sure* Áed is in there?"

Erin was worrying with both hands at the edge of the saddle. "I tried my best to eavesdrop on Fionnlagh when he went to speak with Neasa, but all I could get was something about the consort and sending a message to the other courts. Next thing I know, we're assembling an army." She shook her head. "But all seven low courts are here. Whatever it is, it's important."

"Áed wouldn't want to be anywhere else," Éamon said. He turned to Erin. "He's got a stronger sense of duty than anyone I've ever met. I mean, he took the throne of the human realm at *seventeen*. This…" He looked back to the battle, and Echdían shifted under him as the horse pawed at the ground. He seemed almost impatient, and Éamon stroked his neck. "If this fight is important, then Áed is here."

Erin muttered something under her breath. It sounded like a curse. Then she raised her voice. "I'm riding the horse with you." She slipped off the hind and gave it an affectionate scratch. "This hind is a little too skittish."

"Echdían's a warhorse," Éamon said proudly as if he had any reason to be proud of a horse that wasn't his. "He won't falter. Come on, then."

"You sound so pleased," Erin grumbled.

"It hides the fear." He offered his hand, and Erin took it, hooking the tip of her toe into the stirrup next to Éamon's boot to hoist herself up.

"I'd forgotten how high it was up here," she muttered. She clasped both of her hands over the top of her head like a helmet. "I feel like a target."

"I'm going to get us in," Éamon said, adjusting in his seat to accommodate Erin behind him. "You have the shield. Keep the arrows off us."

"We might be about to die. You realize that, right?"

"You have less to worry about than me. You're hard to kill." Éamon drew his sword and gave Echdían a nudge. The horse started quickly into a trot. He tossed his head proudly, and Éamon got the distinct feeling that he was excited. "You'll be okay."

Erin held his waist tightly with one arm, holding the shield with the other. "I wish this shield was bigger. Or that we had a chariot."

"You can drive a chariot?"

Erin scoffed. "Please. I can stand on the yoke when the

horses are sprinting, and I won't fall when the charioteer turns."

That actually sounded remarkably impressive, but Éamon couldn't let her have it. "So you're not the actual charioteer, then."

He heard her irritated growl, and then she poked him. "Well, I could be!"

Éamon only chuckled. It was much better to tease Erin—and for Erin to be annoyed and poke him—than for either of them to think too hard about the fact that they were headed for a seething mass of flesh and blades.

When they met it, it was chaos.

Already, the ground was red. Around them, cavalry, infantry, and unhorsed warriors clashed deafeningly; horses screamed as arrows and swords missed their mark and sank into equine muscle. Identifying who was who was nearly impossible as the world devolved into a whirling field of earth tones and crimson.

Éamon kept an unwavering grip of Echdían's reins, his teeth clenched hard enough for his jaw to ache as he did his best to keep pace toward the gate. It wasn't possible. Bodies blocked the way, some hot with battle-fury and some already cooling and still on the ground. A great flow of white fire billowed toward them from above, and with a yelp, Erin threw up the shield and ducked her head against Éamon's back. The flames cleared a momentary passage, and with a cry, Éamon dug his heels into Echdían's sides.

The horse tore into the open space without hesitation.

The battle closed around them quickly. A wild-eyed faerie whose sword sparked with flames took a swing at Éamon from the ground, but Éamon yanked on Echdían's reins, and the horse reared. The faerie's sword connected with Éamon's left leg. It slashed a wide cut in the fabric of his trousers before glancing off, and the faerie's face filled with shock.

"Sorry," Éamon muttered as Echdían's front hooves met the ground again with a jolt. The strange, translucent material of Éamon's leg showed through the slash in the fabric of his trousers. "Someone else beat you to that one."

Erin dropped the shield for a moment, enough for Éamon to see that three arrows were already lodged in its hide-covered front. Erin glanced at them with wide eyes before hurrying to lift the shield again.

They were getting close to the gates, where Éamon could see the spiked bottoms of the portcullises hanging at the top of the gateway. If Áed was in the battle itself, there was very little chance that Éamon would be able to find him. The chaos was too dense; there were too many people, too much smoke, too many fallen. Besides that, Éamon didn't think Áed could physically hold a sword in the way he'd need to participate in such a fight—and against high fae, even Áed's inhuman skillset still wouldn't do much good. If he was inside the castle, though…

"He has to be there," Éamon growled. He redoubled his grip on Echdían's reins.

Shifting his sword in his grasp, Éamon used the flat of the blade to smack a high fae soldier out of his path. Echdían only barely evaded stepping on the fallen soldier's legs as, with experienced precision, he navigated the fray under Éamon's guidance. An arrow whizzed by, dazzling Éamon's eyes with ice-white flames, and buried itself somewhere behind him. Erin clung to his back, still holding the shield high. It was hard to tell, given the rhythm of Echdían's gait, but Éamon could see her arm quivering with the strain of it.

"Hang on," he shouted. He leaned over Echdían's neck,

his eyes fixed on the gate. "We're almost there."

The gate was clogged with people. Éamon steered Echdían along the wall, dashing off would-be attackers with his sword. They made it through in what could have been either minutes or hours; the sound of ringing metal on metal, along with the shouts of fury and pain, made the tunneled gateway sing with deafening noise. The courtyard was only slightly less hectic, but after the gate, it felt like a reprieve. Éamon directed Echdían toward a quieter corner, where an empty henhouse butted up against the castle wall, and let out his breath. His heart was flying. "Gods. I never want to do that again."

Behind him, Erin was panting. "My arm hurts like mad."

Still catching his breath, Éamon surveyed the courtyard. It was wide and flat. Directly across from where he and Erin sheltered, wide double doors stood stoically at the top of a staircase. If Éamon had to guess, those doors led into the main wing of the castle—the throne room, feast hall. Through the doors on either side of the courtyard, he thought he'd be more likely to find servants' quarters, perhaps a granary, smithy, kitchen.

Erin swung herself down from the horse, landing with both boots firmly on the cobblestones. "Need a hand?"

Éamon got his bad leg over Echdían's back and kept his weight on his good leg in the stirrup for as long as he could before making the short jump to the ground. He grunted and had to squeeze his eyes shut as the roll of pain passed. "No," he said, slightly strangled. "I'm good."

"What now?" Erin was holding her sword defensively, her shield raised in front of her.

"Well," Éamon said through a heavy breath. "We've broken out of a mound, stolen a horse, snuck into a fae army, met up with six *other* fae armies, and stormed a castle." He shook his head. "Now, we make it worthwhile."

CHAPTER FORTY-FIVE
ÁED

R ian had fallen silent. It was terrifying.

The hallway was low, dark, and narrow enough to make Áed's heart pound faster. Rian held a palmful of firelight ahead of them, but in such close quarters, Áed wasn't sure how it didn't blind him. "This wasn't on the map," Áed said quietly.

Rian didn't respond. He hadn't responded to anything in at least five minutes, and Áed was getting seriously on edge.

"Rian," he tried again anyway. "Where are we *going*?"

To that, Rian only growled quietly.

They were underground. They had to be underground, because the walls were weeping with moisture, and the air smelled like earth. Brackets for torches, all empty, lined the walkway—a walkway which, Áed was growing more certain, sloped downward under their feet.

"Is she in the vaults?"

Rian wheeled on him without warning, and Áed jumped back. "Áed," Rian growled. He closed his eyes and seemed to make an effort to calm his tone, but that angry snarl over his already low, battered voice had sent a knife of pure, primal fear down Áed's spine. "Look," Rian said, more steadily. "I know you're worried about Ronan. And your people. The human realm. That makes *sense*." He clenched his fist tighter around the bundle of papers. "That's why we don't have time to stop and talk." He started walking again, his stride stiff but purposeful. "The armies are already here. We've put the pressure on her. For all we know, she's already opened the gate."

"Which means killing…" He couldn't say it. Crippling nausea overtook him at the very thought of 'Ronan' finishing that sentence. It couldn't be. It just couldn't.

Rian nodded. "And if she opens the gate, she's *gone*. She'll have the human realm—all its people, all its resources, every single human mage—under her thumb by the next festival. Humans are even more susceptible to emotion magic than fae are. She could command legions at once." Every step he took made him grimace, but he strode fast down the cramped hall. "I *know* her, Áed. I know her better than anyone in the entire Goddess-forsaken *world*. This is just like her. She's been ahead of us."

"Once she has the human realm," Áed murmured, "then…"

"Then she marches back here in force," Rian spat. "Reclaims her resources with yours. The low courts won't stand a chance. Your realm will be hers. This realm will be hers. Everything will be hers."

Áed's stomach felt like it was being fed by a drip of ice water. "Then where is she?"

Rian handed Áed the bundle of papers without looking at him, and Áed unfolded it to the page on top. "That drawing," Rian said. "The background. You see that?"

"I'm not sure," Áed said. He turned the paper, trying to tell what he was seeing in the flickering shadows cast by Rian's fire. "Water?"

"A river." Rian picked up his pace with a wince. "It's a

river. And there just so happens to be one that runs right beneath the palace." He accepted the papers back and jammed them into his pocket. "If we'd gone to the other end of the vaults, we might have heard it through the walls."

There was something unsettling about that, but Áed bit his tongue. He only moved faster. "Then we need to hurry."

⦚

Áed really didn't like this hallway. It was something about the smell, he thought, that combination of darkness and damp and cold, clean stone, that brought back memories he didn't like to think about. That along with the cramped darkness and the fact that they were definitely deep underground had him rubbing nervously at his arms and the back of his neck. He quashed those nerves as forcefully as he could. His time in the White City dungeons had been seven years earlier, and he wasn't about to let the lingering anxiety distract him.

After another few minutes of walking, Rian drew back his light without warning. Áed had to press a hand over his own mouth to keep from yelping at the sudden darkness that pressed in on him, opaque and dense.

He felt Rian's hand find his shoulder lightly. "Áed?" Rian whispered through the dark.

"What's wrong?" Áed whispered back.

"Nothing. But we're close." His hand traced down Áed's arm until he folded Áed's hand into his. "I'll lead you. I can tell where the tunnel is."

"With magic?"

"With magic." Rian's hand was warm and dry in Áed's. "Come on."

Despite the pitch-darkness, Áed kept his eyes wide, blinking blindly in front of him. The only guidance was the sound of Rian's footsteps ahead of his, and Rian's hand tugging Áed's forward.

In a moment, they stopped, and Áed realized that light was seeping through the darkness ahead of them, like ink through paper in reverse. Together, they crept forward to see.

The hallway opened up before them. The pathway led down into a natural-looking hollow; stalactites hung from the ceiling, and, in places, met with their mirrors to create rippled pillars of liquid-looking stone. At the far end of the cave, a waterfall tumbled out of some fathomless black hollow into a deep, dark-glass pool, and from the pool, a river slid through the cave into another hollow on the opposite side. The whole place was cast in the stark, shifting shades of white fire that blazed from two upright torches, set on poles that had been hammered into the rock.

For a heartbeat, Áed thought it was empty.

Until a figure, facing away from them, stepped out from behind one of the stalagmite columns.

Beside him, Áed heard Rian make a tiny, choked noise.

The figure appeared to be pacing unhurriedly. Áed squinted, trying to make out detail. It was a woman, it seemed, in a white dress. Under a silver crown, she had hair that Áed had at first mistaken for a cloak; it poured over her shoulders, down her back, and past her waist until it brushed against the backs of her calves in glossy, night-black waves. "That's her?" Áed whispered. Rian nodded slightly. Áed craned his neck, trying to see the entirety of the room. "I don't see Ronan."

"No," Rian said. His voice was barely audible. "He's not here."

Relief flooded Áed's body, and he felt himself slump. "Oh, thank the Gods." He found himself smiling, despite the danger they still faced. *Ronan wasn't there.* He looked to Rian. If they could finish this… "Can you…" He hesitated. "Can you take her?"

But Rian was only staring at the Queen. His dark-lashed eyes were sharp with concentration, and his face was disturbed. "What is she waiting for?"

"You." The reply floated through the cavern.

Both Áed and Rian froze. The answer had drifted from the bottom of the cave, echoing off the walls in a chorus of tranquil voices. Unhurried, the Queen turned around.

There was a smile on her face.

"I was waiting for both of you."

⟩⟩⟩

Áed moved first, because he could. Rian seemed to have been paralyzed, his face frozen in an expression Áed couldn't unpack—it was deeper and more complicated than fear. Áed slipped around the corner of the hallway, to where the path sloped down into the cave, moving slowly. "How did you know we were coming?"

The Queen only chuckled. "What a silly question." She inclined her head, and Áed got the feeling she was indicating Rian. "Really, I knew *he* would come back sooner or later. That was only a matter of time. If you weren't with him, I'd just use him to find you."

"I wouldn't have helped you," Rian growled, and the Queen laughed again.

"Of course, you would have." She took a step forward, her white dress brushing on the damp cave floor. "You remember your old servant friend, my dear? I kept him around…"

Rian only growled louder. He didn't move.

Áed raised his hands, getting between them. "Okay. Okay, so you were waiting for us." At this point, he was stalling;

he shot a look back at Rian, trying to communicate with his eyes that now was the time. The Queen hadn't opened the gate yet; she was only talking. Rian could take her, Áed *knew* that, if he could pull himself out of his own head for long enough to do so. "*Why* were you waiting for us?"

He had expected the Queen to laugh again, but she didn't. "Well," she said with a short sigh. "I was waiting for my consort because I want him by my side in our new kingdom." She pointed to Áed, letting her hand fall back at the wrist. "And I was waiting for *you* to get me there."

Áed drew back. "What?"

She didn't answer him; she stepped closer. "Rian, dear," she purred. As she drew closer, Áed could see more of her face. She had an alien, perfectly symmetrical beauty, but unlike Rian, her looks were cold. She looked like a doll, all porcelain skin, painted lips, and round, youthful face, and her smile seemed like it ought to crack the ceramic of her cheeks. But her eyes, fringed as they were with impossibly long lashes, were different altogether. Something about them made Áed's muscles lock up.

Her eyes looked ages older than her perfect porcelain face.

Her eyes were primordial.

"Rian, dear," she went on, that smile fixed on her doll-like mouth. "Won't you come here? Bring the boy."

Rian still looked petrified. As if it took great effort, he turned to Áed. There was horror etched on his face—horror and realization. "Áed," he whispered. "Run."

Instinctively, Áed took a step backward. He heard the Queen's delicate laughter.

The next moment, he was on his knees.

When Erin, in her terror, had projected her fear over the room from her bed in the White City palace, Áed had felt it distantly. The waves of induced emotion that had leveled Ronan and the guards had left Áed largely unscathed.

This was not the same.

Áed crumpled under the weight of overwhelming, debilitating pain. The fact that it was emotional rather than physical only made it hurt more; as every degree of guilt he'd ever felt, every tear of shattered loss, every drop of terror and regret, all converged on him with singular, cutting purpose, his mouth opened in a soundless cry.

Áed had felt pain. He knew it well. He knew grief, and terror, and helplessness. He knew broken bones and tortured gouges carved deep into his flesh.

And yet, he had never hurt like this.

Every apology he had never made. Every missed opportunity to say 'I love you.' Every golden moment turned into nostalgia so strong that it forced the wind from his lungs and the life from his limbs. He experienced his worst memories like they were happening again.

He couldn't bear this. He would break.

The world was growing dark.

Rian's voice came to him distantly. Something pleading, begging an outside force to please, please stop.

And as quickly as it had begun, it did stop.

Áed lay on his side, halfway down the smooth path to the cave. He was sweating and gasping for breath.

"Áed," Rian's voice came from above him. "Hey. Hey." The other man had taken his shoulders and was gripping them as if he thought Áed would be lost if he let go. "Are you there?"

Áed gasped a ragged breath. He had not been capable of imagining power like that. He felt raw. Cracked. "I'm… I'm here."

Immense relief passed over Rian's face. "Oh, thank Goddess. Are you all right?"

Áed moved to sit up, and Rian shifted to make sure that he was still in contact with him. "I'm okay," Áed said. He was still shaking. "I think." He touched his temple lightly. His head had begun to throb. "What happened?"

"The Queen," Rian said. His voice quivered. "I'm shielding you right now."

"You're shielding *him*," the Queen laughed. Her crown glinted in the pale firelight. "But I can still come for *you*."

Suddenly, Rian's jaw clenched, and he made a sound like he was choking. He squeezed his eyes shut, his hands tightening on Áed's shoulders enough to hurt. "Rian!" Áed gasped.

Rian grunted, shaking his head hard. Áed felt wisps of suffering slip through his mind as Rian's shield around Áed faltered, but the dark-haired man didn't let it fall. "Stop it," he snarled, eyes still pressed shut. There were tears beading in the corners. "You hag."

The Queen tutted, and with a cry, Rian's head bowed under another onslaught of her power.

"Whatever you want, I won't do it," he managed. Áed had no idea how Rian was even still talking. "You should know by now. This isn't enough." He opened his eyes, letting them burn even as tears traced down his cheeks. "This doesn't work on me."

"Hmm." The Queen tilted her head. "That's right, isn't it? It would have been so much easier for everyone if it did." She turned to Áed, and Rian slumped as her attention shifted away from torturing him. "It's Áed, isn't it?"

Áed tore his eyes away from Rian—who was catching his breath, blinking tears out of his eyes—to glare at the pretty, unearthly creature who stood just a few steps from the waterfall.

"Don't ask me how I know," she said, waving a hand lightly. "I've been watching you since your coronation, Áed. Assume I know *everything*."

"Since my *coronation*?" Áed said faintly.

"Don't listen to her," Rian rasped. "She had me spy sometimes, but she doesn't know as much as she wants you to—ah!" He doubled over again, taking one hand off Áed's shoulders to clutch at his head.

"Stop it!" Áed shouted. "Stop hurting him!"

"Come here, then," the Queen said. "While he's occupied. Just come over to me." She tilted her head. "Then I'll stop."

"Don't do it," Rian panted. His face was still screwed up in anguish. "I can't... I can't protect you when I'm like this. Not if you're far away."

The Queen only blinked.

Rian screamed.

"I can make it so much worse," the Queen said lightly. "Áed, would you like me to?"

"No!" Áed knelt in front of Rian as if he could block the Queen's attacks with his body. He tried to find the protectiveness with which he'd defended Éamon, but every time he tried to press it past himself, it shattered under the Queen's attack. He put a hand on either side of Rian's face, and Rian clutched at Áed's wrist like a lifeline. His eyes were hazy and barely open.

"Don't do what she says," he managed. His words were slurred. "I can take it. Don't leave."

"You know what it feels like, now, Áed," the Queen said. She folded her hands behind her back. "To have me in your mind." She nodded to Rian. "He's experiencing that ten times over. How long do you think he'll last?"

"As long as I have to," Rian grunted. He opened his eyes, evidently with a struggle. "*You* trained me to bear this, witch."

The Queen sighed. "Even I make mistakes, I suppose." She lifted a hand and trailed it through her hair. It parted over her shoulder like the waterfall behind her parted over the rock. "But, Áed, he doesn't *have* to bear it. Just come over to me."

"Don't," Rian whispered. Despite his conviction, his voice was getting weaker. "Áed, she's... she's going to kill you."

Áed frowned at him. He knew the Queen was bloodthirsty, but the way Rian had said it made it sound like the Queen wanted Áed dead, specifically. "Me?"

"Your blood." Rian's grip was still steely on Áed's wrist, and Áed tried to take hope from that, even as Rian's voice grew fainter. "Both worlds... the gate..." His forehead fell to meet Áed's shoulder. "I didn't realize... I wouldn't have brought you here."

The fragmented thoughts took a moment to come together in Áed's head. As soon as they did, he found himself holding tighter to Rian. "The person in the drawing..." The memory of dark ink pooling like blood over a fallen figure seared itself against his frame of vision. "That's *me?*"

"The gate." Rian's brow was glistening with cold sweat. "There's a natural gate." His throat bobbed as he swallowed. "In the waterfall. Very small. Water sprites pass through." His eyes fluttered closed, and he grimaced in pain. "If you die at the gate, she can travel both ways." There were still tears pouring over his cheeks. "Don't go to her. Stay... stay where I can..."

"He's fading," the Queen said. Her mannequin face broke into an even wider smile. "Whether you come willingly will soon be irrelevant."

Áed didn't have to look at Rian to know he was suffering. His anguish overflowed as if into the air itself. Even what Áed detected—which he knew could only be an echo of what Rian felt—was enough to make him feel like crying. Áed stayed crouched beside him, wishing he could shield

Rian the way Rian was still shielding Áed.

"Rian," Áed whispered. "You have to kill her."

Another tear rolled down Rian's face. "I can't." The words came out without sound.

"Rian, dear," the Queen said, and Áed got the distinct idea she was changing tactics. "What if *you* came over here?" She smiled benevolently. "If you do, I'll make the pain stop. I promise."

"Rian," Áed said firmly, keeping his voice as low as he could. "I need you to do one thing. Just one." He shifted so that he faced the Queen. "I need you to use your magic." Keeping the motion as subtle as he could, he freed his mother's axe from his back. "I need you to help me grip this."

Rian's hand gripped Áed's wrist. His eyes were blazing, even hazy as they were with pain. "Have you ever killed somebody, Áed?"

Áed didn't answer.

"Don't do it," Rian whispered. "You never go back to how you were before."

There was a kind of energy building in the cave. It was the low murmur of the waterfall, ceaseless white noise intensifying in the back of Áed's skull. Or maybe it was Rian's trembling. Or maybe it was the Queen's magic, webbing through the air invisibly and filling every shadowed space.

Áed set his jaw. His nerves were buzzing.

Suddenly, Rian's eyes flashed wide. "Get down!" he choked.

The next thing Áed knew, Rian had tackled him. Áed's back slammed against rippled stone as they tumbled down the path, one over the other. Rian's elbow found its way into Áed's diaphragm, forcing the wind out of Áed's lungs, and Rian gave a little cry when his head knocked against the uneven path. Panting, they disentangled themselves clumsily on the cave floor. "What was that?" Áed wheezed. He hadn't gotten his air back yet.

His answer came in the form of Rian shoving himself in front of Áed and throwing up a hand. A split second later, a wave of white fire parted around them both.

"That works," the Queen said. Her tone had shifted to amusement, and it came from very close by. "Hello, boys."

Áed scrambled to his knees, casting about for his axe. It had fallen with them—he supposed he should be glad it hadn't impaled him in the back as he and Rian had rolled down the path. His first try at picking it up didn't work. His stubborn fingers closed on the grip but gave when he tried to lift its weight. He swore. Usually, he dealt with heavy things by getting a hand or both underneath it, not by actually trying to grab it. Unfortunately, axes didn't work like that. All the same, he lunged at it again, and managed with both hands to get it off the ground. He didn't think he'd be able to swing it, but he held it up in front of him and Rian defensively.

The Queen only laughed. "Is that a request? I can certainly use that to spill your blood. One weapon is as good as another."

"No!" Rian cried. His voice sounded strangled.

The Queen kicked him. She put her foot on his shoulder, and without so much as looking, pushed him out of the way. "Don't get up again."

Áed did his best to scramble backward, but with the axe in his hands, he was off-balance. On his knees, he stumbled and fell. The Queen bent at the waist, looking at him curiously. "How close do you need to be to the gate for it to work?" Her lips curled at the corners. "*In* it? Oh, the water would run red."

"Rian," Áed managed. He kept his voice quiet, hidden from the Queen under the noise of the waterfall. "I have."

His gaze held steady into Rian's eyes, even as his heart hammered. "I have killed."

Rian's expression didn't change, but all the same, Áed felt his surprise—and chagrin.

"I've done it twice." Áed struggled back to his knees. "Just help me hold the axe, Rian."

"You'll die if I don't," Rian said faintly.

"A lot of people will." Áed got to his knees again and managed to get the axe into his hands. It was unwieldy. "I won't make you kill her. Just help me hold the axe."

Rian squeezed his eyes shut. The Queen had backed off a step after kicking Rian as if, despite her bravado, she still feared him. But now she was drawing closer again, emboldened by his lack of resistance. "The weapon is only as strong as the wielder," she said with a glassy chuckle. "I made plans for this moment as soon as I heard of your bloodline, *Your Majesty*. You keep quite the secret from your lovely, human people." Her smile widened. "But not from me."

From her doll-like stature, Áed would have expected her joints to move stiffly, like a puppet. From her ancient eyes, Áed would have expected her to falter.

The Queen did neither.

In a movement so fast that to blink was to miss it, she produced a knife from the folds of her dress. In the next fraction of a breath, she had it to Áed's throat.

But two things could happen at the same time.

At the very moment that the Queen moved, Áed saw the flash in Rian's eye.

Áed raised the axe, gripped solidly in his hands. His hands did not change their shape, nor did his fingers grow stronger, but all the same, the axe grew light and natural in his palms.

When the Queen pressed her knife to Áed's throat...

Áed pressed the axe into her chest.

CHAPTER FORTY-SIX
RONAN

As soon as the portcullises were open, Ronan had stuck to the plan. As the armies rolled in and the high court soldiers met them in the bailey with a great clash of people and weaponry, he had hightailed it. Fionnuala had been holding her own still, facing fewer enemies as more guards rushed outside to join the fray or man the archers' positions, and Ronan, seeing this, felt all right making for the safest place he could. According to the plan, that meant the inner keep. He was to stay there until the castle was under friendly control; if it stayed in high-court hands, he was to make for the vault and leave the way they'd all come. But that was a worst-case scenario.

His plans, however, had been interrupted almost immediately.

He was tearing down the hallway that lined the courtyard, heading for the keep, when the ground trembled under his feet. It was accompanied by a flash of light through the lead-paned windows and a sound like an explosion. Ronan felt it in his chest, resonating through his sternum.

If he wasn't mistaken, the sounds of shouting in the courtyard had just become notably louder.

He made for the nearest door and burst out into the courtyard in time for a ball of white fire the size of a person to hit in the middle of the yard. As soon as it did, it exploded. Paving stones and chunks of dirt blew outward, and Ronan saw at least three people blasted bodily from the ground. One of them didn't move when they landed.

Frantically, he searched the open space. It was a motley of low-court soldiers pitted against high court fighters, but while the low-court soldiers looked to the sky, distracted from their combat by the threat of more explosions, the high court warriors pressed their advantage.

Suddenly, Ronan's eyes caught on something. "No way," he muttered.

Two familiar figures were standing in the corner of the courtyard. They looked like they had just dismounted from a gigantic black warhorse.

Without thinking, Ronan darted into the fray. He kept close to the walls, weaving between people seeking respite from the fight. "Éamon!" he called as soon as he was close enough to be in earshot. "Erin!"

They both looked up as he hurried up to them. "Ronan!" Éamon was holding the horse's reins, and Erin's shield hung by her side as if her arm was too tired to support it. All the same, her face brightened at Ronan's arrival.

"What are you doing here?" Ronan asked. He knew he was grinning to see them. "I thought you stayed back!"

"How could we stay away from..." Erin gestured at the chaos. "This?"

On cue, another fireball slammed into the ground in the center of what once must have been a vegetable patch. It exploded in a flare of blinding white, tearing the half-frozen earth to pieces and making everybody duck.

"This isn't good," Erin said. "Those explosions are going to decimate us."

Already, Ronan could see that she was right. Low fae lay scattered across the courtyard, and the ones pouring through the gate to replace them were immediately engaged by the still-standing high faeries.

"Up there," Éamon said, pointing. Ronan shaded his eyes, squinting to follow his gesture. "On the top of the well."

The well was nestled into an alcove, roofed into a little outdoor room by the addition of a tiled overhang. On that overhang, with the wall to her back, a faerie stood. Ronan could see the swirl of flames gathering in her palm as she overlooked the seething crowd below her.

Erin growled softly. "I see her." As she spoke, the faerie on the overhang wound up and hurled her fire into a contingent of low fae who had just come in from the gate. Ronan had to look away when it exploded.

"That's a problem," he said. He could hear the bloodcurdling screams that followed the explosion. "Can every high faerie do that?"

"I'd imagine if they could, they all would be."

Ronan pulled his braid over his shoulder. "We're doing something about this, right?"

Erin turned to look at the faerie again. She squinted, her eyes flicking back and forth as she surveyed the field. Then she turned back around, planting her hands on her hips. "Éamon," she said. "You're a good horseman, yes?"

Éamon looked startled. "I'm—all right, I suppose."

"Not the time for modesty." Erin's stare was piercing. "Are you, or are you not?"

Éamon huffed. "Fine. Yes. Yes, I am actually very good with horses."

"Can you get Ronan and me across this courtyard without dying?"

A little glint slipped into Éamon's eye. "I got you and I into the castle, didn't I?"

Erin grinned. "You did. All right, then, get on that horse. Ronan, you, too."

Éamon and Ronan both obeyed, and then Erin shoved herself up as well, positioning her body between Ronan's and Éamon's. For once, Ronan was glad that he was small enough to fit.

"All right, Éamon," Erin said. Her eyes were fixed on the faerie over the well. "I need you to take us across the yard. Head straight for that faerie." Her eyes narrowed. "And when I say 'turn,' you turn." She twisted to look at Ronan. "This is a team effort. When it's time, I'll need you to catch me."

"*Catch* you?"

Erin grinned. "You'll know when it's time." She poked Éamon in the back. "You ready, aristocrat?"

Ronan could *feel* Éamon rolling his eyes, but he nodded. "I'm ready."

"Right," Erin pronounced. She said the word with relish. "Go!"

The horse snorted, drawing back when Éamon dug his heels into its sides. Then, with a thrust of its powerful legs, it shot forward into the courtyard.

The battle turned into a blur as Ronan struggled to focus on just one thing. White fire flashed at the edges of his vision, and the whirl and glint of swords and shields made his head spin. The horse, under Éamon's charge, wove through the melee like a spirit of war. Ronan gripped the saddle for dear life as they leapt over fallen soldiers and galloped between pairs locked in combat. Another white explosion rocked the ground to their left, but the horse regained its footing and kept gaining speed.

Then Erin was in motion.

In one movement, she pressed herself into a crouch on the horse's back, planting her feet in the saddle.

Then, on the back of a galloping warhorse, she was standing.

Éamon glanced back for a fraction of a moment, his eyes wide with shock. "Erin!"

"Keep going!" Erin shouted. Her knees were bent for stability, but Ronan had no idea how she stayed on the horse's back. In her right hand, her sword flashed. "Steady," she cried. Around them, combat boiled. The world seemed beyond clear as Ronan watched the ends of Erin's dreadlocks whip in the wind. She adjusted the grip of her sword in her hand and drew it back.

They were getting close to the well, not slowing down. Ronan's chest seized.

They were going to crash.

"*Turn!*"

Erin's scream cut through the cacophony. Éamon pulled back on the horse's reins, and the horse reared back into a sharp, half-skidding turn. Its hooves dug up grooves in the yard, clods of dirt flying in the direction of their momentum. At the very moment they began to change course, Erin hurled her sword forward.

It spun point over pommel, whirling toward the faerie on the overhang.

"Catch me!" Erin shrieked, and Ronan's attention immediately warped from the sword to Erin's falling body. Her back collided hard with his chest, threatening to topple them both over the horse's rear. He got his arm around her waist, the other gripping the saddle desperately. Éamon took the horse around the outside of the yard, letting it canter out of its sprint.

Ronan found himself holding Erin tightly to his body, gasping as the horse clopped to a bouncy halt on the opposite side of the courtyard. Erin was sweating and hot, her eyes wide and chest heaving. As soon as they stopped, Éamon turned around in the saddle. "Erin! What was *that*?" He was grinning wildly.

Erin slumped back entirely against Ronan, pressing a hand to her forehead. Ronan could feel her heart racing. "Usually that would happen in a chariot," she said breathlessly.

Ronan knew his eyes must be perfect circles. "Erin, that was—that was—" He was flushing with heat from head to toe. "That was the best thing I've ever seen in my life. Ever. Oh, my *Gods*, Erin—"

"Don't get too excited yet," Erin panted. "Did it work?"

They looked back at the overhang.

The faerie's top half hung over the edge as if she had drunkenly fallen asleep on the sloped surface. The only thing to indicate that she wasn't sleeping was the steady stream of blood pouring off the overhang.

"Yeah," Ronan said hoarsely. "I think it worked." He shook his head. His hair was out of its braid, falling around his face. "Erin! How did you do that!" He turned to Éamon. "Éamon! How did you ride like that?" He grabbed the sides of his head. "I'm so impressed! I can't hold it!"

Erin sat up a little to look at Ronan's face. "How about you?" she asked. "Before we got here, what were you doing?"

"Oh." Ronan felt himself blush. "I just opened the portcullises."

It was Erin's turn to go wide-eyed. "That was *you*?"

Ronan nodded. "Fionnuala helped."

"That's incredible, Ronan," Éamon said, grinning. He

looked tired, but his expression was exhilarated. "Was Áed with you?"

Ronan shook his head. "He's with the consort, somewhere inside the castle."

Around them, the fighting had redoubled now that the low fae didn't need to watch for explosive attacks from above. The high armies were being pushed back as more low forces poured through the gates.

"Come on," Éamon said. He swung himself carefully down from the saddle. "Let's go find him."

Ronan and Erin followed his lead. "He and Rian were meant to be disabling the torch signaling system," Ronan said as Éamon led the horse into a corner, out of the way.

"Let's go inside," Éamon suggested. "I want to make sure he's okay."

Now that Éamon had mentioned it, Ronan was also worried for Áed. Áed could handle himself, and he *was* with the most powerful faerie in the world, but Ronan still wanted to check. "Follow me."

Inside the castle again, Ronan was struck by the quiet. He hadn't realized that his ears were ringing until a foot of stone lay between him and the din of the battle.

Almost immediately, though, Erin frowned and moved to one of the windows that opened to the courtyard.

Ronan peeked over her shoulder. "What is it?"

"Some kind of fuss," Erin said. Everything about her body language was wary. "Look."

'Fuss' was a strange word for it. Indeed, the view from the window could have been described as *lack* of fuss, but given the context, that was strange.

Everybody in the courtyard had stopped fighting.

Bloodied swords that had been raised to strike or parry hung uncertainly at soldiers' armored sides. The clamor of shouts had died to quiet murmuring—Ronan could see lips moving beyond the glass, but sound no longer leached through the castle walls to reach them. The world had gone still.

Ronan shrugged. "Back outside, I suppose."

He pushed back out into the clouded sunlight and immediately found himself standing on his tiptoes to see over people's heads.

At the top of the staircase that led to the great doors, Áed and Rian stood. Rian looked worse for wear; his face was pale and haggard. Áed stood beside him, positively drenched in blood. His shirt, his skin, and the axe on his back were all crimson.

"Áed!" Ronan shouted, and before he'd consciously given himself permission, he was sprinting through the crowd toward the staircase. He heard people murmuring—*that's the consort, that's His Elegance, who is that with him?* He barreled up the stairs, not giving anyone else a second thought. "Áed! Are you hurt? What happened?"

He didn't slow down when he met Áed, and Áed staggered back as Ronan collided with him. Right away, Áed gripped him tightly in a hug, burying his face in Ronan's hair. "*Ceann beag,*" he murmured. "You're safe. Thank the Gods."

"I'm fine. I'm great." Ronan didn't release the hug. "What about you? Whose blood is this? What happened?"

In response, Áed nodded in Rian's direction, and Ronan drew his face out of Áed's shirt. He was bloody now as well, but he didn't care.

Rian stepped forward. He was holding something in his hand, and as Ronan pulled away from Áed, Rian raised it. It was silver and round. It looked like metallic, glittering vines had wound about each other to make it.

With a flick of his wrist, Rian tossed the crown down the steps.

The entire courtyard seemed to hold its breath. The crown

hit each stone step with a *clink*, picking up momentum, and it rolled along the paving-stones at the bottom. People moved out of the way.

"The Queen," Rian said deliberately, "is dead."

CHAPTER FORTY-SEVEN
RONAN

Rian's rough voice rolled over the crowd, and Ronan could hear when it met the stone walls and echoed back. The announcement was met by stillness.

"The Queen Líadan, my lady, is dead." Rian's eyes swept the crowd. Even clearly weary, he cut a striking figure. He was beautiful in a way that people just weren't supposed to be.

Ronan was aghast. "That wasn't part of the plan," he whispered to Áed.

"Plan changed," Áed whispered back.

"But…" Ronan shook his head, still processing. "Then is the war over? Who's Queen now?"

The response came not from Áed, nor from Rian.

At first, it was only one person. Then it was two, and then the crowd was rippling with motion as others joined.

One by one, every high faerie knelt.

Something about it felt curious. A number of them threw themselves to the ground immediately as if terrified. Others looked at Rian more fondly and got to their knees with what looked like respect. The rest followed, obeying the precedent of their fellows.

Áed leaned to whisper in Ronan's ear. "About twenty minutes ago, I learned that the royal consort is next in line for the throne."

Rian descended the steps slowly and began to walk through the crowd. Those closest to him deepened their poses as much as their armor would permit. "Stop your fighting," Rian said. The weariness in his voice somehow made it seem lower, authoritative. "This conflict is over." He raised his voice as he moved. "Bone," he said. "Moon. Garnet and Sand. Meadow, Glass, and Gold." At his words, Ronan saw low-courters perk up. "My court's aggression against yours ends now."

There was no cheer. Fae looked at each other in disbelief.

"Tend to your wounded," Rian said. "The fighting is over."

Again, a moment of pause, but people began to move. The atmosphere was of confusion, but people began to do as Rian said. Ronan watched faeries turn to their kin who lay bleeding. Someone was pulling the faerie down from the overhang; she wasn't quite dead, it seemed, but she certainly wasn't throwing any more explosions. Ronan took a brief pause to thank the Gods they'd eliminated her before Áed stepped into the open.

Still, despite Rian's announcement, the air wasn't settled. The sound of fighting hadn't fully died, even though the only skirmishes in the courtyard were happening on the fringes between fae who apparently hadn't been able to drop the grudge. In the corner, Éamon was struggling with his horse: it was rearing up, and Ronan could hear it whinnying as it lashed out with its hooves. It was shying away from Éamon when he tried to take its reins. Ronan had never seen the horse behave that way toward Éamon. Frankly, Ronan was surprised that Éamon hadn't hurried over to Áed as soon as Áed came out of the building. Had he missed something?

Unsettled, Ronan started down the stairs.

Right away, he saw Erin pushing through the crowd. "Ronan!" she shouted. "Áed!" By gratuitous use of her elbows, she managed to stumble into the clearing of the stairs. She ran up them two at a time. "Fighting," she panted. "There's fighting in the bailey."

Áed frowned. "They must not have heard Rian's announcement."

Erin shook her head. "That's not it." At Ronan's questioning look, she jabbed a finger over her shoulder. "There are no Moon fae in the courtyard," she said. "They're all outside." Her expression was intense. "The Moon army is in the bailey, attacking Bone."

⸿

Ronan couldn't explain why, but his first instinct was to look to the corner where Éamon had been struggling with the horse. The horse was still there, ears pinned and nostrils wide, but Éamon was nowhere to be seen.

Áed was already in motion. "They must have planned this," he said as Ronan and Erin hurried to follow him. Erin was right; there was not a single Moon faerie in the courtyard, not so much as a flash of white hair.

Except—

"Éamon!" Ronan called. He saw Éamon's ivory head over the top of the crowd, moving through the gates. Éamon didn't turn back to look at him. "Áed, Éamon's going to the bailey!"

"Éamon is *here*?"

They reached the gates. The sound of fighting, now all too familiar to Ronan's ears, echoed through the enclosed space from the bailey without.

When they reached the end of the gateway, all three of them stopped.

It was clear that the Bone fae were outnumbered. After

all, a portion of their forces was inside the courtyard, while all of Moon had stayed outside to attack. Ronan could see Fionnuala fighting off three opponents at once, clearly tiring but holding her own. Nearer to the wall of the castle itself, Neasa was fighting as well. Her face was streaked with war paint, half-covered by that fang-skull helmet, and she was wielding two jagged swords.

"There's Éamon!" Erin said, and Ronan followed her pointing finger. It was difficult to identify him through the shifting battle, but Ronan managed to pick out Éamon's familiar face. "Nobody is striking at him."

Ronan frowned. "You're right." It made sense for Bone not to—many of them knew Éamon as Áed's crossling. They had spent enough time at the Bone mound to become recognizable. But the Moon fae were actively stepping aside to let him pass.

"What is he doing?" Áed was shading his eyes against the bright, clouded sky. His hand was sparking, but he didn't seem to notice.

Éamon reached Fionnuala and raised his sword. He brought it down on her nearest attacker, making Ronan wince; even at a distance, he could see the blood spray. Fionnuala finished off the other two, one with a vicious thrust through the chest and the other with the flat of her blade cracked hard against her enemy's masked face. She turned to Éamon, and Ronan watched her face fall into surprise. It was impossible to hear what she said, but Ronan watched her lips move. She seemed confused.

Éamon didn't lower his sword.

He stepped forward, and without a beat of hesitation, he shoved the point of the blade into Fionnuala's gut.

"*No!*"

Áed's scream brought Ronan back to reality.

He couldn't process what he had just seen.

Erin was standing frozen. Ronan could hear his own heartbeat. Áed was already in motion, tearing his way through the crowd toward his half-sister.

Ronan stood, stunned. "What…?"

"Éamon's moving," Erin said. She sounded as shocked as Ronan; her voice was distant. "That *was* Éamon… right?"

Ronan blinked, seeking Éamon again in the fray. He couldn't find the words to answer her. Nothing that had just happened made sense.

Without a plan in his head, Ronan took off into the chaos.

His visual on Éamon came and went as he wove through the battle. He bent to snatch up somebody's fallen shield, holding it close as he ran. Éamon was heading in the direction of Neasa, Ronan realized, and a chill dropped into his gut. "Éamon!" he shouted, but his voice was lost to the tumult.

What was going on? What was going on?

Ronan lost sight of Éamon as the fighting closed around him, but he must have been close because he heard Éamon's voice. "Neasa," Éamon called, and another chill zipped down Ronan's spine. Somehow, it didn't sound like *Éamon*. It was his voice, but something about it was profoundly wrong.

He shoved his way into the open just in time to see Éamon approaching Neasa. At his arrival, the Moon soldiers fighting the Bone leader backed off. Ronan stared as they melted into the battle.

"Neasa," Éamon called again. "I have a message for you."

Neasa looked to the battle seething around her and then beckoned Éamon closer to the wall, where it was clearer. Though her face was unreadable behind her helmet, her body language accepted Éamon as an ally. "Speak."

Éamon was close to Neasa, now, and she had lowered her blades.

In a flash, Éamon's sword was free of its sheath. It was still red with Fionnuala's blood as, faster than Ronan could blink, he hurled it in a rapid, deadly arc across Neasa's chest.

Metal crashed against metal.

Neasa held her swords in a cross, trapping Éamon's blade an inch from her sternum. Her eyes were blazing behind her helmet. "I knew something was wrong," she growled, and then she was whipping her arms downward, throwing back Éamon's blade. Éamon barely got his sword up in time to block two lighting strokes from Neasa's weapons. Sparks fizzed out from the contact. "There is something wrong with you, crossling."

Éamon stumbled onto the defensive as Neasa's swords whirled. Something in his eyes looked hollow as he parried blow after blow.

"You're absent," Neasa snarled. "Éamon sleeps. Where is my son's crossling?"

The unsettling, manic grin hadn't left Éamon's face. "Right here."

Neasa's lip curled fiercely. "You wanted a way to get close to me?" Her swords were a blur. "That was your mistake."

Éamon barely blocked two more attacks in rapid succession. As Ronan watched, Neasa dropped the point of one of her swords low to the ground. It was with expert precision that she slotted its tip between the odd, translucent bones of Éamon's prosthesis.

A smile split her own face, as sharp as the fangs on her helmet.

She twisted her sword.

Time seemed to slow down. Ronan heard clearly a single, ringing *click*, like a crack darting through crystal.

And then, with a resonant, singing crash, the material shattered.

Éamon stumbled as his leg gave out from beneath him. Shards of the thing scattered across the clearing; Éamon's boot stayed flat on the ground while the sharp, broken ends of his shin stayed affixed to his body.

For a moment, Éamon blinked. A look of confusion stole over his face.

Then Neasa, with a pitiless snarl, cracked the butt of her sword into his head.

CHAPTER FORTY-EIGHT
ÁED

Áed didn't like staying in the castle. It had been a surprise to him when he caught himself wishing he were back at the Bone mound as if it were home. But after everything, he supposed it made sense for him to never want to see the high court again.

At that moment, he stood in one of the stairwells—the northeastern tower, he thought. He had wandered there without much aim. He was looking out one of the windows, feeling the damp wind on his face as he stared across the plain, to the forest, to beyond.

Footsteps on the stairs made him turn. "Rian," he greeted. The sun was only barely up, and it felt right to speak quietly.

Rian nodded his hello. "Did you sleep last night?"

"A bit." In truth, Áed had spent much of his time pacing the dark halls of the castle, trying to sort his thoughts. After all, there was good news. The fighting was over. After Éamon's attempt on Neasa's life had failed, the Moon court forces had gotten skittish. Rian had arrived in the bailey minutes later, and with a wave of simmering magic, halted every Moon soldier where he stood. It had been hard to sort through later—un-freezing each of them individually so that they could be handcuffed together and locked up until somebody decided what to do with them—but it had been done. Besides that, Ronan and Fionnlagh were safe.

But where there was good, there was dark as well.

Fionnuala was injured badly. She was alert enough to joke about it, but the fact remained that she had been stabbed in the gut. Only time would tell what damage had been done. Fortunately, the blade hadn't been iron. Áed had been assured that made a big difference.

Áed had not been able to believe that Éamon had pushed a sword into Fionnuala's stomach. Even when Éamon had immediately attempted to kill Neasa as well, Áed had found himself unable to accept it. It didn't make sense.

But it was true.

"Fionnuala's awake," Rian said. "She's asking for you."

There hadn't been much time to talk in the aftermath, so Áed followed Rian right away. Already, he knew, Rian had visited as many of the wounded as he could. Healing might be beyond his capacity, but Rian *could* take away pain, and he did for anyone who asked.

Fionnuala hadn't asked. When Áed had heard this, he'd expected her to have a rationale along the lines of 'pain makes you stronger,' but apparently, she just needed it to keep her in bed. If she didn't feel it, she said, she wouldn't be able to stop herself from moving for long enough to recover.

Fionnuala's room was dim when Áed arrived, a single candle glowing behind a latticed wooden screen. Fionnlagh sat with her in the chair next to her bed. His shoulder was bandaged, and his arm was in a sling.

Rian vanished before anyone could ask him to stay or go, and Fionnuala settled back against the pillows with a sigh. Her curly hair was loose; it spread over the bedding down to her waist. She looked warmly at Áed when he came in. "How are you?"

Áed managed a smile. "Shouldn't I be asking you?"

"We need to talk," Fionnlagh interrupted, characteristically brusque. He didn't bother with greetings. "It's about Éamon."

Áed looked to the floor. *Of course.* He wasn't sure what name to assign this feeling. He'd never known that betrayal could feel so much like grief. "I hadn't ever thought he would..." He gritted his teeth. "I didn't know."

Fionnuala piped up. "You still don't believe he could have done this, do you?"

Áed hesitated. He couldn't deny what he had seen, and the proof was right in front of him. Fionnuala had been stabbed. The point of the blade had emerged through her back. But Áed couldn't meet her eyes. "The Éamon I know and the person who did this... they aren't the same."

When he managed to look at Fionnuala's face, he expected it to look accusing or disappointed. Instead, her lips were quirked in a bare smile. "Well, there's good news," she said, "and there's bad news."

⦚

The good news is, you're right.

The words were buzzing in Áed's head. He had taken a seat on the end of the bed and was staring blankly at the floor. "His prosthesis?" He looked up to Fionnlagh and then to Fionnuala, as if either of them could be lying to him. "*How?*"

"Connectivity magic," Fionnlagh said grimly. He held up the arm that wasn't in the sling and shook down his sleeve. He hadn't yet taken off his pollen bracelet. On the bed,

Fionnuala tapped her own so that Fionnlagh's flashed. "The moon crystal."

The bad news is, you're right.

"I started to suspect something was wrong when he sleepwalked into the woods, heading for the Moon court," Fionnlagh said. "Then the next day, Iarlaith said that he dropped off some battle plans at the atheneum and told him he wasn't sure how he'd picked them up. He said he'd found them on his person when he woke up in the forest."

"So…" Áed's voice was faint. "The Moon court is in his head?"

Fionnuala shook her head. She was obviously making an effort to be calming. "We don't think so. It's more like…"

"It's more like he's a puppet," Fionnlagh said bluntly. "They can use his body. They can see through his eyes."

"A connection like that would have taken a long time to mature," Fionnuala said. She had shot her brother a glare at his puppet explanation but hadn't refuted it. "Which is probably why it started with sleepwalking. His mind couldn't fight the magic's progression while he was unconscious."

It felt like someone had doused Áed with ice water. "Éamon is—" His breath snagged in his chest. "He's still *Éamon*, right?"

Both of the Fionns nodded immediately. "Completely," Fionnuala said. "When he's conscious, that is."

"In other words," Fionnlagh explained, "his personality hasn't been corrupted. When he's in charge, he's all Éamon. When he's not, though…"

"He's someone in the Moon court," Áed breathed. With a flash, he remembered Lachtna's soft, pale face. The Moon leader had nudged them to travel to Bone and been so pleased when they had announced that was their plan. In truth, he had been planting a silent asset directly into the heart of his enemy's court. As soon as the high court was out of the way, and Moon had no further need to ally with Bone, he had turned Éamon from a spy into a weapon.

Áed thought he might throw up. "How long have you known?"

The Fionns exchanged a look. "Like I said, we *suspected* when he sleepwalked into the woods," Fionnlagh said. "I confess that when I suspected, my instinct was to eliminate him." He looked away. "It was meant to be him, with the water horse. Before he joined us, we had intended to go around that lake." He looked up, and Áed couldn't read his expression. "But then he saved your life, and I realized that he was still *present*, he was still *Éamon*. I had read the situation incorrectly."

Áed opened his mouth at least twice before he managed a word. "*Eliminate* him?"

"I'm sorry." Fionnlagh looked down again. "I was wrong." He shook his head. "At any rate, my suspicion was confirmed on the way back to the mound. They tried to take control while he was riding. He fought it, and they released him when I covered his eyes; they seemed to be seeking information about what we were doing."

"That's—" *Horrifying. Evil. Sickening.* Áed couldn't finish. He shook his head hard. "You're going to need to do better than 'I was wrong' for trying to *eliminate* my b—" He felt himself grow slightly warm. "My *best friend*." He dug his hands into his hair. "He told me he didn't like that prosthesis. He told me that it made him uncomfortable." He looked up helplessly. "Should I have done something?"

Fionnuala hurried to assure him. "There is no way you could have known. What the Moon court did was crueler than any decent person should be expected to think of."

"That does bring us to the next thing, though," Fionnlagh

said. His tone was dark. "The bond isn't broken."

Áed blinked. "But Neasa—"

"Broke the prosthesis, yes. But for as long as moon crystal remains in Éamon's body, the magic will, too."

Fionnuala, as usual, said it more gently. "He's going to need surgery," she said. "A proper one, this time."

Fionnlagh nodded. "And we'll make him a new prosthesis if he wishes it. One that aligns with what he wants."

Áed was still reeling, but he nodded. Only one thing was absolutely clear. "Excuse me," he said. He stood from the bed. "I need to go see him, now."

≀≀

Éamon was confined to a cell.

It was comfortable, as cells went, with a furnished bed and windows—albeit barred—to let in the light. Áed approached cautiously, peering around the corner.

Éamon saw him immediately. "Áed!" He used the bars to stand and leaned against them as Áed approached. "I kept asking after you! Are you all right? How are the others?"

"I'm fine," Áed said. He knew his voice was a little subdued. "Fionnuala seems like she'll recover as well."

At that, a funny blank look stole over Éamon's face. His eyes glazed, and without warning, the expression dropped off his face. A moment later, it was replaced by a starch-stiff smile. "Oh, that's right," he said. His voice sounded the same, but the cadence was all wrong. "I stabbed that one." He banged both of his palms against the bars, making them crash and rattle, and Áed jumped back with a start.

In the next second, Éamon was staring at his hands like he didn't recognize them, awareness seeping back into his eyes. "Oh." He pressed a hand over his mouth like he thought he

446

might be sick. He sank to a seat again, still holding the bars for stability.

A breath slipped past Áed's lips. "Oh, Éamon," he murmured, and he felt his eyes growing hot. "I am so sorry."

The day was saved: the human kingdom would be secure on its festival nights, the fae refugees could emerge from their hiding and return to their homes. Rian was King of the high court, and Áed knew that he would strive to heal every hurt he ever inflicted. Ronan and Erin were holed up somewhere in the castle, having stolen every blanket they could find, and were probably still sleeping in a mess of pillows and adolescent limbs. Everything was supposed to be at peace again.

But Éamon was not.

"I should never have brought you across the veil." Áed crouched in front of the bars. "You would have been better off if I hadn't."

Éamon shifted so that he could lean against the bars, closer to Áed. "Stop that," he said. "*I* chose to come." His voice was firm, but his hands were shaking slightly. "Did… did they tell you what's wrong with me?"

Áed nodded. "Did they tell *you*?"

Éamon nodded. "Yeah." He looked at the shards of prosthesis still affixed to his leg. "It's, uh… the most terrifying thing I've ever heard." His breath hitched quietly. "I feel absolutely violated."

"Éamon—"

"Did you speak with your mother?"

Áed blinked. That was a very direct change of subject. "No," he said. He looked down. "I don't want anything to be rushed. I'll wait." He wasn't sure what there was to talk about, anyway. Winning a battle didn't have any bearing on their relationship or lack thereof, although he did want to tell her that he had slain the Queen with the axe she had given him. "Éamon," he tried again but trailed off as Éamon slipped a hand through the bars. He didn't reach for Áed's; he just let it rest there. A question, perhaps. An invitation.

Before Áed could think about it, he put his hand over Éamon's.

He dared a peek at Éamon's face to find that his caramel skin had flushed a dusky coral.

"I'm sorry," Áed said softly. "For everything. For—for pushing you away." His lashes brushed at his cheek when he blinked, eyes downcast again. "In that I should have noticed more that you were struggling, and also—" He swallowed hard. "Also, in what you told me in the woods."

Éamon gave his hand a squeeze, but his face was guarded. "I don't want you saying this just because you feel bad for me or something." He looked disquieted. "That's not what's happening, is it?"

Áed shook his head definitively. "You're my best friend." He stared at their hands instead of looking at Éamon's face. "I've always been afraid of losing that. And then there's…" His voice faded.

"Ninian," Éamon finished softly.

Áed nodded. "It's been a really long time," he said. "It never felt like long *enough*."

"That's okay," Éamon said. His tone, Áed noticed, was held very carefully steady. "Áed, I don't want you to be uncomfortable for me."

"Well, that's just it." Áed fidgeted. "After everything, I mean." He knew he was blushing like a flustered child. "It's… starting to feel like long enough."

After the silence had stretched on long enough to be worrisome, Áed looked up.

Éamon was staring at him as if Áed had just slapped him dumb.

"Gods," Áed murmured. "You're still there, right? Éamon?"

Éamon shook his head sharply. "I'm here. It's me." He dragged a hand through his ivory curls, puffing out his cheeks. "Sorry. When you came to see me, I was honestly expecting something a little different." He let out a dry chuckle. "Since apparently, I stabbed your sister, and have been sporadically possessed, and need surgery that'll probably cost more of my leg." He pressed his eyes closed and then opened them again as if making sure reality was sticking around. "I didn't expect you to say *that*."

Áed felt heat spread across his own cheeks. "This was such a bad time. I am so sorry."

"No, no!" Éamon leaned closer against the bars. His blush had gotten deeper. "I'm actually..." A smile played on his lips. "I'm really happy to hear it, actually."

Áed let out a relieved breath. "When all this is over, maybe we can... talk. A little more."

"Talking sounds good," Éamon agreed. "Yes. Talking."

Áed's chest was fluttery as he leaned his head against the bars. It felt incredible to have something to look forward to.

Nothing felt like it was over. The remnants of battle had yet to be cleared up, the dead buried, the wounded healed. The rift between Bone and Moon wasn't going away anytime soon. And Áed had family that he wanted to know better outside the context of war. But when Áed thought of that future, he didn't feel dread.

He shifted his hand so that its broken shape fit better into Éamon's palm, feeling a smile creep over his face. "All right, Éamon," he said softly. "Let's see what tomorrow holds."

EPILOGUE
ÁED

The sun shone through chilly, humid air. The forest was still skeletal, but the snow had melted; over the great yard, a few birds practiced acrobatics, chasing the insects that had begun to emerge from the thawing ground.

Áed leaned on the windowsill, several stories high. The Bone mound was full of its usual smoky, pleasantly acrid aroma, and the damp wind blowing in from outside ruffled Áed's hair.

Fionnuala slouched against the wall beside him. She had taken to wearing even shorter cropped tunics as if to showcase the dark scar on her stomach. It was something Áed had come to recognize about the Bone court. They wore their scars like emblems of victory. His half-sister stretched contentedly in the sun from the window, oblivious to the late-winter cold. "Are you ready for tonight?"

"Of course, I am." Áed looked back over the forest. That night, the veil would be opening to mark the advent of spring.

That night, sometime before daybreak, Áed would go home.

"No, no," Fionnuala said with a grin. "I mean, are you *ready?*"

Áed rolled his eyes. He had been hearing about this festival for weeks now. "Sure," he said, rolling his eyes.

"The humans will have a good time, too," she said. "Iarlaith's been working on finding a way to make half-decent food that Ronan and Éamon can actually eat."

Áed found his gaze being drawn back over the wooded vista. The sun was just beginning to spread a haze of orange across the western sky, preparing for sunset.

"Staring won't make time move any differently," Fionnuala chided. "You have all night before you need to go."

Áed reluctantly tore his gaze away from the view. He knew she was right. But the knowledge that in a few short hours, he would be leaving all this behind… it made his chest feel tight.

"Come on," Fionnuala said. She put a hand on his back. "You should go get ready for the party."

⸲⸲⸲

Éamon was waiting for him in the hall when Áed emerged from their room in finer clothing. When Áed stepped into the corridor, Éamon greeted him with a sprig of yellow-flowered gorse. "Happy festival," he said as Áed accepted the flowers. "That's the only thing I could find blooming this time of year, and I think I got all the bugs off it."

Áed snorted. The spiny stem of the sprig held on well when he fixed it in the pocket of his shirt. "I think it looks nice." He looked up at Éamon more fully and raised his eyebrows in appreciation. "*You* look nice."

Éamon wore a black, open-backed shirt and trousers that he had tied off neatly under the stump of his thigh. He had taken to wearing his hair clipped back with something, playing with the idea of showing the scar over his eye, but now, it was falling out of the clip in a graceful mess.

"You do, too," Éamon said, propping his crutches under

his armpits to pull Áed into a hug. Áed was only as tall as Éamon's collarbone, which meant that he was quite enveloped. He didn't mind. "You smell like smoke," Éamon said after a moment. "What have you been doing?"

In truth, Áed had been fidgeting. He didn't like this waiting. And fidgeting meant twining a little rope of fire between his gnarled fingers until he nearly singed his sleeves. "Nothing."

Éamon sighed, clearly believing none of it, but he didn't press. "Let's go help set up," he suggested. "Keep busy, right?"

The great hall was a long, candle-lit chamber on one of the mound's underground levels. It fit more tables than Áed could imagine using. The place was bustling with energy when Áed and Éamon arrived as faeries strung up garlands of gorse and blackthorn and arranged chairs around the countless tables. The smell of food wafted from someplace, rich and enticing.

"Iarlaith!" Éamon called over Áed's head, and Áed looked up to see his half-brother directing three faeries who carried, in turn, a live, squawking goose, a gigantic bowl of some honeyed alcohol, and at least three bolts of spring-green fabric embroidered with tiny skulls. As soon as he heard Éamon's call, Iarlaith dismissed them and hurried over.

"Éamon!" he said. He sounded happy if a little frenzied.

"Áed, too," Áed said. "How's everything going?"

Iarlaith looked harried. "Normally." He shoved his hands through his densely curled hair. He was wearing an apron, and it was stained with what looked like glitter. "Which means it's a mess. What did you two need?"

"We wanted to help," Éamon said.

"Help? Oh, you might regret offering that." Iarlaith turned and pointed vaguely in the direction of the room's far corner.

"There's a basin over there with about three hundred morels in it. The cook needs them cleaned. Bundles of rhubarb next to it. Take off the leaves."

It was good to see Éamon and Iarlaith getting along again. After they had all returned from the high court, it had taken Iarlaith about a week to stop being irritated with Éamon for sneaking out. He had kept bringing up something about wet poetry books, which Éamon insisted he'd had nothing to do with, but eventually, the whole thing had been forgotten. After all, the fighting was over, Fionnuala had healed well, and Iarlaith hadn't been able to justify being irritated with Éamon while Éamon was recovering from surgery. The healer had taken what remained of Éamon's knee, and a few inches of his thigh; the operation had been difficult, but successful.

"Áed," Éamon said urgently, and Áed was immediately snapped out of his thoughts. Éamon nudged him to look toward the back of the great hall. "It's Neasa."

"Oh, you had better go," Iarlaith said. "I heard she was looking for you."

Áed's stomach tensed. Despite having lived in the Bone mound for the winter, he hadn't talked with his mother much. He didn't feel unwelcome anymore, and he had spoken to her without horrible awkwardness on several occasions, but it was still very unusual for Neasa to seek him out. "Is that good or bad?"

Iarlaith shrugged. "I haven't run into her all day. Been busy." He made a shooing motion with his hands. "Go on."

As Áed had noticed was her tendency, Neasa didn't come over to them; instead, once she was sure that they'd seen her, she waited for them to come to her. "Neasa," Áed greeted formally, with a little bow. Éamon inclined his head respectfully.

Neasa's copper tresses were arranged into a loose roll at

the nape of her neck, and her freckled face was devoid of its usual paint or soot. She held a glass of wine. "Áed," she greeted him in turn. She took a sip of her wine, regarding him over the edge of the cup. When she had swallowed, all with great poise, she exhaled faintly. "I want you to dine with us tonight," she said. "With me."

Áed's eyes widened. He had never dined with the family, although he knew that they ate together on most nights. "Really?"

Neasa nodded slightly, affirming with only the barest bob of her chin. "We will be at the head table at moonrise. After the feast, you may, of course, enjoy the revel. But I would have you with us tonight."

Áed found himself breaking into a smile. "Right," he said, still stunned. "I'll be there. Thank you."

"Don't thank me."

With that, she stepped past them to weave away through the tables.

Áed turned to Éamon, needing to make sure that he had heard correctly. He was grinning fully. "She wants me to eat with the family."

"One more thing," Neasa said.

Áed yelped, jumping. "Where did you come back from?" He clutched at his chest; his heart had nearly just leapt out of it.

Neasa raised an eyebrow but only turned to face Éamon. "There's something for you in the atheneum." She began to walk away again, and this time, she sent a smile over her shoulder. Her smiles were keen. "I think you'll like it better than cleaning morels."

§§

They found Iarlaith waiting for them in the atheneum.
He hadn't lit any candles and didn't seem to realize that

he'd forgotten, so Áed held out a palmful of fire for himself and Éamon. Iarlaith was still wearing the glitter-dusted apron, and he was out of breath. "Mother does *not* give much warning, does she?" he said. "She told you, who are supposed to be surprised, before *me*, who is supposed to surprise you." He shook his head, incredulous. Áed subtly lit a lamp. "Oh, well. I don't think it's too surprising of a surprise, anyway."

He beckoned, and they followed him to a table in the center of the shadowed shelves. On it sat a wooden box, about as long as an arm, and a few hand-lengths across.

"I was going to give you this later tonight," he said, walking around to the opposite side of the table. "But I suppose this does have a nice atmosphere. Besides, I don't know how sober you'll be later tonight." He shrugged. "Faerie wine is the stuff of folktale, after all."

Éamon cocked his head at the box while Iarlaith set about unfastening the latches.

"Éamon, do you remember the questions I asked you a month or so ago?"

"Questions? After my surgery?"

Iarlaith nodded.

A light dawned in Éamon's face. "Wait," he breathed. "Iarlaith, you didn't…" He trailed off.

With an understated flair, Iarlaith opened the box.

Inside, resting on a bed of cloth, there lay a prosthesis.

It was made of warm, glossy wood. In the socket where it would meet Éamon's stump, it was cushioned with soft fabric, and a leather strap, affixed to a buckle, lay loose at the top. The knee and ankle were articulated. "It's made of wild cherry wood," Iarlaith said as Éamon stared at it dumbly. "That's for no reason other than the craftsman thought it was pretty, and it will hold up over time. The knee and ankle are built with a spring around the axis of the joint, so they'll bend when you're walking and straighten when you take a step." He backed up to let Éamon, who was bracing himself on the table with both hands, lean over the box. Áed held the lamp closer for him, and it gleamed off the polished wood. Iarlaith inclined his head. "It was built to your exact specifications."

Tentatively, Éamon touched it. Then, with an expression akin to reverence, he lifted the prosthesis from the box. For a moment, he simply held it. He still hadn't spoken a word.

"You shouldn't try it yet," Iarlaith said. "It hasn't been long enough since your surgery, and since this leg is completely and entirely free of magic…" He shrugged. "Well, as good as that is, it does mean that you're going to heal at the normal human rate." He paused, and Áed noticed that he'd begun to worry at the hem of his apron. "So… what do you think?"

Éamon swallowed, and Áed realized he was choking up. He set the lamp on the table and stepped against Éamon's side to put an arm around his back, careful not to knock out his crutches as he gave him a gentle squeeze. Éamon's eyes were not dry. "It's incredible, Iarlaith." He drew a shaky breath, eyes running up and down the glossy wood. "It's perfect."

Iarlaith let out a breath. "Oh, thank Goddess." He broke into a smile. "When you cross back home tonight, I'll make sure it's with the rest of your things. If it needs any adjusting, the human realm still has craftspeople, right?"

"Plenty," Áed said when it was clear Éamon was still engrossed. "And I would find only the best."

Éamon gently set the prosthesis into the box again, and Iarlaith closed the lid. The latches fastened with a series of *clicks*. "It really has been an astonishing journey for you, hasn't it?" Iarlaith brushed off the front of his apron, clearly unaware of the sparkle that transferred to his palms. "For both of you."

Áed and Éamon shared a glance. "Yeah," Éamon said, at the same time as Áed said, "It really has."

Iarlaith chuckled, and it turned into a sigh. For a moment, silence hung. Then Iarlaith's smile was back, and he pressed his hands together. "Then I suppose we had better make tonight count." He started around the table and caught both Áed and Éamon on the way. "Let's go have a good time."

⁂

The revel was a party like Áed had never experienced.

The great feast hall glowed with hundreds of candles in the enormous chandeliers, and the music was hypnotic in a way that made Áed feel drunk without even a sip of wine. He was also riding a bit of a high from dining with Neasa and his half-siblings—the Fionns and Iarlaith had been delighted to have him there, and Neasa had even asked him a couple of questions about himself. Afterward, Iarlaith had beamed at him, and Fionnlagh had cuffed him affectionately on the back while Fionnuala knocked her mug of mead against Áed's glass. "That was excellent," Iarlaith had whispered excitedly, and Áed had had to agree.

Ronan, for his part, was already drunk. Áed had been strongly tempted to drag Iarlaith off to the side and demand to know why he'd thought it necessary to make *alcohol* that Ronan could drink, but he'd thought the better of it; it was one night, and Ronan was obviously having fun. At that moment, Áed could spot him in the center of the whirling dance floor. He had linked hands with Erin, and the two were spinning each other around, faster and faster. It wasn't dancing, but they were both whooping as they tripped over people in their way.

Áed knew for a fact that they had promised to meet each other at the next festival. He wondered how much chaos that would sow.

Éamon startled Áed by coming up behind him and dropping an arm over his shoulders. He leaned close. "Care for a dance?"

Áed turned around to face him, already smiling. "Of course."

Éamon accepted Áed into his arms, again tucking his crutches into his armpits, and they swayed gently to music that was much too fast and energetic for swaying.

It was hard to believe that by the end of the night, Áed would return to being King. His kingdom would be in some kind of a state, that much was certain, but he would return home bearing good news. Besides, at least Ronan's sole directive as Crown Prince had been to put somebody responsible in charge before he left.

Áed frowned thoughtfully. After everything that had happened, he had to wonder if Ronan would be more or less inclined to accept the responsibility that came with his title. He looked over again. Ronan and Erin had moved to the top of one of the tables and hooked elbows to dance around and around. Ronan's hair was intricately braided with tiny white blackthorn flowers and sprays of gorse, and yellow buds flew out with the enthusiasm of his movement.

Well. Áed couldn't help but smile to himself. Maybe that was a conversation that could wait.

Áed cast his gaze around the revel, at the grinning, dancing fae. He would go home, to his palace and his responsibilities. There was work to do. He had plans for the kingdom about which he cared so much.

But the people around him were his people, and this court his court. He had belonged ever to two worlds, and now he knew both of them. He would never truly be able to leave this place, just as he would never be able to leave the Gut.

So he wouldn't. Every festival night, he knew where he would be.

Áed closed his eyes, rested his cheek on Éamon's chest, and smiled.

Thank you for reading this book!

If you enjoyed this book, you can be an author-reader matchmaker by leaving an honest review on your preferred book-buying platform.

Post a picture of the book on Instagram, Facebook or Twitter and tag **@egradcliff**!

ACKNOWLEDGEMENTS

For all of my words, I cannot express quite how it feels to finish a series. I'm proud. I'm in shock. I'm excited for the future. But most of all, I would say that I am grateful. Having the opportunity to work on *The Coming of Áed* for the past three years has been the most incredible privilege, and it wouldn't have been possible without the people who helped me.

Firstly, as always, Erin Radcliff. She's been at my side since the very beginning, and it's her dedication that truly enabled the completion of this project. From using her impressive administrative skills to help me keep the series on track, to offering her ear as a sounding-board, I could not have achieved this without her. She has given an immense amount of time to *The Coming of Áed*, and her extraordinary generosity merits recognition. Thank you, Erin.

To Tim Radcliff, I extend my gratitude for his unwavering support. His belief in me kept me moving, and he remains my role model for both kindness and patience. I would also like to thank Blake Snow, my wonderful friend and fellow author extraordinaire, who let me FaceTime him in the wee hours of the morning when I needed to vent about convoluted plot outlines. He helped me see the forest for the trees when I had been working for too long to see clearly, and his perspective pulled me out of many a creative rabbit hole.

These acknowledgments would be incomplete without recognizing readers who took time from their busy lives to read early versions of *The Wild Court* and prior books in the series. They include members of local book clubs, public and high school librarians, my newsletter subscribers, book bloggers, fellow authors, and dyed-in-the-wool bookworms: Jesse Nolan Bailey, Sue Bavey, Mimi Black, Lorraine Bondi, Briana C., Angela C., Catherine D., Meg Evans, Leah Gleason, Michelle Haller, Nico I., Amanda K., Kat at KBBookReviews, Alyssa Murphy, Mark Reed, Halo Scot, Charlotte S., Doha S., Estelle Grace Tudor, Woody Ward, Alyssa Williams, A.N. Willis, and many more. To those of you I may have missed—as this is being written as we go to press—my gratitude to you is undiminished.

Thank you to the fellow writers, readers, and passionate book bloggers on Twitter and Instagram, all of whom make the writing community one of the best corners of the internet. I have to give a special shout out to the members of the Writing Community Chat Show Support Group. They are extraordinary and generous, with helpful fellow authors always ready to lend a hand.

My writing support squad, of course, is completed by a wonderful team of professionals: Kelsy Thompson, my developmental editor, offered her acute insights into the narrative and its characters. Her talent proved itself once again in *The Wild Court*, and I am so grateful to have had her input throughout the series. Margaret Diehl, my copy editor, likewise remained phenomenal--a true professional, she was flexible, patient, and absolutely brilliant in her suggestions.

Last but certainly not least, the incredible Micaela Alcaino designed the cover of *The Wild Court*. Her artistic eye once again blew me away, and as always, collaborating with her was a genuine pleasure. It was a privilege to work with each and every one of these immensely gifted individuals.

ABOUT THE AUTHOR

E.G. Radcliff is a part-time pooka and native of the Unseelie Court. She collects acorns, glass beads, and pretty rocks, and the crows outside her house know her as She Who Has Bread.

Her fantasy novels are crafted in the dead of night after offering sacrifices of almonds and red wine to the writing-block deities.

You can reach her by scrying bowl, carrier pigeon, or @egradcliff on social media.

CONNECT WITH E.G. RADCLIFF

www.egradcliff.com
info@egradcliff.com

@egradcliff

Join the mailing list from **www.egradcliff.com** for news about upcoming books in the series, giveaways, blog updates, and limited edition book swag!

BOOKS IN
THE COMING OF ÁED TRILOGY

www.ingramcontent.com/pod-product-compliance
Lightning Source LLC
Chambersburg PA
CBHW051551100726
47898CB00001B/49